Some Assembly Required

ROBIN WINZENREAD

CHAMPAGNE BOOK GROUP

Some Assembly Required

This is a work of fiction. The characters, incidents and dialogues in this book are of the author's imagination and are not to be construed as real. Any resemblance to actual events or persons, living or dead, is completely coincidental.

Published by Champagne Book Group
2373 NE Evergreen Avenue, Albany OR 97321 U.S.A.

~~~

eISBN: 978-1-926681-54-2

Cover Art by Melody Pond

www.champagnebooks.com

Version_1

*To Mom and Dad for blessing me with a
colorful childhood, and to my children
Tiffany, Jackie, and Jordan, for
blessing me with more wonderful, chaotic stories*

Chapter One

As my young son's cries echo through this diner, I'm reminded again why some animals eat their young.

It's because they want to.

"Hey, Mom! Nick farted, and he didn't say excuse me!"

Normally when Aaron, my spunky six-year-old, announces something so crudely, we're at home, and his booming voice is muted by the artfully arranged basket of dirty laundry I've shoved my head into in hopes of hiding like an ostrich from a tiny, tenacious predator.

This time, however, Aaron yells it in the middle of a crowded diner in the small, stranger-adverse, southern Illinois town we're about to call home and, frankly, we don't need any more attention. Thanks to my semi-feral pack of three lippy offspring, we've already lit this place on fire, and not in a good way.

Despite our involuntary efforts to unhinge the locals with our strangers-in-a-strange-land antics, this dumpy, dingy diner, minus its frosty clientele, has a real comfortable feel, not unlike the ratty, stretched-out yoga pants I love but no longer wear because a) they don't fit any more and b) I burned them—along with a voodoo doll I crafted of my ex-husband (see my Pinterest board for patterns), after I forced it to have sex with my son's GI Joe action figure (see downward-facing dog for position).

Crap. I should have put the pictures on Instagram. Wait, I think they're still on my phone.

"Mom!" Aaron bellows again.

Right now, I'd kill for a pile of sweaty socks to dive into, but there's nary a basket of tighty-whities in sight, and that kid loves an audience, even a primarily rural, all-white-bread, mouth-gaping, wary one.

Frowning, I point at his chair. "Sit."

More than a bit self-conscious, I scan the room, hoping for signs of defrost from the gawking audience and pray my attempt to sound parental falls on nearby ears, earning me scant mom points. Of course, a giant burp which may have contained three of the six vowel sounds just erupted from my faux angelic four-year-old daughter,

Madison, so I'll kiss that goodwill goodbye. I hand her a napkin and execute my go-to look, a serious I-mean-it-this-time scowl. "Maddy, say excuse me."

"Excuse me."

belch

Good lord, I'm doomed.

"Listen to me, Mom. Nick farted."

I fork my chef salad with ranch dressing on the side and raise an eyebrow at my youngest son. "Knock it off, kiddo."

"You said when we fart, we have to say excuse me, and he didn't." Finally, Aaron sits, unaware I've been stealing his fries, also on the side.

Kids, so clueless.

Nick, my angelic eight-year-old, is hot on his brother's heels and equally loud, "We don't have to say it when we're on the toilet. You can fart on the toilet and not say excuse me. It's allowed. Ask Mom."

Aaron picks up a water glass and holds it to his mouth. "It sounded like a raptor." He blows across the top, filling the air with a wet, revolting sound, once again alarming the nearby locals. "See?" He laughs. "Just like a raptor."

I point at his plate and scrutinize the last of his hamburger. "Thank you for that lovely demonstration, now finish your lunch."

Naturally, as we discuss fart etiquette, the locals are still gawking, and I can't blame them. We're strangers in a county where I'm betting everyone knows each other somehow and, here's the real shocker, we're not merely passing through. We're staying. On purpose.

We're not alone, either. My brother, Justin, his wife, Olivia, and their bubbly toddler twins kickstarted this adventure—moving to the sticks—so we're eight in total. Admittedly, this all sounded better a month ago when we adults hashed it out over too much wine and a little bit of vodka. Okay, maybe a lot of vodka. Back then, Justin had been headhunted for a construction manager job here in town, and I was in a post-divorce, downward-spiral bind, so they invited the kiddies and me to join them.

For me, I hope it's temporary until I can get settled somewhere, as in land a job, land a purpose, land a life. When they offered, I immediately saw the appeal—the more distance between me and the ex and his younger, sluttier girlfriend the better—and I decided to move south too.

Now I can't back out. I've already sold my house which buys me time, but I've got nowhere else to go. Where would I land? I've got three kids and limited skills. Plus, I don't even have a career to use as an excuse to change my mind or to even point me in another direction.

In other words, I'm stuck. Whether I want to or not, I'm relocating to a run-down farmhouse in the middle of nowhere Illinois to help Justin and Olivia with their grandiose plans of fixing it up and living "authentic" lives since, according to Instagram, Pinterest, and lifestyle blogs everywhere, manicured suburbs with cookie-cutter houses, working utilities and paved sidewalks don't count. Unless you're stinking rich, which, unfortunately, we, most definitely, are not.

Let's see, Justin has a new career opportunity, Olivia is going to restore, repaint, repurpose, and blog her way to a book deal, and me…and me…

Nope. I got nothing. No plans, no dreams, no job, nada. Here I am, the not-so-proud owner of a cheap polyester wardrobe with three kids rapidly outgrowing their own. I better come up with something, and quick.

Where's cheesecake when you need it? I stab a cherry tomato, pluck it from my fork, and chew. The world is full of people living their dreams, while mine consists of an unbroken night's sleep and a day without something gooey in my shoes. I take aim at a cucumber slice, pop it in my mouth, and pretend it's a donut. At least I don't have to wash these dishes.

Across from me, Olivia, my sometimes-vegan sister-in-law is unaware I'm questioning my life's purpose while she questions her lunch choice. Unsatisfied, she drops her mushroom melt onto her plate and frowns. I knew it wouldn't pass inspection. She may have lowered her standards to marry my brother, but she'd never do so for food. This is why she and I get along so well.

Olivia rocks back in her chair and smacks her lips, dissatisfied. "There's no way this was cooked on a meat-free grill. I swear I can taste bacon. Maybe sausage too." Her tongue swirls around in her mouth, searching for more hints of offending pork. "Definitely sausage."

Frankly, I enjoy finding pork in my mouth. Then again, I have food issues. Though, if I liked munching tube steak more often, perhaps my ex wouldn't have wandered. The bastard.

Justin watches his wife's tongue roll around, and I don't blame him. She's beautiful—dark, luminous eyes, full lips flushed a natural pink glow, cascading dark curls, radiant brown skin, a toned physique despite two-year-old twins. She's everything I am not.

She tells me I'm cute. Of course, the Pillsbury Dough Boy is cute too. Screw that. I want to be hot.

Regardless, I expect something crude to erupt from my brother's mouth as he stares at his lovely bride, so I'm pleasantly surprised when it doesn't. Instead, he shakes his head and works on his stack of onion rings. "What do you expect when you order off menu in a place like this, babe? Be glad they had portobellos."

Across from me, she frowns. Model tall and fashionably lean, she's casually elegant in a turquoise and brown print maxi dress, glittery dangle earrings, silky black curls, and daring red kitten heels that hug her slender feet. How does she do it? She exudes an easy glamour even as she peels a corner of toasted bun away from her sandwich, revealing a congealed mass of something.

"This isn't a portobello. It's a light dove gray, not a soft, deep, charcoal gray. I'm telling you this is a bad sandwich. I'm not eating it." She extracts her fingers from the offending fungus and crosses her bangle bracelet encased arms.

Foodies. Go figure. No Instagram picture for you, sandwich from hell.

Fortunately their twins, Jaylen and Jayden, adorable in matching Swedish-inspired sweater dress ensembles and print tights, are less picky. Clearly, it comes from my chunky side of the family. They may be dressed to impress, but the ketchup slathered over their precious toddler faces says, "We have Auntie Ro's DNA in us somewhere."

I love that.

Justin cuts up the last half of a cold chicken strip and shares it with his daughters, who are constrained by plastic highchairs—which I can't do with my kids any more, darn the luck—and, in addition to having no idea how to imitate raptors with half-empty water glasses like my boys or identify mushrooms by basis of color like their mother, they are still quite cute.

Love them as I do, my boys haven't been cute for a while. Such a long while. Maddy, well, she's cute on a day-to-day basis. Yet, they are my world. My phlegm covered, obnoxious, arguing world.

Justin wipes Jaylen's cheek and checks his phone. "We need to get the bill. It's getting late."

I survey the room, hunting for our waitress. Despite the near constant stranger stares, this place intrigues me. It feels a hundred years old in a good, cozy way. The diner's creaky, wood floor is well worn and the walls are exposed brick, which is quaint in restaurants even if it detracts from the value in Midwestern homes, including the giant moldering one Justin and Olivia bought northeast of town. Old tin advertising posters depict blue ribbon vegetables and old-time tractors in shades of red and green and yellow on the walls, and they may be the real antique deal.

They're really into primary colors, these farm folks. Perhaps the best way to spice up a quiet life is to sprinkle it with something bright and shiny. As for me, I've been living in dull shades of beige for at least half a marriage now, if not longer. Should I try bright and shiny? Couldn't hurt.

Red-pleather booths line the wall of windows to the left, and a row of tables divides the room, including the two tables we've shoved together which my children have destroyed with crumbs, blobs of ketchup, and snot. Of course, the twins helped too, but they're toddlers so you can't point a finger at them especially since all the customers are too busy pointing fingers at mine.

Bar stools belly up to a Formica counter to the right, and it's all very old school and quaint, although I would hate to have to clean the place, partly because Maddy sneezed, and her mouth was open and full of fries.

Kids. So gross.

Three portly gentlemen in caps, flannel, and overalls overflow from the booth closest to our table and, clearly, they're regulars. They're polishing off burgers and chips, though no one is sneezing with his mouth open, most likely because his teeth will fly out in the process. I imagine the pleather booths are permanently imprinted with the marks of old asses from a decade's worth of lunches. Sometimes it's good to make an impression. The one we're currently making, however? Probably not.

Nearly every table, booth, and stool are taken. Must be a popular place. Or it may be the only place in this itty, bitty town. It's the type of place where everyone knows your name, meaning they all stared the minute we walked in because they don't know ours, it's a brisk Tuesday in early November, and we sure aren't local.

Yet.

Several men of various ages in blue jeans and farm hats sit in a row upon the counter stools, munching their lunches. A smattering of conversations on hog feed, soybean yields, and tractor parts fills the air. They all talk at once, the way guys tend to do, with none of them listening except to the sound of his own voice, the way guys also tend to do, like stray dogs in a pound when strangers check them out and they're hoping to impress.

Except for one of them, the one I noticed the minute we walked in and have kept tabs on ever since. Unlike the others, this man is quiet and, better yet, he doesn't have the typical middle-aged, dad-bod build.

While most of the other men are stocky and round, square and cubed, pear shaped and apple dumpling-esque, like bad geometry gone rogue, he isn't. He's tall with a rather broad triangular back and, given the way it's stretching the confines of his faded, dark red, button-down shirt, it's a well-muscled isosceles triangle at that. Brown cowboy boots with a Texas flag burned on the side of the wooden heel peek from beneath seasoned blue jeans, and those jeans cling to a pair of muscular thighs that could squeeze apples for juice.

God, I have a hankering for hot cider. With a great big, thick, rock-hard cinnamon stick swirling around too. Hmmm, spicy.

This Midwestern cowboy's dark-brown hair is thick with a slight wave that would go a tad bit wild if he let it, and he needs to let it. Who doesn't love surfer curls, and his are perfect. They're the kind I could run my fingers through forever or hang onto hard in the sack, if need be. Trust me, there's a need be.

His body is lean, yet strong, and beneath his rolled-up sleeves, there's a swell of ample biceps and the sinewy lines of strong, tan forearms. It's a tan I'm betting goes a lot further than his elbows. His face is sun-kissed too, and well-defined with high cheekbones and a sturdy chin. A hint of fine lines fan out from the corners of his chocolate-brown eyes and, while not many, there're enough to catch any drool should my lips happen to ravage his face.

Facial lines on guys are so damn sexy. They hint at wisdom, experience, strength. Lines on women should be sexy too, even the stretchy white, hip-dwelling ones from multiple, boob-sucking babies, but men don't think that way, which is why I only objectify them these days. Since getting literally screwed over by my ex, I'm the permanent mascot for Team Anti-Relationship. I blame those defective Y chromosomes myself. Stupid Y chromosomes.

Regardless, it's difficult not to watch as this well-built triangle of a man wipes his mouth with a napkin. I wouldn't mind being that white crumpled paper in that strong tan hand, even if I, too, end up spent on the counter afterward. At any rate, he stands, claps the guy to his left on the back, and I may have peed myself.

The sexy boot-clad stranger pulls cash from his wallet and sets it on the lucky napkin. "I've got to get back to the elevator, Phil. Busy day."

Sweet, a Texas accent. How very Matthew McConaughey. Mama like.

A pear-shaped man next to him raises his glass. "See ya, Sam. You headed to George's this afternoon?"

"I hope so. I need to get with Edmund first, plus we have a

couple of trailers coming in, and I've got to do a moisture check on at least two of them." His voice is low, but soft, the way you hope a new vibrator will sound, but never does until the batteries die which defeats the purpose, proving once again irony can be cruel.

And what the hell is a moisture check?

I zero in on the open button of his shirt, drawn to his chest like flies to honey, because that's what I do now that I'm divorced and have no husband and no purpose—I ogle strange men for the raw meat they are. Nothing's going to happen anyway. Truth be told, I haven't dated in an eternity and have no real plans to start, partly because I've forgotten how; just another unfortunate aspect of my life on permanent hold. I've been invited to the singles' buffet, but I'm too afraid to grab a plate. At this point in my recently wrecked, random life, I would rather vomit. Hell, I barely smell the entrees. I'm only interested in licking a hunk of two-legged meatloaf for the sauce anyway. There's no harm in that, right?

Where was I? Right, his chest, and it's a good chest, with the "oood" dragged out like a child's Benadryl-laced nap on a hot afternoon. It's that goood.

Of course, as I mentally drag out the "oood," my lips involuntarily form the word in the air imitating a goldfish in a bowl. While I ogle this particular cut of prime rib, I realize he's noticed my stare not to mention my "oood" inspired fish lips, which is not an attractive look, despite what selfie-addicted college girls think. Our eyes lock. An avalanche of goosebumps crawls its way up my back and down my arms and, I swear, I vibrate. Not like one of those little lipstick vibrators that can go off in your purse at the airport, thank you very much, but something more substantial with a silly name like Rabbit or Butterfly or Bone Master.

That, my friends, is the closest I've come to real sex in two and half years. Excuse me, but we need a moisture check at table two, please. Not to mention a mop. Okay…definitely a mop.

For a moment, we hold our stare—me with my fish lips frozen into place, vibrating silently in my long-sleeved, heather green T-shirt and jeans, surrounded by my small tribe of ketchup-covered children, and him all hot, tan, buff, and beefy, staring at us the way one gawks at a bloody, ten-car pile-up. All too soon, he blinks, the deer-in-the-headlights look fades, and he drops his gaze.

C'mon, stud, look again. I'm not wearing a push-up bra for nothing.

Big, dark, brown eyes pop up again and find mine. All too soon, they flit away to the floor.

Score.

Damn, he's fine. Someone smoke me a cigarette, I'm spent.

I scan the table, imagining my children are radiating cuteness. No dice. Aaron imitates walrus tusks with the last of his French-fries, Nick is trying to de-fang him with a straw full of root beer, and Maddy's two-knuckles deep into a nostril. And I'm sitting next to Justin.

Figures. My big, burly, ginger-headed, lug of a wedding-ring-wearing brother is beside me. Does this hunk of burning stud think he's my husband? Should I pick my own nose with my naked, ring-less finger? Invest in a face tattoo that reads "divorced and horny?" Why do I even care? He's only man meat. After all, was he really even looking at me? Or Olivia? Sexy, sultry, damn-sure-married-to-my-brother Olivia? I whip back to the stud prepared to blink "I'm easy" in Morse code.

blink *blink* *bliiiink*

With a spin on his star-studded boots, Hotty McHot heads toward the hallway at the back of the diner, oblivious that my gaze is rivetted to his ass and equally clueless to the fact that I have questions needing immediate answers, not to mention an overwhelming need to scream, "I'm single and put out, no strings attached" in his general direction.

Olivia pulls me back to reality with her own questions. "I mean, is it that difficult to scrape the grill before you cook someone's meal?"

She's still honked off about her sandwich, unaware I'm over here having mental sex with the hunky cowboy while sending my kids off to a good boarding school for the better part of the winter.

"I didn't have many options here," she rattles on, "even their salads have meat and egg in them. Instead of a writing a book, I should open a vegan restaurant. I was going to give them a good review for the ambiance, but not now. Wait until I post this on Yelp."

Eyeballing the room, Justin polishes off the last of his double-cheese burger. "Sweetie, we're moving to the land of pork and beef. Vegan won't fly here, and I doubt the help cares about Yelp. Did you notice our waitress? She's got a flip phone. Time to put away your inner princess and stick with the book idea."

Long fingers with bronze gel manicured nails rat-a-tat-tat on the tabletop. She locks onto him with dark, intelligent, laser-beam eyes. "Would it kill you to be supportive, honey bunch? You might as well say, uck-fay u-vay."

Apparently channeling some weird, inner death wish, Justin

picks up an onion ring, takes a bite, then pulls a string of overcooked translucent slime free from its breaded coating. He snaps it free with his teeth, then offers it to her. "Your book is going to be great, babe, and it will appeal to a larger audience than here. Remember the goal, Liv. As for me, I'm trying to keep you humble. No one likes high maintenance."

The limp, greasy onion hangs in the air. She ignores it, but not him. "Okay, this time, sweetie, I'll say it. Uck-fay u-vay with an ig-bay ick-day."

Jaylen looks up from her highchair and munches a chicken strip. "Uck-fay?" she repeats through fried poultry. "Ick-day?"

Behind her an older woman, also fluent in pig Latin, does a coffee-laced spit-take in her window booth. I hope she's not a new neighbor.

Justin chuckles and polishes off the offending string of onion. Olivia stews. Time to implement an offense. Clearly, we need an exit strategy.

Where's our waitress? I spy her delivering plates of food three booths down and wave. She nods, so I use these few moments to ward off any drama. "Suggestion, you two. Let's not piss off the help. This may be the only place where we can hide from the kids and eat our feelings. Not to mention drink. Agreed?"

Justin snorts, but says nothing. Olivia rolls her eyes, but also says nothing. Success, although it's tentative. Time to leave.

Water pitcher in hand, our waitress returns to our table. She surveys the left-over lunch carnage, unaware my sister-in-law is both unimpressed and pissed off, and it's fairly obvious that, if we're all going to be regulars here, a sizeable tip, different children, or the offer of a kidney is in order. A middle-aged woman in jeans, T-shirt, and an apron with short, no-nonsense, dishwater hair, she refills our water glasses, possibly so I'll have something with which to wipe the seats or drown our young. Or both. I can't be sure. But I'm open to options.

She sets the water pitcher on the table and starts stacking dirty plates. "Ready for dessert?" She's a bit harried, and, with the possibility of an eruption from Olivia hanging over our heads, I pick up a napkin and start wiping. "We have cherry cobbler."

An indignant cry erupts from the booth behind us. One of the three portly gentlemen hollers—this is the kind of place where you holler— "Save me a piece of cobbler."

"Yeah, yeah, in a minute, Ernie." The waitress scowls. "What else can I get you? Pie? Cake? The coffee's fresh."

"Yeah, but it ain't good though," barks the man named Ernie.

A fresh wave of snorts erupts from his companions.

I stifle a laugh, but it's a challenge, especially since Aaron's been flicking my salad croutons in their general direction throughout most of the meal and, despite my scolding, he's getting quite good with his trick shots.

"I bet you've done this before," I say to the woman whose name tag reads "Anna."

She glares at the booth. "Yep, they're regulars. Of course, I call 'em a pain in the butt, myself."

"Good to know, Anna."

"Name's Sarah. This is the only tag we had left."

Of course. Naturally, the crusty old guys are regulars in a diner where everyone knows your name, so you wear a tag that isn't your own, presumably for strangers who rarely show up on a Tuesday. I like this quirky town, even if it doesn't like me.

"Where are you all from? Chicago?" pries the waitress formerly known as Anna.

Olivia avoids eye contact and spit shines her twins. "Is it obvious?"

Curious, Sarah takes in the dress, the earrings, the bright red shoes. "Yep. What brings you through town?"

Backs stiffen throughout the room. Heads swivel in our direction. The general roar of conversation drops a decibel or two, all the better to eavesdrop, I assume.

I confiscate Maddy's spoon and add it to the pile of flatware on my salad plate, then plunge on before anyone at our table offers an unwelcomed critique of the menu. "We're moving here. They bought a place on Stockpile Road, Thornhill."

Eyes stare from all corners of the diner. Bodies sit taller. Ears bend toward us, and whispers swim across a sea of faces.

"Thornhill?" Sarah cocks her head. "You mean old lady Yeager's place? I hope you're good with a hammer."

"It needs a bulldozer," shouts a voice from the back.

"Stick a sock in it, Ernie. Men," she mutters.

"I've got a toxic ex and a lot of frustration, so…" I imitate a manic hammering motion, but, getting no response from the masses, I load up Aaron's spoon with croutons and keep talking. "Justin's in construction—he's starting a new job here next week. He'll put us to work on the house. Should be fun."

Olivia stares at the hunk of sandwich left on her plate before looking pointedly at our waitress. "I plan to blog about the experience—articles on reclaiming the house, restoring the gardens, growing our own vegetables and herbs, recipes, homemade soaps. Think avant-garde Martha Stewart. It's what I do."

Sarah blinks rapidly as she digests Olivia's words. "Ah." She hesitates. "Want a doggie bag?"

Justin chokes on the last bite of his burger as he examines his phone. "Not necessary, but thanks. Can we get our bill though?"

A finger-painted, ketchup rendition of a farting raptor rambles across Aaron's plate. Sarah sets down her stack of dishes, rips our bill from the order pad in her apron pocket, and picks up my son's plate without so much as an appraisal. "So, you all are moving here. Good to know. I haven't been up there in years." She adds another plate to her stack, obliterating his finger art. "I hear it's a real project. Anyway, good luck, and welcome to town." She spins on her heels with arms full of dirty dishes. "You can pay at the register."

Justin tucks his phone in his pocket and wipes his mouth, pleased with his greasy, meaty lunch. "We need to get going. The movers will be here within the hour."

My heart does a double thump. Time to head to the new homestead. True, I'm a hanger-on in this adventure of theirs, just a barnacle on their barge, but I'm excited too even if I haven't been to the place yet. Desperate to reignite my life, the promise of a thousand potential projects, plans, and ideas leap to mind, calling out to me with hope. Maybe this is where I'll find myself. Or a purpose beyond wiping tiny hineys. Something. Anything, really.

Ready to settle the bill, I toss two twenties at Justin. "Here's my cash. Can you pay mine too? I'll run to the restroom, and then we'll get out of here. Sound good?

He grabs the cash. "Yep. Get going, sis. I got this."

My imagination whirls with anticipation as I rise. Roughly fifteen minutes from now, we should be there, home. Can a fresh start be far behind?

Oblivious to my growing excitement, Aaron considers me for a moment as I push back from the table, ready to roll. "Mom, if you fart in there, are you going to say excuse me?"

Nick polishes off his root beer and sets his glass on the table. "I bet she won't. I bet she'll sit there, fart, and say nothing."

Good gravy, will they get off this topic already? My stern gaze falls on blind eyes. Ignoring them, I make a hasty exit to the restroom, but Aaron once again sends shockwaves through the diner with his cry, "Will you tell us if you fart?"

sigh

Maybe I can outrun his voice. I rush away and turn the corner sharp, seeking sanctuary in the women's room. Instead, however, I spy something even better. Speeding toward me from an open door at the end of the hall is Hottie McHot-Stuff, the good-looking cowboy with moisture on his mind.

We both stop short. I sidestep right, as he sidesteps left into my path. We chuckle. Immediately we both dance the other way, blocking one another yet again.

I flash him a smile and grin. "Sorry about that. How about I stop, and you walk on by?"

Hints of vanilla, pine, and leather waft my way. He nods agreement, and our eyes connect. For a moment, we hold yet another stare.

Damn, he's even better looking up close and personal. I could get used to this. Heat rises in my face—where'd that come from? Moisture rises in my jeans—I know where that came from.

All too soon, he breaks our gaze and sidesteps around me. "Excuse me and thank you." Boots clack on the wooden floor, and he saunters away, dragging a steam cloud from my body in his wake. It's a wonder the candy-striped wallpaper in the hallway doesn't peel.

Happy to have a new hobby, I peek over my shoulder and gape at each swaying butt cheek. "You're welcome," I mumble as his blue-jean clad McNuggets disappear around the corner. "You are very welcome."

Into the diner restroom I go, daydreaming about hot cowboys and diner sex. A random inspection of my breasts, hoping they impressed, halts my midday revelry. Because, naturally, there's a hunk of crusted ketchup clinging to my left boob.

Perfect. At least there isn't a French fry in my cleavage. Or is there?

I scrape at the hardened blob with marginal success, preferring to study this fresh new stain on my old, dumpy T-shirt rather than the current flustered face in the mirror. I hate mirrors. The view always disappoints, even now after I've dropped a few dozen post-divorce, pissed-off pounds. But, as I de-crust and wash my hands, I finally look up.

Stain or no stain, I want to see what the cowboy saw.

A round, pixie face with a smattering of freckles that in twenty years when I'm pushing fifty everyone will assume are age spots. Bright green eyes with ex-husband anger issues and a twinkle of insanity. A hint of frown lines spreading across my pale, translucent forehead, explaining my new-found love of long, wispy bangs. Reddish blonde hair thanks to a box from the grocery store. A great big mouth built for yelling and eating. Yep. That about sums it up.

I pinch my cheeks for color because, nowadays, for sheer self-respect alone and in spite of my self-imposed dating ban, I'm making an effort. The truth is, in my full-time baby-making years, I'll admit I didn't most days. A relentless, nonstop tug of war between keeping it together or giving up and letting everything go to seed waged inside me as I confronted dirty diapers, dirty dishes, dirty underwear, and dirty socks. Clad in sensible shoes and something stretchy most days, I only wanted to be comfortable.

News flash. Husbands hate comfortable.

Which is why I am comfortable no more. Time to flush and flee. My old chubby life swirls down the crapper, and my new, uncomfortable, slightly less chubby, but even less focused one awaits. Halle-freaking-lujah, I'm a stalled work in progress.

Drowning in my personal funk, I toss a paper towel in the trash and bolt from the bathroom, far away from the mirror when—slam!

A tall, thin, elderly man sways, reduced to a sapling in a strong breeze, threatening to collapse to the floor under the weight of my rapidly advancing body. He's bundled up in a thick coat, and thank heavens, too, because his right lapel is the only thing that kept him upright.

I cling to it now, gripping with all my might as he steadies his skinny legs beneath himself. His dusty brown bowler hat tilts far forward on a patch of thin silver hair, and there's a spare quality about him.

A tired, watery stare falls upon me, and his initial alarm gives way to anger. "Young lady, watch yourself!"

Why couldn't I have slammed into the cowboy? I could have grabbed something more substantial than this old man's coat.

Letting go of the gentleman's lapels, I lurch backward. "Oh, my gosh, I'm sorry!"

He stands erect, but even with his dignity restored, his anger grows. "You, young people. You don't think, none of you. You have no concept of your own actions, no sense of responsibility!"

Holy crap. What do I say to that? I'm tongue-tied. After all, I did mow him down with my mom thighs. Plus, he thinks I'm "young people," and he sounds like he means it, possibly even enough to pinkie swear.

However, neither of us whips out a tiny digit. Instead, we stand there, locked in stony silence. "Sorry," I repeat for want of anything else to say.

Finally, he turns with a huff and disappears around the corner into the dining room.

Great. We've barely been in town an hour, and I am far from making friends.

Shaken, I hesitate. Please let this move be the right decision. Please?

It has to be because, right now, I'm a freaking mess. Somehow, I managed to abdicate control over my life to a man who eventually chafed under the responsibility. Now? Now, post-divorce, I'm a rudderless ship, a floating piece of flotsam bobbing downstream, willy nilly, with no real goals or plans other than to make this move, which may or may not be a smart move. What if this proves to be a dead end too? I can't have any more dead ends. Wasn't my marriage enough?

Everyone else has it together. Why the hell don't I?

Desperate for hope, I settle for a plea to the universe instead. Alone in the hall, eyes closed, back against the wall, I give it a go.

Hey, universe, will you please let this move be the right decision for me and my kiddies? Please? With sugar on top?

No one answers, God, Karma, the universe, or alien overlords for whom I am a rapidly failing SIMS avatar, nothing.

Was I expecting an answer?

sigh

No.

I'm alone in the hallway. No skinny old men or hot, buff cowboys walk my way. Regrets, fear, and second thoughts burn behind my eyelids, threatening tears. Steeling myself, I open my eyes, ready to swipe them away before any should fall when I notice it.

A bulletin board anchors the opposite wall, demanding my attention. It's plastered with everything from hay for sale (first cut too, which I assume is the deepest) to pictures of mixed-breed puppies alongside notices for church chili suppers. Bluegrass music drifts in from the dining area, and I drink it in, savoring the ambiance, searching for a sign.

Wait, what's this? An employment ad? For an actual job? Who in the hell advertises on bulletin boards in this digital age? Better question, is it a sign from the universe? A random act of coincidence? A magical stroke of luck?

Who cares? It's an ad. I lean forward and read.

"Local businessman with multiple enterprises seeks organized, responsible individual to serve as part-time office manager with potential for full time available. Knowledge of basic accounting a plus. Requires good communication skills, customer service, and an ability to type. Pleasant office demeanor a necessity."

Oh my. It's a real job.

Snapping a picture with my cell phone, I give thanks to my short-lived pre-baby history of minimum-wage, part-time jobs at gas-stations and mini-marts. Customer service? No one rang up a carton of Marlboro Lights faster than me. Responsible? The Circle K condom dispenser in the men's restroom was never empty on my watch.

Is this my sign? It sounds like a stretch. Can I really do all that? I, mean, I wasn't exactly bred for this job, was I?

Bred for it? Ick, parent sex. There's an early Saturday-morning memory from age ten I don't need to recall right now.

Scratch that. It's time to be bold and bring on the next chapter of my life.

Lord knows, I need it.

Chapter Two

My SUV hugs the road as we trail behind Justin and Olivia, headed to our new home. Our new home. Geez, that feels weird, false somehow. Is it my home too? I can't shake this notion I'm clinging to my brother like a used dryer sheet in a basket full of bath towels. At least I smell good.

Low, amber-colored hills undulate around us as we climb through the valley, hauling children and ass along the main road out of town, Poseyville, Illinois to be exact. These rolling hills are capped here and there with painfully neat farms, towering pines, and woods shedding leaves in clouds of red, brown, and yellow. Justin plows through a massive clump, and a storm of dead foliage whorls into my path, eclipsing me with color. I bust through it in six-cylinder glory, growing ever closer to our home.

Nope. Not happening. Still feels weird.

Justin's turn signal snaps on, and I follow him onto a gravel road next to a large red barn. Fat, docile cows hunch together under a large maple. Making the turn, I lower my window. "Moo!" A few black and white heads gape in my general direction, but otherwise they take no notice.

Olivia's voice calls to me from my cell phone on the dash. "Did you seriously moo at those cows?"

I back off Justin's bumper and continue to window gawk. "Yep. I've got to make friends somehow. Cows seem a good place to start. They feel like a judgment free zone."

She ignores my attempt at socializing with the locals. "Cows are so pretty. Too bad they smell."

Forget friendship and fragrance, now steak fills my thoughts. I step on the gas, wishing I burned calories as easily as my SUV. "Tasty too. My favorite cow color is medium rare."

Her sigh sizzles through the speaker. "You're killing me, Ro." My brother's laugh echoes in the distance too, but she ignores him. "You're not planning on eating Bessie, are you?"

"Bessie? You've already got her named?"

"I don't know, maybe, if we ever actually have a cow, which, honestly, I can't imagine. But Gertrude's good too."

Braking into another curve, I fly through a tunnel of trees. "Not

Gertrude. I'm saving that for a goose."

Aaron kicks the back of my seat, possibly aiming for a kidney. "Mom, are we getting a goose?"

Maddy's eyes never leave SpongeBob on the DVD player. "And a cow?"

This is turning into a real pet parade.

Olivia interrupts with a dose of common sense. "I was kidding about the cow. What do any of us know about farm animals? I'm happy to start with herbs."

Wait, aren't animals a requirement in the country? I hope so. "Kids, we'll talk about pets later."

"If we get any," asks Aaron, "are we gonna eat 'em?"

"No!" yells Maddy before I can reply.

"No!" chimes in Olivia.

"Definitely," Justin remarks.

"Guys," I holler back, "there will be no eating of pets. At least not while Livy's vegan."

Justin's snort echoes from my cell phone followed by the distinct sounds of muffled arguing.

Nick catches my reflection in the rearview mirror. "Mom, can we get a guinea pig? They're small."

Aaron kicks the seat again. "They eat guinea pigs in Peru."

"Mom...," Nick whines.

"Aaron...," I warn, "and how do you know that?"

Soothing the rising tensions from one vehicle away, Olivia interrupts, "Maybe we should start with a cat. They can live outdoors, can't they?"

I glare at Aaron in the rearview mirror, and I cut him off before he can start. "Keep quiet, kiddo. Yes, they can," I bark at the dash.

The children chat on, excited about our future cow, goose, guinea pig, and cat. Maddy contemplates a flock of penguins, and I ignore the ensuing argument about where they live and if Aaron can eat one, should we coax some to Illinois. We pass another herd of cattle as we tear down the road and I can't let it go. "Maybe if we get a cow, I can milk her."

There's silence from the cell phone.

Should I sweeten this deal? Time to appeal to her inner blogger. "Wouldn't it be fun to make our own cheese?"

Ever the foodie, she takes the bait. "Good question. It might be fun. I'll try anything once."

"That's why I married you," adds Justin.

Oh, I love this. It's working. And ick. I ignore him and work on planting the pet seed. "Sounds fun, doesn't it? We can start our own cheese farm."

She laughs. "I believe the word is dairy."

Oh. Right. "Thanks, itch-bay."

Still, I don't think she's embracing my hopes of future cow ownership.

"We don't need a cow to make cheese," she explains, "only raw milk. Plus, I'm not sold on dairy. I wonder if we can make it with almond milk. Or soy?"

My pet dreams deflate. "Moo?" I press.

"Meow," crackles from my cell phone. "Let's start smaller. Think cat."

The left turn signal blinks in front of me, interrupting our conversation, and we grind to a halt under a canopy of leaves. A narrow gravel drive cuts through the hills, angling upward through a stand of trees, disappearing beyond sight in the dappled sunshine. A rusted metal gate, complete with chain and lock, clings to two wooden fence posts, barring our way as it thrusts a rusty sign declaring, "No Trespassing" in our path.

We're here.

A twinge of anxiety fills my chest. Am I trespassing? Should I even be here?

I don't know. Maybe?

Images I've memorized from Olivia's blog posts, pictures, and emails come to mind, the huge brick house upon a tree-lined hill, empty and forlorn. Massive shade trees hug its flanks. High-ceilinged rooms drip with woodwork and character. Wide-plank wooden floors tell a tale of paths traveled over time. Huge stone fireplaces anchor room after room, fueling my imagination as they once heated the home. A broken, forlorn greenhouse, locked in silence, calls out for glass and seedlings, cantaloupe and care.

My heart beats a cry, "We're home, we're home," even if, technically, it's not my home. I clutch the steering wheel hard, desperate for a sense of stability in the whirling dervish of my life. Anticipation and anxiety overwhelm me.

Bright shiny stars pop into view, and a tiny ache materializes above my right eye. *You're holding your breath, Ro. Breathe, breathe, freaking breathe. One day at a time, remember? One day at a time.*

They've offered to sell me land—they have plenty, acres and acres of it—they've said so several times. I could build a tiny house, plant a garden, start a project of my own. I desperately need a real project, a substantial project, something beyond trying to fit into skinny jeans, though I have no clue what it might be.

Justin hops from his truck and fumbles with the rusted lock and chain. After a momentary struggle, he pushes the gate open with a bladder-piercing shriek and returns to his truck, pausing long enough to give me a wave, a grin, and, naturally, the finger. I flip the bird back. With a laugh, he climbs in then turns his SUV onto the lane.

Once more, I do what I do best. I follow.

My cell phone sparks to life. "Wait until you see it," Olivia's voice tingles. "It's so beautiful. You'll love what I want to do with the kitchen and the dining room? Oh, my, those floors! You can't find wide-plank oak anymore, at least, not in our budget."

Her plans filter through the air waves. It's thrilling when she goes into full-on air-raid mode. Sometimes, it's even contagious.

Will I ever be contagious?

Emotions overwhelm me. "Sweetie, thanks again for including us," I reply. "I mean it. I owe you guys big time for this. It won't be for long, I promise."

A hesitation. "Ro, stop it. We want you here. Don't forget it."

Justin's voice booms out. "Yeah, sis, we love free labor. Those floors aren't going to strip themselves."

smack

"Ow!"

Brothers. Such idiots.

I love those two.

Hallmark moment over, we drive single file up the narrow lane. Ruts mar the path, demanding my focus, but I'm desperate to catch sight of the house. The kids are silent, riveted to the scene as we crawl along the winding lane. It cuts through hills thick with trees, skirting a ravine laced with mottled tan and white sycamores. Tall, wide trees hug either side of a meandering creek, its bed carved between the hills, heading toward parts unknown.

"Mom," Aaron pipes up from the cheap seats, "this looks like a place where people disappear. For good. You know, like in those movies you won't let us watch."

I knew the silence wouldn't last.

Justin's voice crackles from my cell phone, "Good one, kid."

We climb the last hill under a canopy of yellow and gold when it emerges.

Thornhill.

A gray moldering hunk, the huge L-shaped house perches on a ridge, surveying the land below, a tired, old queen on her throne. She's massive, a three-story behemoth. I'm surprised she doesn't sport a flying buttress or two. A wide porch crowned with an equally wide balcony spans her broad front, overlooking the valley below. Large shuttered windows and a pair of French doors take advantage of the ample view.

Olivia wasn't kidding. It is beautiful, achingly beautiful. Haunting, proud, alone, yet, somehow, so beautiful. What did she say, again? Oh, right, the old gal's got good bones.

But battle scars mar the once proud home, etching her façade with the cruel, relentless markers of time. The high-pitched roof sags in spots—at least I can wear a bra—and the once white-painted brick gleams in faded shades of neglected pinks and browns. Clumps of thick weeds sprout between the porch boards, and the effect reminds me of my calves, which I no longer shave because winter's coming and what's the freaking point anyway? No one grabs them in the dark, and the friction keeps my socks up.

It hits me, then, a kindred connection to this poor, sagging gal, and it washes over me. Already, we have so much in common. Perhaps we need each other.

The west side comes into view, as we crest the hill. Another set of French doors overlook a courtyard behind the house, anchored by the sad, diminutive greenhouse of my dreams. Skeletal remains of wild rambling rose vines clamber over it and into it through absent panes of glass. Olivia's Instagram-inspired visions may be hijacking my imagination because if I squint, I can almost make out the plan—rows of lettuce, pots of tomatoes, beds of basil, thyme, and oregano, and a tall lemon tree bursting with bright yellow fruit. I'll plant a fig tree in a pot, and I'll keep it alive, I promise. Daffodils, too, I'll plant daffodils. My nana always grew daffodils, wide, yellow swathes of daffodils.

Thoroughly devoid of gardening plans, Aaron strains in his seat behind me. "Wow. What a dump. Are we really going to live here?"

Nick presses his face against the glass. "Is this it?"

Great. Me? I picture daffodils, but not my boys. Maybe I should set them up with a Pinterest account. Or make them read their aunt's blog, then quiz them afterward for cookies. Couldn't hurt. I focus on Nick in the rearview mirror and ignore Aaron. "Yep, this is home."

His sweet, sensitive face melts into a frown as he contemplates the giant, rundown house. "It looks haunted."

Sensing an opportunity, Aaron stretches across Maddy pinned in her booster seat all the better to torment his brother. "I bet there's ghosts in there that'll rip our faces off."

Her gaze whips away from the house to the rearview mirror,

catching my attention. "Are there ghosts, Mommy?"

Geez, that kid. Don't blame me, he gets it from his father.

I flash my foulest stink eye at Aaron but answer the other two. "No ghosts. Would Justin buy it if it had ghosts? You know he's a big old wuss about that stuff."

"Hey," echoes from my brother.

Ignoring his protests one-car away, I plunge on. "There are no ghosts, ghouls, or monsters, just plenty of room. Not to mention history, lots and lots of history."

Another kick lands on the back of my seat. "Yuck," Aaron moans. "History sucks."

Clearly, not a good selling point, though great punishment material. "Keep it up, kiddo, and I'll make you memorize the Constitution."

Addressing my cell phone, I holler at Olivia, "The charm of the place is lost on the rug rats."

She chuckles. "Makes me glad the girls are too young to have an opinion. I'm hanging up now. Let's go explore."

"You got it."

Nick studies the house, his curiosity piqued. "We get to go exploring?"

Oh, I can work with this. "Of course. We're on an adventure. That big, old house is full of nooks and crannies. Don't you want to take a look?"

A tempered smile lights his face. "Yeah. I guess so."

Okay, we're getting there. I channel my inner confident mom voice. "Good, so, let's go exploring."

Ghosts forgotten, Maddy squirms in her booster seat, ready to roam. "I want to go exploring too."

Aaron stares through the window. "I bet there's rats in there. I'm gonna catch 'em and train 'em."

Heaven help me, train them to do what? I can almost picture it—large, well-skilled rats in tiny argyle sweaters and itty, bitty hard hats run through an obstacle course of children's books, hunting for hunks of processed cheese. Embracing the sweet bliss of occasional parental ignorance, I shake off that intriguing, but disturbing, mental image and don't pry for details.

Cresting the last knoll, I park and release my three rabid hounds. They break into a run, erupting into banshee squeals, no doubt sending any would-be ghosts far into the distance hills. The rest of us follow in hot pursuit.

The excitement is palpable. Justin and Olivia talk over each other, imagining future garden plots here and future orchards there, discussing priorities and making plans. They're one step closer to their dream. Must be intoxicating.

The air is fresh, crisp, with no hint of the ever-present smell of exhaust coming from the nearby highway overpass of my former home. Crickets and bird song fill the air. A gentle breeze rustles the trees overhead, sending yellow and gold falling before us. We amble up a wide flagstone path past a clump of large blue spruce when I notice my kids standing motionless in front of the house. I pick up the pace, break free of the trees, reach the front porch, and gasp.

High upon the landscape we stand. It's deceptive, this prominence, its height disguised by the rolling elevation around us, not to mention the plentiful trees. An expansive view of the valley stretches before us, and we gawk, all of us, even the children. I want to drink it in. I want to watch the sun rise from this spot. I want to twirl around in the yard and sing about how the hills are alive with the sound of music, I want—

"Mom?"

"Yes, Aaron?"

"Can I have a rocket?"

"No."

Hill after tumbling hill sprout up to the south, each capped with tidy farms and gold and burgundy trees. A glimpse of the creek sparkles below us in the sunshine, and beyond it lies an orchard, long since relieved of its harvest, near the turnoff with its substantial red barn anchored alongside the road. The pasture corner is empty now, but in the distance, more cows stroll in grass-filled fields. Poseyville remains out of view, though the water tower winks its flashing red light in the afternoon haze. Farther past it, the tip of the Methodist Church steeple hugs the edge of town a few miles distant, pointing toward heaven.

Nick scans the horizon. "This is cool." He swivels my way. "Isn't it neat, Mom?"

Boy, is it. I ruffle his hair. "Yep. No wonder they put the house here."

Aaron clears his throat. "I bet I can spit really far from here." He works on a loogie, ready to fire one off into the valley below.

Ugh. I've said it before, and I'll say it again. Kids, they're beyond gross. They're disgusting. "No spitting, Aaron."

Naturally, he swallows it.

For the love of God...

I stifle a gag. Olivia stifles a gag. Leave it to him to make it even grosser.

Justin gives his nephew an appreciative stare. "Dude." My six-foot-three brother offers a fist bump, and my youngest son reciprocates.

Guys. Also so gross.

My equally disgusting brother steps behind me and bumps me with his shoulder, getting my attention. "Penny for your thoughts, sis."

Good question. What am I thinking beyond gross, disgusting, and, finally, back to wow? I look left, then right. What a view. "You got a great place, little bro. Pictures don't do it justice. What are your thoughts?"

A smirk swims across his face. "Honestly? Now, I'm thinking about getting a bottle rocket."

Olivia turns Jayden loose, sending leaves scattering under her tiny toddler feet. "Nope." She laughs.

He puts his arm around his wife and pulls her in for a hug. "Ah, come on. Party pooper."

Uninterested in public displays of affection, Nick kicks at the ground and squirms in his shoes, desperate to burn energy after our lengthy road trip. "Can I throw rocks down the hill?"

First spit, now rocks. What next? Sticks?

Justin scans the valley, probably wondering how far he can throw too. "Sure. I might give it a try myself."

Yep. Thought so. They're gross, but not complicated.

Establishing parameters, I point at a large stone and ward off Nick. "Not that one. Small ones only. And only down the hill."

He pivots on his heels, ready to rock. "Thanks, Mom."

Aaron spins after him. "I want to throw some too."

"Wait a sec." I snatch his collar before he can take off, stalling his progress. "Small ones, kiddo. I mean it. Be really careful. Don't throw them at your brother. Or your sister. Or your cousins. Or the house. Definitely not the house."

So many disclaimers with that child. My conversations with him are walking footnotes dripping with asterisks.

Nick sprints to the drive, leaving a trail of swirling leaves behind him. "I bet I can throw further than you!"

Released from my grip, Aaron dashes after him, pumping his arms as he flies after his older brother. "Bet cha' can't!"

Content they have a plan, but wary of its outcome, I brace myself for the unknown, preferring to take in the view. It's easy to do, this letting go of responsibility, even for the briefest of moments. I want to savor this—I would paint it if I knew how.

Instead, I settle for my cell phone. At least it can zoom, and

Olivia's been after me to be more active on Instagram. I open my camera app and snap picture after picture—Maddie cavorting with the twins, Justin kissing his lovely wife in the dappled sunshine, the long-distance view beckoning with its palette of reds, oranges, yellows, and greens, a true technicolor force of nature.

Circling around, I hunt for my boys, ready to capture them in action as they hunt for rocks, preparing for their epic throwing contest on the hill. Instead of finding them hunkered over the gravel drive, however, I spy them between the blue spruce trees, laughing, bending, chatting, and petting. Because they're not alone.

A cat, plump, yellow, and happy to meet them too, headbutts Aaron's knees. The fat feline leans into my son with his wide-angled head and glides across his legs. A long, swishing tail flicks back and forth in pursuit. Running out of boy, the fluffy kitty turns and tucks into another rub in the opposite direction, sliding back across Aaron, headed straight for Nick. Back and forth it goes, rubbing, spinning, and swishing across my boys' legs.

Nick catches me watching them with their new four-legged friend. All innocence and joy, he points at the kitty. "We found a cat."

"Cat?" Olivia and Justin grind to a halt in mid kiss, their happy-homeowner dance suspended.

Livy's mouth drops open, the word barely off her lips, no doubt reliving our pet conversation during our drive minutes ago. Who knew it would be so prophetic?

Justin squints at the boys, an eyebrow arches up, and a hint of tickled wonder blooms across his grizzled cheeks. "What'd you know? Looks like we got ourselves a cat."

Blinking in slow motion, she scrutinizes her husband. "Did you plan this somehow?"

He raises calloused hands in the air, "Honest, hun, I had nothing to do with it."

"Mom," Aaron interrupts, "can we keep it?"

Ah, the inevitable cry for kitty-cat ownership, right on schedule. He sits now, cradling the fat feline. Nick hovers alongside him, scratching an ear. From here, it certainly smells like adoption.

Tiny girl ears catch the word cat on the breeze. Maddie and the twins brake to a halt, then launch headlong at the boys, squealing. To its credit, the chubby kitty remains undisturbed and, rather than bolting for the weeds as any sane creature should do, it sprawls across Aaron's lap, soaking up the attention, ready for more.

My youngest reaches the cat and drops to her knees, swooning with instant love. "Oh, you, poor baby, I'll take care of you. Mommy, we've gotta keep him. He'll die if we don't."

Oh goodie, a guilt trip too. It's not even my birthday. How generous.

We join the children and study the cat. Shushing Maddie with a finger to my lips, I bend over my son and visually inspect the feline rump fluff from a safe distance. "Are you a fella?" I make eye contact with Olivia. "Should we peek under the hood?"

She tilts away avoiding its bottom. "Probably, but you do it. Quick, Ro, take a peek."

"Nope, sorry." I shake my head. "We haven't even been introduced yet. I feel like we should get to know each other first, maybe have dinner together."

"Oh, for heaven's sake." Justin squats between the children and examines the cat's bottom. "Congrats. It's a boy."

I lean over Aaron to the sound of purrs. "You sure?"

Standing straight, Justin wraps his long gorilla arms around his wife and rests his chin on her head. "Yeah, I can tell the difference between the naughty bits, sis. You may have forgotten, though."

Ouch. What a turd.

Olivia interrupts our squabbles, eyeballing the cat. "He can't be a stray; he hasn't missed many meals. Lost, maybe, but not a stray."

I kneel beside the kids and search for a collar, but find none, although I do find ample evidence of fat rolls. "Boy, he is a butterball. Do you think someone dropped him off?"

My sister-in-law, however, holds her ground. "What if he got out on accident? What if there's a kid crying right now because he can't find his pet? We should probably call the shelter. If he's lost, someone may have reported it."

An avalanche of no and why can't we pour from the mouths of children who only want to love this fur ball. Is that so wrong?

With that chub, however, he probably does belong to someone. Ah, reason, why must you suck so?

Justin and I deflate. He steps around his frowning wife and pets the purring pussy. "I guess we should probably call the shelter. Maybe tomorrow. We're too busy to deal with this today, what with the movers and all. He can sleep in our room tonight. You know, so we can keep an eye on him, make sure he stays out of trouble."

Flailing her hands in frustration, Oliva fails to take the bait. "Oh, good grief. Are you already attached to this cat?"

"Look at him, Liv. What's not to love?"

Determined, Maddie digs in, ready to fight the good fight. "Please, Mommy, can we keep him? Please?"

Nick takes up the gauntlet too, ready to impale my guilt-tripping, parental heart. "Yeah, please?" he implores. "You said we could get a cat"

I shoot a glance at Olivia who shoots one back.

Growing increasingly tired and cranky, my daughter whines even louder. "We'll be good if we can keep him, we promise. Even Aaron."

"I'm not making any promises," Aaron back tracks, ever the politician. "I can catch mice for him, though. I bet there's plenty in the house. Look at it."

"Hey," Justin yells for the second time in ten minutes.

My boy rambles on, making plans. "I'll make traps to catch them and everything. Please?"

Sporting a mischievous grin, Justin aims it at Olivia with a pretend pout, "Yeah, please, Mom? Can we?"

"Please?" repeat Nick and Maddy as they take up their uncle's rallying cries.

"Pwees?" Jaylen and Jayden coo in sync, radiating their personal brand of precious toddler charm.

"Yeah, 'cause Dad isn't around to sneeze anymore," Aaron insists, going for the kill, expertly playing the child-of-a-recent-divorce card. "Mom, you always said we couldn't have pets 'cause of Dad. He's not here now. Can't we at least keep the cat?"

Ah, that boy, he has this guilt thing down to a science.

Sensing the children need reinforcements, the cat rolls onto his back and displays his ample white tummy, declaring in his own kitty way, "Scratch me, minions." Our babies giggle and comply, under the magical spell of homeless kitty cuteness.

I attempt to impart reason into this conversation, careful not to wreck any teeny, tiny dreams or piss off any large, grown adults in the process. "Listen, kids," I begin, "we'll get a pet eventually." I will them to understand, but the looks on their faces are so hopeful. I falter. "…I want to keep this guy too." I hesitate. Tiny chins quiver and tiny eyes turn to glass. Sniffles penetrate the air. "He probably belongs to someone. He's too fat and happy to be a stray. We need to find his owner."

Ratcheting up the darling factor, the four-legged interloper paws at my daughter's pig tails, putting on a show as she hugs him, sprouting tears. He catches one pigtail between his paws and chews the end. The children laugh, even Maddy, and she teases him with strawberry blonde curls. "He wants to play with me."

Resolve melts. Plans go astray. I dissolve into lukewarm

gelatin.

Parenthood, it's such a badass kick to the head.

Fortunately, Olivia isn't immune either. Giving in, she sighs. "Okay, he can stay for a few days. We'll call the shelter on Friday and," she caves, "if no one claims him, we'll keep him."

Squeals of delight erupt on the hill, including the loudest from Justin. She shakes her head, laughing. "If it does belong to someone else, we'll all take him back, and then we'll get another cat. Deal?"

"Deal," we all agree.

I lift the cat from the swarm of children and hand him to Justin, who cradles him close. "Now how about we go explore the house? Did you forget we haven't even seen it yet?"

My children swivel toward the gray form hulking behind us. Nick fidgets in the grass. "Can we bring the cat?"

Instantly we all face Olivia. She looks from child to child to husband. "Oh, all right. You can bring the cat."

"Yay!" fills the air.

Happy, excited, and, finally, curious, the kids make for the house. Nick hip checks Aaron and sprints to the porch, determined to be first. Never one to be beaten, Aaron tears after his brother yelling louder than a high-school cheer block at a championship game. When God handed out inside voices, that kid must have slept in and missed it.

The rest of us trail behind them, ready to explore, but already I'm slipping back into daydream mode. First a cat but what next? A dog? A hamster? No guinea pigs though.

Cat crisis momentarily resolved, we stroll through the lawn, making plans. Olivia points to a spot for lilacs. Justin mentions a grape arbor. I imagine scooping litter boxes. Can we use it as fertilizer? I could sprinkle it around the roses.

Maybe I can learn to garden. They both offered to show me. I'll eat fresh vegetables for a change, not canned. Surely, I can manage that.

Summers filled with tomatoes, wouldn't that be nice. Come autumn, we'll be knee deep in a pumpkin patch. Winter? Sledding parties and snowball fights—won't that be fun. I'm starting to see the vision now. It's fuzzy and foggy, but at least I'm cleaning off my glasses and peering at the furry, weedy future.

I'll ask Olivia to give me cooking lessons that go beyond opening a box, adding water then stirring until ready. I can learn to grow herbs, cook with them, make pies from scratch, simmer homemade stocks—all that good stuff she goes on and on about in her blog. Justin can teach me to be handy around the house. Surely, I can beat stuff with a hammer.

Maybe I will buy a few acres, build a modest house, plant my own garden, get a cat, and start new traditions. I'll put down roots too, and not merely the vegetable kind. Better rooted than rootless, right?

They say when one door closes, another opens, but lately too many of those closed doors slammed in my face, and the only ones I've opened since I had to pry at with a freaking crowbar. Now I have the chance to build a new life here, and it's becoming more concrete with every passing second.

I join my family on the porch of our new home, ready to start our adventure. Things are starting to look up.

I think.

Chapter Three

Rain slick roads stare back at me. I tear through the countryside in Justin's pile of crap-on-wheels, cussing the early-morning drizzle while practicing questions that define me to strangers. Questions like, what are my skills, and where do I see myself in five years, and what are my strengths. Underworked and rarely paid, I'm scrambling for answers, because the bulletin board ad in the diner morphed into a part-time job interview for which I am spectacularly unqualified. Lord knows, I should plan something for the inevitable questions that will arise, questions that circle the black-hole expanse of my post college-drop-out years.

Oh great, I thought of another one. *Tell me, Ro, what have you been doing with yourself beyond wiping tiny bottoms and yelling incoherently? Any filing? Emailing? Number crunching? No, sorry, chewing doesn't count.*

What do I do better than chewing?

Perhaps I should mention self-control. After all, Peter, the ex, told me about the younger woman on a Monday night after I fed him dinner and washed his underwear, and I didn't kill him. That's got to count for something. On the other hand, mentioning a former murderous fantasy I managed to quell only because the children were in the next room might not set the right tone. Bummer.

A giant puddle spans the road ahead. I swerve into the empty left lane, barely missing it. I've got to miss it. This beat-up clunker has a hole in the floorboard bigger than my thighs, thus puddles are fraught with danger. After hitting a tiny one and getting sprayed from the kneecaps down, I've learned my lesson. Can I get a hallelujah? And a baby wipe?

Or possibly a human sacrifice, because that's not even the worse of it. I awoke to a flat tire on the morning of my first interview in years. Stupid Murphy's Law, right? Channeling my inner independence, I was determined to change it, but after a frustrating wrestling session with the car jack that reminded me of teenaged sex on prom night, my progress ground to a halt. No amount of pushing, pulling, kicking, cussing, screaming, or crying would break those lug nuts loose on my SUV. Even after inhaling way too many pancakes for breakfast and jumping on the tire iron, they wouldn't budge. Bastards.

To make matters worse, Olivia had already left to take the boys to school, and Justin was headed to a worksite in another county, leaving me to my last option, his current car project, a twenty-year-old rusted VW Beetle with one working wiper he inherited with the barn at Thornhill. Desperate as hell, I took it.

Making the best of this calamity would be easier if my left temple weren't throbbing like the lead in a porno though. Stupid caffeine addiction. It was a toss-up between having my morning coffee and avoiding caffeine withdrawal or skipping it in hopes I can get through this interview without having to pee. Of course, now, I have a pounding headache and *still* I need to pee because, thanks to Aaron, who weighed forty pounds at birth, I have no real functioning bladder control and my one superpower is generating a quart of piss from desert dry air. *Good call, Ro. Good call.*

Thank God for over-the-counter pharmaceuticals. Digging in my purse, I hunt for an aspirin. There should be at least ten of them in here somewhere—I never leave home without them, but I keep coming up with rock-hard goldfish crackers and cereal instead. Ah, lovely. Now, there's crud under my fingernails too. I hope it's cereal dust—that I can get out on the way to the interview.

My lips engulf my index finger and I suck. Great, pencil lead. I hope it doesn't make me stupid.

Where're those aspirin? Reaching back in, I search for sweet blessed relief, but I'm heading straight for a blind curve in the woods, so I let up on the accelerator, ease into the turn, and pull my hand from my purse.

Only I no longer care about the pills.

Because the bright and shiny grill of a large semi flies around the curve half in my lane. Instinct takes over. I swerve to the right and jam on the brakes, praying they don't fail when the heel of my pump catches the ragged edge of the worn carpet and, with a lurch, peels off my right foot and disappears through the hole in the floorboard.

That's when it hit me.

I should have gone with the double-buckle Mary Janes.

The car grinds to a halt. Shoeless toes rest on the brake pedal, wondering what went wrong. I glare over my shoulder. Behind me, the rogue semi hauls ass, disappearing in short order. Does someone local drive NASCAR on the side?

Oh no, here comes another semi—incoming!

What is this? Ice Road Truckers?

Blaring lights, shiny metal, and perfectly inflated tires careen past, dousing Justin's turd mobile with a gritty spray. A faint cloud of mist swirls up from the hole in the floor, tickling my ankles. I flip off the driver as the truck blows pass, inches from my front fender and, feeling vengeful, I check my side mirror for a reaction.

What the hell…oh, crap.

The second semi heads straight for my brand-new shoe.

This is ridiculous. I'm running late. I don't have time for this. Yet, thar she blows…the truck's front tire nicks my new shoe and sends it cartwheeling through the air into a ditch.

Double crap.

Back in the day, when I was younger, I used to do cartwheels too. Once upon a time, I loved having my feet over my head. But even on my honeymoon, I didn't cartwheel as high and as fast as that twelve-dollar pump. I don't know who Murphy is who created this law but killing him now tops my bucket list.

With one cheap pump on and one off somewhere in the weeds, I climb from the car and listen for more trucks. Except for tweeting birds and rustling leaves, nothing but blissful silence greets me. Good. All the better to drop a few more f-bombs, my dear.

Feeling vengeful, I slam the door and bunny hop down the road, vomiting profanities. Trust me, it helps.

Of course, there's mud—thick, sloppy, suck-out-your-soul deep mud. I ease my way into the ditch and instantly regret it. Damp earth tugs at my one good shoe, threatening to eat it alive. I chance another step with my right foot. Oh, yuck. This is so gross. Bits of dirt, twigs, and chunks of dead leaves cling to my pantyhose. That's right, I said pantyhose. Sure, they may be out of style everywhere but Illinois, but I can live with it because they're a lovely shade of fake "suntan" that makes my legs look like they take beach vacations without me. I do so love the beach. This dead caterpillar oozing between my toes? Not so much.

Naturally, the ditch is steep. A trickle of brown water courses along the bottom, weaving its way through the muck, drenching my missing shoe. Could be worse. My shoe could be floating halfway to town.

If I can find a stick, I might be able to stab it. Figures, though, everything long and pointy is on the other side of this freaking ditch too. I've no choice. I'm going to have to retrieve it.

Should I take off my one good shoe and pantyhose first? Embracing the plan, I slip off my pump, look left, look right, look left again, then shimmy out of my hose and shove them into my shoe. With it tucked safely in the grass, I stagger farther into the steep, narrow ditch. Slipping, sliding, sinking, I reach the muddy water, hike my skirt over my knees, then straddle it.

When's the last time I straddled something good? Not today, that's for damn sure.

Impaled deep in the muddy bank, my shoe makes a weirdly suggestive sucking noise as I free it from the muck, leaving me a tad bit jealous. I give it an unfortunate shake. Dirty water dots my navy skirt. *Brilliant, Ro.* Is it possible the pencil lead is already kicking in, because that was pretty darn stupid.

Un-straddling the stream, I scramble toward the road and grab a protruding root for leverage. It gives in the soft earth and, for a moment, I'm weightless, poised on the edge of disaster, falling backward. At the last second, it holds.

Success.

Lord, I'm seriously running late. Not good, so not good. Shoes in hand, I dash to the car, jangling with interview nerves and bare, wet feet. The day ought to get better from here, right? I mean, sometimes things can get worse because Murphy's cousin, Karma, is probably still angry about the sex with the ex and the voodoo doll, but sometimes they get better, don't they?

Not necessarily.

Because things just got worse.

The door handle resists my tug. I jiggle it and pull. Nothing.

No. It can't be.

Here I am, pantyhose in hand, with one decent shoe on, a scraped up, muddy shoe off, late for my first real interview in my unfocused life, and the door to my brother's beat-up clunker is locked, stubbornly, hatefully locked. Through the dirty window, the ancient, golf-tee-like lock taunts me, a rotten, petulant, plastic child, and me without a wire coat hanger.

Frantic, I pull the back-door handle. Locked. I hop around to the passenger side. Nope. Front passenger door? Not happening. It's locked tighter than my ex's bank account.

I'm totally screwed. Mom always told me, if it's got tires and testicles, it will give me trouble. I'll be damned if she wasn't right. Again.

Hot tears sting my eyes.

No, no tears! One, I'm a grown freaking woman. Two, I'm wearing makeup for once, and raccoon eyes never look good, even on goth girls. And, three, I'm pissed off, and pissed off doesn't cry. No, pissed off gets even. Time to toughen up and solve this problem.

I peer through the window, and my cell phone winks at me from the cup holder. That's of no help. How pissed would Justin be if I busted open a window with a rock? Amused pissed? Out-of-beer pissed? Move-out-of-my-fucking-house-Ro pissed?

Nah.

I'm about to search for a boulder when salvation appears in front me. In addition to my cell phone, something else teases me from inside.

Pavement. There's that giant hole in the floorboard.

Once more I look left, look right. Hesitant, I unzip my skirt and wiggle it to the ground. Ditching my navy jacket and blouse, I'm reduced to only my ultra-reinforced foundational underwear on the side of a road in a countryside probably more familiar with the theme song to *Deliverance* than necessary. But there's a job interview waiting for me at the end of this nightmare. Time to get creative.

Tossing my clothes on the hood of the car, I drop to my knees and roll over onto my back. The asphalt is wet, cold. Stuff sticks to my shoulders, my bottom, my feet. The edge of the hole is close, so close. I grab it and pull. Heat radiates from near the engine. I knock my scalp against sharp metal. "Ow!"

It'll be nice to have a memento of this occasion, even if it's only a scar. At this rate, it sure won't be a job.

I yank myself under the hole and look up. Well, there's a view you don't see every day. From a sizeable distance, the door lock beckons, more tempting than cheesecake. Stretching with all my might, I promise myself an actual piece of cheesecake if I pull this off. Hand stretched, fingertips flailing, arm fat swinging, I reach…

What's that sound?

Oh, no. Say it isn't so.

There's another vehicle coming.

Stupid Karma. I bet she's on her period.

It slows to a halt behind Justin's rusted hunk of junk. A door opens and shuts. Hard-sole shoes pound on the pavement. I yank my arm to my side and move to the left so whoever it is can't make eye contact with me through the window and the hole.

Because, unlike everything else that's happened this morning, that would be weird.

The stranger's shoes draw closer to the car, and I hazard a glance. How I wish I hadn't. Because they're not shoes, they're boots, and there's a burned-out Texas star staring back at me from the heel.

Son of a sea biscuit, this sucks.

It's the Grade-A hunk-of-raw-meat in boot heels. The moisture-check man with the apple-pressing thighs.

Why did it have to be him? I'm on the ground in my

underwear. Great set up for a porno film, but in the grand scheme of romantic meet cutes, this is not the scenario I would have picked.

Yep, the good-looking cowboy from the diner—what's his name...Sam—just rode in on his white horse to rescue me, but I would rather be ugly naked in front of Peter's girlfriend, Ms. Fanny Fucks-a-lot.

Karma, you are such a bitch.

The boots grind to a halt. "Hello? Need any help?" A generous dollop of a fresh Texas accent hangs in the air.

I could respond with a bright and cheery, no, thank you, but do I do that? Absolutely not. Instead, the stupidity of this situation hits me harder than a wet washcloth to the face. What do I do? I snicker. Despite the damp pavement, and the locked car, and the approaching lateness of my interview, I freaking snicker. Yeah, that sends a message I'm sane.

Shifting farther away from the hole, I bite my lip. "No, I'm fine, thank you. Just having trouble with the door."

A pause. "The...the door?"

That's all it takes. Laughter bordering on the maniacal seeps from my soul and erupts from my chest.

Get control of yourself, Ro.

I bite my lip to rein in the laughs, but it's not easy. "Yes, the door. Listen, thanks for stopping. I appreciate it, but I've got this."

The boots shift slightly on the road. "Are you sure? Seems an odd way to fix a door," muses a sexy voice from far above.

Indulging for a moment, I picture the inevitable puzzled expression on his gorgeous, grizzled face. If I remember correctly, it's a nice face and a hell of a good body too. Suddenly, he's invading my thoughts, clad only in ass-less chaps, climbing imaginary stairs—damn—this is not helping. After all, I'm already damp from the wet pavement.

The last thing I need is more moisture. "Yeah, I get it, this must sound crazy, but I'm staying put until you leave."

Another pause. "Any particular reason why?"

I hesitate, then blurt out, "I'm in my underwear."

"Oh."

Cue awkward silence.

Any chance he's picturing me in my underwear? I lay there, frozen, yet tingly at the thought.

Something hot lands on my forehead. Is my cut bleeding? I touch my scalp and inspect my finger. Wonderful. Motor oil is dripping into my hair.

Well, isn't that just perfect.

Gorgeous as he is, especially in the black leather, ass-less chaps hogging my brain cells, I need him to leave. Time to take charge. "I have an interview in town and didn't want my clothes to get dirty. But I'm running late and, as much as I appreciate the offer of help, I need you to leave so I can get this door unlocked and get going. Please?" My plea erupts in a single, relentless explosion, a tsunami of insensible sounds. "Thanks though."

A delay, then, "You have an interview in town?"

Is that amusement in his voice? Why is there amusement in his voice? Where did the confusion go? I liked it better. "Yes, I do."

"You want me to leave?"

"Yes, and sooner, rather than later. This ground isn't getting any warmer."

"Ask and you shall receive." With that, the cowboy with the buns of steel turns on his star-spangled heels then heads back to his vehicle.

Committed to my new hobby of butt ogling, I contemplate smashing my cheek to the pavement to cage a lingering peek of butt cheek but hold off. "Thank you!" I holler instead.

"Don't mention it," he hollers back.

A door slams shut in the distance. I haul myself back under the hole with my sights set on the lock near the base of the window, so tantalizingly close and, yet, so far.

Tires roll on damp pavement. He pulls alongside the car. "You sure you don't want me to call anyone?"

Stretching to the limits of my short arms, I reach, reach, reach for the lock when inspiration strikes. Above me and much closer, the ignition sprouts the key like a dandelion in a yard, begging to be plucked. My fingers grasp at the key chain and yank. It catches, holds, and—thank you, Jesus—falls from the ignition, dropping through the hole in the floorboard, smacking me on the cheek.

It's happened. I did it. Peter isn't here, the key is in my hand, and the problem's solved. I managed it on my own, offer of help notwithstanding. A surge of pride courses through my Lycra-tortured torso, and I kick Karma's fat, nasty ass to the curb.

Boom, baby!

"Nope," I yell back. "I'm good."

"Okay," replies the cowboy, headed to who knows where. "Good luck with the interview."

~ * ~

Miracle of miracles, I'm in the office at the end of the diner hall being questioned by a Winston Churchill look-a-like, and I'm okay with it. He's giving off a comforting vibe, a combination of kind, wise, patient, all the things you want in a future boss or former Nazi hunter.

He sits behind a desk covered in clutter, analyzing my past as he cradles my future in arthritic hands large enough to palm a basketball. It's a crazy, messy space in here, overflowing with an odd combination of books, papers, coffee mugs, shipping boxes, car parts, and tools, but it suits him. His deep set, light blue eyes under sparse, pale lashes behind thick glasses scan my resume. Round, ruddy cheeks cover a veil of blueish veins—or are they arteries—and they huff and puff as he asks probing questions and sometimes smiles at my spontaneous answers. Unfortunately, a cascading web of interwoven wrinkles coalesce into even deeper valleys across his forehead when my answers don't elicit a smile. I'm not okay with that.

I'm lucky to even be here talking with him, as I was woefully late. After I finally made it back on the road, I called to explain the situation—and he claimed he understood—so I went into damage control mode and flew down the road like a demon possessed.

With one hand on the steering wheel, I scrubbed motor oil from my hair with an old rag from the back seat, but to no avail. Now, rather than channeling a confident interviewee vibe—which I never had in the first place—I ooze a certain slick-backed-reject-from-a-1950s-boy-band charm. Not a good look. My fallback was the classic approach of pulling my hair into a ponytail to hide the bad stuff, but all I could find swimming among the cracker crumbs and pencil lead at the bottom of my purse was Maddy's bright-pink sequined kitty-cat patterned scrunchie. Also, not a good look.

As for that elusive aspirin? Not a one. Maybe the fish shaped crackers ate them.

With my 10W-30 tresses pulled tight, mismatched roots span my forehead like a broken picket fence. I can't hide those, but if I turn my head back and forth in time with Winston Churchill Jr, I'm hoping he won't catch a glimpse of the sparkly kitty patterned scrunchie grinning away at the back of my skull.

My polyester suit and cotton blouse are none the worse for wear. Yay for small miracles. But that's the only freaking thing working in my favor. I ditched the mud-splattered pantyhose, opting instead for pasty white calves that look like stubby icicle radishes sprouting tiny, furry roots, and it's too late to rethink that bad decision. Although it has me pondering a shaving schedule, say, like when I change the calendar. Or the smoke alarm batteries.

My shoes, however, are the real issue. One perfectly fine pump cradles my left foot like a holiday hug from Nana, and I'm literally putting my best foot forward as often as I can. The right pump is another story. Black skid marks trail along both sides, which isn't too bad since they're navy, but the color scraped off completely in several spots and a lovely beige pleather peeks through instead. I tried touching them up with an ancient black marker from the console, but it was as dry as a Monday-morning, sexless vagina. Thinking fast, I smeared burnt motor oil from my hair on the spots and it helped. But not a lot.

As for the heel on my right shoe, well, it's a serious problem. It's hanging on by one disturbingly thin pleatherette thread. I briefly considered ripping the heel off the other shoe and passing them off as flats, but when I reached the edge of town, I remembered Aaron's confiscated package of gum in my purse. They can have the occasional piece or two, but when he uses it to stick signs on the car window saying he's been kidnapped, I draw the line. Regardless, taking a lemon and making lemonade, I dug his gum from my purse and started to chew.

When I got to the diner twenty minutes ago, I hopped in on one good shoe and one tenuous shoe with ten sticks of gum wedged between my damaged heel and sole, the only things standing between me and a face plant. Sarah, my future possible new best friend for lack of other options, must live here, and she gave me a what-the-hell stare as I hopped through the diner door. Immediately I shut her down with crazy eyes and a question about where to go, and she had the good sense to look away and point at the restroom hall.

Now, I sit like a disheveled schmuck while W.C. Jr. sizes me up, framing another question. As I tripped through his door, I popped open another button of my blouse with plans to distract him with middle-aged mamma cleavage. After all, a mamma bear has got to do what a mamma bear has got to do to feed her young, even if it means flashing flexible boobs at a senior citizen. It might be working. He hasn't looked at my feet or mentioned my hair or flinched at the sight of my hairy calves.

Despite the mishaps and missteps and lateness and the questions and the minty freshness wafting up from my broken shoe, the interview is going well. I think.

He peers at me over my resume and bombards me with another question. "You say you had car trouble this morning, so I have to ask, do you have dependable transportation?" He has a voice that could sell oatmeal. I love oatmeal. Explains my thighs.

Determined to show confidence, I nod firmly. "Yes, I do. This was a freak thing. I picked up a nail, but I'll get my tire fixed this afternoon."

He smiles, accepting my answer. "You need any help with that?"

How kind. I like that.

"No, I'm good, thank you. I moved here with my brother and his wife." I cross my legs, remember my stupid shoe, uncross them, and tuck it behind my left foot. "He'll help me. Justin is the new project foreman for a construction company here in town."

Mr. Hollister raises an eyebrow. "Ah, he's the man Charlie hired. Good to know."

A whiff of motor oil threatens to distract me. I focus harder. "That's him. They bought a big house and about thirty acres, and they're fixing it up. I've considered building a house there too, someday, if I can find a job. For now, we're sharing housework, bills, taking care of our kids—they've got twins and my youngest won't start kindergarten until next year. Sharing a place makes sense, at least until I can get my own place. Plus, my sister-in-law is a crazy good cook. Sometimes I wonder if I only came along for the meals."

Edmund considers me for a moment. "Interesting."

A pair of granny panties reach new heights in my ass crack, demanding immediate attention. I shift in my seat. Bummer. They remain stubbornly lodged in my nether region. "I plan to stay, if you're worried about it. I have nowhere else to go." Just like these big old panties.

He stares at me with my resume in his big, meaty hand, but I cave and focus on it instead. Fortunately, it doesn't look back. Or stare. Or judge. Though it does disappoint. Much like these panties.

We've been at this for about fifteen minutes, and I've held my own for the most part. Most of the questions were routine, and I did prepare, thanks to Google and practicing with Justin and Olivia. But I suck at this. I put my hands in my lap and twist my fingers back and forth. Great. Now I want pretzels...with butter and salt...and hot mustard...some cold beer wouldn't hurt.

I seriously need hobbies.

My all-too-sparse resume taunts me from his hands. Mr. Hollister re-examines it and scans his notes. I sense the end is near.

He clears his throat. "First off, young lady, thank you for applying, and for moving here too." He's all business now, and my heart kicks up a notch. "We don't get many new people these days, not since the battery factory closed down. Can't even keep the young people around anymore. Only ones who stay are the farm kids. That does bring me to my one concern."

"See, I've got a diner to run, not to mention a grain elevator across the street, and a few rental properties to boot. They generate a lot of paperwork, and I need someone I can count on. You're an unknown quantity."

The older man closes a notebook on his desk and sets my resume on top. At least it's not in the trash. Yet. He taps it and gives me a placating smile. "Vera Ackerd's boy, Travis, also applied, and I know where he goes to church, who he hangs out with, and how often he's been arrested. Becca Olsen applied too, and heck, I've known her family for years."

He pauses. "On the other hand," he continues, altering the over and under odds of my interview success currently playing out in the running tally in my mind, "Becca isn't the most motivated kid in the world. As for Travis, he can't speak up for himself. I blame his mom. Hell, when I called the house to talk to him about an interview, she told me he was taking a bath and took the phone right to him. I couldn't even look him in the eye during the interview. Kept wanting to call him Bubbles."

He nods at my resume. "Then there's you. I don't know you, Sparrow Andrews. Tell me, just who the heck *are* you?"

What?

Who am I?

I swallow hard. What kind of question is that? Fingers twist. My stomach growls. Part of me still wants pretzels.

What was the question again? Oh, who am I. Crud. I didn't Google that one.

What now? The hamster running in the wheel of my mind has stopped moving its fat, tiny legs, and it's spinning helplessly around and around and around, desperate to leap off and vomit. "Who am I?" I repeat, playing for time.

Other than the sound of his wheezing attempts at sucking wind, the room is quiet.

Bummer. There's no getting around this one. I'm going to have to take a stab at it. "Mr. Hollister, I'll be honest, I don't know who I am."

Patient, determined, he holds tight, waiting for more.

Good lord, am I going to have to do this? Define myself in concrete terms? I'd rather eat broken glass.

Steeling my nerves, I exhale deeply. Here goes. "Sir, I'm a single mom with three kids who needs a job. The ex left me for a younger woman, his support payments are few and far between, and, I've got to make it on my own and take care of my kids. I need a job that helps me pay the bills and build a future but also allows me to be a mom." I swallow hard, not sure if I'm helping or hurting my case. "I may not be what you want in an employee, but what I lack in education and experience, I make up for with desperation. I will give you a hundred-and-ten percent because I don't have a choice. I have to. I have to make this work. That's who I am."

I trail my hand along my thigh and pinch it hard, hoping to rein in the trembles bubbling beneath the surface of my wigged-out appearance. Nope. Not working. "Mr. Hollister, I would die for my kids. Filing your paperwork and paying your bills will be a blessing. I will clean the toilet with my tongue if I have to. Also, please call me Ro." I exhale again and stare at my lap. "My mom is a nut job."

He says nothing. I can't read his expression because I'm focused on my lead-filled fingernails. Silence fills the room. He lifts the coffee mug on his desk and takes a slow sip. I cross my legs and squeeze. Naturally, I still need to pee.

He sets his mug on the desk and tents his fingers over my resume. "Tell you what, run across the street to the grain elevator and have a chat with my foreman. If he's got no concerns, I'll put you to work on a trial basis. My decision, of course," he clarifies, "but I trust his judgment."

Maybe the gas station is hiring…wait, what? Heaven help me, did I just get a job? "Oh, my gosh, Mr. Hollister, thank you."

His puffy cheeks break into a smile. "Call me Edmund, and remember, it's a trial. You've got three months to prove you can do it." He reaches his hand across the desk.

I grasp it, overwhelmed. "Thank you, Edmund. I won't let you down."

Edmund picks up a phone on his desk. "Don't mention it. I'll call Sam, let him know you're headed his way." He holds it in his meaty hand, ready to dial.

"Sam?" I repeat.

Perhaps I shouldn't have kicked Karma quite so enthusiastically back on the road.

"Sam Whittaker. He's my right-hand man. You'll be working across the street in the afternoons. His opinion counts too, but you're in luck. He likes people with strong character. I'm sure you two will hit it off. Give him this," Edmund hands me my resume. "Tell him I gave you the thumbs up for a trial run, pending his approval. He'll be the good-looking guy with the Texas accent."

Texas accent?

Oh, holy hell.

~ * ~

A geriatric desk phone rings faintly through the glass of the grain elevator's office door. I steel my nerves and push it open, wondering what awaits me.

The man seated behind the counter doesn't answer the desk phone. Instead, he's on his cell phone, listening to someone who does all the talking. Hopefully, it's Mr. Hollister and he's saying kind, supportive things about me. The man on the cell phone frowns. Scratch that. I hope it's someone else.

As expected, the man at the desk is the guy with the kissable face, the star-spangled, boot-wearing hero who offered to rescue me less than an hour ago as I lay half naked under Justin's shitty-shitty-bang-bang of a car. I can't catch a break.

He's not alone, either. A middle-aged, stocky man in crisp jeans and a camel-colored work jacket rests against the counter between me and Sam's desk. At the sound of the squeaking door, the other fellow turns in my direction and examines me from head to toe with a come-hither expression I neither want nor acknowledge. Sandy blonde hair in a Sheldon Cooper haircut frames a quizzical face. Something registers—oh, no, I'm still sporting mamma cleavage—and he perks up.

Stupid mom boobs. I hang back. How do I fix this freaking button with him watching?

Oblivious to my boobs, Sam talks on his cell phone, his eyes staring at his desk. Dark, delicious surfer curls frame a rugged face etched with concern. His voice is deep and smooth as butterscotch. He purrs into his phone. "Thanks for calling, Greg. Your dad was a good man. I'll swing by next Monday. Until then, keep me posted on the viewing."

His voice spills forth in a heady Texan rumble that has me desperate to attack the Alamo. I make new plans and consider popping open another button.

His strong, tan fingers skate through those curls. He stands and addresses the other man in the office. "Harold Walton passed away last night."

I hang back, mentally sucking hard candy, watching, waiting, listening.

The middle-aged man examines me with curious eyes. "Boy, he fought it hard, didn't he? How old was Harold?"

Finally, Sam notices me, clutching my resume in the background, and beckons me forward. "He was eighty-seven." Before I reach him, though, his gaze lands on the row of office windows facing the diner across the street.

Oh no, does he notice Justin's car? It's sitting right there, not more than fifty feet away. Heat fills my face, swamping me from stem to stern with raw embarrassment. Why, oh why, did I park the turd mobile across the street? I left it there to sit, shedding paint flakes and rust like a diseased cat sheds germs and fur. Is it too early to blame the pencil lead?

The other man clears his throat, bringing Sam back to earth.

Sam moves away from the windows. "Sorry, Charlie, I need to call Edmund, and I have another customer. How about you bring those wagons over first thing tomorrow morning. Sound good?"

Charlie waves agreement at Sam, "Yeah, that'll work. I'll have them here early." Plan in place, he scurries my way and stops a bit too close for my comfort. "Hello, young lady. Having a good morning?"

Well, that's a loaded question. Given my earlier experience on the road and Sam's probable knowledge of it, how I answer is a veritable minefield. I can't lie, and I certainly don't want to relive it. What do I say?

Off topic, is this my essential problem? Do I read too much meaning into everything? Over analyze every conversation until it has the potential to go nuclear? Run negative scenarios to death for every possible action and reaction until I'm convinced there's no good response, so I overreact instead? Should I stop thinking for a change?

Answer the man, Ro.

"It's been an interesting one," I blurt. There, enough said. Truthful, but hedges the question. The devil is in the details.

Instead of continuing out the door, this nondescript man grinds to a halt, picks up Karma's spear, and impales me with it. "Oh, you don't say? I gotta ask, what interests a cute thing like you?"

Crap. Would it have killed me to say yes? And did he call me cute? Does Sam think I'm cute? Isn't this all rather sexist? Am I being hashtag me-too'ed? Why do I care if he thinks I'm cute? Am I seriously that desperate?

You're doing it again, Ro.

Stupid brain. Someone slap me, and help me find my self-respect too, because I left it in the didn't-see-it-coming divorce aisle, alongside the boxed wine, cheap chocolates, party-sized potato chip bags, and discount bins of entire self-loathing.

Act natural, Ro.

I shrug. "Just car trouble, but everything's fine."

Sam says nothing. Charlie, however, wags a finger at me. "Good to know. Cute gals shouldn't have to worry about a thing. Ain't that right, Sam?"

Sam remains silent, neither confirming nor denying the existence of any equally chauvinistic tendencies within himself. After a brief moment, he asks, "What did you say, Charlie? I was thinking about Harold. Mary too. This has to be hard on her, even if it was expected."

Charlie chuckles and opens the door. "Don't worry about it." He struts away, calling behind him, "I'll have the trucks here in the morning. Later Sam. Adios, cutie."

"Bye, Charlie."

I say nothing. The door closes with a thud.

Silence fills the room. I'm alone with the hunk. Again.

Giddy up.

Sam rests his hands on the counter. "Can I help you?"

Shoulders back...slow exhale...show confidence. *You can do this, Ro.* Get in there and bring home the meat. Bacon, I mean, bacon, totally meant bacon. Or a good thick sausage log.

Gingerly, I prance across the room, tiptoeing on wobbly shoes, extending my resume before me. It wavers in the air, fluttering like a kite in a stiff breeze, betraying my nerves. My blood pressure kicks up a notch. It pulses in my neck veins, my wrists, even my forehead.

I need this job. I need this job. I need this job.

Did I mention I need this job?

His eyes meet mine. Muscles stand in relief under a white, button-down shirt. Jeans hug hips absent any shadow from a muffin top.

whoosh My gut sucks in. My suddenly alert vagina crackles like a pile of dried leaves in October. Nipples stand at attention. I'd forgotten I had nipples.

My body says hello, big guy. My brain says snap out of it, Ro.

I may need therapy.

I offer him the quaking, shaking paper illustrating my lack of a work life. "Hi, I'm Ro Andrews" *Stop quivering, dang it.* "Mr. Hollister—Edmund—wants to hire me. On a trial basis. For three months."

Sam takes it. "Hello, I'm Sam Whittaker." He reaches to shake my hand.

Please don't notice the cracker dust. Or the pencil lead.

Strong fingers, warm and callous lined, envelope my own and I no longer care about cereal crumbs or misplaced graphite. Somewhere in my addled brain Enya chants winsomely to harp music. Goosebumps erupt under polyester. Thighs grow moist and this time it's not because

I need to pee.

Stupid, traitorous body. It's my own fault—my sex life both before my marriage and after my divorce has been a self-imposed, Catholic tragedy of timidity. Trust me, I have sampled from a shallow, limpid pool. Filled with toads. None of whom turned into princes when I kissed their wet, warty lips. Given my life-time lack of experience and present lack of available options, it takes little to jumpstart my engine these days.

Unaware I'm reliving my ten-second sex life in my head, his grip is firm, confident. "You bought the Yeager farm, right? I met your husband at the lumber yard the other day. Nice man."

"Brother!" I shout in my clearest, brightest outside voice. "He's my brother. I'm not married." I whip my left hand up and twirl my ring-less finger in the air, nearly endangering his eye.

Smooth, Ro.

He studies my hand. A puzzled expression washes over his face. Does he remember me from the Texas two-step we did in the diner hallway? The puzzled look departs. Or perhaps he remembers me surrounded by a pack of rabid children.

Figures. He probably thinks I'm a whore.

"Divorced," I shout again. "I'm divorced."

"I'm sorry to hear it."

I open my mouth to say, don't be, he was a lying, cheating jerk, realize how that sounds, and stop. My mouth flaps open, a hungry bass searching for a worm. A big, juicy worm.

Geez, I need to get fresh batteries.

"It's fine. I'm over it," I mutter.

Yeah, right. The ex, yes. The hurt? That's a big, fat no.

God, I hope this mental conversation in my head is proof I can multi-task.

Sam indicates a chair near his desk, and I sit, thankful to hide my dust-filled fingernails and my one bad shoe. If only I can get a grip on my flustered feelings and intermittent horniness, I might be able to retain a shred of self-respect.

He sits and studies my resume, immune to my tsunami of misguided pheromones currently daring me to climb him like a tree. My lips part. Sweat challenges my anti-perspirant. Pheromones whisper louder.

A distraction, I need a distraction.

Looking around, I study the office, detouring my thoughts with details, when I realize this won't take long. To call it spare and utilitarian is an understatement. A trash can beside the desk is empty.

No dust—cereal, cracker or pencil lead—coats the nooks and crannies of the metal bookshelf behind him. The computer monitor on the gray metal desk is finger-print free. Papers are stacked, their edges aligned. The file cabinet drawers behind him are closed. Even the windows appear washed.

Unlike Winston Churchill Jr., Sam, it seems, is a neat freak.

This morning's breakfast chaos leaps to mind, five kids yelling for chocolate chips in their pancakes, syrup dripping from forks onto laps, down chins, and even into one of the twin's hair. Olivia throwing socks in my general direction. Justin spilling coffee on the stove. Last night's casserole dish soaks in the kitchen sink. One burnt pancake, forgotten as I tied shoes and wiped noses and poured milk, hardens on the griddle.

Can I trick Justin into eating that pancake later? Before I can plot how, however, something else distracts me. On the bookcase behind Sam's desk, all polished and gleaming, it sits.

A wedding picture.

That was a whole lot of hormonal hell for nothing. Of course, he's married. Why wouldn't he be married? Why hadn't it occurred to me? Have I completely excised the "M" word from my vocabulary? Well done, brain, well done.

Besides, I only wanted to use him for sex anyway, right? Right.

Sam leans back in his chair, reading my resume, which is interesting since there's not much to read, and I examine his left hand. No ring, though. What gives? Is it a work safety thing?

Curious, I examine his office for vacation pictures, finger paintings, crayon drawings, macaroni art, any evidence of a family, but there's nothing else, only that one solitary picture. That's weird. Does he have children? Again, why no ring?

Repeat after me, Ro. You're. Not. Interested.

Sam interrupts my thoughts. "So, Edmund's ready to give you a trial run?"

"Yes, can you believe it?"

Sam laughs and, of course, it's adorable.

Stop it, yells my left brain, *he's married. But look at those eyes and those arms*, pleads my right brain, which wants validation and a little nookie. *Forget about him, you're a strong, independent woman,* Olivia reasons in my mind. *Get a grip, you're acting like an idiot*, my brother screams somewhere in my subconscious. *Fuck him*, demands Mom.

Ro, you're a freak, I mutter to myself.

Sam looks up from my resume. "What?"

Preferring Mom's suggestion to the other alternatives, I want to ogle his muscular chest but fight the urge instead. "Nothing, I'm out of practice in the interview department."

He lays my resume down. "Don't worry about it. If Edmund wants to give you a trial run, I'm fine with it. He's been at this a lot longer than I have." Sam rises from his chair and extends his hand yet again. "Welcome aboard."

Am I employed?

"Seriously?" I inquire.

"Seriously," he replies.

I leap up and grab his oh so firm hand. "I can't thank you enough."

I pump it, and it's still warm, and I still tremble, but it's okay, because I have a part-time temporary job with no insurance, and healing has to start somewhere. Plus, this interview supplied me with enough fantasy material to get me through the long, dark winter nights too, and that's something.

Sam lets my hand go and casts his big, brown eyes to the floor, in the direction of my feet. "Interesting shoes."

Uh oh.

For Christ's sake, Karma, give it a rest already, will you? What kind of a humiliation quota are you running here anyway?

Slowly my sexy new boss lifts his head. It blooms in his eyes, the dawning realization I, most definitely, was the crazy, half-naked, nut-job under the car.

Panic knocks at my composure. "It's complicated." *Please, please, please don't ask for more.*

Fortunately, he doesn't. Instead, he flashes a rakishly handsome grin, and I try not to melt into a puddle of goo, one because he's married so I can't be interested anyway, and two because I need to build self-respect and self-control and all those other selfie words that sound good in my head, even if they are next to impossible to put into practice.

Maybe one day he and I will joke about my adventure under the car. We'll do so over coffee in the diner while his beautiful wife stands at his side, clutching his hand, marking her territory, as my snot-covered, farting children scale my legs like cats, also marking theirs. Yay. Life goals.

"Did Ed tell you when to start?"

"No, he didn't. Should I go ask him?"

"Don't worry about it. How's this Monday? We can get you started at 8 AM. Come to the diner. If Ed's not in when you arrive, come over here, and I'll get you started."

Oh, start me, baby, start me.

Damn it, Ro, get a grip.

My second new future boss talks on, oblivious. "We've got plenty to do around here, so we'll keep you pretty busy."

Dual urges—one to climb him like a tree, and two, to release a primal scream—wash over me, but I fight them both. Instead, I respond with a perfectly normal, adult-like, "Yes, Monday, 8 AM is perfect."

Emotions bubble below the surface. Tingles bubble below my skirt. Gum bubbles beneath my right heal.

Sam walks me to the door, ready to send me on my way. "Don't mention it. I'm sure you'll make every effort to be here on time. See you Monday."

Chapter Four

"This here is your office, and I'm right sorry about that." Edmund Hollister points to the red pleather booth farthest from the diner door. It faces a faded brick wall lined in tin advertising posters and a large mirror reflecting me looking expectant next to my new boss as he welcomes me to work on Diner Day One.

Several cardboard file boxes fill the bench seat against the wall. "We got mold in Esther Mae's old office—the roof sprung a leak," he sighs the words. "Until it's taken care of, it's best you sit here. It's not ideal, but it's the best we can do. 'Course, most afternoons you'll be at the elevator, and it's more private there. Again, this is temporary."

Half the town is in the diner eating breakfast, including Ernie and his cohorts and, while the bacon and eggs smell good, they apparently aren't good enough to pull every pair of eyes in the room off me. Fortunately, I'm getting used to it. "This is fine, Mr. Hollister."

"Edmund," he says, "call me Edmund."

"Edmund," I repeat, "this works for me. I'm thrilled to have a chance."

He claps me on the back. "I appreciate the flexibility. Let's get you to work on these papers for your W2s. Afterward, you can bring out Esther Mae's computer from her office—hold your breath while you're in there—and I'll show you the accounting program. We'll start you off slow."

After tossing my purse onto the table, I take off my jacket. "No need, I want to prove I can do this job."

Edmund yanks a file labeled "Tax Forms" from a box. "Understood. I have a feeling you won't let me down." He waves at the back grill. "Now get to these forms and help yourself to some coffee. Coffee's free when you work for me."

Orders dispensed, he saunters down the hallway, leaving me alone at my office booth.

Anxious to get to work, I slide onto the bench seat with my back to the staring crowd and search for a pen in my purse. This should be the easiest thing I do all day, after all, it's me. Although, I'm filling out forms framing my life, yet I can't even remember my address. What is the zip code again? Flipping through my phone, I scan emails with pertinent details, when—pop—out of nowhere a paper wad lands on the table in from of me.

Huh. *Where did you come from?*

Giving my shirt sleeves a shake, I check for more. Once, during church, shortly before *The End of My Marriage*, I reached across the ex to give Nick a tissue and a potato chip fell from my sleeve into Peter's lap. So, there's a precedent.

Back to the forms. What's my Social Security number again? Can someone please tell me why I've memorized the calorie count for French fries, but not it? Priorities.

Rifling through my wallet, I search for answers when another paper wad lands on the table in front of me, bounces once, and disappears into my purse.

What the hell?

I check over my shoulder. To my right a pair of older women in polyester argue the benefits of different Tupperware products, hardly candidates for any Aaron-like shenanigans. Sarah tops off coffee mugs for the standard issue row of farmers in ballcaps at the counter. Two booths back, however, sit Ernie and the Burts, hunkered over mugs of coffee in color-coordinated flannel. Plus, they're snickering.

Men. Go figure.

Where was I? Right, my Social Security number. I refocus on the forms. Can I deduct the new cat if we keep him? A fresh onslaught of paper wads lands in my hair.

Fellas, if you think this will rattle me, you haven't met Aaron.

A chorus of "Oh my" and "My goodness" and "Ernie, stop that" erupts from the older women presently plotzed near us. In between their clucks of disapproval, footsteps approach. I ignore the sound—my only adult course of action with Ernie and the Burts—and remain buried in paperwork. A body halts beside me, but I feign ignorance, ready to join in on the joke. I could fake a seizure, maybe even drool, when it hits me, a whiff of vanilla. Is that leather and pine too? Peeking at the floor, I spy them. Boots, great big, beautiful, Texas star-studded boots anchor blue-jean clad legs.

Sam.

What is it with this man and his timing?

"Ro?"

Naturally, my body responds with goosebumps, because, frankly, it's not fully embracing my new ten-step program of self-denial. Sure, I can tell my brain we're celibate and single from here on out, but my vagina never gets the message. Stupid, selfish vagina.

Slowly, I look up. His chiseled, sexy face towers above me. A shower of paper wads cascades from my hair, land on the table, bounce on the booth seat, and tumble to the floor. He must think I have the weirdest case of dandruff ever. I recall the neatness of his office. This isn't helping.

Sarah hustles past carrying several breakfast plates, bearing down on Ernie with intent as she slides past my booth. "Dang it, Ernie, I know it was you. I don't have time to clean up your messes this morning. Keep it up and no more refills."

With a swift swish, I sweep paper wads off the table into my palm, dumping them into my purse to feed the stale fish-shaped crackers swimming at the bottom. "Good morning, Sam."

Strong tan fingers pluck one from my hair. They linger near my tresses. Leather and vanilla with a hint of pine waft through the air and, together, they smell a hell of a lot better than divorce. I breathe deep— it's okay—breathing's allowed. I have to breathe. I'll die if I don't.

Sam rests it on the table. "Don't let them get to you. They're harmless, unless you're Sarah. It'll be a miracle if she doesn't kill them one day."

Like clockwork, she stomps back the other way, carrying a tray piled high with dirty breakfast dishes. "It'd be easy too." She huffs past, bound for the kitchen. "They'll eat anything I set in front of them, no questions asked."

Sam stifles a chuckle, revealing dimples deep enough to free dive. Damn, this man is fine. What was I doing? Something with forms and taxes and leather and vanilla.

He studies the sheet in front of me, all boss-like and business-minded. "Good, Edmund's got you working on the W2s. I imagine he'll get to the accounting next."

Hopeful another paper wad clings to my split ends, I brush my hair back behind my ear, waiting for big, strong Texan fingers to set it free. "Yep, that's the plan."

Sam examines the table and ignores my locks. He shifts from one foot to the other as if in a hurry or nervous or both. "Did he mention having you work at the elevator this afternoon?"

I shake my head. "Not yet. After I finish these, I'm supposed to move stuff from Esther's office, then he's going to show me the software."

Sam edges closer to my booth, giving Sarah room, as she whizzes along carrying a tray laden with pancakes, orange juice, and coffee. He's so close…fingertip close…but it's fleeting. Sarah rushes past and Sam retreats in her wake. "Okay," he continues, "I'll see what he has planned for this afternoon. If he can spare you, I'll put you to work on a stack of invoices. I could use the help."

A somewhat horny smirk tugs at the corners of my mouth. Oh, I can help, all right. Maybe polish your belt buckle with my tongue? Scratch an itch with my left nip, perhaps?

Wait, Ro, wife alert, remember?

Crud, I forgot, he's married. I bet she's perfect too. Probably a size four, the world's most obnoxious dress size. Small enough to be firm, large enough to have curves, in all the right places.

I smile an imperfect smile at Sam. "Sounds good to me."

"Great." Another wad whizzes over my left shoulder and lands on the table in front my non-size-four waistline. Sam chuckles. "Ignore the guys. They'll get bored eventually."

I add the wad to the growing collection in my purse. "It's fine. I have a six-year-old with a Ph.D. in pranks. This is nothing."

Sam hesitates. Is he going to ask about Aaron? I half expect a question, but he gives me a polite nod then disappears toward Edmund's office.

"Well, I'll be. Is she blushing?" Ernie's question blasts from the booth at Mach one and flies through the diner. It ricochets off stainless steel, polished wood, and old brick, and bounds down the hallway after Sam, threatening to undercut my pretend poise.

I cage a glimpse down the hall and discover Sam's already in there talking with Edmund. Whew, close call. Oh, no, are my cheeks pink? I whip back around and catch my reflection in the mirror. Great. What a lovely shade of cranberry.

Ernie's shout thunders through the diner. "She is, she's blushing. I bet she's sweet on Sam."

Sarah blows by with a carafe of coffee. "Who isn't sweet on Sam? Half the female population in Poseyville is sweet on Sam and a good portion of the male one too, so leave her be, Ernie."

Argument ensues as they debate the possibility I was blushing and whether or not any local men have a crush on Sam. I wink at Sarah and make a mental note to buy her a new car should I ever win the lottery. At the sound of Sam's footsteps echoing in the hallway, however, the argument dies off and I'm back on the menu like Monday's meatloaf.

"Here comes Sam again," Ernie bellows for all to hear. "Let's see if she blushes."

Immediately, I blush.

Smooth, Ro. Think fast.

"It's a hot flash!"

"You're too young to have them," retorts one of the Burts.

Dang blasted old coots. Do orneriness and testosterone ever

expire?

Sam rounds the corner and strides past me with a polite hint of a smile plastered on his chiseled, dimpled face.

Please make a clean exit. Please...please.

Ernie clears his throat. We catch each other's gaze in the mirror. Sam reaches his booth. Ernie opens his big, fat mouth. "Hey, Sam, who's the new gal?"

Son of a turd biscuit.

Sam grinds to a halt.

Frozen in my booth, I'm laser focused on Ernie's stare, but it's difficult because if I shift my view to the right, I can ogle Sam's tush in the mirror instead. To take a peek though, even one, quick peek at cheek while Ernie scrutinizes me for weakness is a risk I'm not willing to take. Which is unfortunate, because it's such a fine ass. Like biscuits rising in a hot oven, begging to be brushed with butter.

God, I need laid.

"Morning, fellas. Ro Andrews, she's Esther Mae's replacement."

Wow. He remembered my last name. Time to imaginary high five myself.

Burt One breaks the who-in-the-hell-is-Ro spell. "Damn strange thing what happened to her house. That's why I don't let cats inside."

"It wasn't the cat's fault," argues Burt Two. "It was the candle's fault."

"The candle wouldn't have burned down Esther's house if the cat's tail hadn't gotten in it," challenges Burt One.

"You don't know that. Candles burn down houses all the time."

"Yeah, but candles don't go running around the house setting everything on fire with tails covered in burning wax, do they?"

"Whatever happened to the cat?" inquires Burt Three.

"Edmund said it lived. But it don't have a tail no more. I heard what's left of Esther's house smells like brisket too," replies Burt One.

"Ignore them." Ernie breaks his stare with me and addresses Sam. "What's up with the new gal?"

Normally I would beg to hear more regarding the house and the cat and the candle, and a part of realizes we haven't had brisket for supper in far too long which is a shame since Olivia won't fix any on her current vegan kick and I do so love brisket. On the other hand, a huge part of me wants to hear what Sam has to say about the new gal, so, shut up, fellas. Mamma needs validation.

Sam fakes left, earning my gratitude, despite my curiosity.

"Sorry guys, but I'm needed at the elevator. Let's give her time to settle in, and I'll introduce you to her later this week." Not waiting for an answer, Sam slaps Ernie on the back and exits the diner.

Ernie peers at the mirror again, but I feign ignorance and get back to work.

Just like that, miracle of miracles, it seems to be enough. The paper wads have stopped, their interest wanes and they argue about the cat and the candle.

The question is, will it last?

~ * ~

It didn't last.

After the initial thrill of paper wads died away, Ernie and Burt One decided to watch me through the mirror. If we made eye contact, despite my desperate efforts to avoid any and all glances, stares, and winks, they celebrated, hooting and hollering and yelling, "I got one!" Between their hoots and Sarah's threats, brilliance struck like lightning. I got up, stomped to the wall, grabbed the stupid mirror and hid it in the women's room under the men-repelling tampon dispenser.

Problem solved. For now.

By 11:00 AM, the breakfast rush is over, lunch is just getting started, and the guys have called it a day. They've waddled off to bug who knows whom, about who knows what, who knows where. I've managed to relocate the computer and files to my temporary office and, after a brief run through with Edmund, I'm plowing my way through my first set of invoices. Fortunately, it's the plug and chug kind of program, and I rest easy, although this, too, may be temporary.

I finish an invoice and hit save. As I do, a plastic dish tub filled with freshly washed flatware and paper napkins lands on the table behind my monitor, rattling my coffee mug and me. With a plop, Sarah, sporting a T-shirt splattered with coffee stains and a brown smear I hope is bacon grease, drops into my booth across from me and gets busy.

She picks up a set of clean flatware and, with practiced hands, wraps it into a tight napkin bundle then sets it on the table. "Them fellas sure are a pain in my ass. I swear, if the old folks' home had a roving bus, I'd call 'em for a one-way pick up."

A snicker escapes my lips. I grab the next invoice, type in the account number, and hit enter. "Do you think they'll ever get tired of hazing me?"

"Nope. But Esther Mae's office ought to be done in a month or two. Then you can slam the door in their wrinkled old faces."

I like this woman. She gets me.

Focused, practiced, she makes short work of the flatware. "Edmund says to introduce you to everybody. This won't take long. The other server is Rachel."

A fifty-something brunette cleans a table near the door and waves a wet rag my way. "Hi Ro."

I wave an invoice back. "Hi Rachel."

Sarah indicates the fry cook with a hasty head bob. "Back on the grill we have Eli." A young man with a spatula waves over the coffee station in my direction. "He has this silly notion he's going to get me up in a hot air balloon, but I keep telling him, hell no."

Eli's wide grin spreads across a fresh-faced young man in his early twenties. "Are you talking about my balloon?"

"You ain't got a balloon yet, so how can I be talking about it?" Sarah yells, before turning back to me. "We got three other servers, but they work evenings and weekends. That's pretty much it for the diner."

I type in numbers and hit save. "How many people work at the elevator?" I try to sound normal and innocent and casual as can be, even crossing my toes for insurance. Did I pull it off?

Nope.

Sarah's stare is palpable. "You mean tell you about Sam." She wraps the flatware, building an impressive pyramid of napkin bundles, and doesn't miss a beat. "I seen the way you checked him out. Hell, we all look at him like that. He's a good-looking man."

A hint of heat tickles my cheeks. "I suppose, if you go for the rugged, handsome type. After all, looking is all we can do since he's married." A bead of sweat threatens my upper lip.

For the slightest of seconds Sarah falters, recovers, and continues working. "Wrong, he's a widower…"

Wait, a widower?

"…and he's even better on the inside. Let me tell ya, he's a keeper. Problem is, none of us know how to catch him."

"Oh." I pretend to concentrate on the next invoice, but inside my pulse races and darts, careening faster than a horny teenager with a new driver's license.

That sexy hunk of man meat is single?

Sarah studies me close. "I don't think he's dating anyone, either."

My pulse pounds. I open another file.

He's a widower. Maybe he doesn't date because he's still in love with his wife. No matter how sexy he is or how horny I may be, I'm not hitting that.

Still, poor Sam.

Finishing another line on this invoice, I hit save again. "What happened?"

Sarah takes a sip of coffee. "Cancer. It was already pretty advanced when they discovered it. She died about two and a half years ago."

"How sad. Do they have any kids?"

Coffee break over, Sarah gets back to work on the flatware. "No, they never did."

A widower neat freak with no kids? Is this a potential red flag?

Red flag? For what? I've sworn off men, remember? He's nothing but a meat sack. A hunky, muscular, rock-hard, available meat sack. Not to mention, my boss.

The diner door opens with a bell ring and, whether drawn by coincidence or burning ears, in comes Sam, followed by the ever-present chauvinist named Charlie.

Does he have a crush on Sam too? If so, I can't blame him.

"Speak of the devil." Sarah raises a single eyebrow—a skill I have never mastered—and manages to cock it my way.

The computer screen glows before me, demanding attention. Instead, I attempt to raise a brow in reply and fail. Settling on a new goal, I aim to keep my cheeks pasty white and blush free. Figures. No dice there either. It's a lost cause. My horny, single-mom Spidey sense tingles. Not to mention my inner thighs.

Body, why do you betray me so?

Sam heads to the register. "Ro, have you eaten lunch yet?"

Again, I blush. Sarah studies me. I admire her inability to blink. Her second eyebrow rises and joins the other in an upright and locked position. I hide behind my monitor. Warmth radiates from my cheeks. For a moment, I almost miss Ernie.

"Ro?" repeats Charlie.

Oh, no.

My skin crawls. I clear my throat and ignore him. "Not yet, Sam. I've been working on invoices. Does it matter when I take my lunch?"

"No, but I was wondering if we could get our lunch to go and you can run over to Harold Walton's with me. I realize it's a bit early, but we can chat on the way, and you can take notes for me while Greg and I talk. He has several silos not to mention a herd of cattle we might purchase. Or do you have lunch plans?"

Charlie leans against the counter but gazes my way. "Sure, she has lunch plans." He sizes me up like I'm cattle available for purchase too. "I'm taking her out for a bite today, aren't I, darling?"

So much for my Charlie-has-a-crush-on-Sam theory. Bummer. Sarah studies me.

Okay, that invitation needs derailed and fast. "I have no plans, boss," I yell for all to hear.

"Ouch." Charlie shifts and licks his wounds. "Give me a sweet tea to go, will you, Rachel."

Sam casts a quizzical smile at Charlie. "If you don't mind, Ro, go ahead and check with Edmund. If he's fine with it, place your order and, if you could, when your lunch is ready, will you bring my lunch to the elevator too?"

"Sure thing."

"Great, thanks." He swivels around to the counter. "Rachel, give me the special and put whatever Ro's having on my tab."

Charlie, who apparently sucks at taking hints, reaches for his wallet. "No, I'll get it."

I grab my purse, ready to put this potential favor to rest, and slide to the edge of my office booth. "That's not necessary. I can get it."

Rachel joins Sarah in the mile-high eyebrow club which, frankly, would be less obvious if they both invested in a good waxing.

Clearly oblivious to their interest, Sam rattles on, "I've got it, Charlie. Don't worry about it, Ro," he continues, "I'm taking up your lunch time. It's the least I can do." Conversation over, he heads for the door.

Undeterred, Charlie pulls a wad of cash from his wallet and flashes it in the air. "Oh, hell, Sam, you don't need to haul this pretty little thing all the way out there to take dictation, do ya?"

Sam stops.

Crap, crap, triple crap. Is he considering Charlie's plea? Don't, don't, don't. Panic tinged with irritation builds inside me. Stupid Charlie.

I better put an end to this and quick. "Maybe another time. I need to meet our customers first." Not bad. Almost sounds plausible.

Rachel gives Charlie his drink, he tosses her a few dollars then shuffles toward the door. "Okay, darling, but I'm going to hold you to it."

Sam opens the diner door wide, letting him pass. It's a simple gesture with no real meaning aimed at me, but I find it sweet in a get-the-hell-out-of-here-Charlie sort of way.

Deflated, the town's resident irritant marches from the diner, muttering, "I guess she's all yours, Sam."

Silent, Sam follows him, even as the words, "she's all yours" echo in my over-twerked brain.

Until another thought overtakes me.

I'm having lunch with Sam.

Rachel stands frozen at the register, staring at the door. Sarah sits silent, flatware in one hand, a napkin in the other, both brows permanently etched at right angles against her forehead. Finally, she returns to the last of the flatware. "I'll be. The tide seems to be turning for Sam. I guess somedays even a blind dog finds a bone."

Say what? I've no idea how to respond, and I'm not sure what it means, plus, I don't even know if I'm the blind dog or the old bone, but, regardless, I need to splash cold water on my simmering face, talk to Edmund, get our lunches, and go.

~ * ~

No dust clogs the nooks and crannies of Sam's very clean pickup truck. No crud-encrusted pennies fill his cup holders, no ketchup packets litter his floor like landmines. The entire cab is store-plastic-bag free. A mountain woods air freshener dangles from the rearview mirror. A hint of Windex competes with the cedar.

How does he do it?

Oh, right. No kids. Gotcha.

I'm impressed and a wee bit frightened. Seriously, my SUV wasn't this clean when I bought it. People live like this? Scarier still, the dash is fingerprint free, and there's not a stale flake of cereal or cracker to be found. Anywhere. While I'm thoroughly enjoying the ride, it wouldn't be much fun in a zombie apocalypse. At least in my SUV with its sizeable, rock-hard cereal stash, we wouldn't starve.

Would Sam worry over a few handfuls of kid snacks scattered about? For zombie apocalypse survival, of course.

Oh, Peter the Ex? He cared. Always.

Careful of crumbs, I eat my ham on wheat. The sandwich is good, despite a lack of cheese and mayo, which I want but avoid as I regret every past Ho Ho, Twinkie, cheese doodle, and Pringle snack pack that's ever disappeared into the black, gaping hole that is my voracious mouth. Because they're still here, hanging around like millennials who said, "screw adulthood, let's live off Mom forever."

To make matters worse, while this straight-up hunk of a single man sits within arm's reach, all Grade-A, prime-rib juicy, my focus is glued to the spreading mass of my chubby mama thighs jiggling away in his shotgun seat. And, dang it, I'm wearing corduroy.

Life can be cruel.

Tearing the remaining crust off my sandwich, I toss it in the paper sack between my feet. It's been a quiet ride, partly because we're eating and partly because I'm sitting with my legs apart so Sam can't hear the corduroy. Also, I can't think of a darn thing to ask him. I have him all to myself, I'm fully dressed this time, my hair is motor oil free, but I can't even ask about family since he doesn't have one, and I don't know enough about work to ask any good questions. It's perplexing.

Fortunately, though, it's short lived.

Sam breaks the silence first. "Can I ask you something?"

Mayo-less bread goes dry in my mouth. I swallow ham on wheat. "Sure, go ahead."

"Why did your mom name you Sparrow?"

I knew this would come up. "Because my dad hit a bird with the car."

"A sparrow?"

"Yep." I take a bite of my sandwich and chew.

"Ah."

"I got off pretty easy," I continue with my mouth full. "Had he hit a groundhog or a possum, I'd be screwed."

"Of course," Sam laughs. "What was special about this sparrow?"

"Nothing. Mom was in labor, Dad was driving like a mad man, when *splat*! It flew into the windshield. Mom thought it was a sign. She's a bit of a nut job. It might not have even been a sparrow. Could have been a tufted titmouse for all I know. Imagine what hell high school would have been with a name like titmouse." I take a swig from my water bottle. "Can you imagine the nicknames?"

Sam rounds a bend in the road. "No, I can't."

"Dad finally had a say in her name choices when my brother came along. Me? I get a silly animal name. Does Justin? Obviously, a big, fat no. I would have stuck him with Blue Jay or Buzzard but, no, a regular name it is." I risk a glance in Sam's direction and he's smiling. It looks great on him.

"I take it your mom's a free spirit?"

"No, she comes with a pretty stiff price," I joke, "but, yes, she's a free spirit and I love her, especially from a distance." I brush breadcrumbs from the troughs of my corduroys and dump them into the paper sack. "I'll be explaining my name to people until I die."

Sam laughs, and it's musical and soothing and sounds like sex on a rainy day.

I fill my mouth with the last sandwich morsel, hoping it will stifle the moans bubbling beneath the surface. This truck may be crumb free, but it's overflowing with pheromones.

Changing the subject, Sam drives on, ignoring my chewing

mouth. "Thanks for coming with me. I figured it would help you get the lay of the land."

"Thanks for bringing me," I manage. "It's a pretty drive."

We're in the countryside now, but instead of watching the scenery or regretting my chubby curves, my gaze drifts to his side of the truck cab, and it's a much better view. Thank goodness, he's a responsible driver. With every curve he applies the brakes, tensing his quadricep, swelling it against his blue jeans. I may not surf, but I love a good swell and, while it's only a thigh, it's a hell of a bulge.

sigh

Sam indicates the plastic hump of truck separating us. "There's a notebook in the middle console and a pen too. I used to have tablet, but it died, and I haven't replaced it yet. Anyway, when we get there, I'll rattle off some numbers for you to write down."

"Sounds easy enough." I drink deep from my water bottle to avoid drooling. "Sam, can I ask you a question?"

"Shoot."

"What's with the boots? Are you from Texas?"

"I'm from Austin."

"That explains the accent. It's nice though. I've never been to Texas." It's my turn to switch gears. "What brought you to Illinois?"

A hesitation... "My wife."

"Ah."

Way to go, Ro.

Sam concentrates on the road. "We met at Purdue. After we graduated, she went to work for her dad's fertilizer business in Dunreith and we settled here."

"Ah," I repeat.

"She passed away almost three years ago," he volunteers. "Cancer."

I squirm in my seat. "I'm so sorry, Sam."

We sit in silence. Fences, trees, and farms whiz past in a blur.

I take a risk, "Can I ask you another question?"

"Shoot."

"Do you have any plans for Thanksgiving?"

More silence.

It's too soon, Ro. You barely know each other. He's a widower, and you're not touching that, remember? Plus, he's your boss. Not to mention, you need to drop ten pounds. Or fifteen. Also, the house is an unfinished disaster. And, red flag, he's a neat freak. Let's also not forget, Sam may have a possible aversion to kids, and your three are feisty, feral heathens.

Oh, shut up, already.

Life is short, and I'm a people person. After all, it's only dinner with no strings attached. Can't I feed a co-worker? I mean, seriously, what would Jesus do?

A valley of dead corn surrounds us. Sam slows for a train track slicing through the road and fields. "My in-laws invited me to go with them to my sister-in-law's in Cincinnati, and I'm tempted," he replies. "I might drive over for the day and come back on Friday, just haven't decided yet."

Finished with the last of my water, I stuff the empty bottle in the bag at my feet and play off my rushed invite. "Oh, sure. If you decide not to go to your in-laws, and if you have any interest in a great meal in a big house with small children, you're more than welcome to come to our place. Word of advice, though, if you come, don't believe anything my son Aaron tells you. I took a lot of hot baths when I was pregnant with him. He may be overcooked."

Sam chuckles.

I do my best to act nonchalant.

"Thanks for the invitation. I'll consider it."

"Good enough."

Chapter Five

An older man in overalls and a green cap waits near a large red barn in unseasonably warm November sunshine when we arrive at our destination. Climbing from the truck, we join him, and Sam shakes his outstretched hand. "Hi Greg. That was a beautiful service Saturday. Your dad was a good man."

Greg Walton examines the bright blue sky with clear hazel eyes and a ruddy complexion born from decades in the elements. Collecting himself for a moment, he smiles. "Thank you, Sam. He thought highly of you too. The elevator at Dunreith is closer, but he would never take his crop anywhere else. Thanks for coming. I appreciate it"

"I'm happy to help. This," Sam introduces me, "is our new office manager, Sparrow Andrews. This is Greg Walton."

I offer my hand "Ro for short. Glad to meet you."

A friendly grin emerges on his wrinkled face and he gives my hand a sturdy shake. "That's an interesting name you've got there, young lady."

I smile. I nod. I plan my mother's funeral. "Yes, it is. Long story short, I have a crazy mom."

Greg shoots another grin my way. "Enough said. My daughters have one too."

Funny. I like this guy. Why can't he sit behind me every day instead of Ernie and the Burts?

Greg points at the barn. "The cattle are in here. I want to get something done with them before Martha and I leave for Florida." He opens the door and motions us in. "Ladies first."

Excited, I quicken my pace. "Thank you. It's my first barn."

Greg peers at Sam. They exchange a look, and I kick myself.

My first barn. What am I, five?

Trying to regroup, I enter the semi darkness in silence. Scuffling sounds find my ears. Peering through the gloom, my eyes adjust, and they come into view. Several large animals shift farther away from the door. A few tepid moos erupt from dark shapes hulking together near several hay bales. The heavy scent of fur, wet straw, and fresh feces smacks me in the face.

Wow, this place literally smells like shit. I've never come this close to steak on the hoof before and it's definitely more pungent than expected.

Greg flips a light switch, illuminating the cavernous space. Two thirds of the barn teem with life. Solid black cattle keep close tabs on our every move with bright, dewy orbs the size of baseballs. He points to his left.

"There's a dozen steer here, all Angus, near full market weight. Over here," he gestures in another direction, "we have eight heifers almost ready for breeding stock. Grable already came for the bull and the mature cows. If you have any interest, they're yours. What you don't want, I'll take to the auction in Taylorsville."

Sam opens the gate, and I follow, clutching the notebook, but he halts me and enters the pen alone to examine the cattle which dance aside when he approaches. They ogle him with big, brown eyes, much like me with my green ones, though none of them lick their lips like me because, when they're not sidestepping Sam, they're too busy licking the insides of their noses instead.

Watching intently, I'm focused on Sam who's focused on the steers when something tugs at my sweater.

What the hell?

With a start, I spin around as the tug becomes an outright pull. Behind me, a velvety pair of gray lips beneath a little black nose stretch between wooden rails, and those cute lips are latched to the tail end of my sweater, chewing away.

Greg doffs his cap by the brim. He whacks the cute nose hard, and it lets go of my sweater. "Knock it off, Oscar."

"What?" I stare into the pen.

A dark gray, miniature donkey stares back.

The older man draws closer to the fence. "Ignore him, he's a jackass. I ain't kidding either. He's a mini though. Cute fella, ain't he?"

Luminous, jet-black eyes lined in dark wispy lashes blink at me between the fence rails. After retreating from the great hat attack, a donkey no bigger than a collie dog advances upon me once more. He reaches the fence, and velvety lips nibble in thin air.

A sucker for all things tiny and cute, my maternal instinct kicks in. I touch his damp nose with my finger, and he dances back with a snort. "He's precious," I coo. "A mini? Is he full grown?"

Greg returns his cap to his head as I pet his tiny ass. "Yep, he ain't getting any bigger. You like him?"

Fuzzy lips stretch toward me again. "I do." Endlessly they wriggle, desperate for my sleeve. Finally, Oscar snags my hem and tests it with his tongue. "What a sweetie!"

Greg shifts closer. "Want him?"

Mid scratch, I pause. "What?"

"Do you want him? He's gotta go too, and Walter and Cronkite." Greg nods at the back of the pen.

Beyond Oscar's undeniable cuteness, I spy them. Sauntering our way, no doubt wanting to cash in on an ear scratch or two themselves are a fat blond pony and an even fatter black and brown goat.

The farmer pulls a few ears of corn from a bag leaning against a post and offers them to me. "Tell you what, if you want 'em, I won't charge you a dime. I'd love for them go to a good home together. They're buddies."

Walter the pony joins Oscar the ass along the fence rail. He extends his pink and blond nose, interested in a courtesy sniff and corn. Cronkite the goat takes things a bit further, for upon arriving at the wooden fence, he steps onto the upper edge of the lowest rail and stands tall. Velvety goat lips nibble in the air, interested in a little tasty sweater-hem action. I'm the star attraction at a four-legged lip party, and all I can think about right now are my kids. They would love this.

Greg rubs Cronkite between his long, floppy ears. They wiggle back and forth, swaying to and fro. As if reading my thoughts, the older man smiles and goes for the jugular, "Got kids?"

I know where he's going with this. "Sure do, three under the age of ten," I reply, "all of whom are begging me for a cat."

Unable to reach my sweater, the goat nibbles at Greg's coat sleeve, but he shoves its nose away. "Oh, cats are good for catching mice, but if you want some real fun, these here stooges will keep you entertained. Oscar here pulls a cart, and both he and Walter are broke to ride, little ones only, though. Cronkite, here, will eat his weight in weeds. They'd be a lot a fun for your kids. Ain't no better way to teach 'em responsibility than to get pets. Got any interest?"

Finished with the steers, Sam exits the pen to examine the heifers. He says nothing as Greg finishes his sales pitch, and instead studies the cattle with a practiced eye, though his ear remains cocked in our general direction. Is he listening to our conversation?

Grabbing another cob, I feed corn to the animals who inhale every morsel. Desperate for more love and snacks, they nudge each other, slobbering all the while. "What happens if you can't find a home for them?" Oscar under-cuts Walter and stretches through the lower rails to chew the hem of my slacks. Unhappy with the taste of corduroy, he sniffs the top of my shoe instead.

Greg pushes his hat back off his forehead, revealing a furrowed brow. "I'll take 'em to the auction. Mostly likely, they'll be split up. The goat will probably end up in someone's freezer."

"No!" I cry, though it's ironic considering I'm surrounded by a barn full of cattle all headed in that general direction. Sensing my internal conflict, Cronkite looks me square in the eye, which is difficult since his are on opposite sides of his head.

"Yep. It'd be a damned shame. I got a saddle and bridle to go with the pony. They're yours for fifty bucks. I can't give the cart and harness away, but I'll make you a deal on them too."

Is he nuts? I can't bring home a donkey, a pony, and a goat. What would Justin say? Or Olivia? It was a struggle to agree on a cat. It's a crazy idea, ludicrous, even. I stroke Cronkite's ear. Why do they have to be so cute?

Because it's tempting. After all, they can stay outside—that's a plus, right? Although, we know nothing about farm animals. That's a minus. What do they eat? Do we have to bathe them? Do we give them shots? I can't bring home these animals. It's insane.

And yet...

Can I?

Sensing my inner turmoil, Greg leans in, going for the kill. "Tell you what, I'll throw in the saddle and the bridle too, to sweeten the deal. Don't your kids deserve a pony?"

Oh, he's good. I bet he and Aaron would hit it off.

It's the moment of truth, and, better yet, I know what to do. We didn't come here to sit in a moldering old house and let life pass us by while we watch TV and stare at our cell phones. If that's all we wanted, we could have stayed in the suburbs.

No, we moved here to change our lives. To really get into the spirit of living in the country. Gardens, walks in the woods, fishing in the pond, bonfires and, yes, even animals, don't we want it all? Not just me, either. Justin and Olivia want it too, although Olivia may not realize it yet. Imagine her blog posts. Eventually, she'll thank me.

Won't she?

Fortune favors the brave. Here goes.

"I'll take them."

Holy crap.

We have animals.

An unfortunate detail occurs to me. Do I have to take them now?

Rot ro, Shaggy, way to overlook a detail, a big, fat detail.

Good sense and judgement always wait until after I commit to something stupid to rear their boring, responsible heads. Party poopers.

Lacing my fingers deep into Walter's thick mane, I pray for time and hope for the best. "How soon do I have to take them, though? I don't even know if we have fences."

Greg scratches his chin stubble. "How about no later than January second? If you change your mind, it gives me time to get them to the auction on the tenth."

Relief washes over me. Thank God, it's not today. Doing the mental math, I consider it for a split second. We have at least seven weeks to bring them home, possibly enough time to bring Olivia over to the dark side. Justin will be an easy sell. Olivia, however…

Imagine the children, Ro. Let's do this.

"That sounds great, Greg."

"Wonderful!" He claps his hands together with delight. "Sam, you can bring her here any time."

Sam exits the heifer pen and joins us. He scratches Cronkite between the ears but says nothing.

With a tug, I extract a shoelace from Oscar. "I have so many questions, though. What do they even eat? Where do I get it?"

Bewilderment greets my stare. Greg examines me as I bask in my suburban ignorance. Shifting slightly, he faces Sam. "You did say she's your new office manager, right?"

A rather sheepish grin spreads across Sam's handsome face as he studies his boots. "It's her first day, Greg. She's from Chicago."

"Ah, Chicago." He chuckles. Amused, the older man nudges my side with his elbow. "Young lady, they're farm animals. They eat hay and grain, and you work for a grain elevator. You get it from Sam."

Huh. I never made the connection.

~ * ~

Cradling a notebook filled with cattle, corn, and soybean prices on my lap, I dial my cell, calling my brother while Sam drives us back to town in his neat and tidy truck. The smell of donkey spit lingers in the air, but it can't be helped. Instead, I focus on my call.

"What's up, sis?" Justin barks into my ear, "I'm working here."

Happy to share what I hope is good news, along with a selfie of me next to a jackass who, this time, isn't my ex, I put him on speaker, "Sorry big guy, I figured you were at lunch."

A crisp crunching noise crackles from my cell phone speaker. "I'm just busting your chops." I picture him as he eats the last of the Granny Smith apples we wrestled over in the fridge this morning. Darn gorilla arms. He munches into my ear. "So, what's going on? Aren't you working?"

"Yes, but quick question, do we have any fences?"

"Fences?"

"Yeah, you know fences. Posts, wire, wood. Fences. Do we have any pasture with fences?" I clarify.

Justin chews, swallows, then replies. "There's a small pasture behind the barn with fence around most of it. A few trees are down on part of it and the gate isn't up, but it's in the barn. It's a fence in the technical sense of the word. Why?"

"Okay, don't get mad..."

"Oh, shit, Ro," he swallows, "what did you do?"

Best to start small. Crossing my fingers and hoping for the best, I take the plunge, "I adopted a goat."

Silence greets me. I pray he's chewing something soft now, like a sandwich, and plunge on. "And a tiny horse. And an even tinier jackass."

Silence.

"Wait until you see them, bro, they're adorable."

More silence.

"Justin?"

Suddenly, we hear it. Laughter, loud peals of laughter. Followed by choking, probably from the apple.

Oops.

"Are you all right?"

Harsh coughs fill the air. Finally, he replies, "Yeah, I'm fine. I'm glad you're finally getting on board with this country living idea, sis. Though I didn't realize you were going to kick it into high gear so soon."

"No time like the present, right?"

"Point taken. How soon until they move in?"

I sigh in relief. This is going well. So far. "We have to bring them home at least by the first week of January. I'd love to do it sooner though. Listen, I realize fixing fences wasn't the first project you planned to tackle, so I'm happy to do most of the work if you show me how. I'm serious. I want to learn"

"We can probably get the fences fixed in a week or two," muses Justin, "and the barn's in good shape. Won't take much to fix up one of the stalls. Still," he plunges on, tempering my delight, "I got a question for you, sis. Do you have any idea how to take care of these things? What do they eat?"

Settling back against the truck seat, I grin. Look how much I've learned already. "Sure, silly, they eat hay and grain and, the best part is, I work for a grain elevator. Seriously, I can't believe you didn't know that."

I mug a goofy face at Sam and, be still my heart, he cracks a huge smile. God, he has a great smile. And those dimples. They're deep enough to hide a Hersey kiss…hmm…chocolate.

Justin breaks the dimple spell and interrupts my spontaneous eye contact with Sam. "What did you get again? A goat, a jackass and—what else did you say?"

Sam focuses on the road, so I direct my reluctant attention back to my brother. "A horse. A tiny horse. Seriously, he barely comes to my hip. He's so stinking cute."

"Okay, a tiny horse." Justin takes another bite of apple. The sound of him chewing fills the cab with juicy, crunchy noise. "I don't know anything about tiny horses."

"Neither do I, big guy. We'll Google it."

"Sounds good. I'll read up on fixing fences, you read up on those critters, and we'll take it from there. Deal?"

"Deal. Thanks, bro."

"Don't mention it. One last thing, Ro. You get to tell Olivia. Bye." Before I can protest, he hangs up, making a clean get away.

Yikes, Olivia.

shudder

I'll think of something.

Daydreams of happy, excited children distract me. Hugs, screams, tears of joy, it all comes to me, even Olivia smiling while she watches her girls dancing with delight around those sweet critters.

Sam's voice penetrates my revelry. "Ro, have you ever ridden a horse?"

Visions of happy children disappear. The road materializes before me. Sprawling farms fill my vision. Reality makes itself known. It looks like apprehension. I smack it away. "No, I've never even had a pet. My dad left when I was eight, and we rented which meant no animals. Also, most of them eat meat, which is seriously frowned upon by my obnoxiously vegan mother. She thinks even dogs should be vegetarians. Anyway, I doubt I'll be riding Walter and definitely not Oscar." I point at my saddlebags—what a dumb thing to do—and plunge on, "He's so itty bitty. Who knew asses could be so small?"

Not me, obviously.

Sam taps on the steering wheel. His other hand fidgets on the console. What's the deal? Is he nervous? "I figured not, but do you know how to saddle a horse or put on a bridle?"

"Nope." Pictures of happy children on Christmas morning, bonding with their new pets, fill my imagination. It's a satisfying, joyful scene, even if the edges of my mental picture are somewhat fuzzy from ignorance. "I'll Google it too. I bet I can find a few YouTube videos. It's amazing what you can learn on YouTube. We'll figure it out or die trying."

Sam exhales sharply. "Listen, I can give you a few pointers if you're interested." Suddenly he glances my way, but all too quickly, he shifts his attention back to the road. "What I'm saying is, I have horses. I can teach you. If you want. We can go on a trail ride too. If you want," he repeats.

I stare straight ahead.

What did he say?

Instantly, I no longer picture happy children dancing around baby jackasses.

Holy shit-a-row-knee. The hunky Texan offered to give me riding lessons, at his place no less. Suddenly, my studly boss is wearing nothing but a smile in the windmills of my mind. The fires of Mount Vesuvius erupt in all quadrillion of my cells, filling my face—and a few anatomically correct things—with pulsing flames. I'm hot, I'm bothered, I'm flustered.

I like it.

The scent of burning corduroy fills the truck cab, crowding out the lingering hint of donkey phlegm. Separating my legs to prevent his truck seat from smoldering, I gulp, "You'd teach me?"

Naturally, Sam is oblivious to my internal combustion. He's all matter of fact, intent on driving, unaware I've reached my melting point. "Sure," he replies. "It's always more fun to ride with someone else. As soon as you get Walter home, your kids will want to ride him. It'd be good to be prepared."

The dash vent bathes me in hot air, fanning my internal flames. I clamp my water bottle between red-hot loins, expecting it to boil. "Good point. Thanks, I'll take you up on that."

Damn straight, I will.

Sam brakes into a curve. Muscles bulge. More heat rises. I contribute to climate change and melt a polar ice cap. Sam keeps talking. "You're welcome. How's Friday morning? Right after Thanksgiving?"

Now heat isn't my problem. Pounding is. My jackhammering heart clogs my throat. "Works for me," I croak.

Sam stares straight ahead, composed, relaxed. "Good. Should be fun."

I peek at his cheek, searching for telltale signs of fluster, but see nothing. Chiseled, tan control greets me. He's all calm, cool, and collected. Me? I'm burning with the heat of a thousand flames lighting my soul. I pretend to admire the passing scenery, but, instead, I indulge in a daydream.

Sam is shirtless, sweaty. Muscular legs grip white horse flanks. Biceps bulge. He reins in his powerful steed. A sax plays something lusty in the background.

My own sweaty steed gallops alongside his. I'm perched upon it, a tight but curvy Lady Godiva. My mom boobs are magically pre-baby perky. They bounce just enough to be super slutty, not sloppy slutty, as we ride, ride, ride. It's all hot and sexy and a whole hell of a lot of fun to savor, even if the body in my daydream was at least two overdue babies ago.

Sam's voice penetrates my thoughts as we dismount in my daydream. "What did your brother mean when he said this country thing? Is that why you moved from Chicago?"

Chocolate and sex and sweat linger in my imagination. I cross my legs and squeeze, too hard, forcing me to stifle a moan. *Earth to Ro, answer the man.* "Yeah, pretty much. We all needed to get away. Just wanted something more wholesome."

Sam watches the road. "I get it."

Like a thirsty duck drawn to water, my gaze wanders to his blue jeans. What was the question? Right, why did we move. Got it. "Olivia and Justin have wanted to move to the country for a while, but this job offer pushed them into it. Once they decided, they couldn't get here fast enough. Me? I hadn't even considered it until they suggested I come too. At first, I turned them down."

A Saturday afternoon from a lifetime ago comes to mind. I shift in my seat, remembering the irritation, undecided if I should share. Might as well. I ramble on, "The straw that broke me was this party my six-year-old went to. It was a gluten-free birthday party, which, fine, whatever, but this kid's mom wanted them to create finger paintings of the birthday boy, who happens to be a real dick.

"And Aaron—who also knows how to push the envelope—decided to paint his version of an asshole," I continue. "Trust me, that went over like a lead balloon, partly because he's talented for his age, and it was a great likeness of an asshole. And the kid. Plus, he labeled it asshole. That pretty much got him kicked out before the soy ice cream was served."

Beneath raised eyebrows, Sam chokes on a sip from his water bottle. "Soy ice cream?"

"I know, right? Afterward I decided it was time to move to saner waters too. So, here we are."

Hold on a sec…have I shared too much? Worse yet, do I sound

like I'm bitching?

I sneak another peek, surprised to find Sam is smiling.

Wait, of course he's smiling. He's probably grateful it's me, and not him, who's wrangling kids and birthday parties and crayon interpretations of assholes and soy ice cream.

"Ro?"

"Yes?"

"What time should I be there on Thursday?"

Thursday? What's Thursday?

Oh, right, it's Thanksgiving.

Holy snowball in hell. Did Sam confirm for Thanksgiving?

Be cool, Ro. Act sane. Or try to, at least.

Quietly I calculate how many miles I need to jog to lose ten pounds before Thursday. How fast can I re-educate my children in the fine art of acting neat and clean and tidy for a day? Realistically? I mean, can my three devils even act like angels for an afternoon?

Probably not. Maybe I should prepare him for the worst instead. Okay, time to sound confident. "How's 12:30? We eat at 1:00. That'll give you time to arm wrestle the boys for a seat at the grown-ups table and coat yourself in Purell. Wear something washable."

Sam laughs.

"I'm not kidding. Avoid flammable fabrics. Safety first."

"Can I bring anything?"

"I have three kids under ten," I remind him for some idiotic reason. "Wine is always appreciated for the adults, fast-acting Benadryl for the kids, but we've got this covered. On second thought, I have Benadryl."

"Okay, wine it is. Thanks again for the offer."

"Don't mention it."

Sam stops at a crossroads and checks for traffic. I take advantage of the opportunity and collect myself. Sure, I will need to go into commando mode to prepare, not to mention spit shine and polish my children beforehand, but it's worth it.

Sam is coming for Thanksgiving, and he's promised to teach me to ride a horse on the Friday afterward. Last Thanksgiving, with its post-divorce vibe, sucked balls big time. But this year's holiday, with its addition of a sexy hunk of man meat, is looking up.

Maybe it'll suck balls in a much better way. One can only hope.

~ * ~

I type cow quotes into a spreadsheet and calculate the total, but my thoughts are stuck on a tiny ass, not to mention a pony and a goat.

Who would have imagined in my bright and shiny new undefined life, I would be sitting in a grain elevator typing up quotes for heifers while contemplating ass ownership? Not me, especially since only a few hours ago I didn't even know what heifers were other than a horrible nickname Beth Miller called me in sixth grade. As for asses, my ex is the extent of my experience, so this four-legged cutie is definitely an upgrade.

Honestly, I figured I'd spend the bulk of my post-marriage life curled in a fetal position powerlifting multiple bags of Doritos while chugging a bottle of Glenlivet to avoid dehydration. But quoting cattle and rescuing a goat? Not on your life.

My dented metal desk in the grain elevator office sits behind the chipped Formica counter, hidden away in a cramped alcove to the left of Sam's desk. This might have been a big closet many moons ago, but regardless I like it. It's cozy, comforting, and, best of all, it's mine.

Last year's insurance calendar dripping with wildlife pictures almost covers a hole in the plaster and a gray file cabinet with a high school football schedule taped to it stands sentry beneath the calendar. The walls are an industrial flaky beige, which matches my pale, pasty Irish complexion and if I sit perfectly still, I imagine I will disappear into the plaster. I like that in a wall. Yep, this snug office of mine has a real Bob Cratchit feel to it, although Sam is a far cry from Ebenezer Scrooge, even if I do want to haunt him, and hump him, in the night.

Sam's desk anchors the main area directly in front of me and whereas he faces the office door, I face him and the row of windows across the street from the diner. It's such a nice view, Sam, not the diner. If I lean to the right of my monitor, I can eyeball him in profile, backlit by late autumn sunshine, all sexy and smart and competent in his blue jeans and buttoned-down shirt. Such a nice profile. Rugged, chiseled, built like a sports car I want to ride to Vegas. So handsome…what was I doing again?

Right. Cattle.

Regrouping, I study my notes from the dark, fragrant barn, ready to quote steers next when the office door slams open with a bang. I jump, Sam jumps, we both look up, and I rise, ready to tackle my other responsibility—greeting visitors to the office.

I grind to a halt.

Please don't be Charlie.

Pushing away from my desk in my warm, safe cubby, I ready myself to face our customers when I hear it. Squabbles. Outside voices shattering the inside. Coat zippers flying apart. Little feet trampling on worn, wooden floorboards. Olivia's voice. Yelling.

This can't be good. Has she heard about the menagerie already? Surely Justin didn't spill the beans?

Why, oh why couldn't it have been Charlie?

Sam and I exchange a knowing grin, pictures of rescued animals filling our minds. I lift a finger to my lips and whisper, "Shhhh. Ixnay on the nanimalsay."

He sits ramrod straight, digesting pig Latin, staring at my thundering family herd. His face glimmers with a hint of something. What is it? Amusement? Curiosity? Annoyance? Fear?

If he's smart, it'll be fear.

Olivia's voice fills the room. "Ro? Kids, stop it! Maddy, don't take your hat off, we won't be long. Ro, are you here? The waitress at the diner said you were. Have you got a sec?"

I lower my finger from my lips, tear my gaze away from Sam, brace myself, and step into view.

"Mommy!" Maddie breaks into a run, shedding outerwear on the floor, advancing upon the break in the counter.

Aaron marches behind her, his coat already falling from his shoulders. "Gross. This place smells funny." He curls up his freckled nose and inhales deeply. "Oh, yuck, what is that? It smells like old oatmeal…"

Great, now Sam probably questions both my cooking and cleaning skills.

"…gee, Mom, it's weird," he whines. Another exaggerated inhale. "Barf!"

Unperturbed by any weird smells, Nick holds Jaylen's sleeve and tugs her behind himself, practically yanking her out of her glitter-trimmed turquoise snow boots. "Mom, that kid I told you about in class, Cameron. He likes bugs too, and he has one of those hissing cockroaches. Can I go to his house sometime and see it? They won't let him bring it to school anymore."

My babies come at me like a wave, chattering in unison, dripping scarves and mittens to the floor, each voluntarily oblivious to what the others are saying. I plaster patience on my face and exhale. "Isn't this a pleasant surprise?"

Olivia rushes behind them, carrying Jayden on her hip. "Kids, hush." She makes a beeline toward me, flustered, determined, in a mood. I can tell. I know her moods, and this is the exasperated one.

She tugs her purse off her shoulder and slaps it hard on the counter. "Sweetie, I am so sorry to do this to you at work, but Aaron has a field trip tomorrow and if we don't get this form signed and turned back in today, like in the next half hour, he can't go. He'll be sitting in the library doing who knows what. Can you sign it?" She sets Jayden down and opens her purse. "The school secretary leaves at 4:30. It's now or never."

She's here for a permission slip? Thank you, Jesus, I'll live another day, though if I mention the menagerie after supper I could die tonight. I peek sideways at Sam. He remains at attention, stiff, frozen in place. Any chance he's upset they're here?

Unconcerned with things like neat-freak bosses and office protocols, Maddy flies to me and attacks my legs with violent, sticky hugs. "Mommy, I put my baby doll dress on Paw Paw today and he fell over on the floor. It was so funny. Can I take a picture of him with your phone when we get home?"

I shoot a shocked expression at Olivia, pictures of an overweight, angry orange cat dressed in pink chiffon waltzing through my brain, then tilt Maddy's chin up to face me. "He's not still in it, is he? You didn't leave that poor cat in that itty, bitty dress, did you?"

Olivia pulls the slip from her purse. "I made her take it off. The girls were playing dress up and he wandered in there and had to be nosey."

Aaron peels behind the counter and drops his parka at my feet. "We're going to a dairy tomorrow. They said we can have ice cream. Yogurt too. Do you think they'll let me milk a cow?"

Thawing from his initial paralysis upon their arrival, Sam shifts forward in his chair. "That would be the Meyers's farm. They do this every year. It's a big operation." His voice belays a hint of amusement as he reassures my youngest son. "You'll have fun. I'm not sure if you'll get to milk a cow, but they have calves you can pet."

Aaron considers him for a moment before joining him at his desk with Maddy in tow. "Those are baby cows, right?"

Sam nods. "Right."

Nick shakes off his little cousin and joins us. "What do they call baby cockroaches?"

"Gross," answers Olivia, "they call them gross. Can we stop discussing bugs please? Put your coats back on. We can't stay."

I toss Aaron's parka to Nick and point at his brother. "Give this to him. Put it back on, kiddo," I order with eyebrows raised in the international mom symbol for I mean it, so do it. "Listen to your Aunt Livy."

She raps the worn worktop with her knuckles. "That's right, you heard her. Listen to me." Finally, with a wave she acknowledges Sam. "Hi. You must be the boss. I'm Olivia, Ro's sister-in-law. Sorry to bug her at work. Kid emergency."

Surrounded, Sam rises from his chair, "No problem" falling from his lips, his hand ready to shake hers.

She, however, stops him. "You might want to take a raincheck, there's whooping cough going around the school, and Maddy's already sneezed on me." She points at a dark stain on her gloved palm. "That's going to have to soak."

I search for a pen under the counter as I scold, "Maddy, what have I told you about covering your mouth when you sneeze? Do it."

"Oh, she did," replies Olivia, "only she used mine instead of hers."

Giggles burst from my daughter. Amused, but determined to hide it, I focus on the form. Parenting, it's such a roller coaster.

Invisible germs threaten me with sick days I haven't earned as I read. I print my name, hyperaware my babies currently encircle my boss who may be voluntarily childless, not to mention a raging neat freak, all while they spew communicable diseases in his general direction. Is it possible to encase my three heathens in plastic bubbles and roll them around until they're twenty? It's an idea.

Nick scratches his nose and wipes it on his coat next to Sam's knee. "We sleep in the dining room."

I frown. "Nick…"

Olivia drums her fingers on the surface in rapid fire, tap, tap, tapping away. "We're redoing the rooms upstairs first." She reaches into her purse and digs out paint samples, rethinks it then shoves them back inside. "The minions are temporarily camping in the dining room. It's wall to wall mattresses in there, but it works."

No doubt happy to share embarrassing details too, Aaron tugs on Sam's sleeve. "Mom's sleeping in a closet under the stairs."

What a lovely picture that paints. *Thanks for sharing, son.* "It's temporary too," I explain, "and it's handy to the dining room. It's better than it sounds."

Maddy wiggles beside Sam, all smiles and curls and innocence, but she's not fooling me. It won't last. What embarrassing tidbit does she have up her itty, bitty coat sleeve?

Tentatively she chews on her mitten, hesitant. Finally, she taps on Sam's elbow, "I have a kitty named Paw Paw…"

"He's not your cat," Aaron interrupts.

Timidity banished, Maddy channels her inner demon onto her brother. "Yes, he is, he's my cat!"

"No, he's not," Aaron yells into Sam's right ear. "He's everybody's cat." Not missing a beat, he addresses Sam, "I want to catch mice for him, but Mom won't let me play with the traps."

I print my cell phone number. "You need your thumbs, sweetie."

Unconcerned with little boy digits, Olivia looks pointedly at them, no doubt ready to do damage control. "We don't have mice. The house is a work in progress. It was empty for a while, but it's clean. Squeaky clean. Eat-off-the floors clean"

Sam twists in his chair to face her. "I wouldn't blame you if you do have them. Around here during the harvest, they're everywhere. They leave the fields for shelter. Most of us are struggling with mice this time of year."

She grins. "Seriously?"

"Yep. Trust me, you're not alone if you do."

Aaron pokes Sam's shoulder. "Do you have mice?"

A chuckle escapes his lips. "I had a few in a bag of horse feed this morning."

"Can I have one?"

"No," Olivia and I answer in unison.

My son puffs his bottom lip into a full-blown whine. "Why not? It's for Paw Paw."

An involuntary shudder rattles its way through Olivia. "Oh, yuck. Anyway, he's not our cat," she continues. "He belongs to someone, I'm sure of it. Seriously, Ro," she turns to me, "we need to call the shelter. It's been a few weeks now."

Children erupt into complaints behind me. I raise the pen and wave it in the air. "Hush, all of you." Facing Oliva, I speak the inevitable, "It's been on my mind too."

"Mom, no," Nick complains.

Maddy stomps her foot, and it's frustratingly charming. "No, Paw Paw's my cat, just like Poo Poo Pink Princess!"

We stop. Heads swivel toward my daughter.

I halt in mid signature. "Poo poo what?"

Maddy curls her arms into a hug and rocks an imaginary baby. "Poo Poo Pink Princess. She's my pet too. Like Paw Paw."

Aaron makes google eyes at Sam before rolling them at his sister. "You don't have a pet named Poo Poo."

She stops rocking and stomps her foot again, harder this time. "Yes, I do! She's big and furry and sweet, and she plays with me when I have my tea parties, and she lives in a tree house and loves Fruity Pebbles and marshmallows."

Interrupting their squabbles, I inquire, "Marshmallows? My marshmallows?"

Aaron ignores my snack issues. "Geez, Maddy, we're talking

about real pets." He shrugs at Sam. "Paw Paw's real. Mom's got a video of him licking his butt. It's pretty funny. Want to watch it?"

"Aaron," I scold, but it's too late. Damage done. Maddy's found my marshmallow stash, and Sam probably thinks I'm into weird hobbies. Perfect, just perfect.

"Poo Poo is real!" squeals my tired daughter. Determination etched on her face, she questions Sam. "You believe me, don't you?" She searches him with shiny, tear-filled eyes pleading for agreement.

Sam hesitates. He peers at Maddy. "Poo Poo sounds real to…"

But he doesn't finish his sentence. Instead, my adorable four-year-old phlegm monster sneezes directly into his face, interrupting him with an impressive, flying, substantive loogie.

Oh. My. God.

"Maddy, cover your mouth!" I launch myself at them, already offering the hem of my sweater, stiff with donkey spit from our morning field trip. "Sam, I'm so sorry."

Startled, Maddy breaks into sobs, overwhelmed and overwrought. I want to blame the tears on imaginary pet loyalty, but we all know who the real culprit is. My big, yelling mouth.

Grimacing, Sam grabs a box of tissues from a desk drawer and gives one to Maddie. "It's okay, it happens." He grabs a second for himself and starts wiping.

Dropping my donkey-chewed sweater, I help Maddie blow her nose. "I'm so sorry."

Sam tosses his tissue into the trash can and offers me another. "It was an accident, Ro."

No doubt sensing the end is near, Olivia brings us back on task. "Kids, time to go. Now. Move it."

I lift my tired, sobbing baby into my arms, and she drapes herself across my shoulder, exchanging her snot-covered tissue for my hair. Returning to the counter, I set her on it, finish my signature, and fold the form for Olivia. "Thanks. I owe you."

She thrusts it into her purse. "Nah, it kinda feels like I owe you. Tonight, we'll kill a bottle of merlot. Kids, c'mon, let's go."

"Deal."

Grabbing Maddie, I return her to the floor, and help her into her coat. "Time to skee-daddled, kiddos, Momma's got to work."

Marching en masse, my phlegmy, sniffling, arguing family ambles toward the door, yelling goodbyes as they go. With a bang, the door shuts behind them, leaving blessed silence in their wake.

My back to Sam, I follow their progress through the window as they descend the stairs. "Sam?"

Over the squirt from a bottle of hand sanitizer, he replies, "Yes?"

"Are you still coming for Thanksgiving?"

A pause.

"I wouldn't miss it for the world."

~ * ~

My first workday in years ends with me against yet another counter at the local animal shelter, waiting on a receipt for a bulk order of dog food I delivered for Sam. As I wait, I set an alarm on my cell to remind me of my Friday morning riding tutorial with my hunky boss—like there's any chance I would forget—before adding another note to schedule a full-body wax, seaweed detox, discount Botox, and liposuction to boot.

It's going to be a busy week.

A middle-aged woman sits at a desk across from me and fills out the receipt. Behind her an older, overweight golden retriever lies listlessly on a large cushion. White whiskers surround its muzzle and speckle its coat.

"Hey there, fella, you got a name?"

A soft tail hesitates, then rises from the ground. It wags in slow senior time.

The woman tears the receipt from the pad. "That's Lucky. He's not a happy camper these days."

"Why not?"

"He doesn't like the shelter. He misses his home and his owner. Mr. Jenkins passed away a month ago, and his nephew didn't want him. It's a shame, too, because he's a good, old boy." She spins around in her chair and pets him. Lucky lifts his head in response. "He doesn't like the other dogs barking all the time. It gets on his nerves. I sure would like to find him a good home." She swings back around and faces me with a grin. "His adoption fee is waived. He's ready to go."

Soft, hurting eyes watch me. The seed of yet another wonderful idea lands in my brain, takes root, and grows.

What is it with me and dead people's pets today?

Who knows? The point is, I can save this dog.

Olivia leaps to mind. I beat down her image with a fluffy puppy tail. "So, this big sweetie needs a home, you say? I've been wanting to get a dog. Can I pet him?"

Immediately, the woman forgets about the receipt. "Heck, yes, you can pet him."

Coming around the corner, I kneel next to Lucky. He pushes himself into a sit with arthritic bones and his tail wags a wee bit faster.

"You're a big old sweetie, aren't you?" He hesitates, before stretching toward my face. A hot, wet tongue dances lightly against my cheek. "A kiss? For me? How sweet."

Lucky inches upward from a sit to a stand. His tail zips through the air, wagging to and fro, his trust growing. He catches the scent of goat and pony and ass, and his nose explores my arms, my sweater, my shoes. The woman pats him on the back. We're both petting away, happy to love on this sweet old dog, semi oblivious to the sound of the closing door.

Throwing caution to the wind, I make my next big decision of the day. "Would you like to come home with me, boy?"

His tail picks up the pace, wagging ever so faster with each second.

"I'll tell you what, I'll take this fella home. Because he's a big ole sweetie," I say in my best puppy voice as I snuggle my newest addition to the family.

A haggard voice breaks up our four-legged make-out session. "Excuse me."

The chair beside me swivels at the sound. "Judge Middleton, hello. Still no sign of Mr. Evans?"

That voice, why is it familiar?

I turn and recognize him at once. Same thick coat, same dusty brown bowler perched on the patch of thinning gray hair, same spare look he had etched on his face that first day in town when I ran him over in the diner. It's the elderly man I hip-checked in the hallway and, lucky me, he's a judge.

Oh, goodie.

"No. It's been over two weeks since I last saw him. No one has called about a large, yellow cat yet?"

The woman rocks forward in her chair. "Sorry, no one's called or brought one in either. If anyone does, though, I'll be sure to call."

Oh, hell no.

Did he ask about a big yellow cat?

There's no getting around it, I'm going to have to ask. "Excuse me, Judge Middleton?" I interrupt. A sinking feeling blooms in my heart. "Whereabouts do you live? Anywhere near Stockpile Road?"

The elderly man sizes me up. Does he recognize me from the diner? Lord knows we were close enough. Did I give him a rug burn with my mom jeans? After all, these hips don't lie, and I came in hot. Any chance he has dementia? Oops, not nice. No wonder Karma plagues me. Can we settle on a smidge of forgetfulness instead?

Steel gray eyes study me. "I believe we are neighbors. You are the woman who bought Mr. and Mrs. Yeager's farm, correct? I live on the next farm over."

"With the cows?"

"No, I'm farther east. I no longer have any livestock. Only Mr. Evans."

"Oh." Lucky licks my cheek. At least someone in this room likes me. I press for more info. "How big would you say he is? The cat? Is he solid yellow or does he have any white on him?"

"He is yellow striped with a white patch from his chest to his stomach."

Of course, he does. Figures.

I sigh, "I may have your cat."

"Excuse me?" he blinks at me.

"I may have your cat. One showed up when we were moving in. Don't worry, though, we brought him in, and he's been taken care of ever since." I chuckle. "He may even be fatter."

His thin lips remain ramrod straight. "You brought him inside?"

Is he angry? Confused? It's hard to tell. I shrug. "He just showed up, and it was going to be dark soon. We wondered if he was a stray or a drop off. Plus, the movers were on their way and, frankly, he entertained the hell out of the kids. Gave us time to unload the truck." I stop, hoping for compassion, understanding, something, anything.

The judge, however, continues the inquisition, unmoved by our lost kitty-cat charity. "You've kept him inside all this time? You never called the shelter?"

Maybe I should switch tactics. A half-hearted smile lights my face, though I get nothing in return. "We didn't want to leave him out in the cold, and when we did put him outside, he hung around on the front porch, crying nonstop. My kids were crying, and all they wanted to do was play with him—they've never had a pet before. We always planned to call the shelter, we've just been busy what with unpacking, and I started a new job. I guess time got away from us. I was actually going to ask if anyone reported a missing cat while I was here." I stop, praying the dog lady remains silent. Perhaps I need some insurance. "I hadn't mentioned it yet."

The judge remains silent.

Lucky collapses onto his side, exposing his own white belly, so I oblige and rub his tummy. He propels a back foot through the air, kickstarting an imaginary motorcycle. "I'm on my way home after I finish here. Would you like to pick up your cat? I'd bring him back, but I'm not sure of your address."

A frozen voice acknowledges my offer. "No, thank you. I'll have my housekeeper pick him up at 6:00. Is the time convenient for you?"

Convenient? Not really. I have so many body parts to wax. Oh, well, it can't be helped. "Six? Works for me."

"Fine." With a tip of his hat, the icy old man blows through the door.

"You're welcome," I mutter when he's out of earshot.

The woman behind the desk closes her receipt book with a snap. "Ignore him. In his line of work, he's seen the worst of it. Domestic violence, child abuse, shoplifting, drugs, you name it. You'd think he'd retire."

"I hear you, but we saved his cat. He at least owes us a thank you." I brush retriever hair from my pants and point at Lucky with a new mission is sight. "Now, help me here, will you? I've got to tell five children to say goodbye to Sandy Poo Poo Claws the First, or whatever the hell they're calling him now, so tell me this. How do I adopt this dog?"

Chapter Six

Streetlights shine through the windows of the closed diner, illuminating my office booth. I sit in the dark, alone, licking envelopes. The taste of cheap mint reminiscent of expired generic mouthwash pervades my lips, my tongue. These envelopes are the only things needing my tongue these days, and I'm getting paid to do it, so I sit, and I lick. Perhaps that qualifies me as a stationery whore. I should probably care. It's telling that I don't.

The dangling bell above the diner door rings, and I check the reflection in the wall mirror. It's a man, silhouetted in the dark, an unknown entity, stalking my periphery. Broad shoulders, narrow hips, and delicious thighs fill the shadows. Boots pound on the wooden floor, headed my way.

I'm not afraid.

The boots march on, drawing the man ever closer. In the glow of the streetlamp light streaming through the window, a face emerges in the reflection.

Sam.

Leisurely, I draw an envelope across my tongue, savoring it. A sting burns my lip as the edge bites my flesh. I fold the envelope closed, set it aside, and pick up another one. My tongue caresses the cut on my lip.

Sam is beside me now. He reaches out, grasping my upper arm. There's pressure, undeniable pressure. He pulls me to my feet, lifting me from my booth. His arms encircle me.

I drop the envelope. Our bodies fuse together, welded like magnets. Sam claws his way up my shoulder, his breath ragged. Finding the back of my neck, he grasps my hair, and turns my face to his own. His mouth crashes down upon mine. He rakes my lips with his tongue, forces them apart, unheeding my paper-cut pout and my minty, envelope tang. My tongue finds his. He kisses me deep, Grand Canyon deep. I kiss him right back.

Fingers grope and squeeze, find purchase, test boundaries. Relentless, he grips my collar and yanks. Buttons fly from the front of my blouse, landing on the table like yesterday's paper wads. Desperate, panting, wanting, me, Sam slides his eager hands down my ribcage, ripping my blouse apart, flaying the fabric, exposing me to the world.

Expert fingers grip my front-hooking bra and make short work of the clasp. He frees my heaving breasts from the lace and the Lycra and the elastic. Boobs tumble out along with a smattering of potato chip crumbs and a school of rock-hard goldfish crackers stashed in my cleavage. Cracker dust coats my upright nips.

Sam is undeterred. Better still, he's even harder than the stale sea creatures released from my bra. He reaches past me and swipes envelopes and crackers to the floor. Gripping me by the waist, he lifts me with ease, and sets me on the edge of the table. My mini skirt bunches at my thighs which, miracle of miracles, are cellulite free.

His belt blocks my way, halting my progress. I grasp it and rip it from his jeans, casting it aside. The button bursts open, sending the zipper cascading down his bulge.

He's at my knees now, under my skirt, parting my legs. I don't question this, I give into it, wanting, panting, needing Sam to take me on this booth, to take me now, now, now, even if Charlie just entered the diner and is seated at the table beside us, rattling on about crop yields and moisture checks.

He flips through a notebook, apparently unperturbed by our after-hours foreplay as he scrutinizes something in its pages. "You won't need to run that load through the dryer, Sam." He stops, writes down some numbers, then studies me with squinty eyes. "She's pretty dry. No moisture check needed. Saves on the dryer bill for sure. Gotta like that."

I don't like that—why am I so dry? Why would anyone like that? I search Sam's face, yet it's morphed into a nondescript blur of formless contours. He warps in and out, overtaken with soft lines and wispy edges.

Armed with a spatula, clear as a bell, Eli, the young fry cook, is beside us. "Want me to flip her for you, Sam? You gotta brown both sides." He slides the metal edge of the spatula under my ass cheek, ready to cook me well and brown me even. Instead, he stops and points past me.

Maddy's here—where'd she come from?

"Mommy, will you wipe my butt?" She holds a wad of toilet paper and waits. Her nose runs. I tear off a piece and wipe.

Surrounded by shadow, slipping away, Sam lets me go as he backs away, zipping and buttoning, disappearing in the dark. My knees slam together with a thunderclap. The sound rolls through the diner. It echoes out of my dry, empty, money-saving vagina, bounces off the walls, and scares the stale fish crackers, which swim away under my booth. My bra snaps back on its own, enveloping my crumb-covered breasts. I grasp at the rapidly dissolving Sam, panting, wanting, needing. He stares at my child and slips into nothingness.

With a start, I snap awake.

Crap.

Sweat dampens my T-shirt nighty as I lie in my bed with the imaginary taste of Sam on my tongue. The feel of his non-existent grip lingers on my arm; his dream hand grasps my hair. My thighs burn, my breasts ache, everything tingles, I'm jittery, hot and bothered, and so very far from dry.

Rustling catches my ear near the open door of my renovation-inducing, Harry-Potter inspired bedroom under the stairs. Maddy stands silhouetted in the soft glow from the hall nightlight. "Mommy, I gotta pee. Can you help me?"

My head falls back onto my pillow. "Sure, baby, give me a sec, though. Mommy was sleeping."

"Will you wipe my butt too?"

"Yes, baby, go on. I'll be in there in a sec."

Backing into the hall, all distinct and crisp-edged, the real-life version of my daughter pitter patters toward the bathroom two doors down. The light snaps on and the butt-wiping clock is ticking.

Yet Sam lingers on my mind.

If I close my eyes, I can feel him, taste him, smell him, even though he's a world away, footloose and child free. What happened to uninterested? Why can't my body—or my subconscious—take a hint?

And why, oh why did I invite him to Thanksgiving? Am I addicted to chaos and complications?

Can't I dream about gardens and recipes and crafty things like painting dried gourds and repurposing old shutters instead?

No such luck. The mind wants what it wants. Or, I should say, the body needs what it needs.

Well, toughen up, body and mind, because we're in a fucking dry spell. Literally.

At least my life wants to screw me.

Still, it never occurred to me to question relocating my single self to a new town with a rather limited male population. Everyone is either illegally young, desperately old, married, or moving away. Or my boss with a capital B. And Charlie? No thank you.

Face it, Ro, you'll never have sex again. Okay, maybe not with another human being. Might as well date my fucking dildo.

Oh, grow up.

This won't do. Tempting as it is, I could dwell on the dream, relive it, possibly even recapture it, although it would be counterproductive. Instead, I launch into mommy mode. I rise from my sweaty bed and push my sweaty thoughts of Sam aside with one goal in mind.

It's time to wipe some ass.

~ * ~

It's D-Day, Thanksgiving. Between Justin and me, we've managed to whine, cajole, and finally convince Olivia to put away her organic, vegan recipes for the day in favor of a retro 1950s era dinner complete with everything she avoids like the plague—canned mushroom soup, French fried onions, brown sugar, marshmallows she insisted on making from scratch, even ranch dressing also homemade the day before. Sadly, though, she's drawn a sharp-edged line at jellied cranberries from a can, and I'm struggling to recover. I love the crap in the can.

While she's not completely sold on the idea of our all-American dinner and despises missing any blogging opportunity—she almost donned 1950s garb for a spur-of-the-moment photo shoot—I'm beyond thrilled. Canned and pre-made are no strangers to me. They're my go-to dinner-time staple.

As a payback, however, she promptly assigned me a recipe I must now conjure from scratch, recreating Nana's stuffing. I pick Olivia's brain for help and, with her guidance, chop onion and celery with abandon and toast slices of her homemade bread, preparing them for my favorite ingredient, a container of oysters chilling in the fridge. Basically, I've got this, so she's partially appeased.

Surprisingly, although I'm not much of a cook, much less a chef like Olivia, I'm enjoying myself. Maybe it's the holiday or maybe it's this big, old country kitchen, or maybe it's because it smells amazing, but this is fun. Who knew?

An old wooden table anchors the center of the kitchen where we chop, dice, peel, and stir. Too often, my attention wanders to the blazing fire in the large stone hearth anchoring the room. It practically screams for Olivia's homemade marshmallows currently dusted with powdered sugar and hidden safely out of sight in an antique hutch, destined for her sweet potato casserole. Desperate to roast one above the glowing coals, I hold off. While I love gelatinized sugar, my thighs do not.

Giggles and chatter roll toward us from the nearby butler's pantry where our children play. The pantry's wonderful old drawers, cabinets, and cubbies do double duty as a playhouse, and the comforting sounds of make-believe tumble through the door. Sometimes, I half expect them to disappear into Narnia.

It's a gray, blustery day. A brisk northern breeze picks up in intensity, knocking the wooden shutters against the outside wall as we work, yet I ignore Mother Nature's hollow threats. After a good first two-weeks at my first real job in years, today is a family fun day. The gray clouds and threat of snow only add to the mood.

Olivia pulls a bag of cranberries from the refrigerator. She tosses it onto the table and dives back in, calling to me as she hunts through a bottom drawer, "Okay, which is more old school American for the cranberries? Walnuts or pecans?"

I'm about to reply, when there's a loud knock on the back door. Rising from my chair, I consider the options–both are a win in my book–when I remember dessert. "Go with the walnuts. I plan to pig out on pecans in pie form." Stepping around the sleeping form of Lucky, our new four-legged addition, I head to the door. Fat and happy, he lies stretched before the kitchen fireplace, farting in his sleep. "Why can't we have the jellied stuff, Liv? It's easy, and totally cool when it comes out of the can. You can see the rings. They're there so you know where to slice it. Nifty, huh?"

Olivia grabs a bag of chopped walnuts. A shudder courses through her shoulders. "Oh, good lord, no." Lifting a saucepan from an overhead pot rack Justin fashioned from an old French door frame, she practically convulses. "You can't be serious."

Pausing in front of the fire, I linger. Heat baths me. Marshmallows tempt me. "I am." I laugh, enjoying her disgust. "I'm serious as a heart attack."

She tosses a generous helping of nuts into the pan and reaches for a colander. "That's probably what it'll give you. I can't imagine the sugar or the sodium count." Moving to the sink, she dumps the cranberries into the colander and starts rinsing. "One more reason not to buy pre-made. I agreed to marshmallows on the sweet potatoes. You can live with fresh cranberries." She gives the berries a few good shakes and pours them into the pan with the walnuts. "Makes it easier to slice...wow," she mutters.

Tearing myself from the fire, I walk toward the back door as another knock lands on the wood frame. "I could eat a ton of your cranberry stuff by myself. Promise me one thing, though. Don't let me."

She opens a cabinet for a bottle of honey and squirts an impressive glob into the pan. "Cranberry stuff? Seriously? *That's* what we're calling it? Wow," she repeats. Yet another knock lands on the door. "Ro, do you mind? I'm making the cranberry stuff."

Headed to the door, I peek in the pan. Plump cranberries and dark lumpy walnut pieces coated with honey stare back. "Okay, but you might want to come up with a better name if you put that recipe in your book."

Olivia laughs and flings a walnut at me. I duck, and it bounces off the window, landing at my feet. "Next time aim for my mouth. You can't miss."

Turning the doorknob, I glance outside, suddenly curious. Who's knocking? It's too early for Sam, and we aren't expecting anyone else. A brisk wind beats against the panes of glass framing the back of a hooded, green-quilted parka I don't' recognize. Bracing myself against the chill, I open the door. "Hi, can I help you?"

The parka whips around. "Ro!"

The hood comes down, processed burgundy curls with silver highlights spring out, bright red lips part baring shiny white dentures, aggressively lined eye lids flutter, earrings, bracelets, and necklaces jingle and jangle. In the midst of it all, I'm speechless. Then, as the shock deepens, I yell. A primal, guttural yell.

"Mom? Oh, my God, Mom!"

Patchouli-scented arms wrap around me, embracing me in a tight bear hug. Kisses land on my cheeks, dotting me with a trail of lipstick prints. I hug back, in shock. My mind races.

Oh, fuck.

I'm screwed.

"Kate?" Olivia appears behind me, eyes wide with shock, an orange in one hand, a zester in the other. "Kate, I can't believe you're here. Justin, come quick, your mom's here!"

Justin's deep voice erupts from somewhere near the hutch where Olivia's homemade marshmallows sit currently unprotected. "Mom?"

"Yes, yes, I'm here. Now where are my grandbabies?" Mom releases me from her tight embrace and rushes past me through the door. "Ro, can you get my bags please?"

Bags? She has bags? As in plural luggage?

Double fuck.

Mom's suitcases bulge at their seams at bottom of the kitchen steps. A tote bag overflows, spilling out presents. In Christmas wrapping paper. This can't be good. "Mom? You brought bags? I thought you were going to Aunt Theresa's?"

She pauses in mid climb. "Oh, don't be a goose, of course I brought bags. I'm here until after the holidays."

I grip a suitcase handle. Dead weight resists my pull. "The holidays? As in Thanksgiving and the Friday after?"

Please don't say Groundhog Day.

"No, kiddo, I'm here through Christmas. Isn't it great? Besides, I've seen Theresa's condo a dozen times. I couldn't wait to see this place." She flies into the kitchen with outstretched arms. Her voice booms out through the door. "I wanted a fixer upper in the country when I was younger too. I knew you kids wouldn't mind."

Screams of joy and the mad pounding of feet on floorboards announce the arrival of Justin and the children as they make their way into the kitchen. Mom embraces Olivia and waves them in for a hug. Lucky is on his feet, wagging his tail, wanting love too.

Oh, dear lord.

She's here through Christmas.

I love Mom. Always have, always will. I've especially loved how she sings her own bizarre, off-kilter, show tune with no regard for other people's requests. But today, I didn't expect to have her sonnet of insanity filling our home. Sam will be here in an hour—he rattles me to the core as it is—plus we're still practically strangers, the new dog is gassy, the kids are buzzing on sugar, we're living among the moving boxes, and Mom—my oddball, whack-a-doodle Mom—is here, amped up in her speeding-semi-that-won't-stop mode, and I have no clue how to halt the impending crash which sucks since I'm the freaking crash test dummy.

There better be a man of steel buried under that quiet cowboy exterior, because Sam's going to need it. Then I remember another potential pitfall.

He's bringing wine.

General, please raise our status to DefCon One. Not only is Hurricane Kate here, but soon she'll be drinking. Kill me now.

I fling the tote bag over my shoulder, grab a suitcase with each hand, then heave them up the first step, the second, the third, and finally through the open door. Shutting it, I lean against cold wood and take in the sight.

My three happy babies and the twins drip from Mom like her favorite dangly earrings. They chatter in their best outside voices and ramble on about cats and dogs, the house, the farm, everything. Justin waits behind her for another hug. Olivia beams beside him. Lucky wags his tail, happy too.

One thing is certain. She definitely livens up the place.

Of course, so does a three-alarm fire.

~ * ~

Mom's things are stowed in the former servants' quarters past the butler's pantry, though we've yet to touch the diminutive room. It has no electricity or heat except what drifts in from the kitchen, but she says it suits her bohemian, make-shift nature, not to mention her hot flashes just fine, and she's willing to make a go of it, even if it means sleeping in a recliner until I can get to the store for an air mattress.

The grand tour of the house has been put aside as roast turkey and stuffing wait for no man or mom. We're back in the kitchen chopping and mixing and roasting in earnest while I try to figure out a safe way to mention Sam.

Lifting the turkey from the oven, I set it on the stove, and shove in a casserole laden with stuffing. "Mom, why didn't you call? What if we weren't home?" Brandishing the plastic baster thingy Olivia forced upon me, I'm prepared to bathe the bird in bubbling hot juice.

Mom whips past me, lifts an orange from a bowl, and zests it into the cranberries simmering away in a saucepan. "Of course, you'd be home. Why wouldn't you be? Where else would you go? Peter's?"

"Mom…"

She waves, clutching the zester, warding me off. "So, sue me. I took a risk."

Squeezing hard, I suck hot turkey juice from the bottom of the roasting pan, filling the baster. "It's just, we weren't expecting you." Channeling my agitation into flying broth, I squeeze, hosing the turkey from its top to its literal bottom, splattering the oven in the process. Like everything else in this world, it must take practice. Or less agitation. Or both. I suck, squeeze, suck, squeeze, and frown at my mother. "Seriously, you could have called."

She stops in mid-zest as I power wash the bird. "Are you saying you don't want me here?"

"No, that's not what I mean," I backtrack. "I wouldn't have invited other guests if I'd known. We aren't even unpacked, and the house is a work in progress. We're making do as it is."

She looks around the cavernous kitchen. "Making do? You have two households' worth of furniture in here, plus the entry hall alone is the size of a McDonald's, for heaven's sake. And guests? What other guests?"

Ah, this is where it gets tricky. Steeling my nerves, I brace myself and plunge in. "Only one, my new boss. I haven't worked in forever, and they only hired me on a temporary basis, so, it has to go well today, okay. Please?"

She studies the turkey with no attempt at hiding her disgust. "Spit it out, Ro, and quit drowning that poor bird. You're practically raping it with that plastic thingy."

See where I get my cooking skills?

Please, God, put some compassion into this woman. Can you get her to dial back the interrogation of Sam? Don't forget, I rescued a dog, a horse, and a goat this week, not to mention an ass. Please?

Prayers pleaded I continue blast-basting today's main course. "Did you hear me, Mom? I need a favor. Okay?"

Something resembling innocence drips from my mother's smile. It's kind of disturbing. "A favor?" she coos. "Sure, sweetie. What?"

Easy does it, Ro. Don't alert her Spidey sense.

"Okay, he...my boss...he didn't have anywhere to go for Thanksgiving," inside my head, the word "*liar*" bounces around my empty skull, peening off the sides like a silver ball in a pinball machine, "and I know you mean well, but I'd appreciate it if you wouldn't grill him with your particular brand of crazy while he's here. You can be overwhelming. To strangers."

"Your boss, huh." Leaning over the stove, she stirs the zest into the cranberries. "You said him, right? As in a guy?"

Danger...abort...

"Yes..."

"Is he gay?"

Throw her off, Ro.

"I haven't asked." Technically true.

Don't blink, don't blink. Don't show fear.

She's like a shark with blood in the water—smells her prey, slips in like a whisper...okay, not like a whisper, more like a foghorn—right before the bloody, gory kill.

Verbally, she crouches, waiting to pounce. "Would this happen to be a good-looking guy? How old are we talking here? Your age," she purrs, "or mine?"

I bang the baster down upon the stove, startling Olivia who sits frozen at the table, listening to our conversation. If I beg, will she take pity on me? "Want to help me out here, Liv?"

Immediately, she drops the peeler and bolts for the hallway. "I think Jaylen's crying."

"Chicken!" I yell after her.

Back toward Momzilla I whirl with new plans for the baster.

Furiously, she zests yet more orange, dusting the simmering cranberries. "I'm being serious, Ro, how old is he? Any chance I might get lucky tonight?"

Ick. No more sweet dreams for me.

Time for a slightly more direct approach. Here goes. "It doesn't matter how old he is, he's only coming for dinner. Meaning, I need you to be distantly pleasant, understood? Distantly—as in often in another room with the children—pleasant."

This time, it's her turn to bang a spoon on the stove. "Distantly pleasant? Where's the fun in that? Avon ladies are distantly pleasant."

"Mom, please…"

A dramatic, put-upon sigh wheezes out of her flapping mouth. "Oh, all right, for heaven's sake. I'll be a veritable Stepford wife of pleasantness. Distantly remote, if not comatose. Happy?"

It's a start. Pushing the stuffing to one side, I return the turkey to the oven, slamming it shut as Olivia peeks around the hallway. "Dated references there, Mom, although, I'll take it. Avon lady and Stepford wife, it is."

Sensing it's safe, Olivia returns, sparkling with fake innocence, and resumes peeling potatoes. "Twins are fine. False alarm," she mutters, concentrating on her task, even as a tiny smirk tugs at the corners of her mouth.

I smirk back. "Et tu, Brutus?"

Before she can reply, the kitchen door bangs open, and, born in on a blast of frigid air, Justin barrels by carrying an armload of firewood. "Guess what?"

"What?" Olivia and I ask in unison.

Stacking wood on the stone hearth, he tosses a few logs on the fire and, with a nod, indicates the bank of windows behind us. "It's snowing."

"It is?" I cry.

We whip around toward the windows. Fat flakes of glistening snow swirl beyond the glass. We've fallen into a snow globe.

Oblivious to the size of our heating bill, Mom rushes to the back door and throws it open, letting in the cold and snow. Silhouetted against the door, she bellows toward the butler's pantry, "Kids, get in here, you have to see this!"

At breakneck speed, children bound toward the kitchen, hoping for more candy from the depths of their Meemaw's purse.

Reaching the kitchen first, Nick stops in his tracks. "It's snowing!"

Aaron darts around him. "Oh, boy!" He makes a dash for the outdoors, followed by the rest of the children. Rushing down the steps, they gamble about in the white whirling mass of flakes, skipping, hopping, and squealing.

"Oops," Mom shrugs.

A loud war whoop erupts from the kitchen table. Dropping a potato, Olivia disappears out the door too. Joining the twins, she takes their hands and catches snowflakes on her tongue.

Mom, Justin, and I size each other up. Moving slowly toward the door, I eyeball them both. "Are you thinking what I'm thinking?"

Justin dumps the remaining logs onto the stone hearth. "I'll beat you to the snow."

Backing toward the door, Mom stares us down. "Not on my watch. Later suckers." Making fast tracks in her black leather boots, through the door she bounds, leaving us behind.

Momentarily frozen, Justin and I exchange a quick look and spring into action. Together, we rush to get outside. I dodge him, but he catches the end of my sweater, hauling me back. We collide. Bodies smash against wood. He blocks me with his ass, grabs the door frame and heaves. Legs and arms flail. With a heave, he wedges past and leaps into the snow, laughing, "I win!"

Hot on his heels, I dash after him. "No fair! Illegal use of giant arms. Penalty flag—no white meat for you."

"Good." He lifts Aaron by the arms and swings him in a wide arc. "I prefer dark meat anyway."

Halting beside Maddy, I bend and kiss her button nose. "Drats, I forgot about that."

Fat snowflakes land on her pink, outstretched tongue. Hugging my leg, she squeezes tight, bursting with joy. "I want to make a snowman, Mommy."

"Me too, pumpkin. Right after dinner."

"Yay!"

The cry has barely left her lips, when it's matched by a pitiful meow from beneath the large clump of spruce beside the house. Low hanging branches sway, a dusting of snow falls to the ground, and Mr. Evans emerges, damp, needy, and pitiful.

No longer interested in me, Maddy runs straight for the cat. "Paw Paw! Mommy, it's Paw Paw. Can we take him in the house? Please?"

Wonderful. Another unplanned guest. "You shouldn't be here, big fella." I sigh. "You have a home."

Maddy's lower lip quivers. Naturally, I cave. "Okay, fine, he can stay until after dinner, then we take him back home. No tears. End of discussion."

Beaming with joy, my baby hops in place, giggling. "Thank you, Mommy."

"You're welcome, sweetie."

Justin joins us and lifts the cat into his arms. "You're a troublesome fella, aren't you?" The purring pussy headbutts my brother's grizzled chin, and we melt. "See, Liv, it's a good thing I didn't shave. Makes for a great cat scratcher."

In rapid succession, Olivia snaps pictures of my brother snuggling the kitty. "It does have a certain lumberjack appeal." She takes another one. "I may have to buy you some flannel."

"Okay, ew, get a room." Recovering from their verbal foreplay, I point toward the house. "Let's toss him inside."

Justin hugs the cat close. "Ew, yourself there, sis," he jokes before ambling to the kitchen door

Uninterested in our wayward kitty conundrum, Aaron surveys the hill, designing his battle plan. "I'm gonna make a snowman army."

Last year's first snow and our former neighbors' angry texts spring to mind. I make a pre-emptive strike. "Stay away from the red food coloring," I warn. "No guts this time. If you touch the sausage links, you're grounded. They're for breakfast tomorrow."

Behind us, the slam of a door fills the air. We whirl around in the falling snow.

Sam stands beside his truck, all hunky and sexy in blue jeans and a dark gray winter jacket. A black cowboy hat sits on his dark curls, and he holds a bottle of wine is in his big, strong grip. "Am I too early?"

What was I saying? Something about sausage. I regroup and wave him in. "No, not at all."

Immediately, I'm aware my children are outdoors in the snow with no hats, coats, or gloves. Better remind him we're from up north, in case he questions my parental skills. Until I stop short. Two red stocking feet dappled with snow dance beside me.

Well, drat. We aren't that hardy.

I halt my youngest in mid twirl. "Maddy, where are your slippers?"

She shrugs and returns to twirling. "On my baby doll."

At least one of us is a good mother.

Olivia makes a beeline toward Jaylen. "Oh, my goodness, girls, where are your slippers?" Picking her up, Olivia passes her to Justin, and sweeps Jayden into her arms, dusting snow from wet stocking feet. "I better delete those pictures," she jokes. "Evidence."

Lifting Maddy to my hip, I force a smile and gauge the damage. Her socks are soaked, as are the bottoms of her leggings. Worse, Aaron wears only one sock. At least Nick, ever the good child, has on slippers.

"Boys, inside, now." Groans fill the air. Small, reluctant bodies are herded toward the back door. "Get your coats and boots on, mittens and hats too, then you can come back out. If we get enough, we'll go sledding later. Hop to it. We don't need any colds next week."

Aaron breaks into a run. "I'm going to build a ramp." He cuts off his brother and disappears through the back door. A ten-foot high monstrosity leaps to mind, launching his little six-year-old body high off the hill into the valley far below. Note to self, check on him in fifteen-minute intervals. With Aaron, better safe, than sorry. Okay, let's make it five-minute intervals.

Sam joins us, and I play off my latest parental blunder. "We only just realized it was snowing." Leather, pine, and vanilla distract me. Would anyone notice if I bury my nose in his neck? As I'm holding my youngest and my mother is here, probably. What a shame.

Sam adjusts his hat. Curls peek out. "I turned my truck off and you ran out of the house so fast, I figured you really liked wine," he says, holding the bottle for my inspection.

Merlot, my favorite. Wow. This man gets me. I get lost in the label and his face. It's easy to do with those dimples and that wine.

Maddy shifts on my waist, breaking the spell of free alcohol and Sam. Time for introductions. "This is my brother, Justin," I begin.

They connect in a strong shake. "Hello."

"…and you've met my sister-in-law, Olivia, and Jaylen and Jayden, their twins…"

He tips his hat. "Good to see you again."

"You too, Sam."

"…and my three, of course," I add. "Last, but not least," I gulp, "this is our mother, Kate, who I did *not* know was coming and who only arrived an hour ago. Unannounced. Seriously. Like, completely out of the blue. We had no idea. Stopped us in our tracks. I'm still recovering."

Mom thumps me on the arm and deadpans a saucy eyeroll my way. "What kind of an introduction is that?" Zeroing in on the hunky cowboy, she checks him out from hat to boot. "So, you're Ro's new boss. I can see why she likes her job."

"Mom…"

Sam offers his hand. "Good to meet you. We've enjoyed having her."

Taking his hand, she lingers. Of course, she lingers. I count one Mississippi, two Mississippi, three Mississippi—prepared to intervene if I get to six Mississippi's—until finally she lets go.

Together, we make for the back door, Justin and Olivia leading the way. I shift Maddy to my other hip and let Sam pass. Hanging back, I cut off Mom who trails behind, probably to check out Sam's ass.

For a moment, I consider doing the same, although, on second thought, it's creepy when we do it together.

She leans toward me with a whisper. "Good impression, my ass. He's a straight up hunk. I may be old, kiddo, but I'm not stupid." With that, she disappears through the back door after Sam, and I steel myself for what's to come.

The day is so young, and we're only getting started.

Thank God Sam brought wine.

Chapter Seven

Our dining room tables—mine and Olivia's from our former lives—don't match. One is an inch higher than the other, and it's ticking her off big time. I like it, though. It defines the adults versus kiddies' division quite nicely. At only five-feet, three-inches tall, I like towering above the children.

At her insistence, Justin cut wooden risers to even things out while I checked on the definition of anal, so everything's square now and hidden under matching tablecloths. We're set up in the huge hallway leading to the front porch because, with a total of ten for dinner, the kitchen table won't do. Plus, our children are currently encamped in the dining room while we reclaim the upstairs, thus hallway dining it is.

The fat, juicy bird sits on a platter before Justin, who anchored himself at the head of the table early, giving him carving rights. Sam sits to Justin's right, and I'm next to Sam, ready to top off Mom's wine glass every time she opens her mouth. Or shove a napkin into it. I'm flexible that way.

Mom helps Olivia with the twins, even if she's zeroed in on Sam across the table from her, watching him like a hungry predator with her sights set on easy prey. I wish like hell I could feed her in the kitchen with Lucky and Mr. Evans, but that might be difficult to explain to Sam, at least, until she starts talking.

Famished, we ring the mismatched tables, tempted by platters and bowls teeming with savory treats. The plump turkey, perfectly browned despite Olivia's vegan reservations, rests on a vintage creamware platter surrounded by roasted root vegetables.

It taunts Mom too, and she frowns, unpacified by the addition of caramelized onions, parsnips, and turnips. "That poor bird," she pouts. "Totally unnecessary."

Olivia chokes down a sympathetic retort, choosing to remain silent instead.

Is she taking pity on me? I'm glad someone is. "Mom," I command, praying it will stick, "don't start."

Can I blink out, ignore her, she's crazy to Sam?

Tantalizing smells waft around us from this veritable smorgasbord. Mom, however, is immune. Straightening Jaylen's bib, she pushes in her highchair tray with a snap. "We could have fixed tofu and Chinese noodles. The kids love noodles."

"I love noodles," confirms Maddy.

Begging for restraint, I bear down on Olivia with pleading eyes—*don't pile on, don't pile on.*

Inner vegan Olivia, however, is stronger than socially acceptable, pity-taking Oliva and, finally, she breaks. "Agreed, everyone loves noodles, and I make a mean tofu bake."

Justin, however, is having none of it. "Oh, hell no, I love you, babe, including your tofu bake, but it's Thanksgiving." Cradling an electric knife, he's ready to carve and pig out with abandon. "Sorry. I'm eating turkey."

"I want turkey," replies Maddy.

Not to be outdone, Aaron raises his glass of chocolate milk. "I want turkey too." He tosses it back and chugs, half standing, half sitting, one foot on the floor, one tiny butt cheek plastered to his chair, drinking like a sailor.

Crap. I know where this is going—there's a history, here, and not a pleasant one. Reaching across Maddy, I confiscate his glass. "Slow down, peanut. You know the rule. One sip at a time."

Mom watches intently as I set his glass out of arm's reach. "One sip at a time? What are you, Ro, the milk Nazi?"

Great. Sam probably thinks I'm the world's sloppiest control freak. Can I kick her from here?

Instead, I scrutinize my plate, prepared to fling a Brussel sprout her way instead. "No, I'm not the milk Nazi." Ignoring her, I address Sam. "I've learned the hard way you can't let him chug his milk."

"Ah," he replies.

From the end of the kiddy table, Nick adds his two cents to the conversation. "Yeah, if Aaron chugs his milk—and he always chugs his milk and his water and his juice—he throws up." He takes a small sip of his milk. "I don't."

Leaning far over his plate, Aaron faces Sam. "One time, I chugged my cocoa and, after I threw up, a mini marshmallow came out of my nose." He trails his finger down his nostril toward his upper lip, the pride evident in his six-year-old voice. "Everything smelled like chocolate too. It was cool."

Sam snickers. "That's...that's pretty interesting."

Nick shudders. "No, it was gross. He ate it too."

Sam halts, his fork poised in the air. Justin shakes his head, no doubt wishing he could claim yet another fist bump from my boy. Olivia stifles a gag. As for me, having witnessed the incident, I'm long past gagging.

Kids. So nasty.

Maddy, overcome with sibling pride, gushes. "It was gross and cool. Do it again, Aaron."

"No!"

Great. Inside voice, Ro.

This is not the conversation starter I had planned. "Kids, enough. No disgusting stories at the table. Ever." I point at the turkey. "Get to carving, bro. Let's fill their mouths with food."

Justin winks at Aaron, powers on the electric knife, and, grinning like a modern-day Jack the Ripper, addresses Mom. "Buckle up, bubba-lou. It's time to carve."

Perturbed, she tosses her napkin on her plate. "I give up. Would it kill us to have a nice salad?"

The electric knife revs to full speed. Justin raises it high, yelling above the noise, "Yes, yes it would."

"Wait," Olivia interrupts. "Shouldn't we say grace first?"

Vibrating knife in hand, my brother shrugs his broad shoulders and powers down.

"Shall I?" I offer.

"I've got this, kiddo," interrupts Mom as I say, "Dear Lord."

Appropriate, right?

"Mom, it's okay, I'll do it. Drink your wine. Seriously, toss the whole glass back, one chug, you can do it. We have more, plenty, in fact."

Ignoring me, she plows ahead, "Dear semi-benevolent deity, or whoever the hell you are, please bless this poor dead bird who didn't need to die and…"

"Exactly," whispers Olivia.

"Okay, it's already dead. Can we stop, please?" I reserve a glowering stare for Olivia. She sits with eyes firmly closed, ignoring me like the plague.

"What?" Mom asks. "Can't I be truthful? This bird didn't have to die, and we have no idea what's up there or who's out there or…"

Where's duct tape when you need it? I add it to my mental shopping list and throw my back against my chair, exasperated. "Jesus, Mom, no spiritual debates today, okay. Isn't it bad enough we're fighting over the turkey?"

Olivia peeks at me with one eye, then promptly slams it shut. A smirk dances at the edges of her lips. Children shift in chairs, growing restless. Justin fiddles with the carving knife. Sam is silent, frozen in place, possibly wishing he were driving to Ohio.

Mom, however, rattles on. "No, it isn't enough, and take Jesus, for instance…what?" She stops as I vigorously shake my head. "You brought him up, not me."

Sam's thoughtful voice breaks our bickering stalemate, "Dear Lord," he begins, his head bowed, a whiff of amusement brimming below the surface, "or semi-benevolent deity…"

"I like him," Mom nods.

"…thank you for this generous meal, for the entertaining company, and for the long holiday weekend. It is very much appreciated. In your name, we pray. Amen."

"Amen," we add in unison.

"Or women," Mom chimes in.

One minefield traversed, five thousand to go. And it's still so early…if only I had a map for what lies ahead I could plan out the necessary detours in advance.

Justin begins to carve, Olivia plops a spoonful of mashed potatoes onto Jayden's plate, Mom butters a roll for Jaylen, as I send turkey to the boys then dole out green bean casserole to Maddy. Brussel sprouts, salad, stuffing, and gravy make their way around the table. Plates are filled, more wine and milk are poured, and I'm starving.

His mouth already stuffed with turkey, Aaron manages to shovel in a forkful of mashed potatoes too. "Momph, can I hafve my milfphk?"

Have I raised them to act like monkeys?

Handing him his glass, I scold, "Don't talk with your mouth full and swallow your food first. Then one sip."

Immediately ignoring my advice, Aaron takes his glass and tips it, just as Mom fills the room with sound. Annoying, irritating, dreadful sound.

"Aaron, you wouldn't happen to know who put plastic wrap on the downstairs toilet this morning, would you?"

Milk, turkey, and a few chewed green beans erupt from my son's mouth. They land on his plate, swamping his green beans, and splatter Maddy and Nick. Little shoulders shake with laughter as his siblings dive for cover. The plastic cup slips from his grip, hits the edge of his plate and sends a wave of chocolate milk into the bowl of mashed potatoes. Maddy jumps toward me to avoid the spray, and her spoonful of sweet potatoes lands in my lap, coating my crotch with warm, toasted marshmallow glazed in a gooey brown-sugar sauce.

Huh. That's interesting. It's oddly pleasant.

Nick surveys the damage to his dinner. "Gross."

Aaron dissolves into laugher—although not as loud as Justin, who never broke stride with the electric knife. Olivia dashes to the kitchen for paper towels in record time, returns and tosses me a wad. Sam and Mom chuckle.

Justin powers down the electric knife and offers Sam a fist bump. "Other people's children—nature's finest birth control."

Naturally, the cowboy, softly snickering, fist-bumps back.

Great. We've been at it for four minutes, and bedlam has already graced our table.

Milk is sopped from plates, soaked from the mashed potatoes, and wiped from shirts, chins, and chairs. Marshmallow is pried from my crotch—unfortunately, by my fingers even if I pretend they're Sam's tongue—leaving me to sport a sticky stain that, weird as it sounds, smells delicious. I snatch Aaron's now empty glass and, despite his loud protests, fill it by a third with water. We settle into our chairs, and a collective sense of relief sweeps across the table which is a far better thing than chocolate milk.

Hopefully, this time, I'll get to taste some turkey. Inhaling the enticing scents of sage and stuffing, I lift my fork, laden with oyster stuffing, when something soft hits my calf. It clings for a half second, falls, and lands on my shoe.

Did I miss some marshmallow?

Dark, thigh meat calls out from my plate. Sam springs to mind...thigh meat. Give me a sec...I'm picturing it.

Yet another un-named thing hits my ankle and sticks.

What the hell?

Acting normal, I survey the table, searching for clues. Olivia's twins devour buttered rolls with tiny fingers. Maddy has flattened her pile of mashed potatoes and carves a gravy moat around the perimeter. Aaron pouts about his lack of chocolate milk. Nick stares at his plate and fiddles with his fork.

Wiping my mouth, I pretend to drop my napkin and lean over to examine my ankle. A solitary green bean covered in cream of mushroom soup sticks like glue. I bend farther and look right.

What on earth?

A fist, a small eight-year-old fist, is under the table. It swings forward, aimed at Maddy's legs dangling from her booster seat. Soup-covered green beans, bits of mushroom, and French-fried onions sail through the air. Sailing too low, they hit the leg of her chair with a *splat*. Deflected bits of bean, soup, and onion careen toward me, hitting my cheek, my forehead, and my chin.

Napkin at the ready, I sit up and wipe. "Nick?"

Caught red-handed, he fills his mouth with turkey. "Whfatf?"

A chunk of green bean clings to my skin. Lovely. I wipe again. "Nick, are you throwing green bean casserole under the table?"

Forks pause in midair. Olivia covers her mouth with her own napkin, reining in a laugh. Justin, however, makes no such effort, bursting forth with yet another guffaw at my expense. Sam does a double take, fights it for a moment, fails miserably, and joins him.

Nick points at his green beans with his fork. "There's chocolate milk on them."

I study the mess in my napkin, hoping I got it all. "Then don't eat them. Leave them on your plate. Why on earth are you throwing them at your sister?"

"I didn't want you to think I didn't like 'em. I wanted you to think Maddy didn't like 'em. But they've got chocolate milk on them. It's gross."

Beside me Maddy stuffs green bean casserole into her mouth, derailing her brother's plan. I pick up my fork once more. "Leave them on your plate, and after dinner, you can clean the mess on the floor."

"Can Lucky do it?"

"No."

He leans back in his chair and joins his brother in a pout fest. "Okay. Sorry."

Great. Sam continues to chuckle. Ten bucks says he's contemplating a vasectomy.

"Ro?" Olivia points with her fork.

I look up from my plate. "Yes?"

"There's a mushroom in your hair."

Of course. And it's not even a portabella.

Napkin in hand, I dab. Cream-of-soup-coated fungi sticks to my roots. We're now six minutes into dinner, and I'm wearing more of it than I've eaten.

Stretching my leg, I shake off the ankle-hugging green bean down below, when my foot touches another foot. And it's searching. Worse yet, it's groping. Sock-covered toes find the top of mine. They slide across it like butter, find the cuff of my jeans, crawl in, and rub my ankle.

I pull back, startled. "Mom! What the hell?"

She winks at me. "Was that your foot, kiddo?"

"Yes, that was my foot. Whose foot were you expecting?" Then it hits me.

Sam's.

Ick. Kill me now.

"Well..." she purrs.

Can I sneak some children's night-time cough medicine into her wine later? One can hope.

Oozing charm like a freshly picked scab, she twirls her fork in her salad. "Sam, do I hear a Texas accent?"

The feel of her toes, now back on her side of the table, haunts my skin. I shift in my chair.

Sam shifts in his. "Yes, it is. I'm from Austin."

Come on, Nick, throw something at Mom. A wad of green beans, a few Brussel sprouts, Olivia's attractively arranged cornucopia centerpiece, hell, anything.

A plump cherry tomato clings to her fork. Mom sucks dressing from it suggestively. "Ever spend any time on a ranch? I saw your boots and wondered if you ride."

My wine tempts me with the promise of a buzz. I chug it, thankful it's not chocolate milk, even if I do want to vomit. Sam squirms in his chair, so I fill his half-empty glass to the rim and top off my own.

He clutches his glass—trust me, I've been there—and addresses my prying mother. "I spent a lot of time at my cousin's ranch. My aunt and uncle raised cattle and they were into the rodeo too. It was a great way to grow up."

"So, you do ride. How wonderful," Mom continues. "I love a man who's good in a saddle."

"Mom…"

"Yes, Ro?"

Sam interrupts. "I do, I have a few horses at home, though I don't do rodeo anymore. Trail riding is my favorite anyway."

Spreading one leg toward him, I guard his boots from geriatric toe-digits.

Another forkful of salad slides into her mouth. Slowly, she draws the fork from her mouth and chews. "Interesting…"

Gross. Is it too late to be put up for adoption?

Wait a minute. I'm going about this all wrong. If she gets a snootful, she'll be sleeping like a lamb in no time. I contemplate the merlot. "Mom has never been on a horse in her life." I refill her glass. "She's never even touched a saddle."

"Not on a horse…"

Shit, Mom, don't go there.

"…but you're never too old to learn." A twinkle lights her eyes. "Plus, I've ridden other things."

Coughing interrupts us. Olivia chokes on something, real or pretend, I don't even care at this point. Barely breaking stride, Justin thumps her back and keeps on eating.

It's high time I stuff another old bird today. Let's face it, though, it'll take two napkins to fill that gaping mouth, possibly three. Where's Maddy's napkin? Wonderful. It's covered in gravy. I can make that work. "Mom, don't…"

"I was talking about motorcycles."

Steeped in sweet potatoes, Justin works his way around his plate, making room for seconds. "No, you weren't, Mom. Everyone here above the age of eight knows what you're talking about."

Geriatric giggles burst from my mother. "So, what if I was? No harm, no foul."

No foul? Let me at her—I'm going to pluck her like this turkey.

Olivia, however, throws me a lifeline. "Ro, we need to make plans for our Christmas tree. When do you want to put one up?"

I love her.

Thankful for a new topic, I turn toward my studly boss. "Good question. Sam, are there any tree lots in Poseyville?"

Pouring gravy on his chocolate-milk-free potatoes, Sam nods. "The Baxters have a lot behind Red's Tavern. They usually have a variety trees, pine, fir, spruce, you name it."

Olivia points toward the ceiling high above. "We could get a big one this year."

Dinner roll poised at the edge of her lips, Mom murmurs toward Sam. "I've always wanted a big one." Before she can lick it— because of course she's going to lick it—I nudge her foot hard, and she settles for biting it instead, her eyes firmly locked on Sam.

Where's a glass of cherry Kool-Aid when you need it? I could stick her next to Aaron and let him chug away. Imagining the stains, I examine the ceiling, willing her to shut up.

As I admire the high ceiling, however, something unexpected snags my attention. A large black sock. It dangles from the chandelier, perched precariously on one brass arm, barely hanging on.

Why, why, why?

Unaware, Justin helps himself to more stuffing. "We could cut one down instead. We've got fir trees growing on top of each other in the far pasture. They need to be thinned out."

Channeling her inner blogger, Olivia launches into hyperdrive. "Oh, great idea! With it snowing, I could get some photos for my blog and my book draft too. I'll make cocoa, and we can bring the leftover marshmallows." A misty, faraway sheen lights her eyes—she's picturing it, planning it, hell, she's probably already living it. Olivia blinks fast and, finally, continues, "We can make a bonfire and roast them on sticks."

That's Olivia for you. Where I only see black socks on chandeliers, she imagines homemade confections, toasted golden brown, dusted with powdered sugar, set on a blue china plate in the snow next to a log fire beside vintage mugs of steaming cocoa surrounded by frosted evergreens and adorable children. Okay, her children.

How does she do it?

It sounds like fun, too. Ever in awe, I laud my sister-in-law's active imagination. "I'm in," I reply. "Let's do it."

No doubt imagining a huge tree too, Justin considers the ceiling. "How about after dinner? There're some pretty big ones out there…we could…what the hell? Is that one of my socks?"

Heads pop toward the chandelier.

He cocks his head. "Hey, babe, there's a picture for your blog."

Mashed potatoes spray from Aaron's mouth. He doubles over in hysterics, showering his plate and the tablecloth in fine film of white.

Gee, I wonder who did it.

"Aaron!"

Tickled by his own antics, he drops his fork, scattering flecks of white on his T-shirt.

Seriously, I need to get that boy a facemask. Or a giant, plastic bubble. Possibly even a passport.

Biting her lip to fight off a laugh, Olivia chuckles in her chair. Justin, again, makes no attempt to hide his laughter. Sam, too, breaks down, his shoulders heaving with humor beside me. Again.

Me? I get to discipline. Again.

"What have I told you about hiding peoples' clothes? Next time, you're grounded." I re-examine the sock, grateful it's not underwear, happy it's black and can pass for a Pilgrim's. Although I'm especially thankful it's not my underwear. I own far too many pairs of granny panties, but don't judge. They're for sleeping.

Riveted, Mom contemplates our unplanned decorating scheme. "It's only a sock. Could be worse. Could be a jockstrap."

Ah, wonderful. Something worse than my panties. *Thanks Mom.*

Her mouth full of turkey, Maddy stares wide-eyed at the chandelier. "What's a jockstrap?"

With my gravy-free napkin, I wipe my daughter's greasy face. "Don't worry about it, sweetie. Finish your turkey." Time to draw everyone back to thoughts of Christmas. I wink at Olivia and sneak a tiny nod in Sam's general direction. "As for the tree, maybe today isn't the best time."

Aaron brandishes a butter knife. "Mom, can I cut down the tree?"

Nick swivels toward me. "No, I want to, Mom! Tell him I get to cut it down. I'm the oldest, and I didn't throw up, and I didn't throw Uncle Justin's sock on the light. And I didn't put plastic wrap on the toilet either. Please?"

Leave it to Nick to summarize. I wink at Aaron. "He's got you there, kiddo."

"I didn't throw green beans," Aaron counters.

"Point, counter point, kiddo" I smile at Nick.

Excited at the prospect, happy to let someone else cut down the tree, Maddy jiggles in place. "I want a big tree."

I tear my eyes away from my arguing boys and sneak a peek at the sexy cowboy...so yummy...so tasty. Boy, do I want a big one too.

Justin takes a bite of turkey. "Sam, care to join us for a trip to the back forty? If we get a big one, I may need help dragging it to the truck."

Would everyone please stop saying big one?

Much to my delight, Sam reaches for the stuffing and piles another helping onto his plate. "You bet. I need to work this off."

Olivia cuts Jayden's turkey. Pointing her knife at me, she remarks, "Ro made the stuffing. It's her grandmother's recipe."

Sam shifts my way in his chair. "It's delicious."

My heart flutters. Maybe I should give this serious cooking thing a try. Heat rises in my cheeks and in my heart, not to mention my crotch, browning whatever is left of Maddy's marshmallows. "Thank you, Sam."

He smiles back and it's enough. My plate grows cold, yet I don't care. Our table is full, the kids are here, and he's staying a while longer. We have a plan for a tree, dessert waits in the wings, and if Mom keeps drinking, she'll be napping soon. Plus, her room locks from the outside, so things are looking up.

Finally, I take a bite of turkey. It's tender and juicy. I give into the meal and relax.

Without warning, Justin's size-12 sock falls from above and lands in the cranberry stuff. The toe—oh, no, is it clean or dirty—sinks into the bowl, sucking juice like a sponge.

Ewww...

Giggles erupt from my three little monsters.

Mom, Sam, and Justin laugh outright. Olivia tries to keep a

straight face, fleeting as it is, as she, too, loses the battle. Like her, I burst into a belly laugh.

There may be lint in the cranberries, but this is all the Thanksgiving I need.

~ * ~

Dishes soak in the sink, three bottles of wine are history, the snow's let up, the wind's died down, and my travel mug of cocoa is laced with bourbon. Mom and Mr. Evans are napping—thank you, Jesus—and Sam's still here. Now, we're on a mission to find a Christmas tree.

Life is good.

After we filled our bellies with everything except cranberries, Olivia staged a few blog photos—a vintage quilt draped across an old trunk, an antique checkered board placed so, a twinkling fire in the background. Lit candles burned brightly on the hearth. My boys, dressed in matching navy polo shirts, knelt beside the trunk for a quick game. Justin lounged behind them in an easy chair, oozing a fatherly vibe and eating a piece of pecan pie clad in a handknit charcoal gray turtleneck sweater he ditched the second she was done shooting pictures. It was quaint and homey and beautiful and pretend, especially as Nick and Aaron spent the better part of the experience smack-talking each other about who was winning.

Photo shoot complete, we decided over pie it was time to burn off some sugar and cut down our tree.

We ride out to the far pasture in Justin's truck, though several of us, including Lucky, make do in the truck bed. I plop down on a wheel well next to Sam, and it's exciting to sit close in the cold, hanging on for dear life as we careen down the bumpy trail. Arriving at the narrow footpath in high spirits, Justin parks, and we climb out, ready for an adventure in the snow.

Thanks to the cocoa-and-booze combo in my travel mug, my new-tradition benchmark is set on high. Nothing short of spectacular will do, and, so far, it's been Hallmark-movie cute. Freshly fallen snow has frosted our woods into a winter wonderland, setting the mood. Hunky Sam is beside me, looking delicious and keeping me warm whether he realizes it or not. Olivia takes pictures here and there as she follows the twins in their sky-blue snow suits. Lucky bounds ahead of us, chasing snowballs thrown by Justin. My children scamper like chattering squirrels, and they're almost, dare I say it, adorable.

Almost.

Aaron spins around, walking backward through the woods. "Mom, I gotta pee."

Naturally.

I rip off my gloves and help him with the tricky zipper on his snowsuit. "Why didn't you go before we left?"

He peels off his hat and mittens and tosses them to the ground. "I didn't have to then."

Sam and I catch up with him, and I rescue his hat from the snow. "Put this back on."

"But I have to pee."

Yanking Aaron's knit hat upon his head, I scold, "Unless it's coming out of your ears, put it back on." I help him with the zipper, then point to a thick clump of trees alongside the path. "Over there. And don't pee on the dog."

Nick slows down in front of us. "Mom?"

"Lucky, move. Justin! Don't throw snowballs over there. You're not helping! Aaron, watch yourself. Not on your mittens or the dog—good God, turn around!" I spin him toward the trees and kick his mittens out of the yellow snow toward Sam, who hops away like a scalded dog.

Oops.

I stick pee-sprinkled mittens into my coat pocket—yuck—and pull out a spare pair. After eight years of this, I travel heavy. I toss them toward Aaron, far from the yellow snow. "Don't get it on your boots."

"Mom!" Nick yells.

"What?"

He kicks at the snow. "I gotta pee too."

Sipping from her travel mug, Olivia is happy as a clam. "I can't believe I'm saying this but thank heavens the twins are still in diapers."

Ax in hand, Justin grinds to a halt beside his wife. "Would you goobers stop talking about peeing? Now I've gotta go."

Well, there goes the Hallmark Channel. Any chance Olivia will photograph this? Probably not.

Sam scrambles a safe distance away, while Justin picks out a tree to water. Nick's already whipped it out, ready to go. I point at another clump of trees. "Go away from your brother, leave your hat on, and no contests. Watch out for the wind. And each other. Seriously. Do not pee on each other this time."

Snickers fill the air.

Not exactly Pinterest-worthy.

Perhaps I should fan the holiday atmosphere flames and catch a few snowflakes on my tongue. Someone's got to get us back on track, plus, I'm not sure where to look right now. Maybe Sam is peeing too.

Cocoa burns my lips as I sip instead...tasty...very tasty.

Finally, zippers are zipped, buttons are buttoned, mittens and gloves are pulled back on, and we're off.

We walk through the dense, leaf-less woods, making tracks through the snow. It's easy going on four-foot-long legs like Justin's, but the little ones struggle. After ten minutes, their excitement adrenaline is fading fast.

Maddy trips over a tree root, falls in the snow, and catches herself with tiny, mitten-covered hands. Down for the count, she rests on her knees, at the mercy of Lucky who immediately bounds to her side and licks her face. "Stop it, Lucky." She shoves him away, verging on tears, and I brace myself for what's coming next.

"Mom, will you carry me?"

This is why I had two pieces of pie. Battle reserves.

Taking a fortifying gulp of alcohol-laced cocoa, I wipe my mouth on my sleeve, pass the mug to Sam, and bend down. "Come on, sweetie." Instantly, I crave more pie. And bourbon.

Aaron stops short too. "Are we there yet?"

Maddy's boots swing into my ribcage as I trudge along, trying like hell to hang onto that Christmas-card feeling. "Not yet, kiddo," I pant. "Hey, bro, how much further?"

He points toward the end of the path. "It's just over there."

The slope gives way to a large stand of snow-covered fir in all shapes and sizes. It's tranquil and beautiful. And so freaking far.

Sam encourages me with a smile. "Need any help?"

Maddy squeezes me with her knees. Figures. I probably should have peed too. "Not yet. I may need help on the way back though."

"You got it."

We reach the end of the wooded path at the top of a gentle slope dotted with thick clumps of fir. With the prize in sight, the boys break into a run, followed by Lucky. Whooping and hollering, they dash headlong down the hillside into the thick of the evergreens.

A revitalized Maddy squirms, kicking me in the bladder. "Mommy, let me down." She slides from my back and chases after her brothers. The rest of us follow.

Reaching the trees, we wander our winter wonderland, searching for the perfect one. Some are tall and wide, others short and stout, a few slender and delicate, each one fragrant, regal, and dusted with snow. Glistening icicles cling to the topmost branches, and a breeze trails down the slope, tinkling them like fairy bells. It's magical.

Now that we're here though, each tree is too alive, too beautiful to cut down. These are our trees, not random ones from some city lot.

Suddenly, I'm having second thoughts.

Olivia scans the firs, her camera a non-stop blur of activity. "How are we going to decide? I feel attached. After all, they're ours."

A ten-footer towers above me. "Me too. Picking out a plastic tree in a box never gave me a guilt trip. This does, though."

Sam admires a full, lush spruce. "Some of these are pretty close together." He pushes aside a few branches and points at a scraggly sapling in its shadow. "See? This one doesn't stand a chance."

Studying the sapling, a new idea dawns. I run my fingers along a sparse limb. Soft green needles course through my fingers, sending a hint of fresh evergreen wafting through the air. "What if we pick an ugly tree?" I suggest.

Justin stops in his tracks. "Let me get this straight, you want an ugly tree?"

"Okay, not an ugly tree," I backtrack, "not a pretty one either. A struggling tree. You know, one that doesn't stand a chance. We'd be doing it a favor. It's neighbors too."

Justin shakes his head, and we go back to strolling among the fir, contemplating our options.

That's when I glimpse it, through a break in the tree line on the opposite ridge, a smaller, albeit, solitary tree. Its trunk curves in the middle and a gaping hole mars its sparse branches. It's not Hallmark worthy, but, then, neither are we.

Sam follows my gaze, reading my mind. "That one? It's a decent size."

This man gets me. If only the children concur. "Hey kids, what about that one?"

Their voices muffled by trees and snow, they break clear of the thicket and gawk at the ridge.

Nick considers the awkward fir. "Maybe."

Aaron, however, is a tougher sell. "It's not tall enough, and it's gotta big hole in it."

Joining him, I plant a kiss on the top of his head, but he squirms away. "It's plenty tall enough kiddo, and we can turn the hole toward the wall."

Olivia studies it through her camera lens. "It's got a great rustic vibe to it, kinda like the house. We could decorate it with homemade ornaments and set it next to the kitchen fireplace. For pictures."

Justin chuckles. "You two would pick the one farthest from the truck."

Olivia nods at a behemoth to her right. "Would you prefer a twelve-footer?"

He considers the taller tree for a moment. "Point taken. Come on, let's go get it."

Together, we follow the children up the ridge. It's hard going, our steepest climb yet, and I may have to bake more pies to feed the stitch in my side. Finally, we reach the tree, and, to me—possibly only me—it's perfect. Not quite eight feet tall, its ashy blue needles call out for white twinkling lights, although upon closer inspection, the gaping hole is larger than we first thought. Yet facing the wall and hidden under tinsel, it won't be too noticeable. Especially with presents stacked underneath.

Justin tightens his scarf around his neck, warding off the chill. "Remember, you all get to help drag it back to the truck."

The first hint of cold creeps toward my toes. "Yeah, I hear you, but when we get back, we'll have earned another piece of pie." I smile at Sam.

His big, brown eyes smile back and, cold, snow, wind, it doesn't matter, I tingle. Goosebumps erupt upon my arms and spill out from under my scarf.

"Cold?" he inquires.

I shrug. "Not in the least."

Justin examines the rise of the hill and the tree line to the east. Concern touches his face as he gazes back and forth.

Olivia follows his head from left to right. "What's wrong, babe?"

He surveys the surrounding hills. "I can't remember where the property line is. We've got to be close."

I'm of no help. "Can't we cut this one down?"

"I'm not sure. The realtor said something about a big oak sitting on the line along this ridge...I can't tell one tree from the next without their leaves. If it's that one," he motions to the left, "we're okay." He points to the right, squinting against the sun, "If it's that one, it's a close call."

Sam glances from side-to-side, following my brother's lead. "I hate to tell you this, they're both oak."

Justin scratches his chin. "Well, crap."

We ponder the tree dilemma, momentarily stymied. Sam, however, focuses his attention on our intended Christmas victim, inspecting the gap in its branches.

I join him. "Thoughts?"

Scaly bark holds his attention. He picks at it, near the hole in the branches. "See this canker? It's diseased. Taking it down might keep it from spreading."

He has Olivia's attention now too. "Diseased? We don't want diseased."

He peals a flaky piece of bark from the fir and examines it. "It's nothing that'll hurt us. That's why the limbs are dying. This one's a goner."

Justin scrutinizes the bark and shrugs. "Sounds logical to me. Now comes the fun part. Everyone, back up." He lifts the ax, prepared to swing.

"Stop!" Maddy cries.

I leap toward her. "Baby, what's wrong?"

She scrambles toward the tree, her eyes wide. "What's Uncle Justin doing? Is he going to hurt the tree?"

Aaron ducks a snowball from Nick, then pauses. "Geez, of course he is. He's going to cut it down. How did you think we were going to get it to the house? With a shovel?"

Maddy's bottom lip shoots out far enough for birds to land. "Don't kill it." Tears well in her cornflower-blue eyes, and my youngest—who should be napping along with Mom—sobs.

This wasn't in the script.

I lift her into my arms and press her face to my chest. Sobs rack her body. She snivels against my chest as I rock her. "Sweetie, this tree is sick. We're doing it a favor." Snot coats my jacket over my left boob. "Plus, it won't feel anything, and it will be warm inside the house. Imagine how pretty it will be covered in lights. Won't that be fun?"

Maddy sniffs, but not strong enough to suck that snot back in. "It won't hurt the tree?"

"No, sweetie, the tree won't feel a thing."

Ready to help in his own, weird way, Aaron trots to her side in big-brother fashion. "Yeah, Maddy, if we leave it out here, it's going to die all alone. In the cold. You don't want that, do you?"

Despite my raised eyebrows, his warped logic does the trick. She wipes her tears with her mitten and sniffs again. "Only 'cause it's sick?"

"Only 'cause it's sick, baby," I repeat.

Justin grips the ax and addresses Maddy. "We good to go?"

Pointing her face away from the doomed tree, I give him the green light. "I wouldn't tempt fate, bro. We're on a minute-by-minute basis here. Go for it."

"Got it." Justin adjusts his grip on the ax, takes a swing, and drives it home. A resounding, satisfying, meaty thwack greets our ears. Maddy hiccups. The boys jump about, excited. Jaylen and Jayden pay no attention, preferring to crawl through drifts, eating snow instead.

Olivia watches Justin with appreciative eyes, taking pictures, as he cuts down the tree. Sam is beside me, radiating sexiness. I hover close by and tingle.

With each whack, the ax bites deeper into the soft wood. Within minutes, Justin takes a final swing and the diseased fir tumbles to the ground, one step closer to gracing our home with lights and love and possibly bugs.

Aaron dives upon the trunk. "I got it." A quick tug, however, draws him up short, dropping him to his knees. He peers out from under his thick wool hat. "It's heavy. I may need some help."

Justin grips the front of his Iron Man snowsuit and lifts him to his feet. "Is that right? How about we do this together, squirt?"

Aaron pushes his hat back. "I could live with that."

Together, they clasp a thick branch and pull. Nick, not to be outdone, rushes in to join them. My little men plunge through the snow with their first real Christmas tree, and it makes a snot-covered mother proud. I set Maddy down, take her hand and follow.

A hint of vanilla wafts my way as Sam walks around me to help drag the tree. I inhale deeply and hold it. Icy air sears my lungs…dang…he smells good.

"Are you sure you aren't cold?" Sam is behind my boys, prepared to lend a hand with either the tree or Maddy.

I sip my cocoa. "Maybe a bit."

Offer to warm me up. Please, offer to warm me up.

Instead, my brother interrupts. "Then help us with this tree." He trudges ahead of us, headed for the truck. "Trust me, you won't be cold for long."

Sam jogs toward my boys and grabs the fir by the crown, lifting it away from the snow. "I've got it."

A shiver wracks my body as I watch his ass.

Cold?

Ha.

Not in the least.

Chapter Eight

Thick, cinnamon-scented dough, a recipe from Sam's childhood, gushes from under the rolling pin on the kitchen table while an expectant crowd of small, upturned faces surrounds me like coyotes around roadkill. Methodically, I roll the fragrant dough, fully aware of their excitement. With each stroke the fidgeting grows. Small hands sway like saplings in a breeze, clutching cookie cutters. I examine the creamy, brown mass, judging its thickness, before attacking it once more. Each pause and push and glance elicits more impatient sighs from the squirming kiddie crowd.

Aaron bounces in place, excited. "That's good enough, isn't it?"

Unaware I'm reveling in their attention Mom joins their rousing chorus of complaints. "For heaven's sake, Ro, stop torturing them already."

A sympathetic snort erupts from Justin. He sits near the fireplace alternately threading popcorn onto a string, feeding kernels to Lucky, and tossing huge fistfuls into his own gaping mouth. Beside him sits Sam who volunteered for the worse possible job, separating strands of Christmas lights. What a trooper.

Yep, Sam's still here.

Originally, I expected him to arrive for dinner, eat, and leave. After all, we're essentially strangers to him and, what with spilt milk, flying green beans, and a sock in the cranberries, who could blame him?

To my great delight, he not only ate, he stayed and, best of all, he participated. Board games, tree cutting, and ornament making, all enticed him to linger.

It's been glorious.

Nick rocks against the table, bringing me back to the present. "C'mon, Mom, they don't have to be perfect, just done."

If the golden child of patience is complaining, I've stretched it to the limit. Time to step back and turn them loose.

I set the rolling pin down and inch backward away from the dough. Maddy bobs and weaves, a chatty duck in a hurricane. Sensing the moment is near, she vibrates, awash in anticipation.

Always in the mood for theater, I sweep my arms toward the

dough, ending in a flourish. "Go."

Three children pounce, attacking it like a high-school football team at an all-you-can-eat buffet. Plastic stars, plastic trees, and plastic wreaths plunge into the dough in rapid succession, making short work of every useable inch. Small fingers peel dough from the cut edges, lifting here and tugging there, and a satisfying number of ornaments find their way to the baking sheets, destined for the oven.

At the far end of the table, Olivia admires their work from a safe distance. "Those are going to be wonderful." She and Mom help the twins, pressing and prodding their own balls of dough. "They smell so good too. Is that clove?"

"Yep," I reply, gathering the trimmings, "and nutmeg." Caging a peek at Sam, I continue, "I didn't quite have enough cinnamon. Hope you don't mind I took liberties with your mom's recipe."

Tangled in a coagulated mass of lights, he carefully threads wire through a knot in the strand. "It's an inspired touch," he murmurs through the colored plastic haze.

Inspired? Sweet...

Waiting for me to rework the dough, Aaron joins Sam, inspecting his boots. "Are you really a cowboy?"

Helping Jayden press a cookie cutter into freshly rolled dough, Mom simmers from the sidelines, shooting me backward glances. "Of course, he's really a cowboy. Look at him. I bet he comes with whips and spurs."

"Mom..."

Although, she does have a point. Sam cracking a whip? In spurs, no less? Dang...someone fan me. Please.

Caught in the daydream, I knead the last of the trimmings into a dough ball. Instinctively, I work the thick wad into a sizeable, succulent log.

Nope. Not the same.

Setting aside two strands of freed lights, Sam contemplates the next lump. "I used to be a cowboy when I was younger." Studying the mess at his feet, he hunts for an end, ready to tackle another strand.

Unable to contain his curiosity, Nick approaches warily. He pauses a few paces behind his brother, examining my boss. "Did you ride a lot of horses?

Silent, I watch my son, willing him to find his confidence. While Aaron warmed to Sam right away, Nick is holding back. Does he miss his father? Or does he feel allegiance to the man who voluntarily absented himself from our lives? Or is it yes to all the above?

Whether conscious of my son's shyness or fully engulfed in his project, Sam remains focused on the lights. Finally, he replies, "I did. Growing up, my cousin and I, we rode practically every weekend. Every day in the summer."

Aaron twirls a cookie cutter, his busy fingers ever sticky. "I sure wish I had a horse. Do you have any horses now?"

Sharing a precautionary glance, Sam and I exchange brief, innocent smiles, thoughts of Walter, Cronkite, and Oscar hidden away. I bite my lip to keep from laughing, not to mention to keep from picturing Sam naked on a horse...okay, not completely naked...definitely in ass-less chaps, though. And that hat.

Crud. Biting my lip isn't working.

Sam tests a strand and they blink on, bathing him in colored light. "I have two horses and a pony."

"Really? Can I ride your horses?" Aaron exclaims, drawing even closer, excited at the prospect. "I bet I could be a real cowboy."

Unplugging the strand, Sam faces my son. "Tell you what, I'll take you riding sometime. And you too," he nods at Nick and Maddy in mid-sentence. "If it's all right with your mom."

"Fine by me," I reply, heading off their pleas. "I wouldn't miss seeing my babies riding for anything."

Mom fondles a ball of dough. "No, of course you wouldn't. You'll be there with boots on."

Ass-less chaps, Mom. Get with the program.

Sam drops the tangled lights and rises from his chair. "Excuse me, bathroom break."

Clutching the rolling pin, I try to focus on ornaments. Despite the effort, my thoroughly undisciplined body parts take on a life of their own. I break into a sweat, everything tingles, and I commit to my latest hobby, ogling his impressive thighs. Seriously, self-discipline? What the hell is that? I want to ogle his ass too, however, Mom's beat me to it.

Again, doing it together? Totally creepy.

Unaware we're mentally undressing Sam, Olivia admires the freshly cut fir leaning in a bucket of water by the back door. "I can't wait to see these ornaments on the tree. They'll be beautiful."

Tearing my uncooperative eyes away from the hall, I admire the tree instead. "I love that we're making ornaments this year. Great idea. It sure beats store-bought plastic."

Gently Olivia pries an unbaked ornament from Jaylen's mouth. "Yes, it does, assuming they survive. The ornaments, I mean."

I chuckle and finish another round of dough. "At least they're organic." Corralling my boys, I holler, "You guys ready?"

Cookie cutters at attention, they rush to my side, and I give them the go ahead once more. Immediately, they pounce. Elbows fly and tiny hands jostle for position, and I back up to save myself. "You guys don't have to attack it like animals." Wiping flour from my hands, I toss them in the air, defeated. "I give up."

Aaron grips the spatula. Brandishing it, he lops off a wad of dough from an unsuspecting cookie. "Aargh, I'm an animal!"

"Hey, that's my Santa!" Nick cries. "Mom, Aaron's messing up my cookies!"

His little brother welds his kitchen weapon of choice high in the air, pointing at another baking tray. "No, I'm not, that one's mine. Yours are over there."

Small boy fists pound on the worn wooden table. "No, they're not!"

I knew the peace wouldn't last. Thank God Sam's in the bathroom.

A loud rap at the back door penetrates the obnoxious din emanating from my children. "Boys, enough." Backing away from the table, I yell, "Aaron, quit beheading Santas. We're not ISIS, for heaven's sake."

An exasperated sigh erupts from my eldest. "He did it again, Mom."

My back to the door, I bellow, "Aaron, I mean it, quit decapitating Santa, or there will be hell to pay." In mid squawk, I open the door.

Judge Middleton glares back.

The brown bowler hat perches above his brow, the dark woolen overcoat is clasped to his chest, and a gray checked muffler encircles his neck in yards of coarse, scratchy wool. He stares down upon me, cold, immoveable, unsmiling.

Wary, I draw my sweater closer around me. "Judge Middleton?"

Please, don't have a stack of Watch Tower magazines under that coat.

Holding the door wide, I motion him inside, "Can I help you? Would you like to come in?"

He studies the chaos within and squares his thin shoulders, possibly preparing to run should it roll his way. "Thank you, no." He considers the fir in the corner of the kitchen and clears his throat. "What a lovely tree."

My Spidey sense engages. "Um...thank you. We started a new tradition today–it's our first real tree ever. We brought it home about an hour ago."

A tired gaze greets me. "Yes, you did, from my property. I noticed it was missing on my afternoon walk. Gauging from the footsteps in the snow, I assumed I would find it here."

Holy crap on a cracker.

I did it again.

Somewhere, out there, in a parallel universe, there's a version of me who has yet to meet this man or, better yet, who has, but hasn't managed to piss him off at every possible opportunity.

Then again, there's probably another version of me who's giving this old man a blow job for freedom, so it could be worse.

Naturally, while I contemplate my multi-verse options, Mr. Evans chooses this opportune moment to channel his inner Neal Patrick Harris. Purring in surround sound, he saunters into the kitchen, pursuing the singular objective of rubbing himself against his owner's skinny, wool-clad, ticked-off, judgmental legs.

What can I say? It's a wonderful life.

Eyebrows raised, indignation loading to a new level, Judge Middleton takes note of his wayward pet. "Mr. Evans? Apparently, my tree isn't the only thing you've confiscated today."

Maybe I can crawl inside the gaping hole in our stolen Christmas tree and wait him out. Or maybe I should try a different tack. "Would you like a piece of pie?" I motion to the stove. "We have pumpkin and pecan."

Judge Middleton remains stoic, silent.

My shoulders sag. The weight of his anger reins in my joy. "Mr. Evans showed up right before dinner." Behind me, the kitchen has grown silent too. Eight pairs of eyes are riveted upon me and the judge. "We were going to bring him back after we decorated the tree, and pie too. Seriously, it's good pie."

Why am I forcing pie on this old man? Of course, remembering the two pieces I've polished off today, it really is good pie.

Praying he doesn't ask for the last of the pecan, I plunge on, "I guess we were confused about the property line. I'm sorry, it's my fault. I suggested that tree, and I'll pay you for it, plus I'll plant five more next spring. I promise."

Ramrod straight, oozing irritation, the judge has yet to thaw a degree. "This tree marked the property line. I planted it there fifteen years ago to avoid confusion. As for Mr. Evans," he continues, his voice carrying across the kitchen, "I would prefer you not bring him into this house anymore. It's impossible for him to come home when he's trapped in here."

Absent a warning alarm, Mom rises from the table, a veritable tsunami of anger, set on swamping the judge in his snow boots. "Listen here, buddy, no one trapped your stupid cat, and my daughter didn't run off with him either. He just showed up, right before dinner. In fact, you're the one who owes us an apology. Your cat keeps coming here, but are we bitching at…"

"Mom, the kids…"

"…griping at you?" she yells, barely breaking stride, despite the mid-sentence self-edit. "No, we're not, and Ro's taking care of the damn thing, thank you very much. It's not her fault your cat would rather be here than hanging out with your frosty old ass."

I spin around toward Mom, "You're not helping," then spin back to the judge, growing dizzy too, which doesn't help. "Please excuse her, she has dementia."

Incensed, she sweeps upon us, an overdressed tornado of terror. "Oh, no I don't, and if that tree was on the property line, it's half theirs even if you did plant it!" She gestures wildly at Justin and Olivia, fueled by the need to fight a battle, any battle.

It's her defining characteristic. Honorable as it is when she fights for a good cause, it's a real pain in the butt when I'm on the receiving end of her particular brand of banshee justice.

I plant myself between her and the judge, and pray he has the good sense to recognize a two-fisted hellcat when he sees one. Either ignorant or stubborn, he holds his ground, glaring at my mother.

I better end this quick. "How much do we owe you for the tree?"

"Sixty dollars will work."

Mom punctuates the air, her extended arthritic digit doing double time before her. "We only owe him half, Ro."

I sneak a peek at her finger. Is it the middle one? Not yet, though the night is young.

Indignant and probably inebriated, she's relentless. "Don't give him any more than thirty. It's a crappy tree anyway."

Nick slams his cookie cutter on the table. "It's not a crappy tree!"

Nonplussed, Aaron confides in the judge. "Meemaw's right. It's a pretty crappy tree. I wanted a big one, not this scrawny one. Plus, it's got bugs and a big hole in it too. Did you know it's got bugs?"

I swear, that kid…probably angling for a discount too.

Mom points at my child, "He's right! Ro, give him twenty."

I swear, that mom…

Emboldened by her brother's defiance, Maddy slams her

cookie cutter too, enraged, not giving a flying fig about the Christmas tree. "His name is Paw Paw, and he loves me!"

Leaning into his sister, inches from her angry, insulted face, Aaron piles on, "It's Sandy Claws!"

Nick grasps his cookie cutter, headless Santas forgotten in the tree-cutting chaos. "Mom, are you going to jail?"

Justin snickers. Olivia swats him on the shoulder.

Things are going downhill faster than an Olympic bobsled team only there's no gold waiting at the end of this fright fest. Reassuring him, I sigh. "No, sweetie, I'm not going to jail."

He squirms. "Is Meemaw?"

...well...

Of course, at this inopportune time I spy Sam exiting the bathroom, but upon hearing the loud commotion, he grinds to a halt outside the kitchen. "Everything okay?" he mouths silently my way.

I nod, and yet, it's not.

Just a simple holiday at home, that's all I wanted. Some turkey, some pie, a few board games with the children, and a fresh start, a new tradition. Instead my hunk of a boss, who haunts my dreams and leaves me sweaty at night, is about to witness my mom going postal on a local dignitary, whom I've pissed off about an ugly tree and a roaming cat, while my already damaged children think one of us is getting hauled off to the jail.

This is why God gave us reality TV. You can't make this stuff up.

Nor would you want to.

It's high time to smother this dumpster fire. Turning from Sam, I find the judge's eyes and lock in, visually daring our unwanted guest to disagree. "No one's going to jail, Nick."

I shoot Mom a glance, declaring with my eyes *don't go there or I will stab you*, and continue. "Sir, I will give you sixty dollars for the tree since we made a mistake, and this spring I will replace it and we will never, ever cross or touch your property line again. Promise."

I take a deep breath. "As for Mr. Evans, I will not apologize," I declare, raising my voice, halting his protest. "He came here, and I can't promise you it won't happen again. If it's raining or snowing, and he's crying at our door, I will bring him in, and we'll call you immediately if you leave a number, so you can come get your cat. But I won't leave an innocent creature out in bad weather for anyone, neighbor or a judge."

"By the way, Happy Thanksgiving. I'll get my wallet." Sermon over, I march to the butler's pantry for my purse.

Justin slips his wallet from his jeans pocket. "Let me get half, sis."

Flying by, I nudge it away. "No, you don't, bro. My fault, my treat."

Justin and Olivia exchange a glance, her whisper carrying to my ears, "I told you she wouldn't take it," and he tucks his wallet in his pocket and crosses his arm.

Sam enters the kitchen. "Hello, Judge. Happy Thanksgiving. Is there a problem?"

Behind me, the judge clears his throat, then stops, stuttering instead, "Ss-Sam?" Taken aback, the shock in his voice is evident.

I slip past Sam, tempted to trip into his arms. "No, no problem. We took his tree by accident."

Fuming, if not momentarily contained, Mom finally sits, although, unfortunately, she doesn't shut up. "Don't be such a push over, Ro," she snaps, determined to press the issue. "Ignore her, Sam, it's half ours anyway. It was on the property line, and this man is an ass."

Fearful she'll rush the judge, I sail back into the kitchen, counting dollars. "Thank you, Mom, for your support. However, we've agreed to a price, assery notwithstanding. Judge, here's sixty dollars. I hope you don't mind ones and fives. My apologies again. I'll plant those trees this spring, your choice. Now, would you like to join us? We have plenty of food. In addition to pie."

"I recommend the cranberries." Mom smirks.

Silence fills the room, though Justin and Olivia are choking down a laugh. Sam too.

Stiff, haughty, the old man examines me, possibly repulsed by the wad of wrinkled cash I thrust his way. Given the number of ones I'm shoving in his face, he probably assumes I'm a stripper. Or perhaps he's pondering the fact that, between Mom and me, we've either called him an ass or implied it to his face twice within the last two minutes. I doubt any of it helps.

He hesitates and considers my money, conflicted, it seems.

Is he about to refuse it? No, instead, he takes it, and slips it inside his coat pocket. Fixing his scarf, he addresses me in a reed-thin voice coated in disdain. "No, thank you," he replies. Only now does he survey the room, taking in the bickering children, the flour-covered table, the baking sheet sprouting cinnamon dough ornaments, the farting dog, and the fire burning brightly, warming us against his contagious chill. His eyes linger on my family for half a second, but it's telling.

Finally, his pale gray blinking stare finds me once more. Tipping his hat, he picks up Mr. Evans, exits through the door silent as the grave, and marches through the dark, snowy gloom, headed for his car. Proud, stiff, unyielding, he cuts a pissy figure through the whirling white, semi-darkness.

Through the door window, I watch him trapesing through the blackness, clenching his cat in the worsening weather. He's probably going home to an empty house. Poor man. Even his Mr. Evans abandons him.

Then again, he is an ass.

Opening the back door, I follow him into the snow and yell, "Judge Middleton!" Howling wind cuts through me, yet after him I run. "Can I offer you a turkey sandwich to take home? We have plenty, and I feel awful about the tree."

He stops, his arms full of cat, his tired face a disquieting blankness. There's no hint of anger now, no sense of exasperation in his face, not even a glimmer of understanding that we meant no harm. Nothing, only cold emptiness, remote, aloof.

It's unnerving.

Mr. Evans squirms in his clutch, mewling softly. The judge, however, takes no notice. "Again, thank you, no. I must be going."

He opens the car door, gripping Mr. Evans, and climbs inside. The door slams shut, shutting out the cold, shutting out me, shutting out the world. Tentative in the snow, he inches down the driveway through the flurries, riding his breaks over every bump and rut. After an eternity, his taillights break free from the brush at the far end of the lane and make their way through the dark winter wonderland until the hills and valley swallow them whole.

Blowing into my frigid fingers, I shuffle back into the kitchen, already planning to bake him cookies. Pie might not be his thing, but who can resist cookies?

The kitchen is warm, inviting, when I step through the door. Mom sits before the fire, drinking Bailey's Irish Cream and keeping tabs on Maddy who's on her knees in front of the oven, watching ornaments bake. Justin eggs on my boys about visiting me in prison while they eat popcorn from the large bowl in his lap. Sam listens beside them, his hands wrangling the last strand of lights into submission, amused by their conversation. Olivia has joined them too and threads fluffy white kernels piece by piece onto a long thread. Jayden and Jaylen sit on the floor at her feet, content to stroke Lucky's bushy tail with a baby doll's brush. It's a charming scene, even if Aaron asked Mom if they feed people in prison. Giving in to the contentment, I can't wait to rejoin them, and the tension from the judge's visit lifts from my shoulders.

Shutting the door, I make my way to the hearth next to Mom to enjoy my family and my own glass of spiked goodness. All in all, despite the mishaps and the messes and the mistakes, it's been a great Thanksgiving.

~ * ~

Shortly after the judge departs, we tackle the tree, swamping it head to toe in colored lights, fresh-baked ornaments, and popcorn strands. Hole or no hole, fungal scale or no scale, it's a satisfying tree—homey, simple, sweet, perfect for our new lives in our new home.

Not wanting to end our fun, we play more board games with full bellies and cranky kids. When the loosing tears erupt, one thing becomes readily apparent. It's time to call it a night.

Nevertheless, the frosty old judge infests my thoughts like a Christmas-tree canker. No one should be alone on the holidays, not even an ass. Spur-of-the-moment, I delegate bed-tucking duties to Mom and decide this is a job for leftovers. It's my turn to visit the judge.

Fortunately, I have no idea where to go and Sam, my cowboy in shining leather, imaginary chaps, offers me a lift to the judge's house. It's good to give, isn't it? I should do it more often.

Kids kissed and ushered to the stairs we depart. Riding through the darkness in his squeaky-clean truck on Thanksgiving Day night, Sam and I leave for the neighbor's house, a teeming plate of leftovers cradled on my lap, though we're missing pumpkin pie which I polished off after the judge drove away with my tree money and his reluctant cat.

What can I say? Food heals.

Something other than pie distracts me now in this spic-and-span truck cab—Sam's thighs of steel. Even in the dark, his well-defined muscles bulge in the dashboard glow. Will small talk distract me from the inevitable embarrassment of drooling? It's worth a shot. I fake composure. "How well do you know the judge?"

Fat flakes beat against the windshield. He creeps along the snow-covered the road, driving responsibly, taking his time. "I wouldn't say well," he replies, "though I've known him for a several years. He keeps to himself. It's the nature of his job, I suppose."

A whiff of stuffing tempts me from my lap too.

Focus, Ro.

I may have A.D.D.

My gaze flits back to Sam. "You're the second person this week who's defended him to me." Studying his rugged face in profile, I falter. Damn…it's hard to remain on topic.

Great. Now I'm hungry on a whole different level. Time for more small talk. Hoping it helps, I watch the windshield wipers ticktock back and forth, sweeping away the flurries. "The woman at the shelter did the same when I delivered the dog food last Monday. Our first run-in was over Mr. Evans. It didn't go well."

Scratch that. You nailed the judge in the hall too, remember? Best not to share.

Sam chuckles, thankfully oblivious to my error. "No, I expect it didn't."

We round the bend, but a nagging notion plagues me. What if Judge Middleton's only companion is a big, fat, runaway cat? I mean, it keeps leaving him, for God's sake—that has to hurt. Of course, if the frigid old fart thawed a smidge, he might have family and friends to spend the holiday with, assuming he doesn't, of course.

Headlights illuminate a small brick farmhouse trimmed in fresh snow. No cars clog the drive, no lights gleam through the windows, save for one small glow near a side door. The front step is un-shoveled. I picture an old man alone, only a whiny cat for company.

Then I picture Mr. Evans trying to claw his way out of the house.

Poor Mr. Evans.

How depressing…sad…lonely…

Don't be the house, don't be the house, please don't be the…

Sam turns into the driveway.

Figures.

sigh

Putting his truck in park, Sam leaves the engine running, his hand on the key. "This is it." He peers at the front stoop. "Are we going in?"

Grabbing the leftovers, I open the door. "No, I'm guessing he's not a fan of drop-by visitors. I'll only be a moment." Hopping from the truck, I nearly upend myself on the icy pavement and slip slide cautiously to the front door. A shuffle here and a shuffle there, I clear snow from the landing and set the plate where a welcome mat should be but isn't. Needing one last touch, I remove a freshly baked, cinnamon-dough Santa ornament with its head firmly attached from my pocket and place it on top. A push of the doorbell, it rings out, and I swish gingerly away hoping not to fall.

Into the truck I climb. "Come on, cowboy, let's ride."

Sam flashes an oh-well-if-you-say-so grin and backs out. We inch away in the dark, watching the rearview mirror and smile when the porch light flickers on behind us.

Success.

Sure, as gestures go, it's not much. Regardless, I pray it does a little good. No one should be alone on the holidays, not even grumpy old men. Granted, our offering doesn't change anything, but at least he's aware someone's thinking about him on this cold holiday evening.

Plus, if he's sad about being alone, he can lose himself in cookies. Like I do.

Sam interrupts my food issues. "That was a nice thing, you did."

"Thanks," I reply, "but no one should be alone on Thanksgiving."

Smooth, Ro.

Sam's own Thanksgiving might have gone the same way had I not invited him. I hope he doesn't think I did it out of pity.

All too soon, my own driveway looms through the falling snow, and he slows for the turn. Instinctively I extend my hand, touching his arm, "Sam, wait."

Muscles tighten at my touch.

Oops.

Instantly, I pull back. Regrouping, I continue, "Can you drop me at the end of the lane? I enjoy the walk."

"In the dark?"

"Yeah. Trust me, it's a hell of a lot safer than Chicago."

Truck parked, he chuckles. "Most likely." The glow from Sam's truck lights shine before us, spotlighting snow-covered trees but, beyond their reach, it's dark, silent, peaceful. The wind has died and plump flakes drift around us.

Sam shifts in his seat to face me. "Thank you for inviting me today, and for the leftovers. I appreciate it. I had a lot of fun. You have a wonderful family."

I struggle to hide a snicker. "Wonderful? We had lint in the cranberries...mushrooms in my hair. Not to mention headless Santa ornaments for our stolen tree and a pissed off neighbor too. Oh, and let's not forget the plastic covered toilet either, of course you missed that lovely after-breakfast adventure, lucky you. Wonderful seems a bit of a stretch."

Brilliant, Ro. Remind him of the chaos.

"Sorry about the shenanigans," I regroup. "My kids can be a nightmare, especially when they're wound up. It's enough to make me scream at times."

His face clouds in the dashboard lights.

Were they that annoying?

Quickly as it came, the cloud departs, and Sam's sexy face breaks into a guarded smile. Dark eyes search my face. I fight the urge to kiss him. It would be easy to kiss him, here in the dark, even if the consequences would be difficult. Before my urge gets the better of me, he shifts yet again, only to stare out the window once more.

Okay, I can take a hint. Time to leave. "Thanks for everything today, Sam, especially the lift to the judge's house. You're welcome any time." Ready to brave the cold, I zip my coat.

This time, his body moves toward mine. Vanilla and leather drift my away. I forget about toilets and cranberries and flying green beans, choosing, instead to think about his lips. My throat is dry, tight. My vagina is the opposite. I try to swallow. I can't.

Fingers tap on the steering wheel. He seems both lost in thought, yet full of questions, agitated.

Me? I'm absolutely weak kneed in the vicinity of this man, and I'm far beyond agitated. A radiant burst of energy cascades along my spine, electrifying every cell. I catch his gaze, thankful we cut down the judge's ugly, misshapen tree.

Strong fingers halt their tap dance. Sam clears his throat. "Is 10:00 good for you tomorrow?"

My overstimulated brain draws a blank. "What?"

"For the riding lesson tomorrow? If you're worried about the weather, it's supposed to be better, though, frankly, many of my favorite rides have been in snow."

"Oh, the riding lesson..."

Ro, you dumbass, how could you forget?

"...yeah, ten works for me. I'm overdue for a good, hard ride." Feeling bold, I wink his way in the dark.

Subtle, Ro, real subtle.

Though Mom would be proud. Wait...Mom would already be in his lap.

"Anyway," I plunge on, trying to drive away a mental image of Mom straddling a reluctant Sam, "can you text me your address?" Any chance he'll wear chaps? And spurs? Please, God, yes.

Sam edges a bit closer. "Will do, when I get home."

Did he notice my wink? "Great, and thanks again for offering to teach me. Promise me one thing, though."

He squirms, this time moving nearer to his own door. "What?"

Why won't he sit still? It's confusing. Determined and horny, I stay put. "Promise me, if I fall on my ass or end up in a ditch, you won't take pictures, movies, Snapchat, or tweet my shame. This will be my first time on a horse."

Amused or sympathetic—I know not which—Sam chuckles, and it's a deep, throaty sound that rumbles like thunder on a hot summer's day. I love thunder…and pounding rain…and lightning, blazing hot lightning.

Calloused hands finger the gear shift, exploring its contours. "Don't worry, I won't." Gear shift explored he taps lightly on the console. "I bet you'll be a natural anyway." Facing the dashboard, ramrod straight, he studies the darkness, his fingers tap, tap, tapping once more. Is he nervous? Frustrated? Anxious to get home?

sigh

Time to leave.

Truck door open, I jump out, landing in ankle-deep snow. "I hope so, Sam, but don't count on it, Karma likes to prove otherwise. Most days, I wonder if God put me here for comic relief."

Dimples gleam in soft light. "Well, I'm glad he did," comes his reply.

Say what?

Is it possible to climb back in? Would that seem weird?

Probably.

I shut the door, and Sam lowers the passenger window. "Good night, Ro. See you tomorrow."

Can I fit through his window? If I leap, I might be able to swing an ankle up there, maybe leverage myself against the side mirror, and claw my way back in.

Instead, I manage a respectable, "Good night, Sam."

He waves then raises the passenger window, thwarting my plan.

I wave back and start walking

Ten feet into the driveway, I stop. This time, it's Sam's taillights disappearing in the distance. A snowflake, white and cold lands, on my eyelash. I brush it away and amble toward my full, happy home dreaming warm, happy thoughts.

Channeling a big ole Texas tingle too.

Chapter Nine

Thank God, it's Friday.

It's a beautiful sunny day. Sometime in the night, the snow stopped, the clouds moved on, and the sun broke through into a blazing blue, late fall morning. Four inches of snow blanket the ground, treetops, and anything else it can stick to, glazing the land in fluffy, white frosting.

Tied to the fence rail in front of me, a large horse towers overhead, eating sugar cubes from my palm, sliming me in the process, and occasionally blocking my view of Sam's ass. I'll forgive him for it, the horse, not Sam, because despite being a slobbery mess, he's cute as can be—solid black mane and tail, brown fur, a white blaze trailing from his ears to his furry nose, and eyelashes wispy enough to make Beyonce's falsies jealous. He blinks at me in slow, steady succession, inhaling sugar, exhaling drool. It's delightful.

The chaos from yesterday's meal fades and I can only hope it's doing the same with Sam. Regardless, I'm ready for a new adventure. Whether it's the leftover cookies I ate for breakfast or the double mug of coffee coursing through my body, I'm feeling plucky and brave and more than a little horny. This, however, may not be the best combo. I get mouthy when I'm feeling plucky…and brave…and horny.

On the other side of the fence rail, Sam works his cowboy magic in the corral, wrangling a variety of leather straps and buckles, and it's all smoking hot and totally sexy and I'm rethinking my life-long S&M boycott. He's wearing his dark barn coat again which, thankfully, creeps high when he bends over, and a pair of faded jeans hugs his muscular thighs and perfect ass, and this isn't helping the plucky, horny, mouthy part of my personality. Seriously, I'm in self-control freefall.

Trying not to explode—or touch, squeeze, grab, maul, or dry hump either—I settle for resting my arms against the wooden rail, telling myself I'm content to merely watch him work, even though it's a losing battle. Maybe misdirection will help. Time for small talk.

Clearing my throat, I ask, "Hey, Sam, aren't you supposed to be wearing a buckle?"

Or nothing at all perhaps?

Sam ties a small black and white pony to the corral fence a few feet from me and tosses it a flake of hay. "A buckle?"

The big bay searches my palm for more sugar. Velvety horse lips tickle my skin. Why can't Sam tickle my skin? "Yeah, a buckle. Don't you cowboys wear big shiny buckles?"

A flake of hay lands in a cloud of fragrant dust near my boots. "Can you scoot it under the fence for him?" Sam asks.

"Sure." Scuffling my cheap boots through the snow, I send it under the rail, and the big brown horse sniffs it once and, finding it to his liking, starts chewing.

Lifting a saddle blanket from the top fence rail, Sam replies, "I'm fresh out of buckles. Besides, that's the rodeo circuit." Reaching down, he snags the last flake of hay.

Naturally, while I feed treats to his horse, I admire his blue jean clad rump that makes my heart thump, and it's a whole lot sweeter than sugar. Yum. I undo straps and buckles, lost in an indulgent daydream, peeling leather away from muscle-bound flesh.

Where was I? Right, buckles. "My mistake." A sigh escapes my lips. "What about chaps?"

With practiced ease, he places the blanket on the back of a nervous, jet-black horse tied a few fence posts away. "Usually not for a trail ride."

"What a shame."

Two icy bits are tucked inside my armpits, hidden beneath Mom's borrowed parka since mine is currently drenched in dried Maddy snot from yesterday's tree meltdown. I'm supposed to keep them warm, so the cold metal won't hurt the horses' mouths, and it's easy to do thanks to Sam bending over every few minutes. I could probably melt iron with my pits at this point. Sorry, critters, hope you like the taste of single-mom sweat. Again, it's Sam's fault.

I offer another sugar cube, and, in a rush of velvet lips and slobbery tongue, it disappears. "This big guy is cute. Do they have names?"

More careful than before, Sam settles a saddle onto the black horse's back as it fidgets. "Yep. The pony is Butterball."

"Cute."

Reaching underneath the nervous horse, he threads a leather strap through a metal saddle ring, cooing soft words of encouragement. The sleek, black beauty paws the ground. "This is Dancer." Sam pulls the strap tight, and saddle on, the horse relaxes. "I'll ride him. He's young and pretty green."

The soft nose nudges me again. "Who's this big fella?" Its large, wet tongue tests my skin.

Sam hesitates. "Well…"

I wipe horse spit on my blue jeans. "Yes?"

Avoiding me, Sam casts his gaze to the ground, though a hint of amusement lights his face. "His name is Dick."

I freeze. "Say what?"

A sheepish grin emerges. "Dick," he repeats, "his name is Dick."

Again, I pause.

"You're kidding me, right."

"I wish like hell I was."

Reveling in his discomfort, I chuckle. "So, basically, you invited me here to ride Dick?"

Sam nudges his black hat back from his forehead. Thick, dark surfer curls escape from under the brim. "Yeah, I guess I did."

Oh, hell yes, now we're talking.

I feign calm, pretending my insides aren't roiling in a hot, buttered stew of hormones. "Interesting."

Sam joins Dick and me at the rail. Taking the large horse by the halter, he rubs its neck. "Dick, meet Ro. You two will be getting to know each other this afternoon, but be gentle. This is her first time."

Time to play along. "Not too gentle," I half joke. "I like it exciting, big guy."

"Oh, it'll be exciting." Sam laughs.

Suddenly, he stops. The words have barely left his mouth when a blush blooms across his rugged, grizzled cheeks. Quickly, he regroups. "Don't worry, though, Ro, he's well broke and loves getting out on the trails. You're in for a good time."

My heart beats in double time, inflamed by the verbal foreplay, brief as it was. Faking composure, I plunge on, "So, you named your horse Dick. What would Freud have to say about that, I wonder?"

Sam tosses a blanket onto the sturdy horse then smooths it across his broad back. Lifting the last saddle from the fence, he then sets it on Dick. "I didn't name him. He was from a threesome, Tom, Dick, and Harry, and he was fifteen when I bought him. Too late to change it." He secures the last buckle and rejoins me at the fence. "Can you hand me a bridle?"

God, he's close and damn fine too, plus, he said threesome. Deep dimples tempt me within kissing distance. A bridle? Hell, I would give him my virginity, if only I could remember what it looked like. Instead, I unzip my mom's parka and whip out a bridle.

Sidling back to Dancer, dragging my eyes behind him, Sam patiently coaxes the young horse to accept the warm metal in his mouth. Instantly, I imagine what kind of lover Sam would be. Is it possible to be jealous of a horse?

Yes. The answer is yes.

Sam latches the bridle behind Dancer's ears, unaware I'm judging his technique and finding it oh, so satisfying. He loops the reins around the saddle horn and shifts his attention to me. "Okay, Ro, your turn. Hand me Dick's."

I snicker. "Isn't that your job?"

Smooth, Ro. What are you? Five?

To my great joy, however, he laughs, and I join him. It feels good to be outside in the cold, wintery wonderland, enjoying each other's company, the prospect of an adventure before us. Happy satisfaction courses through me, and I pass him the other bridle, eager to ride.

Ever patient, Sam walks me through a lesson in bridling a horse, teaching me how to slip it on and buckle it behind Dick's ears. Seems easy and self-explanatory, and it's a shame too, because I totally want to stretch these lessons, but, teachable moment over, he grabs the reins. "I'm going to need you on this side of the fence. Time to ride."

My happy satisfaction dissolves into a smidge of self-doubt. "To be clear, you want me on Dick, right?" I step on the bottom fence board, aiming for innocence, knowing it's a stretch.

Sam fights another laugh, gives up, and gives in, indulging in a loud, lusty chuckle. Thank God, too, because…damn…it's sexy as hell when he laughs. Seriously. He's all dimples and eye crinkles and shiny white teeth.

"Yes," he continues, "time for you to get on Dick."

Nevertheless, I'm wary. Dick towers above me. Why do I have to be such a flat-out newbie, not to mention completely out of my element? Seriously, I haven't ridden anything with feet in over two years.

I swallow hard—ironic since the subject is Dick. Sizing up the big steed, my confidence falters and I stall. "Now?"

Sam nods. "Yep. Now."

Poised on the bottom fence rail, I hedge. "You have no idea how much I want to but, have I mentioned how big Dick is?"

"Ro…"

I shrug. "I'm just saying, he's a bit more than I'm used to, is all."

Sam pats the patient horse on the neck. "You're right, he's a big one."

"See, that's what I'm saying." Buying for even more time, I

point at the fat pony tied to a post. "What about Butterball? We aren't going to leave him here, are we?"

Moving to the pony, Sam slips off his halter, releasing him. "No, he's coming too. Horses are happiest in a herd. He'll pitch a fit if we leave him behind."

Free at last, the chubby pony joins us, desperate for sugar. Out of cubes, I push his eager nose away. Disgusted by my barren pockets, the persistent pony saunters over to Dancer to steal his hay, because, apparently, short as he is, Butterball is a big dick too.

Watching the two horses bicker I contemplate Sam's advice. "Okay, group rides it is. Now back to Dick."

"Ro…"

"By the way, keep your expectations low." Steeling myself for what's to come, I climb higher on the fence to join Sam. Ever the gentleman, he offers his hand, and I take it.

Rough callouses brush against my palm. Each tiny hair on the back of my neck rises in a slutty salute at the touch of his skin. I revel in the combined strength and tenderness of his grip. It hints at raw power, coiled muscles, a gentle touch. God, it feels good.

Jesus, is this all it takes to get me riled up these days? The touch of a sexy man's skin and I melt into mush? No wonder guys dig recently divorced moms. We've got to be the world's laziest lay.

Reluctant to release him, I hop to the ground. Sam, however, pulls away, choosing instead to size me up.

Wait…seriously…is he checking me out?

Hands outstretched, I pivot at the waist, embracing the attention. "You're rethinking the big, shiny buckle, aren't you? Think I could make it work? I can be trendy too," I joke, "these aren't even mom jeans."

Shut up, Ro, shut up.

He shakes his head. Amusement greets me. "I'm looking at your legs."

Say what? My legs? Why?

I perform a semi-sexy pirouette in my relaxed-fit, discount Walmart jeans, borrowed grandma parka, and cheap, slip-on mud boots. "It took me hours to throw together this ensemble."

Dimples reward me. "I'm trying to decide where to put the stirrups. Let's get you on him, first, then I'll adjust them. Ready?"

God, no, but here it goes. I steel myself. After all, I'm ready to mount at least one stud today. "Yep," I lie.

Following Sam's lead, I grasp the saddle horn and lift my foot high, but, short-legged as I am, it falls ten inches shy of its goal.

Perplexed, I shrug. "What do I do now? Jump? Not to sound like a broken record, Sam, but Dick's really huge."

Stepping to my side, he interlocks his fingers and bends over. "He may have draft horse in him. I'll give you a boost."

A boost? Damn. The day after our Thanksgiving glutton fest, and he's going to toss my butt into the air? Life, so fattening and unfair.

Reluctant, I raise my foot again, and Sam lifts me with ease, heaving me into the saddle where I find myself high in the air, sitting on great, big Dick, feeling lighter than I ever imagined.

Wow. I like it.

Oblivious to the back and forth drama carrying on in my brain, Sam contributes a third act to my passion play by briefly patting my thigh. His meaty, beefy hand rests upon it for only a second, though it's enough to send my senses into overdrive.

"Lift your leg for a sec," he murmurs, starting the launch sequence.

Momentarily speechless, I comply. My brain attempts to compute that sexy Sam touched my thigh, and I swear I smell hair burning as it churns. Struggling to compose myself, it's clear I need a reboot, or a bigger, faster mental processor between my ears. Regardless, beside me he works, composed, collected, adjusting the stirrup. The side of his face tempts me beneath the brim of his hat, all sun-kissed skin, a hint of lines fanning from his eyes, the curl of brown locks, the trace of Friday morning stubble outlining his chiseled, kissable jaw.

Good lord, someone slap me. I'm a smitten kitten.

Sam finishes with the stirrups and hands me the reigns, then unhooks the lead rope from Dick's halter. I sit frozen in place, afraid to move and watch as he unties Dancer from the fence. With one fluid, flawless motion, Sam mounts the lucky bastard—I mean horse—pulling the reins tight. He sits on his horse, radiating confidence. I sit on mine, radiating discomfort, like a patient at a proctology exam staring down a big-fingered doctor.

"Are you ready, Ro?"

Unnerved, I clutch the saddle horn. Brisk air fills my lungs, reminding me I'm both alive and scared shitless. My big fat steed swishes his tail back and forth, but otherwise remains immobile. Terrified, yet also elated and excited, I find my nerve and embrace the unknown.

Exhaling deeply, I relax into the saddle. "Ready as I'll ever be. Come on, I want to ride Dick."

Gripping the reins, Sam nudges Dancer forward. "You got it."

And we're off.

~ * ~

After a few practice rounds in the corral, Sam opens the gate and sets me loose on the trail. I have a basic idea what it means to neck rein, and I haven't fallen off or died, so things are going well.

We ride through open pasture, our destination a thick stand of trees, and Dick plods on like a trooper with Butterball trailing behind. Dancer, however, puts on a show, stopping, starting, tossing his head, and kicking his heels. Sam remains cool, calm, and in control, working the young horse with strong, practiced hands. Clearly, Sam has great hands. It makes me want to buck and dance too.

Instead, Dick and I give him room to rein in the nervous colt, and, finally, Dancer regains his composure. Sam turns him toward the trees, and I nudge Dick, prepared to follow suit. This time, however, the big gelding remains rooted to the spot. I chuck him a bit harder, urging him on, when his broad back tenses and his hindquarters buckle inward. A shudder courses through his round, dusty body, sending a wave of panic through me.

I stop, uncertain what to do. "Sam! Something's wrong with Dick!"

Pulling Dancer to a halt, he swivels in the saddle, concern etched on his face. "What's wrong?"

"I'm not sure. He won't move. Should I get off?"

Sam trots our way, and a mischievous smirk tugs at the corners of his lips. "I wouldn't right now."

"Why?"

"Raise your stirrups and stick them straight out." He demonstrates, stretching his boots far away from Dancer's body. "Like this, and hurry."

A rushing noise fills the air.

What is that?

A pungent wisp of warm ammonia floats on the crisp breeze, assaulting my senses.

Is that what I think it is? Pinching my nose, I grimace at the thought. "You've got to be kidding me. He's peeing? Please tell me Dick isn't peeing."

Resting his arms on the horn of the saddle, Sam grins, his dimples deep as valleys. "I wish I could…"

A cloud of stench surrounds me. I raise my feet higher. "He really is a Dick, isn't he?" Tickled at the circumstances, I pat his big neck, and he sighs. "And I thought you were hurt, you big lug." Eventually, the rushing noise stops, and Dick gives his body a stiff shake. Break time over, we saunter through the yellow snow.

Joining Sam, I relax in the saddle. "There's another first for my journal. *November 27th—today was yet another milestone day in the country. A horse tried to pee on me. It was oddly thrilling. I wonder what tomorrow will bring.*"

"Wait until you get the goat home," he replies, "you'll fill your journal in no time."

"I can't wait," I confide.

Onward, we ride, making for a hillside beyond the trees, chatting randomly, enjoying the day. It's peaceful riding like this through the snow, together with Sam, no house, road or car in sight. Plus, I'm getting the hang of it, even if Dick is a huge, compliant sofa of settled obedience doing most of the work. We ride through the stillness, nothing but hills and trees, sunshine and snow, Sam and me, and Butterball who's constantly bolting ahead, stopping to eat, falling behind, rinse and repeat. Who knew a petulant pony would be my spirit animal?

Eventually, we crest the rising land and, in the shallow valley below, I spy a large pond fringed in ice, hugging the hills. A copse of fir cling to its banks and nestled beyond, a diminutive log cabin sporting a rock fireplace anchors the far shoreline adjoining yet another corral.

A pro at this trail-riding thing, Dick recognizes our destination and lumbers forward, aiming for a gate in the fence. Sam, Dancer, and rollie-pollie Butterball follow suit.

We reach the corral, and Sam dismounts. "Would you like a tour of the cabin?"

It's a fluid, impressive, sexy swirl of motion, and I want him to do it again. And again. And again.

Hold on, what did he ask me? See the cabin?

Tingly and aroused, I comply. "Sure."

Who wouldn't?

Getting to work, Sam slips Dancer's saddle and bridle off, then opens the gate and turns him loose. Buttercup rushes in too, his sight set on a round bale of hay by a lean-to. Sam closes the gate then grabs Dick's bridle.

Oh, no, I'm next. I hesitate. Inexperienced as I am, nothing I do will be as fluid and as effortless as Sam is on a horse. "I'd love to see it," I reply, squirming in the saddle, "if I can get off Dick."

snicker

Ignoring my wordplay, Sam steadies my steed. "You can do it. Remember how I showed you."

Still, I'm not reassured. The ground taunts me, so close and, yet, so far away. "This won't be pretty," I mumble, contemplating his instructions in fast forward, praying I can successfully apply the theory, betting I won't, wondering how long I can stall even as I realize it won't get me off this big ass horse. Inevitably, I'll have to come down.

Channeling his instructions, I give it a go…stand in the stirrup, grasp the back of the saddle and horn, kick my foot over, jump, and land like a tough, though surprisingly graceful and possibly sexy, prima ballerina. Okay, the last part was my instruction, not Sam's…

A resounding thud announces my miscue as I over rotate and land squarely on my ass, possibly bouncing a bit.

How lovely.

Sam pulls me to my feet. "You'll get the hang of it."

Doubtful but, who cares? Taking his hand, I'm breathless, maybe from landing on my butt, more likely because I'm touching him. Again. As superpowers go, Sam's hand has the power to turn me to butter. Or pudding. I really like pudding.

He leads Dick through the gate. Once inside, he removes the saddle and bridle, then releases Dick to join his friends. Shutting the gate, he gestures at the cabin. "C'mon, I'll show you my palatial vacation home."

"Lead the way."

Snow crunches underfoot, and birds chatter around us, singing and tweeting, fliting across our path. The woods surrounding us radiates the aroma of pine. A hint of saddle leather catches my attention. Undertones of vanilla waft my way, Sam's signature scent, and it's a far better smell than horse pee. I suck it in. Fragrant, crisp air heightens my senses to their max. I'm in olfactory heaven.

Wood boards creak as we climb the porch, inviting my ears to the party. Taking a moment, I admire the view. Two wooden rockers face the pond, the snow-covered trees, the gently rolling valley. Sam watches me, and studies the valley as well, before opening the front door. Moving aside, he nods. "Ladies first."

"Thank you, Sam."

Curious, I enter, and instantly I'm charmed. It's adorable—rustic, homey, quaint. Ax-hewed logs line the cozy single room, awash in bright light and soft shadow. A fieldstone fireplace, deep yet clean of ash, cradles a cast iron pot hanging from a metal crane anchored in stone, begging for soup, stew, or some other slow-cooked comfort dish. Paned windows gleaming in spotless glass flank either side of the chimney, letting in the late November sun, and dust motes dance their way through the streaming beams of golden sunshine.

Two wooden Adirondack chairs face the hearth, and a small table sits between them, begging for books, coffee mugs, and, in my case, a well-filled glass of wine. Beyond them, next to a window overlooking the pond, stands an antique Hoosier cabinet flanked by a wooden table and two other chairs begging for warm bodies and a good meal.

It's simple, perfect. What must it be like to sit at this table on a snowy night, across from Sam, eating dinner by lamplight, talking about the day? Wonderful, no doubt.

Scanning the space further, my glance falls on the one white-elephant in the room, both taunting and tingling me with its past history and potential future implications. An antique four-poster bed hugs the opposite wall, igniting a spark in places needing sparked.

Better not fan that particular flame. I have to mount a horse later.

Drawn to the craftsmanship, determined to avoid thinking about Sam and his wife contorted in their bed, I amble toward the fireplace to glide my fingers across smooth stonework. "It's beautiful. My sister-in-law would have a field day in here. Seriously, she'd be barking orders and staging a thousand and one pictures."

Closing the door behind us, Sam steps into a beam of light. "She's welcome to use it for photos."

On the mantle, an earthenware vase cradles a single, dried sunflower, its seeds long gone. I caress a dried petal, its frail brittleness evident beneath my touch. "Thanks, Sam, I'll mention it. She'd bring props, food, work her magic, it's what she does. Everything's a stage for one of her homegrown fantasies. Just once, I'd want to picture the world like she does," I rattle on. "It's always way too real for my comfort."

Sam pushes a chair closer to the table, aligning it with the other. "Not enough fantasy in your life?"

I almost, I repeat, almost, erupt into a dry-heave version of a spit-take, recalling only a smidgen of my Sam-induced fantasies. Instead, however, I manage to contain myself. "Most of my fantasies are kiddy books these days. My feet are firmly planted in the real world. I've considered writing a counter point to Olivia's blog," I continue, "just real-life stuff. Diapers plugging the toilet, disappearing children when you're running late, setting the stove on fire, losing your shoe on the road when you have an interview. That kind of thing—not that those things have happened," I backtrack, embarrassed and say, "though, it does kind of sum up Olivia and me. She's the well-dressed fantasy. I'm the comic-relief reality." I shrug and go back to admiring the stonework. "Real life. It's what I do."

Sam studies me from across the cabin. "You should do it, Ro, write a blog. Fantasy is great at times, but the real world isn't going anywhere anytime soon. Besides we need more laughter, and you have a great sense of humor. People need healthy reality more than they need some idealistic fantasy of what some people think life should be."

Born from encouragement, feverishly fed by his attention, my cheeks burst into blushing flames of heat. It's intoxicating. "I was joking, Sam." I laugh. "Who would read a shit-happens-and-it-happens-to-me-so-why-not-laugh-about-it blog? Though, surely, I'm not the only one who's had to sand shellac out of the carpet. Oh, and don't ask. Trust me on this, never take a belt sander to shag pile. Anyway, thanks for the encouragement."

Still, joke or not, it's an interesting idea, the blog, not the belt sander. "I'll think about it. Who knows, maybe I will."

Despite my casual response, part of me awakens to the notion. Should I? I mean, why not, right? Could this be it, my thing? Did Sam fertilize a seed I planted in jest?

Unaware I'm questioning my life goals he inspects the Hoosier cabinet. "You're welcome. Besides, you have a blog expert who can help you. I'm sure Olivia would be a great resource."

His dimples wink back at me, and my pulse quickens. Like before, however, Sam looks away. He opens a cabinet door and tests a hinge, swinging it back and forth, wincing when it squeaks. "I should oil these. They're starting to rust."

The squeak is slight, unlike the obnoxious grating noise which emanated from my back brakes when I arrived at his place today. Any chance he noticed?

Sam contemplates the hinge while I contemplate Sam. His neat streak fills the room, underscoring the obvious, that his reality—hot, single, childless, sexy guy—is so different from my own sticky, child-ladened, hot mess of a life. Books, upright and alphabetized, line shelves on one wall. Cotton curtains in red and gold plaid hang straight, the bed has hospital corners, everything is put away in its place, neat, tidy, organized.

Disheartened, I nudge the iron crane. Well oiled, it swings, meeting no resistance. I sit on the hearth and rest against the cold stone. "I'd love to have a cabin like this. One, it's small and easy to care for and, two, I could hide from the children. What a great place to get away."

Sam closes the cabinet door and joins me. "Do you hide from them often?"

A cranberry-soaked sock taunts my memories. "Only when they're home."

Silent, he sits next to me on the hearth. We stare at the sunshine pouring through the windows. The dust motes bob and weave in the light, both animated and suspended like confused snowflakes, unwilling to fall to earth. They dance and spin, and our breath sends them swirling in spirals.

An evening a few weeks back leaps to mind, me reading *Horton Hears A Who* to my babies. Is it possible, swirling in those motes before me, a tiny version of me is in a tiny cabin with a tiny Sam contemplating an even tinier, itty, bitty dust mote? Any chance she's getting laid by her teeny, tiny cowboy boss in a teeny, tiny bed?

Anything's possible.

A deep, contented, not so teeny sigh escapes my lips. "It's gorgeous." Winter light trails across the floor, inching closer to our feet. Mesmerized, I study the sunlight, the dust. "The last time I saw a beam of light that pretty, Patrick Swayze was standing in the middle of it telling Demi Moore ditto."

Puzzled, Sam cocks his head my way. "What?"

"*Ghost?*" I repeat.

He shrugs, confused. "I don't follow."

Cold from the hearth stones seep through Mom's parka. "The movie? Forget it. What I mean is, it's nice here. Did you and your wife come here often?"

Sue me. I'm curious.

Muscular, boot-clad legs stretch before me. He takes off his hat. Thick, unruly curls tumble out. Like me, he leans against the fireplace and sighs. "No, she didn't care for it. We would ride here often, but at the end of the day she always wanted to go home, said it didn't make much sense to sleep here when we had electricity and hot water at the house." He falters, perhaps distracted by a memory, and chuckles.

The bed tempts me once more. We could start a fire, maybe even in the fireplace. Instead, I caress the smooth rock, trailing my finger along rough mortar. "Did you ever cook on the fire?"

Another sigh. "I have. She preferred a microwave. Or a restaurant."

A stubbled jaw, clenched, rugged and well-defined, haunts my peripheral vision. "Ah," I mutter. Curiosity gets the better of me. "What was she like?"

Dark curls tilt in my side vision as Sam lowers his head and examines the floor. Nimble fingers tug at his hat brim. "Strong, intelligent, free-willed. A dedicated worker for sure, totally into her job. She was a rising star at her dad's fertilizer company. They wanted to expand, and she enjoyed her work."

There's an edge to his voice I haven't heard before. Icy, hard, it rings out in the frozen room. What drives it? Grief? Loneliness? Anger? If so, aimed at whom? God? Himself? Her?

Unaware of my questions, Sam startles me with his own. "What was your husband like?"

Don't say the H word...he's not my husband, he's my ex, he's my ex.

Focusing on the ceiling, I share, "Selfish, cheap, impatient..."
You sound like a bitch, Ro. Rein it in.

"...also, quiet, focused on his work too. Ambivalent most of the time. Loved to golf. A jackass with a wandering eye."
Uber bitchy, Ro.

Sam studies his boots. "Sorry, I didn't mean to go there."

This time, it's my turn to sigh. "It's fine, I'm over it. I just wish he would take more interest in his kids. It gets to them."

Suddenly, the image of Nick's sad, expectant face haunts me. "Maybe that's why I said yes to the animals. You know, to distract them from everything that's happened. Though," I continued, incensed, "how can a parent, any parent, abandon their children?" Anger gives way to sorrow and undercuts my composure. "It's one thing to ditch me, it's another entirely to abandon his own children. I mean, who does that?"

The white-hot sting of tears catches me off guard, rattling me, and a single rebellious drop breaks free. I give a rather indelicate sniff—when my children hurt, I'm far from a delicate flower—and dig in Mom's parka pocket. Finding a tissue, I blow.

It smells like sex. Yuck. Yuck. Yuck.

I shudder and shove it back in her pocket.

Clearly misinterpreting my shudder, Sam puts his arm around my shoulders and squeezes me gently. "Hey, I'm sorry. I didn't mean to upset you. Here you come out for a riding lesson, and I make you cry instead. Some friend, huh?"

The weight of his arm comforts me, even as my thoughts linger on the word friend. "Hey, don't worry about it, Sam, it's not your fault."

"Yes, it is," he murmurs.

My heart in my throat, I stare at Sam. Deep brown eyes drill into my burning green ones. His touch is warm upon my skin. I lift my face to his and he lowers his to mine.

Just like that, worlds collide, stars explode, dogs lie with cats, the Cubs win the Series, and Sam, the sexy, single, smoking-hot cowboy, kisses me.

~ * ~

Once upon a time, a very long time ago in a galaxy far, far away, a boy kissed me. His lips were full and moist, and it was gentle and sweet, and we were young, very, very young, so it wasn't what you would call a hot, sexy kiss as much as it was tender…and sweet.

And then, he stuck his big fat tongue down my throat, I gagged, got mad, and punched him in the face.

Two weeks later, he asked me to go steady.

Boys. Go figure.

This kiss?

This isn't like that. Not even close.

Even though it's freaking cold in this cabin, even though tears streak my cheeks, and after riding around on his fat horse for over an hour, I totally smell like a camel, this kiss is *hot*. Freaking hot, as in melts metals and creates fission and puts the fires-of-hell-to-shame hot. In short, we're smoking.

When Sam's lips meet my own, angels sing. Or, maybe they're devils giving voice to the notions in my head because my brain isn't singing a Sunday hymn. Our lips part. Sam's tongue rakes mine with fire. I burst into an inferno, and my arms engulf him. His tighten around me, so firm, so strong, and we fall into a deep, desperate kiss. We freaking kiss…and kiss…and kiss, oh, my lord, how we kiss.

Right now, my vagina could light China, and possibly even Singapore, if we could figure a way to harness it. Hell, there's extra energy to spare for Australia too, mate.

Without warning, though, it's over.

Sam pulls back. His arms fall to his side. I search his face for meaning, for understanding. Confusion stares back at me.

Rising to his feet, he bolts straight for the door. "We should get back." The door slams shut, Sam disappears, and I'm alone in his cabin, hot, horny, and clueless.

What the bloody hell?

I'm panting like a puppy after chasing its own tail. My arms, knees, legs, feet, everything has morphed into jelly. Not the good kind of jelly which stands up to peanut butter, mind you. No, I'm the discount jelly on the bottom shelf that separates into liquid after it's been open for two days, sitting on a hot counter in July kind of jelly.

I'm puddling into my shoes

Confused, torn, sexed up, and hormonal, I sit, hoping the

cowboy will come back. After all, damn, it was one hell of a kiss. It was, wasn't it?

Plus, there's that big, beautiful bed...

Hold on a sec...what if he's getting a condom?

Leaping to my feet, I rush to the porch, searching for Sam and spy him in the corral, bridling the horses.

We've got a big, fat no to the condom, breaker, breaker, over and out.

Bummer.

Closing the cabin door, reality slaps me in the face as I realize what's about to happen.

Horny as hell, I'll be riding the wrong damn Dick back to the house.

~ * ~

We ride in awkward silence, though it's difficult since I'm aroused and riding a stud, plus, I have no clue what to do or say, other than bite my lip and try not to moan. Awkward, self-conscious, mortified, I follow him as we ride straight to the corral, no more sightseeing or lollygagging. Hell, even Butterball has picked up the pace. The silence settles in harder than the cold, and my steamy kiss-induced joy morphs into an itty, bitty twinge of frustration-induced anger.

Men.

Bah, humbug.

Sam hops off Dancer and opens the corral gate, calling to Butterball who protests at first, before bolting inside. I ride in and make for the fence, and Sam follows.

Remembering my last ungraceful dismount, I rise in the stirrup, swing my leg over, steadying myself with the saddle horn this time, and, miracle of miracles, land on my feet. "Ta da!"

Sam concentrates on his young horse. "Good job."

At least say it like you mean it, cowboy.

A part of me wants to bark at him like a rabid dog, screaming why, why, why, why, why? Instead, I slip the bridle from Dick's head—which is funny if you think about it—and raise it in triumph, hoping to lighten the mood even as I dig deep to hide my irritation. "She *can* be trained."

Sam sets Dancer's saddle and blanket on the fence. He stands beside the rails, frozen in place. "Ro, I'm sorry for what happened back there," he starts. "I don't know why I did it." Eyes cast to the ground he frowns at his feet.

Um, gee, thanks Sam.

I drag the saddle off Dick, a bit more forceful than intended and set it on the fence.

What was it, Sam? Pity, loneliness, lust, opportunity? Pick one. Any chance at all, any possible chance, it was honest attraction? Perhaps even a connection of the heart?

Nah, of course not.

Time to polish off my membership plaque for the she-woman's man-hater club.

That twinge of anger gnaws at my composure. Perhaps I've found my first blog topic, men who suck. I make a mental note to toss back a bottle of wine and jot down an outline after the children go to sleep.

I yank the blanket from Dick's back and throw it onto the fence rail. "Hey, Sam, it's fine, no big deal," I lie. "No apologies necessary." Enough said. I clam up because, hey, I enjoyed it and he didn't. Slipping Dick's halter off, I set the big horse free.

A veritable statue of immobility, Sam remains rooted against the fence.

I scratch Dick's nose and pat his neck, grateful he didn't kiss and run. "Thanks again for the ride. I should get going any way."

Returning to life, Sam finally thaws, snapping to attention, meeting my stare. Shock, surprise, sadness spread across his face, cascading in waves of raw emotion.

Regardless, I don't care.

Boss or no boss, I'm pissed.

A toss of my hand, a short, brisk wave, I pop over the fence and march to my car.

"Later Sam."

~ * ~

Olivia's grandfather clock tick tocks in the hallway, timing my insomnia in my bed under the stairs, where I distract myself from potential kiss fallout by testing names for my future blog. It has to be perfect, especially as I plan to publicly skewer ex-husbands and kiss-and-run cowboys, not to mention cellulite and chin hair, with my own gutsy take on their disappointing reality.

Unfortunately, it's not going well. *Fuckers and Why They Suck* seems a bit aggressive. *Men, Why Bother* has potential. *I Wish I Were A Lesbian* needs pursuing and not just as a blog. *I'm Only Here for The Triple AAA Batteries* hits a little too close to home, as does *What The Fuck Is Going On?*

Maybe I should run these past Olivia.

Despite my ever-growing list of rejected blog titles, my

relentless brain keeps hopping back to Sam. Why did he kiss me? Was it want? Need? Opportunity? Pity?

Worst of all, why did I let him? Seriously, what happened to my anti-relationship life goals? Not to mention my don't-dally-with-the boss rule? Okay, I made the last one up, but…what happened?

Why did he run? Do I have too much sticky, arguing baggage, as in three snot-covered kids, friction-inducing thighs, and a problematic ex? Am I merely a casual hookup to him? After all, I'm only temporary at the diner anyway. Does he think he can kiss, run, and fire me later?

Bosses Be Crazy? No, too specific.

I roll over and peek through the crack of the stairwell door. The kiddies sleep, the house is silent, distractions are non-existent, thwarting my efforts to sidetrack my tortured mind.

Instead, it replays the kiss.

Argh.

Men Are Cocksuckers…not bad. I may have a blog title after all.

If only I can stop obsessing about Sam.

~ * ~

Sam's cabin surrounds me. Naked and needy, I'm sprawled on his bed, exposed…waiting. Moonlight spills across his bare chiseled chest. Biceps bulge, and he straddles me, lowering himself upon me. The weight of him compresses my ribcage. My nips are at full attention. He might be able to write his name in the snow, but I can etch mine in the cabin's frozen glass windows if need be.

His lips grow closer. I can almost taste them now. I know what they taste like too. He's close, so close. Hot breath caresses my nips. It reaches my face, washes over me, and smells like dog food.

What?

Dog food?

I wake with a start.

Are you kidding me?

It's still Friday night, I'm still in my bed, and Sam still ran from our kiss. Beside me the door under the stairs to my mini bedroom now stands wide open and Lucky has joined me. His chin rests on my rib cage, breathing on my face. Seeing me stir, he wiggles, excited. His wide, yellow tail swishes against the doorway in the dark, signaling his gratitude for my attention.

At least somebody wants me.

I rise from my pillow. "Let me guess. You have to pee."

Anxious for a trip outdoors, he dances in the dark. Together, we waddle to the French doors, the pitter patter of old puppy feet and soon-to-be-middle-aged mama feet the only sounds. I let him into the moonlit courtyard where he sniffs the wooden planter boxes Justin and my boys built for Olivia. Stone pavers are piled high beside them, yet another project. Funny, those pavers will be laid before I am. At least Olivia's plans are taking shape, even if mine are unformed and lifeless.

Lucky does his business and I wait. Kicking the brown, dormant grass, he wanders a few more feet and hunkers down, to take a crap.

It hits me then, with blinding clarity, my purpose.

Pride or no pride, I am the piss patron of innocent souls, the butt wiper of babes, the timekeeper of turd making. While my own life may be stalled, I make shit happen for others. Literally.

Lucky ambles to the French doors, prepared to call it a night. I let him in, pat his tired, gray noggin, and send him to the kitchen to dream before the dying embers. As I crawl into bed, praying for sleep, another thought hits me. I have my first blog topic.

My Life Is Shit.

Chapter Ten

Monday mornings suck.

Monday mornings after major holidays and a face-sucking session with an apparently reluctant, part-time, temporary boss really suck. In fact, they suck balls. Sweaty, sweaty balls.

I woke to rain, which sucks. The snow is gone, leaving behind puddles of mud, flooded creeks, dog prints on the floor, and a bad attitude, which sucks. Cranky children, sniffles, a skirt that's too snug, and the thought of facing Sam weigh me down and, guess what?

This sucks.

Account receivables demand my attention in my office booth which necessitates more than one search on Google. My skirt pinches, my bladder screams, three sleepless nights don't help, and I really, really, really need another cup of coffee.

The back counter stretches a hundred miles away this morning, but I make the long-distance waddle anyway and fill my mug. Clutching it with a stiff claw of a hand cramped from yanking one thousand and one carpet tacks from a wooden floor destined to be the boys' future bedroom, I sulk back to my office booth, the definition of a bad mood. Knees creak from too much kneeling, joints ache from too much gripping, arms ache from too much pulling, and my heart aches from too much feeling. Plus, I'm pissed off too. Not a good combo.

Also, because I am Karma's poster child for bad timing, as I hulk across the diner, muffin top spilling out, lapping java like a cow, wincing all the way, in walks Sam. I've heard nada from him since leaving his farm Friday morning, giving me no choice but to I ignore him.

Time to bury myself in work.

Fortunately, the invoice in front of me has numbers, mindless rows of numbers willing to swallow me whole even if the cowboy won't. The computer screen flashes to life, the diner bell rings again, and I hope like hell Sam has left the building.

Instead, however, because Karma has also made me her prison bitch, I hear her bellowing, a cape buffalo on the Serengeti, searching for its half-witted calf. My mother's distinct cry echoes through the room, adding to my personal doom and gloom.

Can I get an oh, crap? Anyone? Hello?

"Ro!"

Dear Lord, shoot me now.

While I dread the thought of her stampeding down the length of the diner to join me where I can do damage control, it's better than what happens next—Mom hollering in her largest, clearest, outside voice.

"Sam!"

Damn.

I'm screwed.

I can't even ignore the impending carnage. Looking up, it taunts me from the dreaded wall mirror, a freak show reflection in all its technicolor glory. Black leather biker boots hiked up over skintight, olive green jodhpurs which anchor her to the floor. Elaborate drop earrings jingle, and red and silver braids—one sporting a beribboned falcon feather—fly beneath a jaunty beret. A multi-colored crocheted tunic with fringe, no less, hangs below her bomber jacket. Still squawking, her grating voice reverberates against brick walls and wood floors.

Jarred awake from their Midwestern coma at the sight of this unnatural imported creature, the locals' heads spin over their deep-fried daily specials as they morph into human Tilt-a-Whirls at the county fair.

I sure wish I had a chiropractic practice in town, because whiplash is officially on the menu.

Hold on...horror of horrors, Mom is doing the unthinkable...she's approaching Sam near the register.

I swear, it's a sign of the apocalypse.

Can I fit myself into the fryer vat behind the grill? End it all with an extra crispy coating? With these thighs, I might literally melt away. But nope. More likely, I'd burn the place down while discovering I'm the other white meat. Like pork, but with more fat and less raving bacon fans.

Mom's voice hits me like a Mac truck, blasting me back to reality. "Wonderful to see you again, Sam." She leans in to hug the man...

Seriously, Mom, a hug?

...and, surprisingly, he hugs her back.

Time to put a stop to that. "Mom! I'm down here."

Ignoring me, she removes her red leather gloves and thwacks them meatily against her palm. Deftly throwing fresh gas on the rumor embers simmering away inside the diner, she focuses on my skittish boss. "We enjoyed having you over on Thursday. You need to come again. Soon too. I make a mean tofu meatless loaf."

Old gray noggins at tables and booths bob back and forth. I listen for satanic music and expect pea soup and dentures to be projectile vomited through the air at any moment, but they only confer, no doubt debating a variety of topics, things like who is this strange apparition, why is she dressed like a Macy's Day parade float, isn't the parade over, what is tofu, can you even *have* a meatless loaf and, most likely of all, why did Sam have dinner with this strange Day-Glo-dressed woman on Thanksgiving?

Sam clears his throat and coughs a reply, "Th-thank you for the offer, Kate. Dinner was wonderful. I especially enjoyed the pecan pie."

Is he nervous? He should be.

Also, mental note, buy more pecans…

Why bother, though, right? Because, I'm pissed about the kiss. Okay, well, not the actual kiss. The kiss was magical, sexy, flaming hot…where was I? Right. I'm pissed. At Sam and myself. That giant brushoff has me steaming like clams.

No pecans. Or pie. Ever.

"Mom, over here. C'mon on, girl," I kiss whistle into the air and pat my thigh.

She waves her hand aimlessly in my direction, and I'm growing desperate. She's essentially clueless to my kiss-the-boss crisis, a potential problem in the making given her presence and Sam's.

Curious for details, she digs into him, stabbing me in the heart, "How was the trail ride? Ro didn't say much when she got back. What happened? Did she fall off?"

The cornered cowboy catches my reflection in the mirror. Immediately, he drops it, preferring to inspect the floor rather than my disappointment. "No," he regroups, "she didn't fall off."

A pro at reading non-verbal clues, Mom senses a story and dives in, face first, for the kill. "Really? She's not the most graceful duckling in the pond. She learned to walk at nine months, which was amazing, but, because of it, she didn't crawl for long, and it hurt her coordination. She could have used more of this," Cruella mimics the back-and-forth, arm-and-hip swinging action of a crappy, crawling baby, sharing my faults with the room.

Can I have her committed? Please?

I swear, if I could choose a superpower, it would be the ability to explode people's heads with one look.

…focus…

Boom!

Ah…satisfaction.

Instead, unfortunately, like a cheap rubber band stretched to its limits, I snap.

"Mom, don't make me come over there!"

At the sound of my voice, Sam peeks at the mirror once more. Our eyes meet. Again. Instantly, his flit away. Again.

This is getting ridiculous.

Worse, Cruella doesn't miss a thing.

Too bad I don't have a typewriter instead of a computer, I could hang myself with the ribbon. Sling it over the light fixture, fashion a good, sturdy knot…stupid advanced technology.

Sarah bolts my way while I examine the computer cord, gauging its length. "Holy crap," she whispers cradling a tray of dirty dishes, marching toward the kitchen, "is that your mother?"

Vigorously I nod.

"Damn, girl…"

Caught in Mom's crosshairs, Sam flinches slightly backward, a stricken animal caught in a leg trap, clawing for purchase as it tries to slither away with its three remaining limbs. Instinctively, he parries my mother with a dodge. "It was a beautiful day for a ride."

He doesn't fool her. Skilled in advanced relationship warfare, she recognizes his noncommittal reply for what it is—conversational fodder—and it only fires a warning shot across her ample, heaving bow. Alert, she settles in, embracing the challenge. "Yes, it was a beautiful day, but did you have a good time? She didn't have a mommy issue, did she? That can't be helped. Well, I guess it can, but not without insurance. Oh, and bladder mesh."

What? What is she saying?

Oh, God, please, take me now.

Livid, I start to rise from my booth, ready to tackle her like a 'roided linebacker only to find my foot tangled in the computer cords. Are you kidding me? Is Karma on her side? Angrily I swing my ankle to no avail. Giving up, I squirm under the table to free myself.

Remarkably calm given the circumstances, Sam lobs another meaningless reply, "No, she didn't embarrass herself at all." From under my booth, his voice sounds odd, not happy, not angry, not sad, just…well, restrained. "She did great."

"Good," Mom purrs, no doubt biding her time, possibly hoping for more intel. She's cagey that way when intel is on the line. Especially if I'm the subject.

Suddenly, the diner bell rings breaking the awkwardness, and Charlie's voice booms like a death knell. "Hello, Sam."

Glancing from booth to hall, I gauge the distance between

them. Will anyone notice if I slither to the restroom on my stomach? I'm already down here, so I might as well.

Several gray-haired women at the next table bend toward me and whisper suggestions on bladder mesh, outpatient surgery, Kegels, and Depends. Oh goodie, one of them has a coupon.

Clearly, this won't be a clean exit.

I extract my foot and pop back up. Perhaps I can vault my way down the aisle and propel myself over my blabbering mother. If I land right, I'll be close to the door.

Whistling a happy tune, Charlie does a ninety-degree turn and scoots my way, blocking my escape. "There she is. You owe me a dinner date, young lady. How's this Friday?"

Oh...no...why didn't I stay under the table?

At the sight of fresh man meat, Mom shifts into high gear. "Excuse me, Sam, but Ro has a fish on the line, and Mamma needs to help her reel him in. She's out of practice. Let's catch up again soon." Plan in place, she trails after Charlie, oblivious to the gawking crowd, sweeping down the aisle, dragging the open mouths of Ernie and the Burts along in her wake like catfish on a stringer destined for the frying pan.

They descend upon me, Mom and Charlie, two thirsty mosquitoes, hovering, swarming my booth office. An expectant grin plasters his red, puffy face as he buzzes in my ear, railing on about a date. Mom halts next to him, trapping me on red pleather.

Immediately, I sweat through my stupid, tight, pinching skirt. Ick.

"Charlie, I...no, it's not a good time," I begin, adamant.

His face remains unmoved. Pasty white and expectant the man claps his hands together. "You won't believe what I've got planned for our date," Charlie announces.

Oh, say it ain't so.

He's making plans.

Did he not hear me? Am I speaking in tongues?

Inside the diner, the collective news quotient passes its implosion point. The locals hum, twittering excitedly, following Charlie, Mom, Sam, and their various conversations, contemplating dinners and trail rides and dates, and pie. Even Sarah has ground to a halt, clasping a coffee pot, watching, listening, most likely judging.

Channeling her inner judge and jury onto Charlie—whether for herself or for me, I can't say—Mom quantifies his value, polishes his flaws, and catalogs whatever good points he may or may not possess. Temporarily satisfied, she begins her further cross examination at my expense. "Hello," she purrs, "I'm Ro's mom, Kate. Are you asking my daughter on a date?"

Without even pausing for an answer, she pokes me in the shoulder. "Go out with him," she orders, as if it's settled.

"Mom, mind your own business. I don't have time."

"Phst." Like Charlie, she discounts me too as the next stupid idea crisscrosses her mind. Frowning, she squints at Charlie. "You're not a pervert, are you?" she asks.

Inspecting him from top to bottom, she searches for whatever visual clues she believes are common to—and observable in—potential small-town pervs. No doubt, Mom's got a list.

Charlie squirms under the glare of her internal pervert-o-meter. "No ma'am, I ain't no pervert. I'm Charlie Turner. I own the largest construction company in the county. Her brother works for me, a tall, lanky blond guy."

Her eyes twinkle. "Why, yes, my son, Justin."

Oddly relieved at the news, he fist-bumps vacant air. "Good to hear it from another mouth. Didn't want to end up in anything kinky. There's a rumor going around she's a lesbian. 'Course I was more worried she was married. Glad to know she ain't either."

"Right now, I wish I was," I offer to no one since they're completely tuning me out anyway.

As the words 'kinky' and 'lesbian' slingshot around the room, two older women several tables away reach their limit. They wave at Sarah and signal for their bills, but she ignores them, instead topping off coffee cups at another table despite the protests of its customers who are, in fact, drinking hot tea.

"A lesbian?" repeats Mom. "That's hardly a problem…for you okay, it'd be an issue, but, no, she's not a lesbian. Though a little kink wouldn't kill her." Mom winks at Charlie before addressing me. "He's funny, kiddo. Go out with him."

"I'm not dating! Not now; not ever!"

"Don't listen to her," Mom coos. "She says she's not ready, but she is."

A few quick taps on the keyboard, I Google the causes of spontaneous combustion, not only for me, hell, Mom, Charlie, Sarah, Sam, even the old lady with the Depends coupon, they're all on my list. I'm ready to toast the bunch of them and dance barefoot in their ash piles. Unfortunately, Google fails me, forcing me to rub my thighs together instead, generating some serious kilowatts as my only back-up plan. With any luck, I'll spark and fry.

Oblivious to my Google search, Charlie squirms, perhaps

excited at the prospect of a little kink. "You know what they say. When you fall off a horse, you gotta get right back on. Dating's like that too, you know…"

"No, it's not," I reply to the walls, apparently.

"…you've gotta just go for it. Tell you what, I'll pick you up on Friday. How's 4:00?" Before I can protest yet again, he hollers toward the front of the diner. "Hey Sam, will you let Ro off early on Friday? She's got a hot date with me."

What the hell? Am I mute? Did I fall into another dimension where I can only be seen and not heard?

This conversation's becoming a speeding car with no brakes, out of control, running down a hill, and I'm tied in the trunk and apparently gagged. This needs to stop.

Have I mentioned I'm tired of being steamrolled by men? And my mother? No?

I am. I'm totally sick of it.

Oddly enough, a steamy, touchy lifeline appears, tossed by the kiss-and-run cowboy, giving me hope. "That's up to Edmund." Sam's voice fills the room, firm, stiff, unyielding, though that's not what I want firm, stiff, and unyielding on the cowboy.

Stop it, Ro. He ran, remember?

Regardless, I grab that lifeline and hang on. "See, I have to work. End of story."

Finally noting my date reluctance, Mom skewers me, visually slicing and dicing me with a keen, knowing expression, though what she knows has never been apparent to me, primarily because she's bat-shit Crazy with a capital C. Frustratingly determined to get me laid, which sucks, she continues her barrage.

"Who's Edmund?" she cries, surveying the room. "Of course, he'll let her off. Ro, go ask this Edmund guy if you can get off early on Friday."

Maybe I should carry a spray bottle of water for occasions such as this, squirt her in the face a few times, dose her in a stream of H2O. I hear it works on cats.

Instead, I forge a mental shopping list and drum my fingers on the table. "Mom, I am not taking off early on Friday."

Except to buy a spray bottle.

Forgetful of the temporary nature of my part-time, uninsured job, she presses, "Why can't you?"

"One, I have to work, and two, I don't want to go on a date."

"Yes, you do, you just don't know it yet. Besides, you're part-time," she exclaims before whirling ninety degrees in the direction of my boss. "Sam," Mom hollers over a half-dozen blue-haired women, two of whom are still arguing the existence of tofu meatless loaf, "isn't she part-time?"

A quick peek in the mirror provides a profile of Sam, terse, agitated, uncomfortable, begging the question, is it because of me?

Immediate answers escape me, leaving my negative imagination to its own devices.

Not good.

At the register, Sam busies himself, paying Rachel. "Yes, she is," he replies, digging for change, "but she's being trained, and I'm not sure what Edmund has planned for her this week." Folding his wallet, he shoves it in the back jeans pocket currently hugging his magnificent ass. "It's his call, not mine."

I drag myself away from Sam's reflection and focus on the invoice. "There you have it, Mom." I smirk. "I'm being trained. You can't argue with that. Plus," I say loud enough for all to hear, shaking my head no, "I'm not ready to date!"

Clearly one for similes—not to mention tuning out uncooperative women—Charlie prattles on, earning my wrath "I think you're Mom's right—time to rip off that bandage. Saturday, it is then. I'll pick you up at 4:00. More time for fun that way. Gotta hop, I'm bidding on a commercial building in Jenkins. Hope you like seafood."

Practically skipping the length of the restaurant, he stops halfway out the door, his face peeking around the frame, a plump groundhog searching for his shadow. "Don't worry, I got your address."

"Forget about it, I'm not going! You're just wasting your time!"

"You're funny, Ro. Catch 'ya later. Saturday, to be exact," he jokes, my protests dying on my lips and in his ears. With that, he disappears, on his way to Jenkins, making plans for Saturday that include me and, apparently, dead fish.

This. Sucks. Balls.

Mentally, spiritually, if not yet physically, I engulf Mom in flames. Thanks to her, Charlie plans to show up on our doorstep this weekend for a date I don't want. On second thought, if whatever seafood emporium Charlie thinks he's dragging me to has a giant lobster tank that's bigger than the fry vat, there's a chance I can crawl inside and drown.

Oh yay. A silver lining.

The computer monitor tempts me with blissful, mind-numbing work, drawing me away from my problems if only for the promise of a few hours. Squaring up to the keyboard, I type.

Unfortunately, it's not to be. Mom, who was never good with hints, takes off her biker jacket and tosses it onto the seat across from me, then plops down, apparently planning to stay awhile.

Lucky me...

A hard-edged knife, Sam's voice cuts through the diner. "Ro, no need for you to come to the elevator today." Behind the counter, her mouth frozen in a what-the-hell-is-happening-O, Rachael gives him a to-go cup and a carry-out bag. "I'll be in the field all afternoon. Whatever we need to work we'll tackle on Wednesday." He shoves the diner door open, the bell blasts overhead, and—poof—he's gone.

Elvis has left the building.

Jesus, that was uncomfortable.

All smirks and smiles and psycho eyes, Cruella wallows in smug satisfaction. "Well?" she cackles.

To the roar of background chatter taking place at my expense, I grow a thicker skin and plug in numbers. "Well, what, Maleficent?"

Lacquered fingernails tap on the table. "Aren't you going to thank me?"

Stunned into silence, I freeze.

Is she kidding me?

"Thank you? Seriously, thank you? For what? For trying to stick me with a date I don't want? I'm not going."

"Yes, you are."

"No, I'm not and you can't make me. I'm not five anymore, and I'm certainly not going to thank you for sticking your big mouth in my business."

An impish sparkle lights her animated clown face. "I'm not talking about your date, kiddo, which, yes, you are going on—"

"For the love of God, let's be clear about this. I'm not going out with that two-legged slug."

"Whatever. I'm talking about stirring up Sam." Light reflects off her pearly white dentures. Insanity twinkles in her pupils.

Too bad she's older and bruises easy. If she were a few years younger, I could kick her under the table. No one would blame me either. Though she's wearing spiked heels, another battle I have no chance of winning today. Cutting my losses, I seek clarification, begging for insight into her whack job of a thought process. "You want me to thank you for pissing off my boss? Am I hearing that right?"

"No, little one, for making him jealous. Lord, Ro, you can be so slow sometimes." The clown smile spanning her face dims in disappointment.

"Wow, Mom, and insults too. This day keeps getting better and better. Don't take this the wrong way—no, wait, do, *do* take it the wrong way. Butt out of my life!"

Concern touches her face, and I'm reminded that, deep down, she believes she's helping in her own odd, irritating way, even if she isn't.

Still, I'm not ready to cut her any slack.

Hiding behind my monitor, I plug in numbers. "Why are you even here?"

She snags my coffee mug and helps herself to a sip. "Olivia sent me. You have the paint samples for the kids' bedrooms. I'm running to the hardware store."

Wow. A legitimate excuse to bug me. Who knew?

Fishing around in my purse, I find Olivia's swatches and mine, then slide them across the table, tapping on a peachy square circled in pen. "Get me two gallons, please. I'll pay you back on Friday. In fact, I think I'll paint Maddy's room Saturday evening. Works for me, seeing how I don't have any plans."

The swatches disappear into her cavernous purse and, circling back to the dreaded Charlie, she clucks at me, "A date with that man won't kill you, and, trust me, I get it, you're not interested."

"Then why on earth—"

"You like Sam. Admit it! It's plastered all over your face," she interrupts, too loudly for my comfort given the surroundings, "plus, he likes you—don't deny it," she raises her palm toward me, halting me in mid-denial. "I'm telling you, that man is interested too, but he's conflicted for some reason. Could be because he's your boss…"

Or is it because I have a house full of young, crumb-covered children and a personal penchant for clutter and chaos? All possible deal breakers for Mr. Clean, perhaps?

"…you've got to come at him a bit differently," Mom reasons, oblivious to my fears, blabbering on. "No full-frontal assault on Sam. Ease into it like a tub of hot water, one toe at a time."

Indulging in exasperation, I scoff, "Do tongues count?"

"Sure," she shrugs, "who am I to judge? Kiddo, go out with this Charlie guy, shake out the cobwebs, and get a good meal out of it at least."

"Geez, Mom, enough, already, no!"

"What? I mean is if he's going to be that much of a pushy ass, you should at least order the lobster. And the steak. But don't get drunk."

Should I bang my head on the table? If I'm lucky and hit it

hard enough, I could bypass this conversation with a soothing round of unconsciousness. It has a certain appeal.

As I have to work, however, I resort to sighing instead. "Jesus, Mother. Please, just stop."

"Hey, Jesus knew the value of loaves and fishes too, and he wasn't above handing out free meals either, but the point I'm trying to make is, Sam needs to understand if he drags his feet too long, he's going to miss out. I'm not saying date this other guy long term, just one simple date," she declares, clearly on a roll. "No rooster wants another cock scratching around in his hen pen, and if Sam's the man I think he is, he'll be crowing a different tune."

There you have it. The dysfunctional logic of the insane.

Across from me, Mom lets her weird advice sink in.

Maybe she thinks I'll come around, which is pointless since I blacked out immediately after she said Sam and cock in the same sentence.

Impatient, she squirms, before blurting, "Still no thank you?"

Both agitated and ticked off, I ignore her and return to my blessed, nonjudgmental numbers. Snippets of nearby conversations buzz past me. Words I try to avoid float on the breeze, catching my ear, sucking me in, words like, "Sam" and "Charlie" and "date" and "dinner" but, thankfully, not "cock."

It's enough to make me scream.

Taking pity for once, Mom rises from the booth, a vibrant, loud-mouthed dragon taking flight, giving me hope for some peace during this shit hole of a day. "Clearly now is not the time," she says, slipping on her gloves. "I'll leave you to your work, but know this, Sam is intrigued by you. Date Charlie, don't date Charlie, whatever, it's your call. But," she finishes, donning her jacket, preparing to leave, "any athlete will tell you to practice before the big game. If Sam is the World Series, take a warm-up run at this Charlie fellow. Work out the kinks and the anger," she continues sharing more logic, "plus, it sure wouldn't hurt you to get laid."

Platters crash a few tables away. Sarah, having collided with a chair, temporarily blinded by Mom's last suggestion, stands frozen in place, surrounded by ceramic carnage, taking in my mother's words with burning ears and saucer-sized eyes bulging from her head.

Trust me, I know the feeling.

To my great relief, Mom picks her way around Sarah's mess— "You need to be more careful, sweetie," she shares in passing—and sweeps toward the door. Floating by Ernie and the Burts, whose dentures must be dusty at this point, she chirps a happy, "Goodbye gentlemen."

Snapped out of his conversation-induced haze, Ernie shakes himself, an old, wet, startled dog, and mutters an awe-struck, "Goodbye."

Together, the trio follows her progress through the diner, sucked in her colorful wake, slaves to curiosity. Happy to acknowledge any fanboys regardless of wrinkles, Mom rewards them with a flirty wink and a princess wave.

Gag.

I slump into my booth and try to clear my mind, conversations around me be damned, but the reality of what she said plagues me. Any chance she's right?

No.

Maybe?

No. No, I've got to cancel this disaster, though I don't even have Charlie's phone number.

Why Mothers Should Be Required to Wear Ankle Monitors…another potential idea to add to my list of future blog posts. That one should write itself.

The spreadsheet calls out, begging attention, but images of Sam consume me. While I desperately need to finish this task, I let my gaze wander to the window where it lands on the grain elevator, seeking Sam.

What the hell?

Another image distracts me from my internal temptation. Animated and gesturing wildly, Mom hogs the sidewalk, engaged in what appears to be a heated conversation with my nemesis neighbor, Judge Middleton, possibly telling him where to stick a tree.

Yay. More good Karma coming our way.

Finally, she snubs the judge and storms past him, her sights set on the hardware store. He glares after her, no doubt both shocked and bewildered, before stomping away in the opposite direction.

It's good she's making friends.

Switching focus, I tear myself away from Mom and her path of destruction to look across the street. Sam's truck is in its usual spot, so tantalizingly close. And yet…

…I'm haunted by the kiss.

Unlike Mom, I'm not convinced he wants me.

Which really, really sucks.

~ * ~

Time flies when you have something to dread and, before I can blink, I'm staring down the tail-end of a Saturday I wish had never come, face-to-face with the date I don't want with Charlie. It threatens like a prison sentence I can't outrun and pardon me while I puke.

Here's my problem—I caved, then I waffled. I let Mom get to me, and I contemplated the disaster until it was nearly too late.

Trust me, when I came to my senses, I tried calling it off, repeatedly, but I don't have his cell phone number, and I'm certainly not asking him for it either. I figured he'd come into the diner Friday, providing me a chance to beg for a raincheck I never intend to cash but, tone deaf as he is, he must smell my reluctance. He stayed far away all week, not unlike Peter's support checks.

Bribing Justin was no help either. I begged him to slip Charlie a note at work, asked him for a number I could text, but no dice. When pressed, my unhelpful baby brother hemmed and hawed and made feeble complaints about not being twelve. Lame, right? Anyway, that option faded too.

The real kicker is Charlie's office. Every time I call—and, trust me, I call, even this morning—he's never around. What a turd.

Zero-hour approaches. Olivia's grandfather clock booms out the bottom of the hour, announcing my doom. I, however, am not going down without a fight. Five moving boxes and counting, I'm searching for my backup plan. It's here somewhere…ah, victory. Wrinkles and all, I throw on the novelty T-shirt Mom gifted me two summers ago. It's a lovely purple-tinged puce which makes my Irish skin look ghastly and clashes with the evergreen phrase *My-Mom-Went-To-Dildo-Island-And-All-I-Got-Was-This-Lousy-T-Shirt* emblazoned across my ta-ta's. Perfect.

Mom's voice bounds up the stairwell. "Ten minutes, Ro. Get your ass down here!"

Can I make a break for it? Hit the road, thumb my way to Canada? Not the worse idea I've had. Contemplating this date earlier in the week qualifies as that one.

Who am I kidding? This late in the afternoon, I'll never make it to Chicago on foot and Mom's hid my car keys. There's no other way around it.

Reluctant date time, here I come.

Once again, I'm screwed.

Not in the good way.

~ * ~

"Look at your watch," Charlie commands in his take-charge voice. His truck is stopped in the middle of a road between two empty fields as we travel who knows where. Like Sam's truck, Charlie's is freakishly neat, begging the question, what is it with the men in this town?

"Humor me," he implores, "look at your watch."

What? More importantly, why? I hold up my wrist, modeling my lack of jewelry, which matches my lack of makeup, as well as my lack of interest. "I'm not wearing one."

Charlie ogles my naked wrist, then me, unfazed by the T-shirt and old athletic bra uni-boob I'm sprouting. "You've got one of those stopwatch apps on your phone, right?" Convinced I'm watchless, he checks out my boob log next.

If he's smart, he better be searching for evidence of a cell phone because it's not too early to kick him in the nuts.

Digging it out of my purse, I brandish my phone in the air. "What next?"

Chubby palms rub together in glee. Anticipation blooms across his clean-shaven, pudgy, oddly boyish face, "Okay, when I say go, start timing."

Confused, but game, I flash my app. "Ready when you are."

"Well, now..." Goofy, fish lips protrude from his puffy face and he stretches my way, leading with his chin. "Well, now." He puckers.

Ew.

"Not for that!" My voice echoes in the truck cab, and I lurch backward.

Should I cut bait and run? What are the odds he has child-proof locks and they're engaged?

Thwarted, he pulls back. Fish lips stand down. "I'm kidding you," he pretends. With hands locked at ten and two, he grips the steering wheel, focused on the long, flat road. "Get ready."

Get ready?

"You're not going to floor it, are you?" My life may be challenged, but I don't want to check out on an Illinois backroad surrounded by corn stubble and pieces of horny, middle-aged playboy any time soon.

"Oh, no." He chuckles. "Get ready...and...go."

A double check of my seatbelt for safety's sake, I push start and brace myself.

To my left, Charlie steps on the gas. Together we roll down the road at a glacial twenty-mile-per-hour pace, hardly what I expected. Whereas I imagined some death-defying road race, instead, he crawls down the road, one hand on the wheel, the other on the console, tapping and twitching, burning adrenaline as we motor in slow motion. A smile lights his wide, expectant face and his country noggin bobs and rattles as we meander between the fields. Puttering on, he shifts from watching the road—though there's really no need at this non-existent rate—to checking his side window filled with reflections of harvest stubble, to smiling at me like some organ-grinding monkey searching for a nut.

It's weird. Worse yet, it goes on and on...and on. Charlie drives and grins. I sit and stare and time the drive, getting creeped out, hoping I'm being pranked.

What the hell kind of a date is this?

We clear the cornfield and Charlie shouts, "Time!"

Startled, my phone slips through my fingers and lands face up on his laser-cut, freakishly clean floor liner where it continues to count my boredom.

In a panic, he hollers, "Get it, quick, shut it off! It won't count if it keeps going."

What won't count? My inescapable desire to be somewhere else, perhaps?

I push stop and pick it up, flashing the time at Charlie.

He squints at the time, frowning. "That's okay. We only need to shave off a few seconds."

A minute-and-thirty-nine painful seconds have crawled by at a glacial rate, a minute and thirty-five if you subtract my clumsy, dropsy three or four, and I have no clue what gives. Shrugging, I pry, "What the hell?"

Inflating, Charlie sits taller. "That field's the longest in the county," he shares. His chest puffs with pride or possibly indigestion. "I own it."

"Ah," is all I can muster.

"See how long it is? That there is the longest field in the county," he repeats, perhaps hoping the magnitude will sink through my suburban ignorance.

It doesn't. I'm dumbfounded.

Underscoring the importance of his achievement, Charlie examines the field in his rearview mirror, enamored with himself, most likely happy in the knowledge that I'm now aware he owns this big-ass field. "Huge, isn't it."

Men, Size, And Penis Proxies...blog topic number forty-two and counting.

Occasionally subtle, but ever ironic, I decide to throw him a bone. "It's good-looking field."

He cruises down the road, shedding a vibe of self-importance my way. "You bet, all nine hundred acres of it. I got a combine with the

GPS system to harvest it—precision steering—and I rent Harley Cooper's too, just for this field. Time is money."

"Speaking of time," I start, hoping this dog will hunt, "I can't be out too late. My youngest isn't feeling well." It's not a total lie. She did have a cough, but I'm thankful she was upstairs when Charlie arrived.

He, however, ignores my motherly concern and drives on. "Oh, heck, she's in good hands."

Ah...*The Great American Male Brush-Off of Womanly Concerns*. More future blog fodder.

What awaits me now? A giant barn? A ball of twine? The county's largest meth lab?

Good thing there's room on my phone for pictures.

We've left the big-ass field behind and travel southwest through a part of the county I have yet to explore. The land is flat and nondescript. Fields of corn stubble tradeoff between fields of soybean stubble with an occasional field of winter wheat stubble included in the mix. The stubble on my unshaven legs fits in nicely. Field after field fly by my window.

"Where are we going?" I ask, desperate for intel.

Gleefully in charge, Charlie whistles a bouncy little ditty. "You'll see."

He's a happy man, I'll give him that much. Of course, lacking any real sense of self-awareness, how could he not be? He probably imagines he's more fun than a barrel of monkeys. And me without an organ to grind.

Not one to be left in the dark, I press once more, "No, seriously, where are we going?"

Unconcerned with my concern, Charlie concentrates on the road. "It's a surprise. Care for some music?"

Beaten, I give up my line of questioning and settle for rubbernecking out the window. "Sure. I'd love some."

Country music fills the cab as Charlie turns onto the next road. We travel through flat farmland while he sings out loud about girls with bodacious ba-donk-a-donk.

He treats me to a suggestive wink.

Wait, oh, no, why did I wear the jeans that make my butt look big? Perhaps if I clench, it'll shave off a few inches. I sneak a peek at my hips.

Wow. It doesn't.

Bound together in this four-wheel prison, we ride on, tortured minute after tortured minute, closing in on the county airport. Finally, it stretches across the spent landscape, and beyond the tarmac, rises the unexpected—a beautiful hot-air balloon. Deep red at the top, it glows against the brilliant blue late-autumn sky as it fades from burnt orange to golden yellow. The car belonging to Eli, the young cook from the diner, is parked next to it, and, for the first time tonight, my spirits perk up.

"Is this the surprise?"

Please say yes, please say yes, please say yes...

Charlie launches into full wind-up monkey mode. His cheeks must ache from the strain, he's smiling so wide. "Sure is. What'd you say? Want to go up in that thing with me?"

A floating mass of color, the balloon fills the sky, gleaming in radiant colors, igniting my imagination. I'm entranced. Life is meant to be lived, not endured, even if that includes a one-time date with Charlie.

Contemplating the splendid adventure before me, I rally. "You bet your sweet ass I'll go up in that thing."

Elated, he smacks the truck console. "Hot damn, now we're talking! Let's go ballooning."

We enter the airport grounds and park next to Eli's car in the shadow of the balloon. From inside its basket, the young fry cook waves. "Hi, Ro."

Leaping from the truck, I rush ahead, leaving Charlie sputtering in the cab. Before me, the tension on the ropes is palpable. Goosebumps erupt along my arms as I step beneath the floating beast towering above me. Overhead it spans the empty air, nothing but color-tinted space, wonderful, wide open, glorious space. Only hot air and fabric will keep me aloft in a matter of minutes. It's beyond exhilarating.

"Hi, Eli. Is this yours?"

He tugs the throttle of a large burner suspended below the massive space. A giant blue tongue of flame scorches the air. "No, it belongs to the airport, but don't worry. I'm certified. Someday, hopefully, I'll have one." Nodding toward an older man standing outside the basket, Eli continues, "Ro, this is my dad. He's helping me launch."

Charlie joins me and greets Eli's father. "Hi, Mark. When you going to sell me your thirty acres in Gowdy? You could use the money to buy your boy here a balloon."

A bemused expression crosses the man's face. "Not today, Charlie, like the last five times you asked me."

"It never hurts to try," he muses. "Let me know when you

change your mind."

Uninterested in Charlie's business dealings, I grip the taut line, and energy reverberates through my arm. Expectation courses through me too. I'm dying to climb aboard.

As if reading my mind, Eli unlocks the basket gate. "Come on in. It's a great day for a ride."

Tripping over myself, I join him and head to the rail, not wanting to miss a second of this unexpected treat. For a moment, I contemplate texting Olivia, but stop myself. Mom must never know I enjoyed myself. I'd never hear the end of it.

Unfinished business tabled for now, Charlie leaves Mark behind and rushes in too. "Don't forget me. I'm paying for this trip, you know."

Naturally…the unenlightened male cry for required economic acknowledgement.

Squared away in the basket, I make room for Charlie, but he snugs in beside me way too close, practically hip to hip.

Basket gate closed, Eli adjusts the throttle and releases a clamp. "We'll go north, beyond Poseyville. I'll shoot for Cagney Park. If we catch a tailwind though, we may make it as far as the soccer fields outside of Dunreith. We'll play it by ear."

His father picks up a tow line, unlocks another clamp from a large hook embedded in the concrete, and steps back. "Sounds good. Have fun. I'll see you when you land."

With that, Eli cranks a large lever. A loud snap fills the air. More clamps open, releasing ropes, and, like an express elevator in a high rise, the balloon rushes upward. We're off.

Harvested fields of corn and soy crisscross the patchwork-quilted land below. White farmhouses, silver equipment sheds, and red barns dot the landscape. Trees, naked of their leaves, run in lines along fence rows and roadways, and pop up in yards and pastures. Church steeples stretch skyward, pointing to the stars. In the far distance, almost lost in the haze, gleams Poseyville, my newfound hometown which actually is starting to feel like home.

"Ain't that something?" Charlie sighs.

Too taken with the view to speak, I stay silent. Our slow ascent to the clouds is quiet, peaceful, the stillness broken only by the occasional sound of the heater keeping us aloft. Gazing upon the town, warmth floods my heart. This town, that home, these people, they're all worming themselves into my life in ways I never imagined.

Charlie drapes an arm over my shoulder, derailing my bliss, and involuntarily I stiffening then sidestep away. Finally taking a hint, he lowers his arm and plays it off as nothing.

What does he think the current dating exchange rate is for hot-air balloon rides these days? If he's smart, he better not be thinking blow job.

Double ick.

Casting off that mental image, I give into the view and lose myself in the joy. Along we glide, cruising through the brilliant blue, a colorful dot meandering without purpose or plan except to ride the thermal currents wherever they take us. It speaks to me, this aimless wandering. Who knew a hot air balloon would be such a relevant metaphor for my life?

The existential nature of our undirected travel is lost on my date, however. Instead, Charlie shifts from one foot to the other, either agitated, bored, restless—it's hard to tell—and, rather than mediate on any possible meaning of life, he settles for vapid small talk. "I almost bought a plane once," he confides.

"Yeah," I mutter, semi-lost in my contemplative daze.

He squirms. "I thought about one of those plane time shares too," he continues, "that way you only pay for what you use."

"You mean like a commercial flight," I poke.

Silence.

A car threads through fields far below.

More silence.

Charlie inches closer. "I suppose, kinda like that, yeah, but not as fun."

"Hmmm," I murmur, content to watch a flock of geese disappearing in the distance.

He sighs. "I figured you'd be more of a talker."

Imagine that.

Me. A talker. Who'd of thunk it?

Treating him to a sideways glance, I chuckle but remain silent.

"Thought you'd have more to say, I mean," he clarifies.

Giving in, I gesture at the landscape. "We can talk in the truck. This," I reply with a sweep of my arm, pointing at the view, "needs savored."

Unsure how to refute the obvious, Charlie settles himself against the rail. "Okay, I guess we'll check out the view."

Should I get out my stopwatch and time him?

Nah.

Content in the silence, I settle in too. We rise, and my spirit soars.

Let's hope it lasts.

~ * ~

When we ascend to cruising altitude, the current turns due north, pushing us shy of Poseyville. From this height, I make out the grain elevator and the diner across the street. Without forethought or effort, I trace the main road from town until I find it, Thornhill, tall and proud, high on the ridge. Its grayish white hulk sits regal upon the hilltop surrounded by its russet crown of trees. Joy engulfs me.

Strange as it sounds, it's becoming home. My home.

We've been at this for two hours, at the mercy of the breeze, floating above the land. The balloon descends into the lower currents, traveling farther north. Against my wishes, my eyes take on their own agenda. I follow the riverbanks alongside a roadway I traveled only hours ago. Crisscrossing the basket, I face west, keeping the road in sight, pretending I'm enjoying the impending sunset, though I'm doing nothing of the sort.

Instead, I search for a log cabin.

Sam's farm is in the near distance, taunting me in the golden evening glow. The barn and corral come into view and, in the pasture beyond, a small black and white dot trots around a larger brown one and a solid black one too, Butterball, Dick, and Dancer out to pasture. I trace the path we took, by the woods, through the field, past the next tree line to the pond...to the cabin.

We're flying straight for it and dropping. As we do, the current ebbs, and we hover over woods and fields, creeping along, a ponderous pace that allows ample time for painful scrutiny below.

Scouring the landscape, I see it. Parked next to a wood pile near the cabin sits Sam's truck. Eagerness and anger mix in varying degrees. While I don't want to, even as I tell myself not to, I can't help but wonder.

Where's Sam?

Against my better judgement I rake the ground, searching for him, seeking evidence of his presence, though he remains unseen. It's torturous, this unprovoked searching. Where is he?

Freshly split firewood lays next to the cabin, calling out to his penchant for neatness, begging to be stacked. Buried in a stump, a gleaming ax waits to split its next hard wood victim, and a chain saw rests on the lowered tailgate of his truck.

He has to be close.

"You might want to come back over here," Charlie calls from the other side of the balloon. "We're close to Flat Rock Falls. They ain't much, but they sure look different from up here."

Uninterested, I scan the ground, searching, seeking.

"You might want to check it out," he tries again. A hint of desperation rings in my ears, yet I ignore him.

Beneath us, the cabin door opens, and Sam emerges. Buff, sexy, and rugged, even from here, he crosses the porch and leans against a post. Whether lost in thought or lost in a daydream, I can't tell, but what I *can* tell is simple enough.

I want him.

sigh

What am I doing? This, it isn't healthy.

After all, he doesn't want me.

Even as I ask these questions, even as I tell myself over and over to stop obsessing over him, to give up on this fantasy, my body, my heart, my soul do what they do best—ignore my mind and flood me with need. Usually it's cookies. Sometimes it's wine. These days, it's Sam.

The world around me dissolves. Having found my goal, I lock in on him.

This, right here, it's all wrong. I'm up here, in this balloon with Charlie, when all I want is to be down there, grounded, with Sam. I hover over him and the cabin where we kissed, in a balloon with a buffoon too oblivious to realize he doesn't stand a chance. It's true, I want a man who doesn't want me, yet despite it all, if the mooring ropes were long enough, even if my arms aren't strong enough, I would risk it and climb down.

A roaring blast of energy breaks the silence. Eli hits the throttle, sending blue flames to lick the air, keeping us aloft, startling me out of my reverie.

Snapping his attention skyward, possibly shocked at the sight of a massive balloon drifting overhead, Sam catches sight of us.

It's too much.

I regroup and wave.

He hesitates, then waves back.

Charlie pops to my side, presses against me, and waves as well.

Stupid Charlie.

Sam drops his gaze, then steps off the porch to amble to the wood pile. He grabs the axe, sets up a log, and gives a powerful swing, splitting it in two, cleaving my heart as well.

So much for going slow, huh?

At a snail's pace we glide over the cabin, beyond the pond, ever onward, leaving him behind.

In our wake, Sam cleaves log after log, driving blow after blow with strong legs, powerful arms, a broad back. At long last he stops and, finally leaning against the ax handle, he gazes at the balloon and watches us drift away.

If I truly were a sparrow, I'd take flight and leave this basket behind, glide down, join him. Or fly away, far, far, away. Both are preferable to this.

Eli's voice cuts through my thoughts. "Hey, Sam." He's on his cell phone making new plans. "Do you mind if we set down in your bean field? The wind's laid down and, at this pace, we won't make it to Cagney Park before sunset."

Growing smaller with each gentle breeze, Sam talks into his cell, forming words I can't hear, while I watch him shrink in the distance.

Is this as weird for him as it is for me?

Probably not. To him, this may mean nothing, just an unplanned intrusion into his otherwise blissful Ro-free Saturday night. For him, it was probably only a simple kiss, opportunistically taken and nothing more.

Well, that hurts.

Stupid brain.

Plans made, Eli replies, "Great Sam, thanks. We'll see you in a few."

No.

Of all the things I planned *not* to do on this date, running into Sam while stuck here with Charlie ranked high on the list. Seeing him from a distance is bad enough. Karma, please don't make me face him now.

Ignorant of personal boundaries, Charlie invades my space yet again. "This has been a real treat. I hope you liked it as much as I did. It's kind of hard to tell." He scratches his chin, his expression somewhat puzzled. "You've been so quiet."

His voice demands attention, though I only have eyes for Sam, yet I manage a respectful reply, "It's been a beautiful ride, Charlie. Thank you."

"You're welcome."

The balloon plummets at a steady rate. We drift beyond the barn, over Sam's house, our destination a large, empty field to the north.

Preparing to land, Eli readies ropes and adjusts the throttle. "Dad's on his way," he shares as we fall from the sky. "He'll run you guys back to the airport."

Our joy ride nearly over, Charlie goes for his wallet. "Good, that works. What do I owe you? Two hundred and fifty, wasn't it?" He shouts the amount, clearly relishing the moment.

What's up with that? Is he desperate for credit for the money he's spent on this ride? That would probably run true to form. I've had him pegged as the kind of man who keeps score and tallies debts owed, even unwanted date debts.

Conflicted, I'm not sure how to respond. Would I have fought harder to cancel this date had I known the cost, both mental and financial? What is he expecting beyond sincere appreciation? Does he want me to dry hump his leg in thanks?

Dating; it's such a mind fuck.

I focus on the impending sunset. The sun drops with the balloon, darkening the blue sky. It erupts in color, taking on deep shades of purple, pink, orange, and red, a masterful abstract worthy of the finest art galleries.

Heedless to the light show, Charlie conducts his business. "A tip is in order too," he announces, adding more moolah to our growing date tally. "How's fifty grab you?"

Ugh.

I should have chained myself to an attic beam.

We're yards from the ground now, too low to make out Sam, his truck, or the cabin. We glide forward and down at the same time until the basket's lower edge scrapes along short stumps of dead plant stubble. The basket's bottom lip touches the ground, finds purchase, and with a tiny lurch and a slight sway we land, gentle as can be.

If only my heart would sink so softly.

Gripping the basket edge, I wait for Eli to signal our departure, desperate to retreat though there's nowhere to go, even as I keep watch for Sam.

Price paid, Charlie hems and haws, seeking a response. "Pretty neat, huh?"

Where's Mark's truck? He's coming, right? He's my ride out of this hell.

Where's Sam's truck? He's coming right? I can't let him see me with Charlie. He may not care, but I do.

"Ro?" Charlie says, "Pretty neat, wasn't it?"

Distracted, I mumble, "I'll say."

Emboldened, my clueless date comes in hot and fast. There's no time to even flinch. He grips me tight.

Startled—not to mention annoyed—I twist my face to his shoulder as he buzz-kisses my hair, and I pat his back, humoring him like a wet dog. Naturally, because Karma is a wicked serial killer who intends to stalk me until my death, Sam pulls in behind us, an uninvited spectator to our uncomfortable, unwanted embrace.

I can't catch a break.

The truck door slams shut. Itching for release, I struggle to extract myself from fat-fingered Charlie who, finally taking yet another hint, lets me go.

From a safe distance away, Sam contemplates the ground.

Eli shuts off the gas and kills the throttle. "Thanks, Sam. I appreciate it." He opens the basket gate and motions for Charlie and me to climb out. "Dad should be here any minute."

The cowboy's face is blank. "Don't mention it," he replies. "No rush. I was finishing up anyway."

Awkwardness lands with the balloon. I'm unsure of what to do next. Taking the safe approach, I examine the colorful canvas. Devoid of hot air, unlike my date, it eases its way to earth, deflating gently. Like me, it's limp, weak, falling, and fading fast.

Busying himself with the mooring lines, Eli secures the basket and keeps talking. "I'll get this all squared away while Dad takes them back to the airport. We'll be out of your hair in no time."

Sam rocks on his boot heels. "Take your time." Finding the ground more interesting than me, he scours it, avoiding my eyes.

Frustrated, I look away. A sigh escapes me.

Once more Sam speaks. "Did you enjoy the ride, Ro?"

Charlie takes my wrist, claiming his territory before I can respond. "You bet we did. It was a real treat."

Repulsed, I jerk it away.

Blessed with keen peripheral vision, the quiet cowboy lifts an eyebrow but says nothing.

Charlie, however, is nonplussed. "I wouldn't mind doing that again someday. What'da say, Ro? You want to go again?"

Great, now what? Say yes and let Charlie think he's got the green light for a future ride while making Sam believe I'm interested in another date? Say no and make Eli believe I didn't enjoy myself, thereby losing the opportunity for another amazing ride?

Or should I stand here, silent, like I didn't understand the question? Giggle like a freaking stooge? Don't men like it when women giggle?

Fuck you, Karma. I'm over this.

Thoroughly ticked off with the lot of them—fry cook excluded, bless his young, innocent, hot-air-ballooning heart—I turn my back on the two older men, and it's oddly, amusingly satisfying. "Eli," I gush because I mean it, "that was amazing. I'd love to do it again sometime, and next time I'll buy," I finish, gaining steam along with backbone.

Charlie's turn next.

Surging with anger-laced gumption, I face my pushy date straight on, prepared to end this charade. "Charlie, thank you for this. I never expected to go up in a balloon today. It was awesome." Offering my hand, I set my own date exchange rate—honest gratitude plus a brief, platonic shake. Sounds even to me. If he wants a tip, I'll chuck him on the shoulder.

Confused, he blinks rapidly, unable to translate. "Hey, the date's just getting started, honey."

So much for an even exchange. Cognizant of the fragile male ego, I switch tactics and opt for a harmless lie. "About that," I start, "I'm going to beg off for the rest of the date. My head is pounding, and I don't have any aspirin in my purse—"

Sam shifts on his boots and interjects, "I have some in the house."

Ignoring my kiss-and-run boss, I plow on, steamrolling Charlie as I do, "—and I'm worried about Maddy. If you don't mind, I'd like Eli's dad to drop me off at the house when we leave. Let's call it a night."

Mouth gaping, Charlie balks. "It's only going on seven. I was going to take you to Dunreith. The A&W has a fish fry on Saturday nights, plus the drive-in's playing the *Creature from the Black Lagoon*. I didn't know if you like old black and white films, but this one's a real treat."

Geez, I feel bad. It's kind of sweet how much effort he's put into this date, but sweetness won't buy my interest any day of the week. Going, eating, talking, it would all be a distraction, delaying the inevitable until I'm forced to make him face the reality that we are simply not going to happen. Better to rip off the bandage now even if the scab comes with it. His simile, not mine.

"Charlie, no," I begin, firm, direct, highly motivated. "And here," I dig into my wallet for my emergency check, "let me pay you for my half of the ride."

"What?"

Brandishing my check, I search for a pen. "I want you to take it, Charlie. I insist."

"Oh, no, hell, no, don't do that." He's offended now. Reality has landed with the balloon, and it hurts. "Look, I get it. You're not interested."

Finally, acceptance. Thank you, Jesus.

Sam drifts a respectful distance away to chat with Eli, who's unaware I'm raining on Charlie's date parade.

"I'm sorry," I reply, wanting to sound sincere, but as he trapped me into going on this date anyway, it's difficult to muster the energy.

Make a note, guys, if you've got to force it, it's never going to work. Nag, trap, whine, cajole—all bad signs.

Though most of you ignore those anyway, don't you?

Yeah. You do.

Well, look at that. Another blog post idea.

I'm on a roll.

Charlie shrugs. Turning his back on me, he faces Sam as Mark arrives in his truck to whisk us away. "Could you do me a favor, Sam?" my dejected date implores.

"Sure, Charlie, what do you need?"

"Do you mind giving Ro a lift home? I wouldn't ask, but one of her kids is sick, and I need to get my truck. Do you mind?"

Sam examines his field, watching Eli secure the balloon, and hesitates, perhaps about to refuse his request. After a brief moment, he answers, "I don't mind. It's not far."

Relieved, Charlie claps him on the shoulder. "Thanks, I appreciate it." He mutters something to Mark and climbs into his truck, ready to turn tail and run, fixated on the distant landscape, avoiding me. Curious, Mark exchanges a quick glance with Sam, hops into his truck then drives off, leaving us alone.

For a moment, neither of us moves, frozen in the dusk.

He studies me. "Ready?"

I meet his gaze, reliving *The Kiss* and its aftermath for the umpteenth time. Embarrassment feeds irritation. My gumption grows, engorging on raw emotion. Because I'm fired up now.

Let's channel that inner irritability, Ro.

Determined, I square my shoulders. "Ready as I'll ever be," I repeat for the second time tonight.

We indulge in a brief staring contest, but I'm confident in a victory. After all, I have yet to lose one with him, so bring it on, boss.

As expected, Sam blinks first.

Spinning on his boot heels, he walks to his truck. "Let's go."

"You got it." I follow him with purpose and climb in, relieved the date from hell is over. This isn't how I expected it to end, but for once Karma might be cutting me some slack.

Or, more likely, she's planning more hell.

You never know with that bitch.

I tighten my seat belt. After all, this could get ugly.

~ * ~

Eureka. I've thought of blog topic number forty-nine. *Dating in Small-Town Illinois—Don't.*

I like it.

Hold on…am I turning into Olivia?

All things considered, it's not the worst thing I've dealt with tonight.

The sun sinks fast, coloring the sky with streaks of fire as we travel through the growing dusk. Sam concentrates on the road. Breaking the silence, he asks, "How's the headache?"

A relevant question.

I hesitate. Neither a pretend headache nor possible blog topic pound my mind into submission at the moment. Instead, our kiss plagues me, replaying over and over on a near-constant loop in my imagination, torturing me with regret. "Better," I lie.

The truck grows quiet, and I busy myself counting telephone poles. One…two…it's not helping…three…I keep coming back to the same question.

What's the deal with that kiss?

And why aren't there more freaking telephone poles, for Christ's sake?

"Sam?" I give in.

"Yes?"

"Why did you kiss me?"

Ah… the dead cat is out of the bag now. No matter how large my mouth, no effort in the world's going to suck those words back down my throat.

Silence.

Impatient, I clench and unclench my fists in my lap. Irritation builds. "Hello? Earth to Sam. The kiss?"

Dial it down, Ro. He's still your boss, remember?

He clears his throat. "I…about that…well…because I really wanted to kiss you, Ro."

Silence.

Say what?

"Ah," I reply.

I hesitate.

"Why did you walk away?" I continue. "Did I need a breath mint?"

"No…" He hesitates. "It's complicated."

Geez. What a total cop-out.

My irritation maxes out. Any second I may cross the border into pissed-off territory, and we wouldn't want that. I stare out the window, gritting my teeth, looking for poles. What's the deal? Do they bury the power lines in this part of the county?

Absent tall wood to distract me, I finally break. "Was it a pity kiss?"

Oh, sure, now we pass a pole.

Sam turns onto Stockpile Road, growing closer to Thornhill. His face glows in the gleam of dashboard lights. "No, it wasn't a pity kiss." He releases his words like a gentle sigh, and they hang in the air, filling the uncomfortable silence.

Not a pity kiss. Okay, better.

I'm not satisfied. We're closing in on the driveway, and I have so many questions, miles and miles of questions.

He reaches the lane. "My turn."

"Shoot."

"Why did you kiss me back?"

Let me show you how it's done, Sam.

I face his profile in the dark. My voice is firm, strong, confident—not my usual go to emotions, especially in difficult situations. "Because I damn sure wanted to, that's why."

"Ah."

Great. Thornhill lumbers in the distance, we've run out of road, yet I'm no closer to understanding what happened at the cabin. The darkness is complete as we crest the hill, but a light burns bright in the barn. I motion for Sam to park next to it, ready to disappear and make tracks.

The barn door opens wide, and Justin walks out, clad in coveralls and a wool cap. "Can I help you?" he calls out.

Sam lowers his window, and I bend toward it, closer to his chest. It rises and falls, an ocean wave of oxygen I'm desperate to ride. Self-conscious and still ticked off, I draw back and answer my brother. "It's me. Sam gave me a lift."

Confused, he joins us at Sam's window. "What the hell?" he questions. "Didn't you have a date with my boss?"

A whiff of leather and pine distracts me. "Yeah," I reply, "that ended a bit early." A hint of pine lingers. I love wood…hard, hard wood…

Again, it's highly possible I'm a touch A.D.D.

Fortunately, Justin brings me back down to earth before I embarrass myself. "Early, huh? Should I ask why? Never mind, ignorance is bliss. Good to see you again, Sam." He smiles. "Didn't recognize your truck right off."

Sam nods. "Good to see you too."

Happy the subject's no longer my date with Charlie, I switch tactics and scan the barn. "What are you doing out here? Everything okay?'

My goofy brother shoves his big mitts in his coverall pockets, and I can tell he's pleased about something. "Yep," he replies with a head bob at the barn. "I finished the stalls tonight and that last section of fence too. You can bring those animals home any time. We're ready."

Peering through the darkness, I try to make out the fences. "Really?" I squint. Yep, I spy a fence and a gate too. He did it.

"Would I kid you, sis?"

"Yes."

A smirk lights my brother's face in the dark as he laughs. "This time, I ain't. They're ready. Let's get those critters home. No sense putting it off till Christmas. Or until Olivia has a chance to change her mind."

"Good idea." Leaning closer to the open window, I invade Sam's sexy space. "Let's do it."

Shifting ever so slightly in his seat, Sam's cheek draws closer to me. Is it intentional? He remains there, addressing my brother. "Need any help? I've got a livestock trailer."

"You do?" Justin asks.

"Yep, and I'm free tomorrow. I can call Greg on my way home. If he's available, it won't take long to get them loaded. We could have them here in no time."

What's happening? Aren't I pissed off? Where'd the irritation go?

Tearing myself away from the window, I rein in my emotions as best I can. The fences are fixed, the stalls are ready, Sam's offering to help, and we can bring home the beasties. The kiddies will be so happy.

Say yes, Ro. We'll tackle the kiss situation later.

Before I can answer, Justin replies, "Great. We'll be ready."

I nod agreement—it's all I can manage at this point. "Yep."

My brother studies us. Catching his gaze, I swivel my eyes, indicating the house, silently inviting him to leave, please.

On cue, he takes the hint. Stretching his long arms wide, he sighs. "It's getting chilly, and I got a beer in the house with my name on it." Stretch complete, he offers his hand to Sam. "I was wondering how we were going to get those critters out here. Thanks. I'd appreciate it. Hopefully tomorrow works."

Sam reciprocates with a firm shake. "Don't mention it. Happy to help."

Back to the barn my brother trots. *Snap*, the light shuts off, he closes the door, then saunters to the house, leaving me alone in the dark with the cowboy.

Okay, now what? Do I do linger? Make small talk? Dry hump him like a junkyard dog, ask forgiveness later, possibly from the unemployment line?

How about I pry instead.

"So," I press, "it's complicated? Dare I ask why?"

Sam's jaw tightens, his full expression lost in the darkness.

Curious, patient, I sit, silent.

His voice cracks as he says, "Yeah, it's complicated."

That's it? Been there, heard that.

Giving up, I reach for the door handle. "Thanks for the ride. Bye, Sam."

Gently, he touches my arm, stopping me. "Ro, wait."

Frustrated, I hesitate.

Sam fidgets in the truck cab. Finally, he drags his fingers through dark curls, then faces me. "I owe you an apology. I shouldn't have kissed you like that, and I shouldn't have left like that either. It was rude, it was wrong, and I'm sorry."

Anguish fills his voice. It melts what little irritation remains from that confusing, unsettling kiss. I touch his coat sleeve, hoping to reassure him. "It's okay. Apology accepted."

His hands twist in his lap, belaying a sense of frustration, possibly even exasperation. He plunges on. "No, no it's not, Ro." Switching course, he grips the steering wheel and stammers, "I can't explain it. Sitting in the cabin with you that day, it felt so right to be there with you, to kiss you. I didn't even ask, though, I just did it. Then I panicked, I'm your boss, for heaven's sake, and what if you didn't want to be kissed? I...well," he stutters, "it's certainly not that I didn't like kissing you...more like...the opposite...my heart said hold you, but my head said run. So, I ran."

Trembling fingers cover his face, shielding his eyes as he finishes, "Jesus, I'm a freaking coward. Plus, I hurt you. I'm so, so sorry for that, Ro, really, I am. Please forgive me."

Oh. My. God.

Did he say what I think he said?

Goosebumps erupt on my arms. My vagina awakens.

He liked it?

Yeah, all that other stuff is good too, but he liked it, the kiss!

No takesee backsees. I heard him.

Be cool, Ro, be cool.

Totally unable to be cool, I practically blather in reply, "Sam, like I said, it's okay."

Suddenly, Mom's unwelcomed advice brings me up short—gee, thanks, Mother. What was it she said? He's a skittish stallion with a history of bolting? Ain't it the truth. Best to ease my toe into the topic like a hot tub set on high.

Mulling her words, I reply, "Apology accepted. For the record, I liked it too. The running away part? No, definitely not. But the kiss? Yeah, that I enjoyed. Immensely."

Sam's fist relaxes. "Are we okay then?"

I smile. "Yep, we're okay."

A huge sigh erupts across his grizzled cheeks. "Thank you, this was killing me."

"Don't be so hard on yourself," I joke. "Remember, I enjoyed it. Anyway, I'm glad we're past this."

"Me too."

Awkward silence tinged in relief fills the cab. Time for me to go. No sense pushing the envelope. I reach to open the door and catch my reflection in the side mirror.

A pale face minus makeup and flat hair gapes back at me. Not to mention, I'm wearing my fat clothes.

Ouch.

Not a good look.

Maybe I should do a little damage control. I fluff my hair a bit and attempt to hide in the shadows. "By the way, Sam, I didn't want to go out with Charlie." I sweep my palms along my disappointing outfit. "I didn't want to encourage him. This is zero effort. He was already too enthusiastic."

Dark eyes sparkle. "You look great."

"Sam, I'm wearing old maternity jeans."

Overcome, he tosses his head back and laughs. It's a joyous sound, loud, lusty, contagious. Regaining control, he chuckles. "It doesn't matter, Ro. You're a natural beauty." His voice is tender without a hint of sarcasm.

Wow. Does he mean it?

Mom jeans for the win.

Emboldened in the dark, it hits me. No risk, no return. I decide to make the first move. "Let me put this out there, Sam," I start. "I like you, a lot. But, right now, I'm damaged goods and, frankly, my life is in a holding pattern. Plus," I push on before my confidence wanes, "I'm getting mixed signals from you, and I'm not sure what the issue is—

maybe you still love your wife, maybe it's because we work together, hell, maybe it's because I have a small herd of crazy, crusty kids," I blabber, gaining speed, "but if you ever get to the point where you want to try dating again, I hope you consider me. Take all the time you want because I need it too, but when you're ready to rip off that bandage, if you're interested, give me a call. I'll probably say yes. Because I'm interested, very interested, in dating you."

Spent from the magnitude of that effort, I suck in air and sigh deeply. No sense dancing around the subject anymore. He can either rise to the occasion or hide from the fallout. Either way, I've said my piece, it felt good, and he knows where I stand. Single, horny, and wanting him.

Inspiring, isn't it?

Goodnight falling off my lips, I face him now, curious, seeking a reaction.

Sam watches me closely. The reflection of the dash lights burns bright in his eyes. Hesitant at first, then gaining confidence as I meet his stare, he moves toward me. Muscular arms encircle my shoulders, pulling me close, gently at first, until our lips meet, then forcibly, drawing me closer still. And, once again, Sam kisses me.

What can I say? I love it.

Unlike that first kiss, this one is slower, deeper, lingering. There's time to think, as in *oh-my-lord-he's-kissing-me-again-and-it-seems-like-he-means-it-this-time-and-I-suggested-taking-it-slow-but-I-don't-want-this-kiss-to-ever-stop* time to think.

Yeah, it's that good.

In fact, it's hot and sexy as hell, but unlike the last desperate kiss which felt stolen in time, this one feels deliberate, meaningful, like it may build to something...something good and substantial, possibly involving eventual foreplay and actual sex.

It's that kind of kiss.

We break, coming up only for air. His arms enfold me in a close embrace. Energy driven by emotion, lust, and hormones courses through my body. I shiver. Sam, ever attentive, cranks the heat.

Me? I try not to lick his face, amazed at my usually limited supplies of willpower.

Casually, softly, Sam caresses my arm, igniting another wave of goosebumps. They stand tall across my body, burning like sentry fires across a mountain range.

"If you're interested," he offers, "and when you're ready, I would like to try a date."

Halle-freaking-lujah.

Instantly, Mom's words of caution smack me down.

Is he ready?

Am I ready?

Good question. I honestly don't know. My life has been stagnant for almost two years now. Plus, it's complicated, he said.

Then again, life is always complicated. Why should Sam be any different? Besides, what if I really do need to rip off the bandage?

Throwing caution to the wind, I jump at his offer. "I'd like that too."

Something bordering on relief washes across his face. Maybe he hasn't noticed my goosebumps, but surely he hears the jackhammer pounding its way out of my chest.

Is that the rip of a bandage I hear?

Trailing a finger along my palm, he takes my hand into his own. Warm skin distracts me as he makes plans. "I'll call Greg about picking up the boys tomorrow," he says with a gentle squeeze. "In the meantime, I'll try to figure out how to top that balloon ride…"

…just show up, Sam…

"…and when you're ready, say the word," he says.

It's official. Dry humping him is back on the table, however, since the moment our lips touched, it would no longer qualify as dry.

His words whirl in my mind. It's difficult to translate them through the rush of heat and light and energy having its way with my body. "Sounds great." Forcing myself to open the door, partially because I need something solid to hang onto even if only a handle, I murmur, "Goodnight, Sam."

"Goodnight, Ro."

Somehow, I manage to climb out, reliving the taste of his lips on my lips, the touch of his fingers on my skin, the strength of him as he wrapped me in his arms.

Damn…I'm spent, and it was only a kiss.

Desperate to fan that flame, reluctant to leave, I shut the door and amble to the house. Reaching the steps, I turn.

He sits in his truck, watching me, smiling at me. He gives me a wave, and I wave back.

The truck starts, and Sam drives down our lane, disappearing behind the trees.

Entranced, I float three feet above the doorstep.

Charlie may have taken me up in a balloon tonight, high above the earth, but it was Sam who took me to heaven.

I hope I never have to land.

Chapter Eleven

Mud gushes under Sam's truck tires as he backs a livestock trailer to the gate beside the barn. Mother Nature tried to screw with our plans by sending an early morning downpour our way, but nothing short of a typhoon will keep me from wrangling farm animals with that sexy man. Fortunately at midday the sun breaks through, rewarding us with only a slightly overcast, semi-soggy Sunday instead, though it's a perfect opportunity to keep the kiddies hidden inside while we set up their surprise. I probably owe Mother Nature an apology for all the cussing.

To my great joy, Justin pops out of the barn the minute we arrive, and I swear he's been preoccupying himself in it since I snuck out on a pretend mission for toilet paper. Using his lanky limbs to his advantage, my eager brother opens the pasture gate, gestures wildly at Sam and swings it to the back of the trailer, forming a makeshift loading chute. We're both excited, and best of all, it almost seems like we know what we're doing.

Trailer in position, Sam climbs out of his truck holding a rope. "Ro, I'll lead Oscar, and the other two should follow. Justin, stop anyone who tries to make a break for it."

My brother spreads his lanky limbs into a large X, forming a blond-headed barrier, while simultaneously peeking inside the trailer. "I'm on it." Craning high, he frowns. "Wow, they really are short. I can't even see their heads."

Across from him, I'm trying to create my own little X, but, being vertically challenged, it's not nearly as intimidating. "I told you, bro, these animals are my people. Close to the ground."

Sam unhooks the door latch. "I like to think of you as fun-sized, like a little Snicker bar."

Blushing, I laugh. "Yum."

Over Sam's shoulder, Justin rewards me with a totally inappropriate don't-make-me-vomit face.

It's pleasant making him gag. I should do it more often.

Inside, the animals seek comfort in each other's company clustered at the neck of the trailer. Oscar the ass chews on a bale of hay meant to occupy them. Walter the pony studies us between thick hanks of blond hair. As for Cronkite the goat, well, he's fallen flat on his side!

"Sam, something's wrong with the goat!" I rush past Oscar, startling Walter in the process. They trot toward the end of trailer where Justin corrals them inside, and Sam flies in, joining me at the goat's side.

Checking for broken limbs, broken ribs, bumps, lumps, something, anything, I work my hands along his torso. "Oh, my gosh, what's wrong?" I cry, desperate for an explanation.

His sides rise and fall with hard breaths, his eyes are wide open, and his furry brown legs stick out ramrod straight from his body, rigid as stone despite any evidence of a cause.

As I make hurried plans to Google the nearest veterinarian, however, his body relaxes, his yellow eyes focus forward, and, thankfully, Cronkite rises first into a sitting position and finally stands. Minus a care in the world, he tugs a mouthful of hay from the bale and chews, content as a babe.

What the freaking hell?

Calm and apparently unconcerned, Sam kneels, petting the revived goat. "Ro, he's okay," he says.

"No, something's wrong with him," I insist. The goat gives a shake, then sniffs the hay. I feel his fur, searching for clues. "He had a seizure. Should we call a vet? Can goats have epilepsy?"

Chuckling, Sam pets Cronkite's back, stops at the base of his tail, and scratches. The little goat's tail takes off, whirling in the air, wagging furiously, a windmill teeming with energy.

"Nothing's wrong with him," he replies. "He's a fainting goat. I guess we forgot to mention that. When he gets scared or startled, he faints. It doesn't hurt him, though. See?" He points at Cronkite, who takes another bite of hay. "He's fine."

Itty bitty Oscar chews on Justin's jeans cuff as my brother gives voice to my shock. "A fainting goat? What the hell? You learn something new every day."

"Why on earth does he faint, for heaven's sake?" I ask, petting the fluffy beast.

Carrying the bale of hay, Sam exits the trailer while Cronkite, Oscar, and Walter follow in hot pursuit. "Someone bred these goats to faint. You put them in with your valuable livestock, and when something like a coyote or cougar goes after them, the goat faints. That way your valuable livestock can get away. It's not pleasant, but practical." He tosses the hay into the paddock and shrugs. "Basically, Cronkite's walking bait."

"Walking bait? That's terrible!"

The horror of Cronkite's genetic fate, however, is lost on

Justin. Instead, he's impressed. "Someone bred a goat to faint? That's brilliant...hey, quit that."

He shoves Oscar who decided a fraying cuff is more tasty than dead grass. Eyeballing his jeans which are now frightfully damp with donkey spit, Justin jokes, "How about we teach this fella to faint? Maybe we should hobble the donkey and give the goat a fighting chance."

He pushes the diminutive donkey away again, excited expectation twinkling in his baby blues. "Should we get the rug rats?"

Surprised itty, bitty faces leap to mind. This is what I've been waiting for...well, that and for Sam to kiss me and touch my boob. Swiveling to face the house, I catch Olivia clearly in suspense, peeking through the backdoor window, watching.

She can pretend all she wants, but she's as excited as we are, I'm sure of it.

"Definitely," I reply, waving at Olivia. Immediately she disappears, no doubt yelling names and grabbing coats and hunting for shoes. "This is going to be epic."

Given a green light, Justin bounds through the gate, shouting as he runs, "I'll get 'em."

"Okay," I call out after him, "but don't tell them."

My giddy, silly brother makes short work of the gap, sprinting in record time. The backdoor creaks open and slams shut with a bang, leaving me pleasantly alone with Sam, if only for a moment.

It's torturous being this near him, yet unable to share only a handful of brief, ecstatic kisses caught in snatches here and there. Sure, we managed a few in the truck though nowhere close to what I consider my required daily quota. How many more kisses can we squeeze in before the kids arrive? Should we go for quantity? Quality? Both?

Yes, please.

I focus on the house, ready for an onslaught of children, and draw nearer to Sam, ready for an onslaught of kisses. "Penny for your thoughts, cowboy."

Sam pulls his gaze away from the house and stares at me. His chestnut brown eyes beam. Dimples tempt me. Handsome as hell, he pats Walter's dusty back—leaving me slightly jealous—and smiles. "I'm thinking this is a good thing, you did," he answers. "Mostly I'm thinking you're pretty darn cute in those mud boots."

"Tuesday," I blurt out, "let's go Tuesday."

Screw the weekend. I'll explode by then. Or run out of double AA batteries, neither of which is good.

Hay and a goat stand between us. Sam sidesteps Cronkite. "I

haven't come up with anything to top the balloon ride yet."

One bale is no match for horny me. Also stepping wide, I clear it and move toward him. "Trust me, you don't have to."

Sam's eager hands find mine. "I'll pick you up at five-thirty. We can go to Glendale. There's a great Italian place I'd love to take you." Muscular arms encircle me. Tender lips draw near.

Panting, I'm excited and not just for carbs. "I'll be ready," I sigh the words, tingling as I do.

The door to the kitchen bangs open, and my whiny brood of babies emerges, arguing with Justin, reluctant to leave their blanket fort in the living room, followed by Olivia herding her equally disagreeable twins.

Startled, Sam pulls back, and we both brace ourselves for the thundering horde headed our way.

Justin ushers my griping three, cajoling them as he does. "Trust me, goobers, you're gonna want to see this."

Olivia is in hot pursuit, marshaling her twins, adjusting knit caps, and fixing last-second zippers. Our loud, excitable tribe argues and yammers and fusses.

Please be good. Don't make Sam have second thoughts.

At least they're wearing shoes and coats this time.

The trailer and Sam loom in the driveway, catching Nick's attention. "Why is he here?" My son stops in his tracks, curious. "Is there something in that trailer?"

Justin nudges him and points toward the pasture. "Not anymore."

Always three steps ahead of everyone, Aaron shouts, "Is that a horse?"

Shock and awe explode across tiny faces.

Never one to miss a teasing opportunity, Justin pokes my boy. "Correction, kiddo, that's a pony. You need to read up on your farm animals," he jokes.

Giggles and squeals erupt from our minions. "A pony!" Maddy shrieks. She breaks into a run, possibly alerting the neighbors of any impending air strikes in the process. Whipped into a frenzy by the sight of fuzzy, four-legged cuteness, she leads the pack, and our children dash headlong to the pasture, scrambling over the fence in full throttle, a horde of small, rabid zombies.

Instantly, Cronkite faints.

Can you blame him?

Olivia snatches the twins by their hoods, drawing them up short. "Ro, what's wrong with the goat?"

"*Aargh!*" screams Nick.

"*Aargh!* scream Jaylen and Jayden.

Maddy freezes. "Mommy, he's dying!"

Images of traumatized children and six-figure psychology bills fill my brain. "No, he does that. It's kind of his thing. He passes out when he's startled." Cronkite stiffens at my feet, casting doubt on my words. Regardless, I plunge on, "Stop screaming like banshees and get in here. Pet him, and he'll know you're not going to eat him. He'll be fine."

Released from Olivia, the twins rocket forward and join Maddy and the boys in the pasture. Olivia takes her camera out of her coat pocket and follows, unconvinced. "You've got to be kidding. You got a goat that falls down whenever kids scream?" She snaps a quick picture. "This is going to be interesting. Quick, Ro, yell again. I want to see how long it stays down."

"He's not a toy," I correct her. Apparently, I'm the only sensitive one in the family over the age of eight. Who knew, right? I guess I better help the goat.

Tufts of hay stick up between Cronkite's legs. He lies rigid at Justin's feet, and my brother prods him with his shoe. "Good thing Mom's in town. You know she'd be making rude comments about stiffies."

Ugh.

Yes, she would.

A tug on my coat pulls me away from that horrid thought. Aaron stares at Cronkite. "Mom?"

Instead, another horrid thought comes to mind. "We're not eating him, Aaron."

He drops next to the small animal and strokes his fur. "I wasn't going to say that. Is he really, okay? Don't worry, fella," he consoles the goat, speaking gently to him, "you don't have to be afraid. We aren't going to hurt you."

Pinch me, it's happening. Aaron's already more compassionate.

Thank you, Jesus.

Slowly, Cronkite relaxes. Rising to his feet, he treats Aaron to a courtesy sniff, then reaches for the tassel on his jacket zipper and gives it a tug. "He's trying to take my coat off," Aaron laughs, yanking it up. He teases the goat with the tassel, and Cronkite grants his wish, jerking it down once more. "You're a silly goat, aren't you?"

Camera clicking rapidly, Olivia comes closer. "He's cute when he's up on all fours." She takes picture after picture as Aaron hugs

Cronkite. She winks at me. "Is it wrong I'm tempted to scream?"

I chuckle. "Yes."

With Cronkite fully recovered—for the moment, at least—Maddy launches into full-blown ecstasy, overcome at the sight of fuzzy, furry pony cuteness. Vibrating with glee, she dances around his chubby body with Jaylen and Jayden, then entwins her fingers into his thick mane.

"I love him, I love him, I love him!" She hugs Walter by the neck, unaware Oscar inspects her straw-colored hair.

I brush the donkey's velvety nose away, and dissuaded, he ambles after Nick, who immediately panics, climbing the fence to safety.

Shushing Aaron before he can taunt his brother, I wedge myself between Nick and Oscar. "It's okay, sweetie, he's a nibbler. Offer him some hay, and he'll take it from you. Cute, isn't he?" I coax Nick from the fence and scratch Oscar's ears. They flop to and fro, and it's irresistible.

Timid but intrigued, Nick approaches. Tentatively, he stretches out his hand, holding a wad of hay at arm's length. Immediately, Oscar's grayish pink tongue darts forward for a taste. Nick stiffens—not unlike the goat—and holds his ground as the small donkey munches the dried grass.

Warming to the tiny animal, Nick pets his neck. "Yeah, he's pretty cute, I guess."

Oh, this is too good to be true. My happy family has four-legged friends, and already we're better people for it.

Should my blog take a different direction too? I feel a post idea coming on, *Life, Sometimes It Works Out.*

I love it.

While not my original plan, because, frankly, I didn't have one, it occurs to me that this is why we're here. To expand our comfort zones into the great unknown. To try the new, to push our boundaries. Plus, our unintentional journey brought me Sam last night and a better ass than my ex today.

Call me crazy and knock on wood, but I think things are starting to look up.

~ * ~

An old bathtub, salvaged from the barn and plugged at the drain, serves as a makeshift watering trough, a brilliant piece of inspiration on Sam's part. Hay bales are stacked, feed sacks are unloaded, and straw is scattered around a stall. Walter and Oscar, who have already earned their keep with rides for our children, are checking out their new surroundings, ready for a well-earned rest.

Goats, unfortunately, know nothing about the two enemies to moms everywhere, tired and cranky, which have set up camp in our children, morphing them into whiny, bratty stinkers. I'm trying to get my three back into the house for baths and snacks, but Cronkite won't let up with the antics. Climbing on the remaining bale of hay we shoved in the stall, he leaps, jumps, and contorts, teeming with acrobatic joy. It's both glorious and hilarious.

Despite their vociferous protests in full view of Sam, I push them from the stall kicking and screaming, and I swear Maddy's breach birth was easier. Further thwarting our plan for a clean exit—as if that were ever possible—Cronkite rears on his itty, bitty back feet and bunny hops at me, issuing non-stop challenges while I shut the gate in his fluffy face. Obviously, fainting is the least of his gifts.

"Will you stop being so cute?" I beg him with one last scratch of his soft nose.

My pleas, however, fall on deaf ears. Mindful of his adoring audience, he executes a swift pirouette on fat hindlegs before ending with a big finale, a well-placed drop-kick off Walter's chubby pony ass.

Impressed, Justin gives him a standing ovation.

Equally amused, though growing more frustrated, Olivia wrangles a sobbing twin. "Want to help me with the girls, sweetie?" she cries, clinging to Jaylen.

Unwilling to leave the goat show, her tired toddler arches her back in her mother's arms, muttering, "No, no, no, I wanna watch goatie."

Justin swoops in and lifts Jayden as she joins her sister's sob fest, wailing, "No, I stay." Feet kick, tears fall, and, love them as I do, at the moment I'm thrilled they aren't mine.

Rocking her frustrated daughter, Olivia sighs. "He's too stinking funny. Can't say that for the girls right now. Here's a thought, I want to build him a jungle gym. We can sit on the patio and watch him play. He's better than cable."

Wrestling a hysterical Jayden, my brother snorts. "You're going to build him a jungle gym?"

"Okay," she replies, soothing her baby, "we. Satisfied? We can build him a jungle gym. Right after we tackle the upstairs bathroom."

With the animals settled in the stall and Cronkite finally out of site, I herd my bickering brood from the barn, equally disinclined to leave our exciting Goat du Soleil. Mentally, I'm planning a massive obstacle course. Perhaps carpentry can be my thing.

Those plans will have to wait another day. The afternoon draws late, and we herd cranky children through the pasture, approaching the trailer where Sam prepares to shut the gate. Ahead of him, Aaron skips to the front, reaches the trailer then pauses to look at Sam. An agreeable nod from the cowboy elicits a grin, and Aaron bounds past him to disappear inside.

On his heels, Nick peeks in after his brother.

Sam nods toward it. "It's okay. You can go inside too."

Grinning slightly, Nick dashes forward only to stop short. He raises a knee, bends a shoulder, and holds out his hands, protecting himself from who knows what. "Don't!" he yells.

Too late. Something dark, round, and moving fast flies out of the trailer, hitting him in the chest. It semi-explodes into clods. Wild laughter ensues inside.

Anger ticks across Nick's face. He wipes his jacket and hollers words I don't want to hear, "Mom, Aaron's throwing poop at me!"

Oh, crap.

Literally.

Launching into motherly combat mode, I make for the trailer. "Aaron, stop it this second!"

Blissfully free of parental responsibilities, Sam covers his mouth, hiding his laughter, no doubt thrilled he doesn't have to scold or scream.

Because that's my job.

Oh, goodie.

Soft mud beckons my eldest. Tempted, he grabs a handful and flings it at his little brother. "What ya gonna do now? You're trapped, stupid."

Here we go. Time to ramp up the mother mode. I let out a primal yell, "No!"

Aargh!" yells Aaron, as mud flies into the trailer.

"*Aargh!*" hollers Nick, as more poop flies his way.

What gives? Am I invisible?

Bolting for the trailer, I scold, "Boys, stop it this—"

Only I don't finish that sentence. Instead of channeling my inner mom, I demonstrate my outer klutz and propel my mom mass forward in high gear only to hit a patch of mud where gravity betrays me. Boots sail into the air, and I soar, executing a perfect butt-first cartoon fall into the gooey, gooshy mud. Wet ooze penetrates my blue jeans, coating me in a delightful layer of brown, sodden earth.

Not to mention possibly a little pee.

Sam rushes toward me and earns massive boyfriend material points for not laughing. Concerned, he inquires, "Ro, are you okay?"

188

Maybe? It's hard to tell in the freezing muck, partly because my ass stings and I don't know if it's from the cold ground or the hard bounce. One thing is certain though, acrobatic as it was, I'm no Cronkite. Still, while he may land on his feet, I'm definitely giving him a run for it in the entertainment category.

Like the jackass he is, Justin brays loud and long, reveling in my predicament, putting Oscar to shame. Olivia, who instantly plopped a stunned Jaylen on the ground, photographs me with abandon, laughing like a she-devil, unaware I have another blog topic, *In-laws Are Expendable,* simmering away in my brain. Maddy cackles. Seriously, she's in neophyte witch territory here. And Jayden? She's staring at her dad with something akin to disappointment.

I like that kid. She's my new favorite.

As for Nick, his scared face bears down upon me, burdened by the growing implications of my fall.

For a brief parental moment, I let him squirm, and ponder whether to ground him and his brother. It's tempting.

Or, I can fan the adventure flames and get this party started.

Decision made, I claw at the mud oozing around me and fling with abandon, shouting, "Incoming!"

Caught unaware, Justin takes a direct hit to the stomach. Goo splatters Jayden's shoe. A drippy clod sweeps past him, smacking Maddy on the chin.

Bullseye.

A three-for-one shot too.

Awesome.

I should totally go pro…

At the unusual sight of his mother nailing a toddler with mud, Nick's face lights with shock and, finally, relief. Arming himself with more mud, he rushes into the trailer and advances on his brother.

"You can't get away now!" screams my eldest. Mayhem erupts from inside. World War III ensues.

It's glorious.

Sam offers me a hand, but I hold up mud-caked palms. "I'm a mess, and there may be a dead worm under my thumbnail."

Bracing himself, he takes my hand anyway. "I got you."

Oh, yes, you do.

Rising from the muck, I'm about to say thank you when…

Wet earth plasters the side of my face.

Justin.

Game on.

We descend into chaos. Mud is tossed, pitched, ducked, and

dodged. Olivia and the twins escape to the safety of the pasture and cheer us on while avoiding errant throws. Sam and Justin heave mud at my boys, who have vacated the trailer ready for war. Bits of hay stick to small, wiry bodies as they bob and weave, squealing and yelling, tossing wet earth and round poop with abandon.

Temporarily grateful for my short frame, I dodge another attack from Justin and come in hot, throwing wildly. He takes aim again. Dropping to my knees, I slide. Slops hits my shoulder, coats my cheek, splatters my hair. It's messy and cold and incredibly fun.

I can't stop laughing.

"Ro, what's going on here?"

Wait…

What?

No.

That voice.

Cold. Penetrating. Judgmental. I'd know it anywhere.

Shit on a shingle.

It's him.

On my knees, mud oozing between my knuckles, I grind to a halt. It takes only seconds and feels like forever. The weight of the world descends upon my shoulders, pulling me out of my joy straight into the abyss. Frozen in place, I can't think, talk, move.

"What the hell? Is that mud?"

"Dad!" yells Nick.

Fuck.

Peter.

~ * ~

The nightmare is real.

Pinching and poking myself won't wake me from this reality. The ex is in the driveway, Nick is barreling toward him, I drip with mud next to Sam, and I'm stunned. Bewildered. Speechless.

Also, semi-grateful. At least Mom is in town doing who knows what, otherwise the kids might get a very real lesson in primitive, hands-on castration.

Reeking of shock and awe, I kneel in the filth. "What the hell are you doing here?"

Again, subtle, I'm not.

Peter lurks beside a blue four-door sedan I don't recognize, wearing slacks and a polo shirt I didn't iron for him, looking like he stumbled off the eighteenth green and got lost on the way to the clubhouse. He's dyed his hair too. It's lighter than usual, possibly to hide the gray, and he's trimmer.

Good. Maybe I'm not the only one to give him food poisoning.

Worse, his home-wrecking girlfriend sits in the car, clean and pristine, while I sit in the muck.

What a bitch.

Dressed in his standard business casual costume, Peter glares incredulous, questioning the mud, judging our antics, no hint of amusement gracing his lips. He checks his watch and clears his throat. "I'm here to see the kids. I left a message on your cell phone. You should have called back, Ro," Peter whines as Nick comes in for a landing. Stopping his son short of a hug with a well-placed palm at face level, my ex immediately makes excuses, "Hey, buddy, slow down, you're kinda dirty. Let's get you cleaned up first before we hug it out, okay? Good." Ever an ass, he's unaware his son deflates in front of him.

Muddy and pissed-off, I rise, a slightly awkward phoenix taking flight from the ooze with one demand. "Hug your son, Peter."

Vigilant against a dirty, love-filled hug, my ex holds his ground, still warding off Nick. "I will when he's clean."

Filthy and clueless, Maddy breaks into a run. "Daddy," she yells loud enough to drop a fainting goat. Bursting with new pet joy, she squeals in delight, "Mommy got me a pony!" Not to be deterred, she hurtles past his arms, ducks, dives, and latches onto him at the kneecap, squeezing tight. Too late to stop her, he gives up and settles on blaming me.

"Satisfied?" he complains, as if that sweet, tender hug is my fault, or something I should feel guilty for. He grips her shoulders and eases her back, holding our daughter at arm's length, worried about his chinos which, unlike his daughter, don't give a flying fig about him.

What an idiot.

Having no regard for my wardrobe when it comes to my babies, I wipe my nasty palms on my jacket and shrug. "No, frankly, I'm not." In full throttle, I bark at Sam's livestock trailer, "Aaron, come out and hug your father."

Aaron appears from the depths of the trailer where he retreated to hunt for more poop. "Dad?" he cries, elated. Sprinting through puddles, he jumps into Peter's arms, oblivious that the outstretched hands of his father are meant to stop him in disgust, rather than catch him with love.

Dirt bag ex. He should be the one covered in mud and shit.

A dramatic, put-upon sigh escapes Peter, and he pats his son gingerly on the back. "Hey buddy." Finally, he wraps Aaron in a quick hug, followed by Maddy, then waves Nick in for a loose embrace.

"Kids, it's good to see you." Smiling for the first time since arriving, Peter embraces my babies.

It's almost tender. Until he wipes his fingers on his children's backs.

Already exhausted from the excitement of a full rich day, Maddie sniffs and sobs and stammers, hugging the stuffing out of Peter's leg. "There's also a donkey, Daddy," she mutters between sobs, "and we have a goat who falls down a lot, and he does tricks too." A good, shiny patch of earth grows on his knee from her coat, and I decide then and there that that child is long overdue for a massive dollhouse.

Regardless, she continues sob talking, rattling on to her father about the animals. "We have a dog too!" Maddy points toward the pasture seeking Lucky who roams about, eating pony poop. "I have a gray baby with a pink tail too. Her name is Poo Poo Pink Princess and she lives in a closet in the house. She likes Cheerios, and I brush her with Mommy's toothbrush."

Peter examines the house. "A pink tail? God, Ro, is she playing with rats?"

It's the house that's wigging him out, I know it is. No doubt, all he sees is the peeling paint, the moldering brick, the slight sag in the roof, and the glassless greenhouse. When it comes to seeing potential, Peter practices selective vision. No wonder he thinks we've got rats.

Perhaps I should adjust his thinking with a boot heel to the junk before Olivia emasculates him…ah, not in front of the children. Restraining myself, I pick damp blue jeans from my ass crack. "She doesn't have a rat. Poo Poo's her imaginary pet."

Howls erupt from our daughter. Livid, Maddy stomps her feet, splashing mud onto Peter's tasseled loafers and defends her invisible friend. "No, she's not!" She tramples the earth into submission. "She's my best friend, and I love her."

Inattentive as ever, Peter ignores Maddy and her nap-needing meltdown and sniffs his fingers. His nose wrinkles, his eyes squint, a grimace floods his face, and he sniffs again. "What is that? Is that shit? Are you letting the kids throw shit?"

Oh, goodie.

He *is* covered in mud and shit.

Life goals…

A triumphant giggle brews in my throat, and I bite my lip. "Poop, actually," I manage, "but I heard you'd gone organic. Embrace it. That's about as chemical free as you can get." My cheeks ache from the effort of holding in hysterics at his expense. Witch that I am in his eyes, I'm desperate to cackle.

"It's shit, Ro!"

A chunk of mud loses its grip on my tresses. It falls to the ground with a suggestive plop, and I smush it with my rubber rain boot, losing patience. "Jesus, Peter, don't be so anal. Your mom screws up your potty-training thirty years ago, and the rest of us have to suffer for it?"

Dial it back, Ro, dial it back.

Fear mingled with sadness washes over Nick's upturned face. Maddy blubbers away, hopping up and down, whining about the sweet, invisible perfection that is Pink Poo Poo Whatever The Hell She Is.

Aaron, at least, soldiers on in true Aaron style. Helping in his own way, he picks a nugget of brown from the ground and offers it to his father. "It's pony poo," he confirms, oblivious to Peter's growing disgust or, possibly, unconcerned by it. With Aaron, you can't tell. "It's shaped like baseballs." He tosses the turd in the air. "I hit Nick with it, and he kinda cried."

Nick shoves him hard. "Shut up," he yells. "I did not."

Taking aim with the turd, Aaron replies, "Yes, you did."

"Aaron, don't," I shout, "that's enough."

I hate dressing them down in front of Peter.

And Sam.

Peter side-steps his poop wielding son and examines the house.

I know what he's doing. He's tallying its flaws, judging, finding it wanting. It's his signature style.

Taking a tone that may cost him a testicle before the night is through, he asks, "This is where you dragged my children?" Repulsed, he holds his arms far from his body and performs a wicked bobble-head impression, nodding and wobbling from his mud-speckled clothes to his thoroughly filthy children, circling back to the less-than-perfect house. "Does that thing even have heat?"

Yikes. He's treading on thin ice now.

Justin grabs Olivia, stopping her before an avalanche of creative obscenities and gel-lacquered nails rain down upon us all. "Liv, the kids."

She strains against my brother's firm grip. "Then take them to the house and let me at the other-may ucker-fay."

Restraining his pissed-off wife, Justin stares down my ex. "Peter, don't be badmouthing our home," he warns.

This is getting ugly.

I step in front of Justin and Olivia. "Ignore him," I aim at her. "We can make another voodoo doll later. I still have underwear. You can even blog about it."

My pale attempts to diffuse the situation fall on deaf ears, however, and Olivia glares past me, choosing to shoot daggers at my ex with dark, intelligent, angry eyes.

You know it's bad when arts and crafts won't dissuade her.

Perhaps I should suggest crafting a shiv from a tree branch with a rock chip. There's a project I think we could both get behind.

Unconcerned by his father's line of questioning, Aaron tugs at Peter's polo, demanding full attention, ready to provide answers. "Yeah, Dad, we have a big fireplace and we fill it full of wood and it makes the room real hot and it's neat too. Uncle Justin puts this one kind of wood in it and it pops and cracks like fireworks. That's my favorite. Sometimes we cook hot dogs over it." Vigorously waving, he demonstrates cooking a hotdog, scattering even more specks of mud and crap onto his father's polo, earning himself three cookies and ice cream for dessert.

That boy is a genius.

Maddy hiccups next to her brothers and chimes in. "We cook marshmallows too," she sobs, overwrought and exhausted. "I don't like mine burnt, but Aaron sets his on fire. Mom always tells him not to burn the house down when he does. It's fu…fu…funny." Her final word trails out long and loud in tear-strung, hiccupping glory.

Ignoring us adults, Peter bends toward the children, pumping them for intel. "Do you have a stove?" He directs the question at Aaron. "You can tell me. Be honest, son."

"Of course, we have a stove!" I reply

Something akin to a growl erupts from Olivia. "Jesus Christ, Peter, what do you think we are? Animals?" She annihilates my douche of an ex with a torrent of angry, frustrated words. "Have you ever known me to not have a freaking oven? God, you're such a fucker."

Oh no, she's skipping the pig Latin.

Not good.

As his wife tips into the dark side, Justin picks up Jayden and thrusts her into Olivia's arms, no doubt hoping a child will keep her from strangling my ex.

Cradling her daughter, Olivia bites her lip and stands down. Justin's plan works.

For now.

Furious at the damage he's inflicting on my family, I fight the urge to advance upon him myself, but it's an internal battle I'm losing. Caving, it's my turn to unleash a hell storm. "Good lord, Peter," I start, edging in his direction, my fists clenched, "we get divorced and you think I can't manage heat and an oven? What the hell? I have a job now, I pay my bills, I'm working toward the future, and, for the record, all of that would be easier if you kept up your support payments, you jerk!"

Ah, it's here, the call of the harping shrew. Funny, it's never far when Peter's present.

Whether justified or not, it's not a sound I care to hear spilling out of my mouth. Sam and my children are witnessing me dissolve into my divorce-induced insanity, and I would rather die from raging dysentery than let this continue in front of them. Practicing great restraint, I suck it back in, trying to contain the fury.

Olivia takes my silent, fuming brother by the wrist and tugs him toward the house. "Babe, let's get the kids up to the house before I end up in jail."

"Yeah," he replies, but remains rooted to the spot.

She shoves Jayden into Justin's arms and picks up Jaylen. "Come on," she orders, "to the house. You too, Nick, Aaron, Maddy, let's go."

Reluctantly, my babies peel away from their father, and Olivia steers them toward the kitchen door. Maddy marches ahead, sobbing in a tired voice pitched so high only the neighborhood dogs can hear her. Except apparently for Lucky who ignores us from the pasture where he wanders to and fro, munching a mouthful of poop.

Where were you twenty minutes ago, Lucky? This could have all gone down much smoother if you had worked your disgusting magic in the trailer first.

No such luck.

A white-hot dumpster fire of an ending isn't what I had planned when Sam offered to bring home the beasties today. No, mandatory family fun time interspersed with snippets of Sam kisses hogged my original agenda, certainly not this descent into bickering hell.

Plus, from the looks of Peter, it's only going to get worse.

~ * ~

I face my ex, ready to throw down, but it's difficult. The kids may be in the house, but Sam's behind me, seeing me at my worst, and his presence only leaves me unsettled rather than solid. Given no choice, I press on. "What are you doing here?"

Peter inspects his soiled slacks. "I told you, Ro, I came to see the children." Dirty handprints and muddy smudges pop against the once pristine navy wool.

Eyeballing Maddie's handiwork it occurs to me, I may need to rethink the color scheme for the boys' bedroom. Blue and brown do go well together.

Mud drips from my earlobe and lands on my shoulder with a *kerplat*. A flick of my finger sends it flying in his general direction. "Our children are not a buffet you can sample when you're hungry, Peter," I scold. "They're your children. You can't ignore them for months and then just show up like everything's fine."

Peter and his girlfriend—Frieda? Frances? Formaldehyde? What the hell is her name?—judge me in stereo, him from the driveway, her from the car. "Save me the sermon. I'm not leaving until I've said goodbye, and if you don't let me, I'll make sure they know it. Next time, I'm taking them for the afternoon, if not overnight." Swelling with self-importance, he stomps toward the car and disappears inside, apparently planning to wait out the children out of reach of flying mud and my screaming profanities.

Damn, I want to throttle him.

No, scratch that, I want to put these thighs of mine to good use and charge him like a hippo, pummeling him into the ground.

Is that too much to ask?

Instead, I blurt, "You're such an ass." The words rocket out of my mouth.

Crap.

Sam.

Again, this is not how this day was supposed to go.

Spinning around, I face him, searching his eyes. Is he judging me? Why wouldn't he—this is insanity. Has his opinion changed at the site of my ex-induced antics? He's certainly not catching me at my best. Dripping with self-admonishment, I falter, "Sam...I'm so sorry about this...I had no idea he was stopping by."

His firm grip finds my arm and reassures me with a tender squeeze. "It's okay," he whispers. Understanding, compassion, patience, it all competes for expression in that rugged, handsome face. "I know you didn't expect this," Sam continues, earning my gratitude. "I should go, unless you need me to stay. Are you okay?"

That kind, sexy face reels me in. Mud, Peter, the girlfriend, all are shoved aside. Something other than anger blooms. Gratitude, borne from Sam's compassion, washes over me and it's a damn, fine, noble thing. "I'll be fine," I stammer, overcome, "but thanks for everything, for helping with the animals, the kids, for understanding." Tears well within me, threatening my composure.

Much like Maddy, I also need a freaking nap.

An aw-shucks-thank-you-Ma'am-it-weren't-nothing grin

spreads across that handsome face. "You're welcome."

Emboldened, I ask, "Are we still on with the big date?"

Brown eyes sparkle. A dimple ignites in a tan, grizzled cheek. He draws closer to me. "I'll pick you up at five-thirty," he answers and, being the sweet, hunky, action hero of my dreams, Sam wraps me in a tight, muddy, heaven-sent embrace.

Tears fall, mud drips, lips part, my heart pounds, and Sam kisses me.

Oh, my God.

I might be falling for this man.

~ * ~

The afternoon grows darker by the second.

Right after Sam exits the driveway, Mom returns from the store. Spying Peter and the girlfriend, she lets loose a stream of creative obscenities, flips a few vigorous middle fingers wildly their way, and nearly shoots an ample, saggy buttocks moon in all her geriatric glory until I remind her they both have cell phones, at which point she considers it for a moment, lowers her parka over her ass, and grabs a box of wine from her car.

Blowing a series of wet raspberries, she trundles up to the house, talking out loud about erectile dysfunction and sluts, while punctuating the air with the words "fuckers" and "whores" and "dick face."

It's one of my proudest moments as her child.

Shortly after Hurricane Kate blew into the house, the children were ushered back out by Justin. He stands guard, now, a faithful pit bull saved from a life of dog fights while the children hunch beside Peter's car, all clean and shiny in jammies and slippers, hats and coats.

Perhaps lying, perhaps making excuses for his absence, perhaps throwing me under the bus, perhaps all three, Peter mumbles who knows what to the children. Blank expressions cling to their sweet faces.

Funny, I'd forgotten he's a mumbler.

It once struck me as cute. These days, I didn't even remember enough to miss it.

Out of earshot at his request, next to Justin who's on red alert, I strain to read the ex's thin, formless, unsatisfying lips. How does Ms. Fannie-Fucks-A-Lot feel about those non-existent lips? Perhaps we have something else in common after all.

Peter spreads around the hugs, wrapping it up.

I remain rooted where I am, determined to put forth an indifferent front even if it kills me.

Finally, he glares my way as the children say goodbye. "Ro, I need to speak with you."

Don't give me orders, ass hat.

Concern crosses Nick's face. I fake a calm smile and reply as upbeat as possible, "Justin, can you take the kids to the house?"

A ticked off, "Hmpft," emanates from my brother. He waves my babies toward him, encircling them with outstretched arms, protecting my brood, and guides them to the house.

Patient while they depart, I turn and study the girlfriend.

Bleachy blonde, perky nose, eyes hidden behind sunglasses, dripping with good posture, she sits, nodding in time to a tune. Her window's up, the car is on, and the radio blares. Not once did she leave it to meet the children, and Peter made no attempt to introduce them, despite their constant, curious peeks in her slutty direction. As she's jams out to some song with way too much base, one thing dawns on me.

I'm essentially alone with Peter for the first time since he told me he was in love with someone else.

Where's a homemade shiv when you need one?

I really do need to plan better.

Come to think of it, is Illinois an open carry state? Instead of a blog post, I might be writing a confession later if I'm not careful.

As usual he expects me to approach.

I don't. He's on my turf, and I'm not budging an inch.

Neither of us gives in. Finally, he breaks the silence. "Our custody agreement says I can have them on Wednesdays, but I can't see them when they're here and I'm in Chicago."

I say nothing.

"Well?"

"Well what? It's not like you spent Wednesdays with them when we were in Chicago. I adhered to the law and stayed in state. It's not my problem if you're inconvenienced now."

"It will be."

My heart does a slight lurch and beats at a faster pace. Blood rushes in my ears.

Arms knit across Peter's chest.

I'm familiar with this pose. He's uncomfortable about something.

What is he getting at?

Finally, his gaze falls to the ground, and he studies his loafers.

Please let them be shit covered.

He looks up. "This arrangement isn't working for me."

Poke the bear, Ro. Poke it.

"Again, not my problem."

Anger flashes across his taught, condemning face.

He may have worn the pants in our marriage, but I'll be damned if I'm going to don a skirt for our divorce. *That's right, Peter. I grew a fucking backbone. Now deal with it.*

Wheeling around on his loafers, Peter marches to the car, pausing to glare at me over the hood. "Yeah, well, like I said, it will be. I'm rethinking the custody agreement, Ro. You'll be hearing from my attorney," he barks. Disappearing into the safety of the blue sedan, he cuts me off, signaling the end to our conversation.

Fear swells in my stomach and rises into my pounding chest. I don't flinch, I don't cry.

I'm frozen.

Ms. Fanny-Fucks-A-Lot turns down the radio long enough to glance my way. Frantic to leave, Peter yammers continuously as he backs the car—his pencil thin lips flap in her ear at Mach One, most likely labeling me a bitch—but she locks eyes on me. Unlike Peter and Sam, though, hers never break. Her stare moves in unison with the car, following me, judging me.

A vague smile spreads across her otherwise still face, but it's not one of welcome. It's a knowing, threatening smile, a smirk actually, and unlike Peter's threat, it fills me with more dread than his words could ever do.

A picture from one of my old high school history textbooks leaps to mind—cowboys in the old West herding buffalo over cliffs, running them to their deaths. It comes to me, clear as day in the growing dark.

My heart thunders like those buffalo, running on the plains. I picture Nick, Aaron, Maddy. I picture the buffalo, running, running, running, oblivious to what's coming.

Peter's word gave me pause, but her expression iced me to my core.

It comes then, the sobs, great, heaving, heart-wracking sobs. Raw emotion, outright terror, red-hot anger, hatred, it all comes in great, roiling tsunami waves. They inundate me, dragging me down, drowning me whole.

I am in the dark, alone, cold, scared, and I do what every mother since the dawn of time has done for her children and will do for her children.

I cry.

Chapter Twelve

Sam will be here in twenty minutes, and I'm panicking. At the moment, I'm clad only in a faded beige slip from the nineties, hot rollers fight for position in my hair, flip flops grace my feet while borrowed polish dries on my toenails, and I'm wrestling with Olivia's eyelash curler that's supposed to make my Irish eyes look smiling, but I don't think it's working and I don't have any idea how to use this stupid metal monstrosity anyway. Besides, my angry green peepers haven't smiled since Peter stopped by dripping with threats, so I have little hope a strange metal contraption will help. And, to top it all off, I can't find my one tube of cheap lipstick.

This sucks.

Making matters worse, Mom shuffles toward me with purpose, and that can never, ever, ever—say it with me now—be good.

To think, last night I could have been doing something useful and productive like putting a lock on this damn bathroom door instead of lying awake mentally eviscerating Peter.

Mistake number one and the week is still young.

Is it too early to start drinking?

Reaching her destination, Mom inspects my reflection in the mirror and, naturally, finds it wanting. "I hope you're wearing decent underwear and right side out this time," she squawks, tapping an arthritic finger against her chin.

Why can't she find another hobby?

"That was one time, and it was an emergency," I reply, examining the lash curler for instructional clues etched on the handle. Nope, nothing. Bummer. Am I using it upside down? Do I have time to Google it? "Anyway," I continue, "it's not like Peter cared." What am I doing wrong?

She snatches it from my hand, flips it over and demonstrates, before slapping it back on the counter. "Maybe he did," she remarks, launching gray eyebrows to ten and two across her forehead.

Ouch.

Picking it up, I press carefully, smooshing thin lashes into submission. "Mom," I glare in the mirror by way of a warning, "I told you not to mention it again."

She waves vigorously, warding me off, unconcerned as usual.

"Whatever. New topic. Did you shave down there?"

Mothers and boundaries…I swear…

Tossing the lash thingy into the sink, I examine my one finished effort. Is it any different? Possibly? "You can't be serious?"

Cruella De Vil, however, is on a mission, though instead of spotted Dalmatian doggy hides, she's dead set on my hair-laden crotch. Which is weird. Leaning against the doorway, she offers cringe-worthy, unwanted advice. "Sweetie, these days, women keep it high and tight in the nether regions."

"I've had three kids, Mom," I fuss. "The only thing tight is my wallet, and I'm too broke to get high."

"Kegels, kiddo, Kegels…"

Kegels, they sound so German. Are they?

"…I can help with the other too," she adds with a wink.

Note to self, don't eat her brownies.

"Stay on topic, Ro," she chides, expertly reading my distraction. "Perhaps you should go totally bare. It's called a Brazilian."

Looking for a hint of curl, I squint in the mirror. Anything? Maybe. I glance at Mom through appallingly flat lashes. "I'm aware what women do these days." Inside, however, I squirm. Imagine the browser results that web search would get me. Besides, why is Mom such an expert on these things? Does she keep it high and tight in the nether regions?

Wrinkled prunes assault my imagination.

Ugh.

Pardon me while I vomit in my mouth.

Oblivious, she prattles on, "Fine, kiddo, but did you do anything about it? What?" She bristles under the slow burn of my green-eyed death ray. "It's a legitimate question."

Giving up on Olivia's torture device, I hunt for my pink and green tube of miracle mascara. "No, Mom, it's not. It's a personal question, and it's none of your business."

Where's that tube? I rifle through my make-up drawer, tossing stuff aside, but it's hopelessly swamped. Maddy's hair clips, the boys' plastic pirates, three bars of semi-used soap, my new toothbrush, a half-empty potato chip bag…no mascara.

Crap.

"Maybe it's not my business," she rambles, "I'm only trying to help. How long's it been? Months? Years? Who knows with Peter and, no, a vibrator doesn't count. Besides, that man never struck me as dripping with testosterone, despite the blonde. All I'm saying, honey, is that you need to be prepared."

Gulp

My post-divorce, out-of-practice, pre-date anxiety stew of nerves ratchets upward from simmer to boil.

Perfect.

Agitated, I slam the drawer closed. "Enough, Mom, you're not helping."

"Fine," she acquiesces.

My senses go on alert…it's unlike her to cave. Is she taking pity on me?

She can't be, Maleficent is never that kind.

I cage a peek in her direction.

Nope.

Maddy makes her way into the bathroom, dodging Mom, and skipping straight to the toilet.

Thank heavens. Time to change the subject.

"Need help, sweetie?" I ask.

Blonde pigtails bob as she pushes her step stool to the toilet, drops her knickers to her knees, then climbs aboard. "Can you wipe my butt when I'm done?"

"Of course, baby girl." Whirling upon my own unhelpful mother, I wave her away. "Shouldn't you be spinning a web in the attic? Or polishing your broomstick?"

Temporarily censured and backing out, Brunhilda the Brazen wanders away, bellowing as she leaves, "You heard what I said, kiddo. Trim the shrubs, climb on that horse, and ride it."

Maddy wiggles on the toilet. "Are we getting a horse, Mommy?"

God bless innocence when it's attached to young ears.

"No, sweetie, Meemaw's crazy. Just poop and tell me when you're done. Mommy needs to hurry."

Searching the next drawer, I find my mascara, and get to work. Thanks to Mom, however, I'm thoroughly distracted. After all, what exactly are Sam's expectations? And what is going on down below? Is it bad I can't remember? Do I have time to shave things? Lots of things?

Before I can check under my slip, Maddy interrupts my train of thought. "I'm done." Precious toddler feet swing in the air.

Crotch status on hold, I grab a generous wad of toilet paper, but as I do, I make another mistake. A no good, lousy, horrible mistake.

Anticipating Sam's arrival, I gaze out the bathroom window.

Son of a bitch.

Cronkite, the fainting goat from hell, has escaped the pen and now stands grazing in the shadow of the greenhouse, munching an extension cord running to the barn where Justin, unaware he's about to cook barbecue, cuts pipe for the upstairs bathroom with an electric table saw.

Holy freaking, flaming goat burgers.

This is bad.

My toilet-paper-free palm pounds glass. "Drop it, you stupid goat!"

Nothing.

Happily chewing away, Cronkite ignores my pleas, which is not surprising since he only speaks goat and, as I'm now the friendly neighborhood snack lady and not a hungry, toothy predator, he's tickled with my attention. Therefore, fainting in fear? Currently, it's not an option.

At any second, I expect him to squeal in mid chew and go rigid, his fluffy body smoking as a thousand volts of electricity barbecue his happy ass on a night when we're completely out of hamburger buns.

Typical, isn't it?

Stranding Maddy on the john, I race through the house, literally running out of my flip flops, and take a short cut through the French doors.

Thoroughly acclimated to his surroundings, Cronkite studies me, unfazed by my haste, extension cord in his mouth, death millimeters from his lips. Sensing he's my target, he backs away, determined to play.

Reaching the courtyard, I grab the cord, brace myself, and pull. "Let go, you idiot!"

Strong as I pretend I am, however, he's even stronger. The feisty fellow doubles down, locking his knees, enjoying this game of tug-of-war.

"No, stop it!"

Lured by the commotion, Justin emerges from the barn and grinds to a halt, no doubt confused.

Twisting in his direction, I dig my bare heels into the damp earth, "He's eating the cord! The stupid thing's eating the freaking cord!"

Terrified the goat is about to die, inspiration finally strikes.

I can unplug it from the house.

Whipping around the other way, I start to tug in the opposite direction, but stop short.

Holy crap on a cracker.

A truck door shuts with a thud.

Sam.

Wearing a shell-shocked look of what-the-freaking-hell on his sexy face, my heart-throbbing cowboy watches me do battle with a goat and an extension cord in my ancient underwear and plastic curlers, while sporting mascara on only one eye which may or may not be curled.

You can't make this crap up if you tried.

Dark washed jeans hug his muscular thighs. Surfer curls frame that face. A black button-down shirt peeks out through his coat, stretched across that magnificent chest, broadcasting a fuck-me-Ro-I'm-worth-it vibe. And he's worth it. Oh, how he's worth it.

Yes, Sam, yes, I'll fuck you!

I forget what I'm doing. Instantly, plans are made to shave everything, literally everything. I can't stop staring at him, he's that freaking delicious, as in better-than-marshmallows-and-pie delicious.

Sensing an opportunity, Cronkite gives a mighty heave and yanks the cord hard, freeing it from the wall outlet, ending his own potential crisis yet elevating mine. Dragging me along with the cord, he pitches me forward. My feet sail into the air, my beige slip flaps wildly, and a cold breeze shoots along my thighs, blasting my fuzzy, furry, unshaven crotch. My arms pin wheel, muffin top jiggles, and I careen downward, landing on my elbows, my boobs, my hips, and, I swear, I even bounce a bit, at which point Cronkite, ever the comedian, decides now is the perfect time to keel over and faint.

Fucking goat.

"Ro?"

Did Sam say my name? I'm not sure. He may have said, "Buh-bye" for all I know.

It's kind of hard to hear since Justin's laughing like a full-sized, non-miniature jackass behind me.

Stupid brother.

Can I get him to bite on this cord?

In front of me, Cronkite is still down, his brown legs rigid, though he's coming around. I'm half tempted to wait for him to climb to his feet so I can shove him back down again. I'll sit on him too. Or maybe shock him. Where the hell's my taser?

As for me, sticky, damp dirt clings to my elbows, my knees, my boobs, and a smear of mud glazes my chin. Who knew country life would be so filthy?

Embarrassed, flustered, exasperated, I rise to my knees, spewing questions. "You're early! Why are you early?" Followed by,

"Shut up, Justin!"

I repeat, stupid brother.

Frozen in place, Sam points at his truck. "I brought a few more bales of straw. I planned to unload it while I waited," he stammers. "There's no rush, Ro, take your time."

Behind me, a small knock rattles the bathroom window, demanding my attention. "Mommy," comes the muffled voice of my youngest. Her tiny face smooshes against the glass as she stands on the toilet and peers out. "Can you wipe my butt?"

It's a glamorous, frigging life.

Regaining my composure, I slip into mom mode. "Maddy, don't stand on the toilet. You'll fall and hurt yourself. I'll be right there."

She gapes at me for a moment, and eventually her strawberry blonde curls disappear from view.

It's difficult to muster dignity with wet grass in my cleavage and a butt that needs wiping waiting in the wings, but I give it a try. Channeling a sliver of pride, I stand...not exactly tall...more like, upright and face my date. "Excuse me, Sam, I need to help my daughter. Then I'll get dressed, and we can go. Provided you're still here when I come back out."

I pick sod from between my boobs and fling it at my brother, then turn to scamper to the house, crossing my fingers, praying Sam doesn't leave, not blaming him if he does.

Because why wouldn't he? Chaos reigns again.

What is the deal with my life?

Desperate as I am to seek sanctuary inside, I risk a quick peek in his direction, fully expecting him to be skipping backward to his truck, fleeing the scene. Surprisingly enough, he's not.

He's smiling.

At me.

The world stops. I forget about the mud, the goat, the embarrassment.

Sam isn't running, he's waiting.

For me.

Across the expanse, our eyes meet. My heart leaps in my grassy, filthy chest. It beats hard against my polyester slip-encased ribs, pulsing in my veins, pounding lockstep with my astonished thoughts, thumping in time to "Sam's still here, Sam's still here, Sam's still here."

And he is. He ushers Cronkite to the barn, but he's locked on me. Amusement anchors his gorgeous, grizzled face, and he gazes in my direction as he walks.

Oh, my gosh.

It's happening.

This warm, burning sensation, I recognize it and, no, this time it isn't heartburn.

It's love.

I'm falling in love with this man.

Seriously.

Please, oh please, oh please...

Let it be mutual.

~ * ~

Maddy's shiny hiney wiped, I flush, only to discover Aaron's latest handiwork. The churning toilet vomits a monstrous tsunami of bubbles from the generous squirt of dish soap he added to the tank at some point in the afternoon and billowing suds swamp my feet. Taking lemons and making lemonade, I clean the mess, scrub the toilet, wipe the floor, and wash my hands in the process, before adding mascara to my other eye.

Motherhood multi-tasking for the win.

Now, the task on deck is my first date with Sam, and we're not off to the best start despite the smiles and stares.

It's time to improvise.

Seeing that man, recognizing the goodness of the kind heart beating in that strong chest, I ditch the beige slip and forget the A-line skirt and the soft, subtle sweater set hanging on the bathroom hook. Going for broke, I don a pair of black leather, knee-high boots and a short denim skirt—borrowed from Olivia's post-baby-days wardrobe—and pair them with a sky blue, button-up, V-neck sweater exposing a generous hint of mom cleavage. Not exactly the original look I planned but, as the man has seen me in a slip more than he's seen me in boots, I figure it can't hurt.

Drastic times call for drastic measures.

When I finally exit the house, he gawks at me with a wide stare that have nothing to do with goats or mud or broken-down cars.

It's a good sign.

~ * ~

We're finishing our dinner in a cozy Italian restaurant thirty miles away in Glendale, oozing garlic and carbs and drooling over the dessert menu. Beside me, my cell phone blinks with another intrusive text message, and apologetic, I show it to Sam.

"Mom again," I confirm.

He tears himself away from the dessert menu and gauges my

level of concerned. "Is it important?"

Silencing my phone, I slip it into my purse. "No, she's complaining about Squidward from Spongebob Squarepants. Apparently, he isn't anatomically correct."

An eyebrow rises. Sam puts down the menu. "Should he be?"

"Given he's a cartoon, I'd say no. From her perspective he should be. He doesn't have enough tentacles. For a squid. It's not like she's expert in aquatic animals, but that woman does love to Google. I'm ignoring her. She's only trying to start a conversation, so she can ask how it's going."

The waitress returns, and we order a slice of molten chocolate lava cake with a scoop of vanilla ice cream to share, although I have no idea where I'll put it as I'm stuffed like a Christmas goose, even if I restrained myself and went with the pork roast instead of a dish teeming with carbs. But sharing chocolate with Sam is too delicious to pass up, even if my contribution is only a bite or two. Or three. Okay, possibly four.

Dessert plans settled, my mind drifts toward tempting thoughts—a lusty good night kiss, Sam's arms around me, and, naturally, molten chocolate lava cake—when he interrupts my mental orgy.

"Have you started writing? Your blog?" he clarifies.

Fiddling with the cloth napkin in my lap, I hedge my answer, remembering my last efforts at the keyboard. "I have, a few personal essays, that's it. It's not easy, but it's satisfying. Nothing's posted online, and there's no actual blog yet. Olivia's trying to help, but it's unnerving. To her, it's a business and demands focus. To me? It's therapy. Totally, free therapy."

Sam wipes his mouth with his napkin. "Therapy's not a bad thing. It helps to get stuff off your chest."

"Exactly," I agree.

Still, as I contemplate sharing chocolate with Sam, a brief wave of panic floods me. What stuff is on his chest and, also, where's my dessert fork?

Finding it under my napkin, I relax somewhat and prattle on even as I contemplate what might weight him down. "Anyway, Olivia says my social media has to be consistent—like I have anything social or consistent in my life—and I need a reoccurring theme beyond chaos, plus a dedicated Instagram feed, a Twitter handle, stuff like that. Oh, and I should build my platform and my brand, whatever that means. She told me to get a tablet too, so I can update and converse on the fly, but I told her one of the kid's old school folders should do the trick.

She threatened to chase me down and beat me with it."

Amused, Sam nearly chokes on his wine.

It's fun making him laugh.

"Yeah," I continue, "aggressive, right? Especially since, when I'm not working, I just want to play with the kiddies and the animals and write funny stuff. Like, get this, Walter? He follows Lucky constantly. I mean, everywhere. Maybe he thinks he's another pony, maybe he's half blind, regardless, it's funny and kind a weird. Oh, and now I want a horse, thank you. But Olivia wants me to be serious about the blog."

Sam toys with his glass. "That can come later, can't it? Isn't the main thing right now just to write?"

I nod. "That's my idea, especially since my writing needs work. Baby steps, I tell her, baby steps. She ignores me and vomits advice."

Sam rewards me with another lusty laugh, and I join him. We revel in the joke and drink our wine, and I'm a content as hell.

This is going well.

Our table anchors a window overlooking a frozen garden decorated in white Christmas lights, and it's magical. Falling snow glistens, lights twinkle, reflections sparkle—it's stunning. Inside, a cozy fire burns bright in the hearth across the intimate room and the only other couple rises to leave. The candle before us glows, I've kept my hair away from the flame, more wine is poured, chocolate is ordered, no one has farted or choked, and I have Sam to myself.

Life is good.

So why can't I just enjoy it?

Because, despite everything, an irritating notion planted itself in my brain along with our prosciutto appetizer, and it's eating at me internally. It's like Sam said. Sometimes we need to get stuff off our chests. Whether we should is another thing entirely.

Oblivious, Sam swirls his glass, studies its contents, and takes another drink. "We may have to get a bottle of this to go."

I regard my own nearly empty glass and picture Sam in his underwear, hoping that excellent image will kill this idea simmering in my brain, which is digging in like a tapeworm, festering like a boil. Momentarily distracted, I cast him a half-hearted smile. "By the way, that's twice you've seen me in my underwear. Eventually, you'll have to even the score."

Dimples appear on those kissable cheeks, and Sam chuckles. "I didn't see much of you the first time, only enough to realize you weren't one of the guys from Jerry's Garage. None of them have your legs."

My legs? Were they shaved when I was under the car? I can't remember.

"Backing away from the underwear dare already," I reply. "Interesting. And thank you."

Candlelight sparkles in Sam's eyes. He draws closer. "Ro, I want to apologize again for leaving like that after I first kissed you. It's just...I hurt you, and I truly regret it."

His gaze plummets to the table and he picks at the tablecloth. "You deserve to be treated better than that." His chin lifts. Big, brown eyes blink at me.

Instantly, I melt. "Sam, don't, it's fine."

This time, it's my turn to look away. Dinner has gone so well. We've chatted about work, about people at the diner, about the animals, about our childhoods, my writing, and we even discussed that balloon ride, but this nasty worry nags at me. "Sam, can I share something with you? Even if I don't want to."

Sam stiffens. "What is it?"

Best to get it off my chest. Reluctantly, carefully I start, "Okay, here's the thing. I have a lot of baggage, not to mention three kids who are a real challenge most days. My life must be a freaking disaster to you. Here you sit, neat and clean, handsome, child free, and missing your wife. Meanwhile, I'm lucky if my shoes match and we don't run short of toilet paper."

Fueled by my glass of wine, I plunge on even if I shouldn't. "This is who I am, though, pure and simple. Sure, I'm barely holding on most days, but my kids are my priority. As for pursuing this, whatever it is," I add, pointing, first at him, then back at myself, "I need you to realize that. There can be none of this without my kids. We're a poorly wrapped package deal. To be honest," I continue to ramble, "I always imagined I would have more. Crazy, right? And if that has anything to do with you running away too, tell me now. I'll understand. I'll be crushed, but I'll understand."

There it is.

Reality.

What a buzz kill.

A final exhale escapes my chest. I sit and let my words sink in, wondering what the collateral damage may be. Whatever it is, I'll have to live with it regardless.

Shock rolls across Sam's puzzled face. Startled, feeling or thinking who knows what, he falters. His shoulders drop, and he studies the tablecloth. Finally, he rubs the back of his neck and lifts his face to the candlelight. Those sexy dimples wink at me.

Is he smiling? Why does he seem relieved?

Is it because I let him off the hook?

Sam reaches across the table and takes my hand, and I brace myself for what's to come.

"Ro," he says, his hand warm on my skin, "you're right, I don't have any kids, and on occasion I do miss my wife, and yes, something drove me away after that kiss."

Oh, crap.

You had to bring it up, Ro.

Couldn't you have least gotten to second base with him first?

I swallow. Words stick in my throat. Somehow, I manage to croak, "Okay, so, what was it?"

Gently, he squeezes my fingers. "First, please understand, I've been dealing with a lot of anger. I only started to come to terms with it during the last year."

Anger? That I get.

I put my other hand upon his and squeeze back. "I do understand. When you lose a loved one, it has to be difficult not to be angry."

"No, no, that's not it," Sam replies.

"Then what?" I hang on his words, confused.

He pulls his hands free and leans back in his chair, hesitant about whatever it is.

He's going to say he's still in love with his wife, that he'll forever be in love with his wife, I just know he is. I bite my lip and wait for the inevitable.

Flickering firelight illuminates his sorrow. He shrugs in the soft glow. "Shelly decided she didn't want kids." He states it briskly, his voice husky, his jaws tight with emotion. He contorts the napkin in his lap with calloused fingers, twisting it and wrenching it in his firm grip. "We talked about having kids, but after we married, she only wanted a career. In a county where procreation is the local pastime, I married the one woman with no interest in being a mom." His voice quivers, relaying an undertone I've not heard before.

"It drove us apart," he continues. "We separated, and I was going to file for divorce, but then she was diagnosed with cancer. Stage four. She needed me, and I stuck it out until the end. For better or for worse, in sickness and in health," he murmurs. A slow sigh escapes his lips. Tension eases from his shoulders, and he rubs his face. When his palms come away, he adds through glistening eyes, "What I'm trying to say is, my walking away had nothing to do with me being in love with her or the fact that you have three kids."

The waitress arrives with our dessert, winning the bad-timing award for the night in the process. Sam stops torturing his napkin and regroups enough to thank her.

Silent, I watch her walk away, willing him to continue as I sit here, clueless. If it's not his wife or my kids...I raise my fork and take the smallest of bites. "It's because you're my boss, isn't it?" Sick at the notion, I drop my fork and replace it with my wine glass. Taking a deep chug, I swallow the last of my wine and sigh. "Why are we even here then?"

A grin as big as Texas rains down upon me. Laughter shakes Sam's body. "That's not it either."

He's laughing? Seriously?

I stab at the chocolate cake. "Okay, what? Tell me."

Pausing, Sam composes himself. Finally, he replies, "Ro, I want a big family, always have, but Shelly wasn't truthful about what she wanted. It hurt. After she died, I was too angry to even wonder what the future might bring. I knew I couldn't begin another relationship until I recovered from that hurt. I dealt with it the only way I knew how. I buried it deep, put my life on hold, and focused on work."

His gaze turned tender. "Then you showed up."

He's serious now. The laughter's gone, and he seems to grapple with his words, as if attempting to explain something.

I wait, patient, expectant, hopeful.

He starts, "You breeze in here with a pack of kids like it's the most natural thing in the world, a flat tire doesn't stop you, you dive into this job with next to no experience and do it well, you're saving animals left and right, you're standing up to your ex, and I'm floored. You're a little force of nature, Ro, and I can't stop thinking about you. You're the most real woman I've ever met. You're funny, you're smart, you're fearless, and you're cute as hell."

"But...?" I interject.

God, I hate that word.

"...you've got a family, a wonderful, crazy family." He searches my face for understanding. Longing, joy, regret burn in those dark eyes while he struggles to give voice to his fears. "You have three wonderful kids, so I was sure you had no interest in more. If life blesses me with stepchildren one day, great, I'll love them with my whole heart. But I walked away because I could get lost in you, Ro Andrews, and then I'd be right back where I started. With no children of my own. That's a dream I can't let go, not yet, anyway."

He chuckles. "Long story short, I figured you'd slammed the baby door shut, locked it, and threw away the key. It's great to realize you haven't."

Hold on a sec...

...back the reveal truck up...

What did he say?

Confession accomplished, oblivious to my wonderment, Sam releases me, grabs his fork, and takes a bite of cake. "This is good." He sighs. "I love chocolate when it's not too sweet. This one's just right."

For once, chocolate is before me, but it's not my focus.

His words linger.

Am I dreaming?

No, I'm very much awake. In fact, I'm a hormonal stew, a churning, seething, roiling mass of excitement and elation and horniness too. I stare at Sam as he takes another bite. "Let me see if I've got this right," I begin, tentative, afraid if I push it, time will reverse, and he'll suck those words right back in, "you've been fighting this because you were afraid I didn't want to expand the booger brigade?"

A sheepish smile creeps across his face. "Pretty much."

"Seriously?"

Dimples tempt me across candlelight. "Seriously."

Holy crap.

Fear, worry, and regret depart. Amusement engulfs me. Tears spring to life, joyful, happy tears. Even my napkin is too small to hide the gloriously loud snort emanating from my mouth. It sends us both into hysterics and, of course, I snort even louder.

Happy tears cloud my vision as I try to contain the giggles. "My God, we really made some stupid assumptions, didn't we?"

Sam continues to laugh, and it's glorious. "Yes, yes we did."

Finally, we regain a sense of self control. I stop snorting and Sam relaxes in the candlelight. Setting down his fork, he reaches for my hand once more. "I realize we're only now getting to know each other, but, for the first time in quite a while, I'm looking forward to life. You're this adorable, surprisingly funny bright spot in my otherwise endless stretch of dull, pointless days, and I'm grateful. Sure, this is our first date, but it feels like a step in the right direction, at least. For now, let's enjoy each other's company and take it step by step. Sound good?"

Sniffing loudly, I fork a gooey morsel into my mouth and murmur through the chocolate, "I don't know what the hell I'm doing, so step-by-step is good. Plus, I'm not going anywhere."

"Good. You're well worth the wait."

Maybe it's the chocolate or the wine or from sitting here with Sam, discovering the truth, talking about our fears, and facing them down. Regardless, while I'm a hot mess dripping with divorce damage, I, too, have hope.

Sam said I'm worth the wait, and he for damn sure is.

Let's not make him wait too long.

~ * ~

We walk out of the restaurant into a whirlwind of snow and drive home at a snail's pace. I don't mind—the more Sam time, the better. The snow falls hard and fast as we approach Thornhill much later than intended, but I have no plans to shorten what I pray will be a passionate make-out session in the driveway. Thank heaven, the restaurant had mints.

Through the swirl of flakes and thick stands of trees, however, I spy lights burning bright in the house. Lots of them, though it's late on a school night.

What the heck?

My silenced cell phone forgotten I finally check it. Ten text messages and three phone calls—Mom, Olivia, and Justin have each called or texted within the last forty-five minutes.

Oh, no.

I ignore Mom's texts and open Olivia's. It's short and to the point. "Get home ASAP. Peter called child protective services. They're here. Now."

That fucking bastard.

We crest the hill. A van with government plates sits next to a sheriff's car. Both are off and empty, and thankfully the sheriff's emergency lights are not on.

Wordless, and leaping from the truck, I sprint for the back door, forgetting my coat, my purse, my goodnight kiss, forgetting Sam. The kitchen is empty, so I make a beeline for the main hall. Justin sits in the semi-darkened dining room, rocking Jayden who's asleep on his shoulder, and he points up the stairs. I take them two at a time. Voices echo in the distance.

At the far end of the landing, a heavy-set woman clutching a clipboard peers above her glasses, talking with Olivia and Mom. A deputy, some young buck named Brent who's visited the diner a time or two since I started, braces himself behind the woman, one hand on his hip, the other resting on his holster. He watches me mount the stairs. As I approach, he bypasses her and steps forward to halt my progress.

Good for him. He recognizes kick-ass crazy when he sees it.

In full-on mamma bear combat mode, I fall upon him. "What's going on?" Black dots dance in my vision. Sucking wind, I bite my lip. Tonight's not the night to faint from lack of oxygen. Unless sex with Sam is involved, and that ain't happening now.

Dripping with authority, the strange woman bypasses the deputy. "Hello, I'm Meredith Scott with Posey County Child Protective Services."

"I'm Ro Andrews. What's going on here? What the hell did my ex say? Good lord, we were playing in the mud. Wait, where are my kids?"

Nick's voice finds me from the girls' future bedroom. "We're in here, Mom."

I lunge between the woman and the deputy into the room.

My three sweet angels sit on the floor, clad in pajamas, playing with a few blocks amid the paint cans and drop clothes. No smiles greet us, no squabbles fill the air, no building block castles grow on the floor. Only three small children who play among the tools and moving boxes, aimlessly jostling toys in a large, unfinished, run-down room.

At the sight of me, Nick leaps to his feet and breaks into a run. Tears cascade down his face. Aaron follows, joining us, and hugs me too.

"Mommy!" Maddy squeezes in between the boys and wraps her tiny arms around my knees like a squid with the requisite number of tentacles.

Overwhelmed, I cling to my children and attempt to soothe them.

Mentally, however, I'm planning a hunting party.

For Peter.

Nick studies me with sad, puppy-dog eyes and whimpers, "Mom, what's going on?"

How can I take this pain away? A mother is only as happy as her saddest child, and I have three who are suffering. Enough is enough.

The woman blocks the doorway. "Ms. Andrews, may I have a word?"

"My children are upset. I'll be with you in a moment." Turning my back on her, I tilt each face in turn and kiss their sweet cheeks. "This is a big, old house, and they want to make sure it's warm and dry, and that we stay safe during the winter."

Unconvinced, Nick presses. "She asked about our mud fight and about sleeping in the dining room."

Aaron twists in my arms, burning nervous energy. "She asked if we go to school and what our favorite subjects are too. I told her I like recess best. She laughed at that. I told her I hit Nick with a turd." He squirms. "Am I in trouble for that? Are they going to take me away because I threw a turd?"

Choking down tears, I sink to my knees. "No, sweetie, you're not in trouble for throwing a turd. Tell you what, let me talk to Ms. Scott and clear this up. Tomorrow's a school day. We need to get you three in bed and pronto."

Though all I want to do is cradle them close, I pry my scared babies loose and flash my biggest, most confident, fake smile. Playfully, I tap Nick's nose. Worry is etched across his face, and it kills me. "I'll be back in a second," I reassure them.

Crossing the room, I follow Ms. Scott out the door. A crowd waits at the top of the stairs, including Justin, minus Jayden, and Sam, who joined us and talks with Officer Brent. As I approach, they stop. Silence fills the air.

Out of earshot from the kids, I face the woman invading my home. "What did my ex tell you?"

Pen at the ready, she taps her clipboard. "Ms. Andrews, I'm not at liberty to discuss our source. We received a report that an emergency welfare check was in order as we had children living in squalor in an unheated home. We were required by law to check."

"And?" I wave my arms about the hall. "Do you see squalor?"

"No, I—"

"Is the home unheated?"

The pen stops tapping. She lowers the clipboard. "No, it is not."

Olivia steps forward. "Damn straight, it's not."

"Easy, babe." Justin snags her forearm, restraining her.

Mom squirms past him. "Let her be. She's got a right to be pissed too."

"Now let's everybody stay calm." Officer Brent raises his hand. "No sense getting worked up."

"Easy for you to say," I snap. Ignoring the deputy, I address the woman judging our home. "This house is heated and clean. We have electricity, plumbing, food. The children are healthy, loved, go to school, and are in no danger. So, if we're done here. I'm asking you to leave. It's late, and they're upset. If you do care about their welfare, you'll call it a night. Am I right?"

Filled with determination, I could win a staring contest with a cat.

Equally determined, Olivia moves closer to me, radiating fierceness. Uncharacteristically silent through most of this nightmare, Mom crosses her arms and joins us. Together, we silently dare the woman to continue.

Ms. Scott tucks her reading glasses into her purse. "Ms. Andrews, my report will show that the children are not in any immediate danger and that the living standards in the home are adequate."

"Adequate?" Olivia barks.

"Presently, we have no cause to remove them from the home. Please be advised, however, that—"

"Mommy," Maddy screams from the bedroom.

Operating in panic mode, I brush by Ms. Scott and dash into the room. "What?"

She waits in the open closet door and points inside. "Mommy, it's Poo Poo Pink Princess."

What?

Ms. Scott joins me in the room with Officer Brent.

Maddy laughs, patting her knees, talking baby talk. "Come here, Poo Poo. Who's a good baby—"

Ms. Scott shrieks, stumbling backward. "Eeek!"

A fat, languid possum waddles straight for my daughter, trailing its pink nasty tail through the building blocks.

Oh.

My.

God.

Maddy plops to the floor. "Where've you been, Poo Poo? I had a jelly sandwich for you, but it's gone." She swivels to face me, awash in smiles and sunshine. "Mommy, can I get Poo Poo another jelly sandwich? I ate hers. Can I borrow your toothbrush when she's done? She likes toothpaste too."

"Madison, come here now!"

Startled, her face snaps my way. She swings from adult to adult, confused, wanting only appreciation for her pet, but instead she's met with fear and disgust. Once more, my baby starts to cry. She shoves the possum away and runs into my arms.

Apparently anti-social, Poo Poo practically pivots on her creepy pink tail and disappears into the closet.

Bracing for action, Officer Brent unsnaps the top of his holster. "Want me to dispatch it?"

"Dispatch it? In our home? Are you insane?" I'm screaming now.

Maddy is screaming. Aaron is shell-shocked. Nick is sniffling yet again. From below us echo the cries of the twins, startled awake by the commotion overhead, and I register Olivia bounding away to soothe her own terrified offspring.

This idiot wants to fire his weapon? In our home? What the bloody hell?

Sam steps behind the deputy. "Brent, I have a live trap at my house. I'll run and get it. In the meantime, don't do anything stupid." He stops in the doorway. "Ro, will you be okay while I'm gone? I'll hurry back, I promise."

Cradling my crying daughter, I muster a nod. "I'll be fine."

Sam flies down the stairs and is gone.

Leaping into action, Justin rushes into the closet after the possum. Momentarily, his voice rings out, "A ceiling tile's missing, and the lathes are cracked at the outside wall. I bet that thing used a branch to get into the attic. From there, it's a short climb into the closet."

Ms. Scott shudders and crosses the room. She glances around the door for confirmation, then sprints back to the safety of Officer Brent.

It's time to end this disaster. I pass Maddy to Mom and address our unwelcomed guests. "This doesn't change anything. We were clueless about the possum, but here's what's going to happen. Sam's going to live trap it, preferably tonight," I add, to Ms. Scott. "We'll patch the hole and whatever it's using to get into the attic. I'll take the possum to the vet for rabies shots, and it can live in the tree outside."

"Maddy, you can set food and water near the tree for it but," I shake a finger at her growing cries, "she is not allowed back in this house, and you are not to touch her. She is a wild animal."

Determined to end this experiment in social hell, I address Ms. Scott directly, "It's way too late, and we are off to bed whether you stay here or not. Understood?" I face them both, toe-to-toe, in full Super Mom mode, daring either the woman or the deputy to disagree.

Bring it, bitches. I'm ready rumble.

Ms. Scott squares her shoulders. "We're done here."

"So, we're good?" I question.

Do wild possums change the child endangerment equation?

She grips her purse close. "This animal needs to remain outside the home. I suggest you dispatch it, but that's your call, not mine. This may warrant a follow-up visit, but, for now, I'm satisfied the children are in no imminent danger. No need to remove them from the home tonight."

Behind me Nick repeats, "Remove them from the home?" but I usher him from the room and propel him to the stairs with Aaron and a sobbing Maddy in tow.

In the dining room, Olivia cradles her babies in a large recliner, worry etched upon her face. Had my children been taken, the twins would have too. Like me, she's shaken to her core, another damaged soul sucked along in Peter's miserable, selfish wake.

I repeat, that bastard.

We herd the children to bed. After a quick promise to come back and tuck them in, I depart the dining room and propel Ms. Scott and Officer Brent through the hallway toward the kitchen.

Until she stops at the bathroom door, delaying my relief.

Crud.

"May I?" she asks.

My blood pressure tick-tocks upward in time with Olivia's clock, and I motion her in. "Of course."

The door closes, leaving me alone with Officer Brent.

He pats his holster. "Let me know if you change your mind about the possum."

On edge and nearly unhinged, I flash fiery green eyes in the dim hallway. "I won't."

From inside the bathroom come the muffled sounds of shuffling. Toilet paper whizzes away on the roll. It seems so long ago when I was dodging Mom and helping Maddy, anticipating my date with Sam, fighting with a stupid goat...

Oh, nut balls.

"Don't flush!"

Too freaking late.

"*Aaagh*!"

Startled, Officer Brent moves for his holster then shoves open the door.

Bubbles stream from the toilet, escaping the bowl, and crawl across the floor to swamp Ms. Scott's cheap slacks bunched at her cankles. Dancing in the suds, she wrenches polyester skyward along her thick thighs, mustering an expression that can only translate into one possible thing...

What the freaking hell?

It's one I understand too well.

Some nights when I can't sleep, I lie in bed and try to imagine what it's like to be a monk. I could run off to a temple high in the mountains, shave myself bald, take a vow of silence. Fast. Meditate.

Or fling myself from the tallest tower.

It has possibilities.

Or maybe I should get better at hiding the damn dish soap.

"Aaron, enough with the practical jokes!"

Mischievous little boy snickers float from the dining room into the hall.

That kid…I swear…

Officer Brent laughs.

Embarrassed, Ms. Scott shakes her wet feet and treats him to a grimace then barks at me. "I'll send you a copy of my report."

Inspection complete, she gyrates around him in her damp, sensible shoes. She shuffles to the kitchen, hell-bent on reaching her van in one piece, ignoring Officer Brent who follows, chuckling behind.

Through the back door and into the flurries they go, and I can't lock it fast enough. Finally, she climbs into her van, and he disappears into his car.

Plastered to the door window, unwilling to breathe, afraid I'll jinx their exit if I do, I watch for their taillights, willing them to leave the lane. Not until they turn onto the road do I exhale in relief.

Brakes lights disappear, and relieved, I tremble. Resting my forehead against the cold glass, I close my eyes.

Tonight, I fought off the demons.

What Peter-induced hell awaits me tomorrow?

~ * ~

It's after midnight, my wine buzz is long gone, and I can't balance these freaking blocks to save my life. Is this another coordination thing? Had I crawled longer as a baby, could I build a better fort?

My back is pressed against the wall in the girls' future bedroom, next to the closet door beside Sam. Our block fort towers an impressive three stories high, no thanks to me, and we compromised on the turrets, despite my inner princess which seriously believes them necessary.

Sam helps himself to my block pile and occasionally eyeballs an electric train set tempting him from the shadows. We wait in semi-darkness for Poo Poo Pink Princess, hoping she discovers a can of dog food in the live trap waiting at her front door.

Stiff and aching, I stretch my back as my block pile dwindles. "Much as I like sitting here with you, it's getting late," I say softly. "You have to drive home, the roads are bad, and we both work tomorrow. I'll check the cage in the morning. If we catch it, Justin can put it in my car. I'll take it from there."

Sam places another block, starting a fourth floor. "Are you really getting it shots?"

"Not only that," I snicker, "I'm having it neutered too." I set a block on Sam's only to collapse a partial wall. I shrug and start sorting. "Oops…sorry."

We sit close, our sides smooshed against each other, shoulder to shoulder, and begin again. Sam chuckles and rearranges blocks. I chuckle too and lay my head on his shoulder. He leans into me, vanilla, pine, and leather swirl in his wake, and his cheek falls upon the top of my hair.

It's more heavenly than the chocolate cake.

"I could sit here all night," Sam whispers, reading my thoughts, "but you're right, it's getting late, and this wood floor is starting to hurt. Before I do…" He hesitates then adds, "there's something missing from our date."

"What?" I joke. "Government officials, wild rodents, and overflowing toilets aren't enough for you?"

"No."

"Bosses are so difficult to please. What then?"

"A goodnight kiss."

"Aha…" I reply. Tingles ignite. "You sure you want to kiss me? I think my daughter's been using my toothbrush on a possum."

Sam bursts into a laugh, filling the quiet house with spontaneous joy.

After this disaster of an ending, it's good to laugh.

We sit in the dark, giggling like mad, two thirty-something people in the middle of nowhere, playing blocks and awaiting a possum with pearly whites. I fall into his arms, he pulls me close, and, possum or no possum, germs or no germs, we kiss.

How is this possible?

It's even better than before.

His lips find mine, my heart races, and I melt into Sam. He's tender, oh, so tender. Our lips part, and I give in completely. Trust enters the picture and morphs into excitement, which bursts into a passion that fills me to overflowing. The outright need is intense. Everything exists in that kiss. Joy at finding him. A hint of anger that it took this long. Contentment in the action itself. Lust at what's to come next. Peacefulness that this may actually be it, that I was meant to find him, that we were meant to be together.

And humor when we hear the snap of the live trap, confining Poo Poo Pink Princess in her gilded cage. Regardless, as the night grows later by the hour, we sit in the darkness and kiss.

~ * ~

With Poo Poo cooling her heels at the vet for vaccines and a quickie surgery so she can go forth and practice safe sex, I burst through the doors of the diner, desperate to get to work while pictures of child protective services, cheating ex-husbands, and pudgy rodents dance in my imagination like spoiled, drunken, sugar plum fairies at a rave.

Trust me, I've had better dreams.

Officer Brent hunches upon a bar stool, cradling a cup of coffee, and re-enacting a bit of local drama to none other than my neighborhood nemesis, Judge Middleton. Catching sight of me, he spins away, choking on a laugh.

Gee, I bet I can guess who's the star of his latest passion play.

Joy to the freaking world.

Good lord, this is embarrassing. A possum and child welfare workers graced our home last night while I was on a date, slobbering over Sam, and now the judge—and possibly the entire town—is aware of it.

Whatever. I'm going to own it.

"Officer Brent, Judge Middleton, good morning," I chirp and stride toward them, a giant grin plastered on my face. I do all the right things—make eye contact, exude confidence, blame the redness of my cheeks on the weather. "Cold, isn't it? Oh, and Poo Poo is at the vet as we speak, to be vaccinated and," I reply as I squirm away to my office booth, "spayed."

The deputy's chin drops to his chest. "Spayed? You're kidding?"

I plunk my purse next to my monitor and take off my coat. "Nope, I'm serious as a heart attack. She's a she. Oh, and lots of people keep possums as pets. I Googled it."

Please don't Google it.

Desperate for caffeine, I grab my mug then head toward the coffee station. After dumping in enough sugar to kick start my pancreas, I fill my mug to the top, inhale steam, then take a cautious sip.

Drats. It needs bourbon.

Turning to my booth, I glide toward it, balancing my full mug. "Who knows?" I remark, hoping they buy it, "maybe Maddy will be a vet one day. That child can tame anything."

Take that, you local yokels.

Safe in the confines of my booth, I risk a peek at Officer Brent through the mirror.

Both he and Judge Middleton, in addition to Ernie and the Burts, gape at me with open mouths and holy-shit expressions. Apparently, taming wild possums and updating their immunizations isn't a regular thing here in Poseyville.

Whatever. They'll get over it.

Taking solace in a stack of invoices, I'm fully aware a roomful of shocked men stare at me in disbelief.

You'd think I'd get used to it.

No. The answer is no.

The diner bell rings, and I ignore it—there's work to do—until Officer Brent's voice demands my attention. "Hey, Sam, did you hear? She went and did it. She took that possum to the vet. She's getting that dang thing fixed too."

Instantly, I forget invoices and look for Sam's reflection in the mirror.

He stops beside the deputy and claps him on the back. "She doesn't want to upset her daughter, Brent. You can appreciate that. How old is Emily now?"

Through the mirror, mirror on the wall, Brent's reflection shifts under the weight of Sam's thoughtful stare. "She'll be three in February."

Judge Middleton, however, says nothing.

"Three? Time flies, doesn't it?" Like that, Sam changes the subject. He nods at the judge, then waves at me as he mouths, "I'll be right there," before he helps himself to the coffee pot.

Holy crap on a cracker.

He's perfect.

Sam fixes himself a cup of coffee and joins me. Pushing my monitor aside, I forget about invoices, officers, and possums, oh, my, and stare at the handsome cowboy sitting across from me.

sigh

"Good morning, Ro."

"Good morning, Sam."

My eyelid twitches—come on, caffeine, kick in—and I clutch my mug and pass it off as a wink.

His hand rests on the table, and I want to hold it. Can I do that? Are we "public" yet?

So many questions.

"Thanks again for helping last night," I murmur instead and twitch. "I had a great time, despite how it ended."

Passionate hot kisses assault my memory.

"Especially how it ended," I add.

Sam blows on his coffee and winks back. "I did too. We need to do it again. Soon."

A quadrillion cells fire on all cylinders, inundating me in flames. I half expect smoke rings to puff from my throat when I speak, and I'm surprised when they don't. "I need to run to Glendale Saturday to do some Christmas shopping," I purr. Chancing spontaneous combustion, I slide my foot under the booth, find his boot, and glide my toes up his shaft—boot shaft, I totally meant boot shaft.

The unfortunate reminder of Mom's Thanksgiving foot massage reins me in, blinding me momentarily.

Yuck.

Damn it, Mom.

Reluctantly, I drag my foot away. "It's not dinner and a movie," I continue, "but if you don't mind romping through a toy store first, dinner is on me this time."

Sam presses his calf against mine, rekindling embers. "Sounds like a plan."

"Good." I gulp.

We drink our coffee, and it's pleasant, despite the curiosity of twenty plus people watching us with far too much interest. If cable TV and the internet aren't doing it for them, the least we can do is be memorable, right?

Sam and I chat with Saturday on our minds until shades of blue and black snag my attention in the mirror. A police officer I do not know approaches from the front door.

Suddenly, Sam's face clouds as the man heads our way, and his attention rockets back to me.

Instantly, I tense. What gives?

The officer halts beside us. "Sparrow Andrews?"

For the second day in a row, every mother's worse fear spreads through me, burning like wildfire, immersing me in terror. Questions I may not want answers to swamp me in my office booth, questions like why are you here, and what happened, and what's wrong?

"Morning Sam," he says while waiting my reply, unaware I'm dying before him.

"Melvin," Sam whispers, acknowledging him.

My throat constricts, strangling me. "Yes," I croak. "Are my babies okay?" I half rise, my stomach in my shoes. My heart lurches against my ribs, pounding in my chest, threatening to burst through my skin.

The strange man thrusts an envelope into my face. "Ma'am, I'm here to serve you papers from the Court of Posey County."

I take it.

"What?"

He points at a sheet fastened to a clipboard. "Sign here, please."

My eyes burn—did I forget to blink? My chest pounds. I've forgotten to breathe. Regardless, I sign my name.

"Thank you." He tucks the clipboard under his arm. "Later Sam. If I don't see you in the next few weeks, have a Merry Christmas."

"You too."

Time stops. Sam, the diner, customers disappear. My world at this moment is confined to an envelope.

My fingers tremble. I tear it open and grasp the papers, wrenching them from it, then read.

It's a summons from Peter.

The bastard wasn't just making a threat to take me to court.

He's doing it.

Peter's coming after my babies.

~ * ~

"Ro?"

Sam pounds on the diner's bathroom door, but I ignore him. I'm on my knees, reeling against the toilet, sobbing, dying, dissolving.

Peter wants my babies. He wants full custody.

With her.

This is hell. I've descended into hell.

Vomit rockets into the bowl.

Sam pounds and yells and questions.

My babies are my world, they're everything I've lived for, sacrificed for, altered my life for, given up a career and toilet paper for. I would die for them without question, without fail. If he takes my babies, he may as well reach into my chest and rip out my still-beating heart.

It goes where they go.

Always.

My head rests against cold porcelain. Tears carve their way down my face.

He wants my babies.

And, God help me, I'm afraid he's going to get them.

Chapter Thirteen

Christmas waits for no man, woman, or court hearing. Peter's threats hang over me like a life-ending icicle, but a mother of three small children has to plow forward when Santa's on his way. In between working and worrying and bugging my attorney, I've bought toys, hidden candy, hung stockings, and made plans that include 'offing Peter.

Just kidding.

Maybe.

In between my near constant breakdowns and hysterics, Sam is my sexy island in a sea of uncertainty. Since Peter's custody bombshell two weeks ago, my days are spent either working at the diner, tending to my children, writing my blog, emailing my attorney, and sobbing in the car. Nights swell with checking homework, making lists, shopping online, wrapping presents after hours, and hiding my tears in the dark. Most evenings Sam joins us. We eat supper, we play games with the kids, we build more block forts, sometimes with turrets, and Sam finally got his hands on the electric train set. His presence gives me comfort and hope and soothes my fears, even if only temporarily.

As toys rolled in these last few weeks, we've bonded over itty bitty screws and bicycle chains, double AA batteries and plastic parts, not to mention wine-laced confessionals and heavenly make-out sessions, while the children slept unaware on the other side of the house. Treading lightly given my current state of near panic, we have yet to make love, but at least most of my moments with Sam have been glorious.

At the moment, however, he helps distract me from my custody fears by tackling advanced prep work on a pile of toys that will require way too much post-eggnog attention come Christmas morning. Already, we've wrapped a microscope set for Nick, a baby doll that wets itself for Maddy, and stuck batteries into a small remote-controlled helicopter for Aaron, which we naturally tested in the kitchen, and we've spooled extra line onto the reels of the boys' first fishing poles.

Tonight's last project is a plastic dollhouse for Maddy. A thousand and one components occupy the kitchen table along with instructions in Japanese. But as the evening wanes, I have second thoughts about building a dreamhouse and more thoughts about shifting our physical relationship into high gear. Instead of putting together toys, I want to unwrap Sam.

He's digesting instructions, all sexy and sweet, reading glasses perched at the end of his nose, inhaling foreign, five-point type. My contribution, snapping pieces of roof to pieces of wall, is finished, as is my wine. I'm toasty warm and, for now, at least, I'm feeling pretty fine.

It's time for dessert, and I don't mean pudding.

Sam takes off the glasses and rubs his eyes. "This makes no sense."

I undo a button on my long-sleeve, Henley T-shirt. "It's in Japanese."

Sam drags his palms down his cheeks. "There's English too, but it's not much help." Tired and worn, his gaze falls upon me. At the sight of the second button popping open, his eyebrow shuts up. His hands fall from his face and suddenly, he sits a little straighter, riveted upon me.

My hunger lingers and grows. I undo another button...and another.

Out of buttons, I refill my glass of wine, and I lick the rim. "What if we save the dollhouse for tomorrow night? I can think of better things to do."

In an instant, Sam springs from his chair. Finding a very willing recipient, he touches my back, my arms, my hair, kissing me with a force I had not expected.

I respond in kind, desperate to get at him.

He reaches behind my shirt, slides his hands beneath it and finds my bra clasp, releasing it. His lips fall upon my own, devouring me.

I grip his waist, drawing him close, then tug at his shirt. Content to let my own fingers do the walking, I climb his ribs one by one. My fingers skate across his chest around to his back. His muscles grow taut at my touch. I caress his lower back, trailing downward, my goal that magnificent, rock hard ass. I can't get enough of him, his skin, his lips, his smell, his touch.

Sam leans into me, pressing me backward, upon plastic and paper in the middle of the kitchen table. His fingers and lips explore my trembling flesh. Gently, urgently, he slides his palms upward and clasps my breasts. Electrified, I gasp. Pushing my shirt and bra up, his mouth finds my nipple, sending me into a frenzy.

My back and neck take on a life of their own, arching in

agonizing need. Wave after wave of want tear through me. I shove aside piles of toy debris, find the table edge and grip it, seeking leverage. Panting, I pull Sam upon me, distracting me from the whirring noise filling the room.

Hold on...

What whirring noise?

A sharp pain cuts through my desire.

"Ouch! What the hell is that?"

Sam pulls back. "What? Did I hurt you?"

Wincing in pain, I clutch my hair and discover stiff plastic. Rotors from Aaron's toy helicopter are buried to my skull. Hanks of hair twist around the shaft, knotted tight, stuck to my scalp like a British fastener, and me without a royal wedding to attend.

I grip the table edge, next to the controller, alongside a fishing pole. It's a miracle I don't have a lure snagged on my ass. I push myself up. My bra, high upon my neck, strangles me, and my disappointed breasts swing in the air, missing Sam's lips, his tongue, his hands.

He plants himself between my legs and examines the toy while I, head down, examine his crotch, regretting every wasted centimeter as it deflates before me.

He moves the helicopter a smidge. "I need to take this rotor off."

"Ouch!"

This is not the head I wanted tended to tonight.

"Sorry, sweetie. Hang tight for a second." He searches the table for a diminutive screwdriver. "It's got to be around here somewhere...here it is. Tip your head a bit."

I have no choice but to sit on the table, keep still, and slide my fingers around his waist. Working my way down his blue jeans, I cup his ass.

Sam works on the rotor. "You're not making this easy."

"Good," I mutter, "I'm trying to make it hard." Verbally, I parry and thrust. God, how I want to thrust.

A tool in one hand, a helicopter in the other, Sam finds my lips and kisses me. It's slow and deep, the way kisses should be. We break only for oxygen.

Exploding with want, I blurt a demand. "Sam, get this out of my hair and make love to me. Please."

His chocolate brown eyes lock onto mine. "You got it, babe."

There's urgency in his efforts, and I'm frozen in place, doing what I can to speed the process. I reach his inner thigh and work my way up, up, up, gratified when I arrive at my goal, satisfied when he moans.

Keys jingle in the back door. The lock turns.

Sam and I exchange feverish glances.

The back door opens.

Shit.

Busted.

Immediately we spring into action.

Mom saunters into the kitchen, humming *Bolero,* carrying her winter coat, mere seconds after I managed to adjust my bra and fix my shirt. Her red hair hangs loose and wild around her big, hoop earrings. A green satin blouse hugs her impressive mom curves above her black leather skirt and killer spiked heels.

"What have we here?" she asks, hanging her coat on the rack and treating me to a closer look.

My, my, my...she smells like wine and pipe tobacco...interesting.

I angle between her and Sam, shielding his crotch. "We were working on toys."

"Toys? Right. Listen, I'm not one to judge, but," she points at my noggin, "what's with the helicopter? I didn't take Sam for kinky."

I'm about to answer, when another sound sends me into an even greater panic.

"Mom!"

Double shit.

A child is up.

"Sam, help me hide this stuff." I pop off the table and lift a shipping box from the floor.

Leaping into action, he sweeps his arm across the table, shoving plastic, paper, and fishing gear flying inside. A chunk of dollhouse roof hits the helicopter remote, sending rotors back into gear. They whirl away at the one millimeter of freedom his efforts bought me, grinding it up in a split second until they can spin no more.

"Crap!" I yank the controller from the box and pry the batteries loose, tossing them into the sink. Sam grabs the box and bolts to the back door.

"Mom?" Maddy calls to me from the hall.

"What do I do?" I point to the miniature scale Blackhawk attacking my tresses.

An impish grin lights Mom's face. "You do get yourself into some weird pickles, kiddo."

"True, but that's not helping!"

She smiles and tosses her purse beside the sink. "I'll take care of Maddy. You go take care of Sam. Ditch the helicopter first. You don't want him to lose an eye." Laughing, she disappears into the hall.

I burst through the kitchen door, seeking my cowboy.

Where'd he go?

Oh, no!

An assortment of plastic lies scattered around my sexy sweetie, outlining him like chalk around a body at a crime scene. He lays sprawled on his back in the snow.

"Sam!"

I fly down the steps and hit the ice. As I soar through the air, bound for disaster, I have to time to ponder things, things like, "this is going to hurt" and "I bet we aren't having sex tonight after all" and "why didn't I buy cat litter for the walkway," not to mention absorb Sam's warning cry of, "Watch out for the icy patch!"

And to think, I spent all that time shaving.

~ * ~

A gooey pad of medicated muscle relaxer sticks to the twingy spot on Sam's back. We've swallowed half a pound of ibuprofen between us and, I swear, it's not enough.

The box of dollhouse parts—*please let them all be there*—and other assorted toys are stored in Mom's room for another attempt at another time. We're ready to call it a night too, but Sam has one last mission—removing Nick's helicopter from my hair.

Yep.

It's still there.

In the bathroom, Sam teases me with his closeness. My back is against the vanity, my chin at my chest, counting the teeth on his zipper while he works. "I hope we don't need the scissors." I sigh.

We've lubed my hair with conditioner to make it easier to pull free—not how I planned to use lube tonight—but now the bastard of a tiny screwdriver is super slippery and difficult for Sam to hold.

"This is going in the blog," I share, "for personal therapy."

Concentrating on my tresses, he teases them from around the rotor shaft. "Want me to take pictures? You know, for your blog?"

His grin sets me tingling.

I backtrack, "Don't you dare."

At my side, Sam bends closer. "Steady...don't move..." His nose is practically in my part.

"Do I have dandruff?"

"No."

He frees another hunk. It sticks up and out from my scalp, joining the other ratty, nasty chunks.

I look like a drunk clown.

"I meant to touch up my highlights, but with Christmas and this mess with Peter and work, I've been super busy."

"Your highlights are fine. Quit squirming." Sam concentrates. He twists the screwdriver.

"Do you see any gray hairs? I have tweezers in there if you find any. Feel free to pluck them." I point at the drawer with my toe.

"I don't see any gray hairs." He loosens another hank. The helicopter budges.

"Sam?"

"Yes, Ro?"

"I've been meaning to ask you. What's a moisture check?"

He halts.

A laugh, loud, strong, and full of life, erupts from my helicopter hero.

"God, I love you, Ro," he chuckles. "You're always good for a laugh."

Suddenly, Sam freezes. His words hang in the air.

I freeze too.

Slowly, I raise my head, helicopter and all.

He lowers his.

Our eyes meet.

I expect him to be terrified, but I don't think he is. Plus, I expect to be terrified, but I'm pretty sure I'm not.

Instead, my eyes burn with tears, happy, joyful, hopeful tears.

"I love you too, Sam."

A tender kiss lands on my nose.

In the blessed midnight silence of the bathroom, Sam, my dear, sweet cowboy hero, goes back to work on the helicopter.

~ * ~

After the sugar-fest that was Christmas, I've reluctantly agreed to start New Year's off with less alcohol and more vegetables. At Olivia's request, I'm helping her make a colorful Mediterranean chopped salad, and I dice baby carrots while she tackles a red pepper. Naturally, we're each racing to finish our individual piles of veggies as we're both rather competitive and neither of us wants to do the purple onion. I can tell from her knife skills however, it's going to be me.

Bummer.

Colorfully dressed as always, Mom sweeps through the kitchen door, scarf flying, hat askew, brandishing a letter in her purple-gloved hand. "Guess what I have." She sets her purse on the table with a thump and thrusts the envelope toward me like a dirty, smelly diaper.

"What is it?"

She waves today's mail in the air and shoves it at me. "Look at it. I know what it is."

Poised over her pepper, Olivia stops. "Who's it from?"

Smacking it against the counter, Mom grimaces. "It's from up north." With a toss, she flings in front of me. "And it ain't a letter from Santa."

What can be in this four-inch-by-nine-inch piece of folded white that could have her so upset? Then again, the last envelope slapped into my face with force pretty much sucked, thus hesitating is a given—not opening it means not knowing. Finally, however, the adult in me kicks in and I grab it.

It's a business envelope complete with a clear, plastic window highlighting the deliciously tempting words, "Pay to the order of," which peek from the address slot.

The sender? My husband's attorney.

What now?

I rip it open. It's a check for child support.

The bastard's getting caught up.

"Are you kidding me?" It's everything he owes me until now.

"Don't cash it." Mom rips off her gloves, seething. "He can't prove you've got it. I can't believe the idiot didn't require proof of delivery. If you don't cash it, you can say he hasn't paid."

"If I don't cash it, he'll send another one and require proof of delivery."

"Good." She sets her gloves on the table then pulls off her hat. "When you get that one, you can cash it too, after the hearing. I mean, hey, if he wants to send money for the kids, who are we to argue, right?"

"You have a point." I fold the envelope and stick it in my bra. "I can't believe he's trying to play catch up at the last minute. What a jerk."

Adding her scarf to the growing pile of accessories, Mom growls. "Kiddo, it's getting close to crunch time. We need a plan."

Pretending it's Peter's limp dick, I massacre a baby carrot. "What do you suggest I do, Mom? Hire an assassin? Pay off his attorney? Disappear in the night? Because, trust me, I've mulled two of those three options, and I bet you can guess which ones."

She plants herself across from me. "Lucky for you, I planned ahead. Now hear me out, Ro, and don't get mad."

I cringe.

"Oh, shit, Mom, what did you do?"

She hesitates.

"I hired a detective."

"You did what?"

Olivia drops a cucumber. Deer-in-the-headlight eyes bulge from her skull. She bends to the floor, feels around for the veggie, then picks it up, not once losing sight of Mom. "A detective?" she repeats.

Practically radiant with glee, Mom beams across the table. "I hired him two weeks ago. Paid him a bundle too. And, surprise, surprise, he found some juicy dirt on Peter. Remember that when you do cash that check. You can reimburse me. Four hundred ought to do it."

Like a puppy begging for a biscuit, Mom wants her reward.

"What dirt?" I question.

"He's doing it for her. She wants to play mom, but she doesn't want to be pregnant."

I gape at her. "You're kidding?"

"Nope. She says she wants kids, but not stretch marks, so they decided to take yours. What a bitch."

Olivia and I exchange a look. "Your PI got all of that?"

"Yep. He stalked her and her family and friends on Facebook, Instagram, Twitter, and, get this, dating sites."

Dating sites?

Ha, I knew she wasn't serious about that jackass. I bet it was his uber-thin lips and the fact he's selfish in bed.

Mom rattles on, "Sure, she says she wants to settle down with Peter, but not enough to blow off a beach house and a wealthy retired businessman on DateMe.com. Interesting, isn't it." She grabs a baby carrot and pops it in her mouth, unaware it's a Peter dick substitute.

Olivia gawks. "Who's the wealthy businessman?"

Mom does a double take. Slowly she chews her carrot. "It's my PI, kiddo. Try to keep up."

Olivia's manicured brows shoot skyward.

Chuckling, Mom sits at the table and chews. "That's not all."

"There's more?" I lean forward.

"Peter hasn't changed. He spends hours at work, hours on the golf course, hours at the gym, hours at the bar around the corner from the office. I bet he only goes home to eat, change clothes, and fuck her."

"Mom…"

"You're right. He probably changes at the gym." She winks at me and grins. "Think this is helpful?"

I toss aside a carrot and rub my temples. "Maybe. I don't know.

I mean, I guess it does throw doubt on their relationship. If we can blindside Peter with the online dating stuff in court, we might rattle him. After all, does he really want to be a single, full-time dad, or is he only doing it for her?"

Is it time to take this to the next level? All's fair in love, war, and custody battles, right?

"Can your PI chat her up, and dig for more?" I ask. "Like, is she serious about Peter? Have him ask her about having kids too, can you?"

Pleased with herself, Mom practically vibrates. "Been there, done that. Wealthy old businessmen don't want to be bothered with kids." Mom rises from the table, searching for her cell phone, and marches to her room. "My PI's paid through the next four days. A lot more chatting can go on in four days. I'll give him a call. If we're lucky, he might get pictures."

"Pictures?" Olivia and I repeat.

Mom grinds to a halt. "Nudes? Selfies? Jesus, and you two are the millennials. Keep up with the times."

Wow.

What horrors reside on her phone?

Also, ick.

Suddenly, a face swims into my vision, Ms. Fanny-Fucks-A-Lot, sitting in Peter's car, judging me while I, dripping with mud, played with my children, children she plans to snatch away like a thief in the night.

Like hell she will.

"Fine, if he can get nudes, I'll take nudes, big, fat technicolor nudes. Get them, and I might even tip you."

Satisfied and clucking, Mom disappears down the hallway, dialing her phone. "Excellent. I love a challenge."

Questioning my own morals, I attack the onion, dice, and chop, ticked off, but hopeful and a little afraid too. A line is about to be crossed, and I'm tumbling over it in comfortable shoes.

Brace yourself, Peter.

It's going to get ugly.

~ * ~

It's officially ugly.

In fact, the uglies scream at me from a manila file folder, like a stripper with fans made of fake feathers. I can't even shut my eyes—her nipples and va-jay-jay are burned into my retinas—but not as much as that bleached asshole.

Great.

One more beauty tip Mom will nag me to try.

At least not now anyway. We're in court.

A heavy wooden table decorated in pen-etched graffiti—*Judge M is a soulless zombie* being my personal favorite—anchors an otherwise unimaginative room where I await my custody-hearing doom. The carpet is threadbare, the lights are fluorescent, the windows are smudged, and the whole thing smells like death by Lysol.

Wooden chairs stretch in rows behind me where Mom, Olivia, and Justin sit nearby, literally having my back. To my left, my attorney reviews his notes.

Cocky and condescending, Peter and his attorney are parked annoyingly close beside us at another table, almost within spitting distance. They aren't alone either. Ms. Fanny Fucks-A-Lot, draped in cashmere and pearls, lounges behind Peter, pretending to be virginal.

As for Sam, he's off in the atmosphere, making scarce at my request, trying not to be a factor. My heart wants him here, but my head says no.

In front of me lies the file folder, its incriminating evidence squared away for now. Fortunately, the pictures only came in late last night, a shrewd delay on the PI's part, making it impossible to include them in the discovery process.

In other words, Mom came through, and Peter has no clue.

And, get this. I'm miserable about it.

Crazy, right?

Is this who I've become? A semi-deranged working mom who pays a stranger to elicit poorly lit nudies from my ex's future ex, so I can destroy him in court? Apparently, hell hath no fury like a mother protecting her young, so, yeah, I guess it is.

Thoroughly at ease with our surprise, David, my attorney, intrudes upon my thoughts. "Don't worry, Ro. Let's stick to our plan, and you should be fine."

I nod imperceptibly, watch the clock, and avoid the folder. My game face is on, and it's backed by full color print outs of T and A and a smattering of Brazilian P.

A door at the front of the room opens, and the bailiff strides in. He scans the room and positions himself near the large front desk. A moment later, the door opens again, and the bailiff announces, "All rise."

A whirl of black robes whip through the door, and Judge Middleton enters, carrying papers and pad, sparing nary a glance toward the audience.

Yeah.

Judge Middleton.

My neighbor, my nemesis, the one individual in this small burg of a 'ville who I've managed to piss off repeatedly with missing cats and inadvertently stolen Christmas trees.

Holy crap, I'm screwed.

Judge Middleton sits behind the desk. "Take your seats." He pushes the papers aside, inspects his note pad, then scans the room. His gaze lands on me and, whether surprised, angry, happy, I have no clue. No expression finds favor on his face. He examines Peter, acknowledges the room, then clears his throat. "Let's get started."

Brace yourself.

Here we go.

My attorney rises as I sit. He states my case, that I'm providing my children with a good home, they're clean, well fed, cared for, protected. They go to school, do their homework, take part in activities, yada, yada, yada. He's summarizing everything, outlining the laundry list of parental responsibilities as planned.

Will the weight of this make any impression on the ex, hopefully bringing him to his senses?

Are you getting this yet, Peter? Hello?

Responsibilities summarized, David launches into a summary of Peter's failings as a parent including the missing child support, the lack of visits, calls, texts, concern, etc. Building to a crescendo, he ends with the big finish, that I've given no cause to alter the previous custody agreement.

A deep sigh escapes my lips. Taking a risk, I swivel around for a peek at Fanny Fucks-a-lot.

Figures.

She's texting.

I swivel the other way, exchange a reassuring glance with Olivia, and a you-got-this chin bob from Justin, then spy Mom on her cell texting too. Finally, Mom senses my stare, looks up and smirks like a loon, then treats me to a wink.

Adrenaline courses through me. I whip back around where it's safe, and my attorney calls Peter to the stand.

Question time.

Peter swears to tell the truth, the whole truth, and nothing but the truth, but I don't buy it for a second. The courtroom walls in Chicago dripped with lies only he and I recognized during our original divorce proceedings.

Let the lying begin.

David advances upon him. "Mr. Andrews, when is the last time you spent quality time with your children?"

"December first. Faith and I made plans after Ro refused to take my call." Peter shifts in his seat.

I simmer in mine.

"Objection, Your Honor. My client did not have her cell phone on her at the time of his call. Please note, he could have phoned days prior regarding his plans."

Judge Middleton scratches something on his pad. "Sustained." Once more he ponders the room, stoic as ever.

My attorney continues, "How long were you with your children when you last visited them?"

Peter studies his manicured nails. "Almost twenty minutes."

"Almost twenty minutes," David muses, "real quality time."

Peter's manscaped fingers link together in front of his chest. He sits taller. "She wouldn't let me stay, probably because that place is a dump."

Behind me, whispers fill the room, the loudest Justin's plea to his wife, "Don't take the bait, Liv."

She mutters softly behind me. The word castration hangs in the air.

David ignores Peter's comment. "When is the last time you saw your children before December first?"

"Aren't you going to ask why it's a dump?"

"No. I'm not interested in opinions, only facts." My attorney peruses his notes. "Please answer the question."

Peter thinks for a moment. "In September."

I shake my head no.

"…right before she took them away to that dump," he declares.

A sharp gasp behind me snags my attention. Olivia seethes. "He better run the fuck out of here when this is over," she murmurs.

"Damn straight," Justin concurs.

Mom, however, is oddly silent.

Then I hear it.

tap, tap, tap

She's still on her phone.

"Objection," David says.

"Sustained." Judge Middleton sighs. "Mr. Andrews, answer the question."

Peter rests his right arm on the chair and rubs his chin. "It's true, thought, the place is a dump. I'm surprised it's not condemned."

Scuffling sounds erupt behind me. Justin restrains Olivia.

Judge Middleton treats us to a cold stare.

We freeze.

Finally, he returns his attention to Peter. "Mr. Andrews, enough. I will find you in contempt if this continues."

Chastised, Peter replies, "I'm sure it was September."

David looks up from his notes. "It was July twenty-fifth, to be exact."

Peter hesitates. "No, that doesn't sound right. I'm sure I've been with them since July."

David pounces. "Provide us with a date. Give us a timeline. Tell us what you did, where you went, when you picked them up. Give us details, a text, anything that will corroborate another date, proving to us that you did, in fact, spend time with your children between the end of July and the first of December when you spent twenty minutes talking to them from your car. Unannounced. At my client's home."

Peter clenches his fist. "It was September, and you can't prove otherwise." He punctuates the air with a fist. "It's her word against mine. And I wouldn't call that dump a home."

I angle sideways and gaze behind me. Justin holds Olivia, and Mom, phone free now, grips Olivia's left arm. My incensed sister-in-law radiates tension, a coiled spring threatening to leap.

I hope she clears me and my attorney when she finally pops. I still don't have insurance.

Judge Middleton raps his gavel and rubs his temple. "Continue, counselor."

David nods. "When did you last visit with the children before that?"

Peter mugs a pained expression, making sure we take note of his long-suffering exasperation. "Jesus, do I have to account for every second with them since the divorce?"

His attorney wags a warning finger at him, and Peter slumps in the chair and sighs. "It was in May. I had the kids the weekend of Nick's birthday."

"His birthday is in April, you moron. Aaron's is in May."

Oh, crap.

Shut up, Ro, shut up.

Silent, the judge douses me with a hard, frozen stare from the bench.

I mouth a silent, "I'm sorry."

He remains silent, his expression unmoved.

That's it. He must be Vulcan.

Peter frowns at me. If he were an oyster, I bet he'd be working on one hell of an irritated pearl.

My attorney refers to his notes. "It was April tenth. Suffice it to say, Mr. Andrews, for a man wanting full custody of your children, you have been significantly absent in their lives these last nine months."

Peter squirms.

It's glorious.

"How many phone calls have you made to my client to check on their welfare?"

"I don't know."

"How many texts have you sent?"

"I'm not sure," Peter mumbles again.

"How many emails? Letters? How many inquiries, Mr. Andrews, have you made regarding your children's welfare?" my attorney demands.

"Objection, Your Honor," Peter's attorney finally shouts. "He's badgering my client. Let him answer."

"Sustained." Judge Middleton sighs again. "Counselor, one question at a time."

"My apologies." David spins toward Peter. "Shall I repeat each question and allow the court to make note of each, individual response?"

Peter fiddles with his tie. "I don't remember how many times I contacted her. It was a lot."

Again, I indicate disagreement, vigorously shaking no at his claim.

"Shall we subpoena your phone records, Mr. Andrews, to verify your claims?"

"No." He adjusts his suit coat and squirms.

"That's fine," David snaps, "I shall share my client's instead."

He gives a copy of my cell history with Peter's sparse calls and texts highlighted in yellow to Judge Middleton.

Briefly, the judge reviews it and passes it to the court reporter.

David draws closer to the witness stand, stalking his prey. "Mr. Andrews, how much do you pay a week in child support?

"Okay, here's the thing—"

"Answer the question," David interrupts. "How much do you pay in child support on a weekly basis? It's a simple question. Answer it."

Peter fumes in frustration. "A hundred and sixty-five a week."

"Interesting," David presses. "You are significantly behind on that support. In fact, more than three thousand dollars behind."

"No, I paid her that."

"That wasn't a question, Mr. Andrews, it was a statement, and where's your proof? Can you provide receipts to the court? A cancelled check? Because we do, in fact, have a statement from the court showing four weeks ago you were behind over three thousand dollars." David pulls another paper from the manila folder.

Overcome with rage, Peter glares at me. "I sent her a check, but she hasn't cashed it yet. She's sitting on it to make me look bad. I got caught up three weeks ago."

"But you admit," my attorney continues, going for the gonads, "you were five months behind until three weeks ago, after you filed for a revision to the original custody order?"

"I'll admit nothing of the kind," Peter yells back, "and it won't matter once she cashes that check."

"On the contrary, it does matter," David notes. "It begs the question. How committed are you to the support and welfare of your children?"

Peter adjusts his suit coat. He loosens his tie. Squirming in the witness chair, he stews but says nothing.

My attorney turns to consider Ms. Fanny-Fucks-A-Lot.

She's no longer on her phone but listens intently now that talk has switched to money.

"To summarize, you have requested the original shared custody arrangement be revised to provide you with full custody of your three children, and yet you haven't exercised your rights to keep them these last nine months. You've failed to make your child support payments for five months, and you've made little effort to contact my client regarding their welfare." He stares pointedly at the girlfriend. "One wonders what's changed to cause you to make this request. Tell me, Mr. Andrews, do you live alone?"

Peter takes the bait. "That's none of your business."

My attorney whips around to face Peter. "It is the court's business to ascertain who will be sharing living quarters with the children. So, I ask again, do you live alone?"

"No."

"Oh?" David asks, feigning innocence. "Who do you live with?"

Peter rolls his eyes and sighs. "Faith Chadwick."

It's Faith? How ironic.

I choke on a snicker.

"The woman joining us in court today, correct?" David clarifies.

"Yes."

"What is the nature of your living arrangement? Platonic

roommates or are you in a relationship with Ms. Chadwick?"

Peter smiles at her. "We are in a relationship."

She gives him a tiny smile back.

I vomit in my mouth.

"Ah," says David. "Is this a serious relationship?"

"Objection." states Peter's attorney. "Relevancy?"

"Your Honor, it is very relevant." David takes two steps toward the judge, halting the word "sustained" on his lips. "It is our contention this man is content to be an absent father and that he only requests full custody as a direct result of his relationship with this woman. That makes the seriousness of this relationship paramount to our case."

Judge Middleton tilts his head for a moment then says, "I'll allow it."

"Thank you, Your Honor," David acknowledges the judge then focuses on Peter. "I ask you again, Mr. Andrews, what is the nature of your relationship with Ms. Chadwick?"

We're getting to the heart of it now. Having worked Peter into a corner, David moves in for the kill shot. Time to grow a backbone and bury my morals.

On the stand, Peter answers, "We're in a committed relationship." He speaks only to me, his voice hard like the room. "She's the love of my life, my soul mate. She completes me."

Yeah, right.

Like you have a soul.

"Would she concur?"

"Of course, she would." Peter snorts, frowning.

Like Thor's mighty hammer, David brandishes the folder. "Mr. Andrews, whose email address is heavensent2020@hotmail.com?"

"What?" Peter freezes. "Why?"

"Answer the question please."

My family rustles in their chairs, and their chatter catches my ears. Mom, Olivia, and Justin exchange satisfied whispers.

Peter falters. "I'm not sure."

"Really? You're in a committed relationship with Ms. Chadwick, but you don't know her email address?"

He inspects the file folder and regroups. "Oh, yeah, sorry, I guess I didn't catch that. Yes, it's Faith's."

Ms. Fanny-Fucks-A-Lot is immobile, frozen, her cell phone forgotten.

Peter shifts his attention from my attorney to his girlfriend. Worry clouds his face.

Is he less confident than before?

David opens the file folder and extracts two more pieces of paper. "Tell me, Mr. Andrews, whose email address is ceo1969@gmail.com?"

"What?" He sits straighter.

I spin sideways for a better view.

The girlfriend blanches a delightful shade of pale, except for two blistering swatches of red blooming across her cheeks.

"Perhaps it will help if I read a few emails addressed to it." David offers a copy to Peter. "Dated yesterday evening, and I quote, from heavensent2020@gmail.com to ceo1969@gmail.com, *Baby, I can't wait to get at you next week. Damn, you have me fucking hot and horny*—excuse me, Your Honor, I'm reading verbatim."

Judge Middleton waves a weary hand.

In this moment, it dawns on me, this, this is why he's a robot. To listen daily to these exercises in human suckitude, to sit through this crap, watching families fall apart and people argue, it has to take a toll. Human nature in its lowest form darkens his doorstep on a regular basis. No wonder he shuns the world.

"*I want to go for a ride in that sports car, baby. I'll be sure to shift your big stick, and you can play with my headlamps. Give me a few minutes and I'll text you pictures to rev up that throbbing engine of yours for when we meet. I seriously need to fuck you, stud, and soon.*"

Wow. This isn't even creative. I mean, come on, throbbing engine? Shift your big stick? Headlamps? My mother could write better porn than this.

In fact, she probably has.

Okay, ick.

I'm actually thinking about Mom and porn.

Double ick.

Peter devours a copy of the email. Unblinking, he flits left to right, taking in the words, the date, the meaning.

His attorney slaps the wooden table and rises to his feet. "I object, inadmissible! We were not provided this evidence, Your Honor."

David approaches the bench and gives his copy to Judge Middleton. "Sir, if you will note on the email, we only received this late yesterday. There was no time to include it during the discovery process as we simply didn't know of its existence until last night."

Judge Middleton takes the email and reads it. "I will allow it."

"Thank you, sir. Moving on, Mr. Andrews, can you please tell me the cell phone number of Ms. Chadwick?"

Here it comes. The big finish. The pictures. I can almost hear the drumroll.

Still…must we do this?

I have no love for this man, and none whatsoever for the girlfriend, but we've made our case, and it needs to end somewhere. Human decency means something, right?

Clearing my throat, I rise halfway from my chair. "David, don't."

He turns to face me.

Peter stiffens in the witness chair, digesting the next request and its implications, bracing for the next blow.

I wish I could see the girlfriend, but I can't. Instead, I implore, "Sir, may I have a moment with my attorney?"

High upon the bench, Judge Middleton considers me. "One minute," he grants.

David closes the folder and comes back to the table. "Ro," he sighs, "we agreed, these photos are compelling."

Behind him, Peter tries to peer around David's back. Giving up, he silently questions his girlfriend, mouthing, "What's going on?" Confusion and pain swim across his contorted, angry face.

It's delightful…and yet…

Why do I feel damned?

It's not like Peter would hesitate. Why do I?

Then it hits me.

I'm better than this, than him.

The words choke in my throat, but I manage to spit them out. "Do you think we've made our case? It's just that, I'm kinda having second thoughts. Are the pictures necessary?"

David is perplexed, and I don't blame him.

I am too.

"We've got nudie pictures that bitch sent to another man yesterday!"

Mom.

On her feet, she displays her cell phone, brandishing a photo of Miss Thang's naughty bits for all to see. She scrolls and, as each picture of tits and ass and va-jay-jay pops on her screen, she thrusts it at the judge and Peter, making sure they get an eyeful.

"Mom!"

"Objection!" Peter's attorney shouts.

"What the hell?" Peter questions.

"No!" cries the girlfriend.

"Yes!" yell Justin and Olivia in stereo.

"Katie!" hollers Judge Middleton. "That's enough!"

Back the truck up…

What?

Did the judge just call my mother, Katie?

Judge Middleton?

What the hell?

He's pounding his gavel now over the tap, tap, tap of the court reporter who types furiously. The bailiff gawks at Mom's phone. Peter's on his feet too, glaring at the girlfriend who collects her things for a speedy exit. His attorney rubs his temples, his mouth locked in a grimace. Olivia's applauding, whistling, bouncing in her chair. Justin fist pumps the air.

It's bedlam.

"That bitch isn't serious about him," Mom rails, swiping right. "She's sending nudies to my private investigator. She thinks he's some rich dude, and she's planning to trade up."

Judge Middleton waves at the bailiff who makes a quick shuffle in Mom's direction, but she's already in the aisle, halfway to the exit, parting words bursting from her lips. "I told you Ro was a good girl, Milton. This bitch just wants to play temporary mom with my grandbabies." She shakes off the bailiff when he reaches for her arm, muttering, "I'm going." Triumphant, she marches up the aisle and disappears out the door with a hearty slam.

Milton?

I'll repeat, what the freaking hell?

"Order!" Judge Middleton shouts, pounding his gavel. "I will have order in this court."

"Your Honor, we need a five-minute recess," begs Peter's attorney.

"Granted. In fact," Judge Middleton says as he rises from the bench and hustles toward the door, "let's make it ten."

Chapter Fourteen

Thirty minutes later, it's over.

Shell-shocked, I leave the courtroom to join everyone in the hallway, shaking and quaking, reeling with adrenaline. Accepting hugs from Olivia, Justin, and Mom, we collectively shun Peter who he sulks from the room alone in stony silence. Shaken, bitter, betrayed, he's not the same arrogant asshole who strolled into the courtroom this morning.

We have no decision yet, but my heart beats with a smidgen less fear. But only a smidgen. Because so much remains undecided.

After Mom blew up the room with her cell phone, and after Peter demanded to see the pictures despite his attorney's objections, I allowed them to be entered as evidence. Afterward, he became a man without purpose. His attorney instructed him through a few brief questions, they grilled me for fifteen minutes to no avail, and I stepped down with more confidence than before.

Yet, it plagues me, the indecision, the unknowing.

More specifically, Judge Middleton plagues me.

Recess concluded, he blasted into the courtroom, frostier, more frozen than a polar ice cap. The hearing concluded far quicker than my attorney predicted, although the judge growled and snapped and glared through each second until he finally swept from the room with nary a glance our way.

As days go, this one is ending somewhat more satisfying than it began.

Yet the nightmare lingers on.

David says expect something within the next two weeks. My plan? Distract myself with children, writing, work, Sam. This is my life now. I don't want to lose it. Still, it means more sleepless nights, more worried distractions, and no appetite while I wait, wait, wait, and wait. Every gray cloud has a silver lining somewhere.

Funny if mine turns out to be a slightly firmer tush.

~ * ~

Time is not my friend. Has it really been only ten days since the hearing? It can't be I've aged a lifetime. Even sitting here, in my boss Edmund's diner office, the seconds crawl by.

What wild goose chase is he sending me on next? A hunt for old Chevy parts? A four-drawer file cabinet the office doesn't need?

Pink light bulbs for the bathrooms? It's sweet—he must think these errands will get my mind off the impending decision.

They don't.

Muttering to himself about something being long overdue, Edmund opens a drawer and withdraws an envelope.

Ah. He's sending me on a field trip. I start to reach for it. "Another bill to pay? Need me to run it to the post office?"

He smiles. "Nope. It's for you."

I hesitate. I don't like envelopes anymore. "What's this?"

Edmund thrusts it at me. "Something you've earned. Go on, take it, it won't bite. It's an employment offer."

Oh, crap, here we go...wait...what did he say?

My kind, elderly boss rocks in his squeaky chair, satisfaction etched on his wide, wrinkled face. "I know you have a week or two left in your trial," he rattles on, "but, what the heck, you're one of us now. This spells out your benefits, including insurance."

My voice falters. "Insurance?" I squeak.

Am I being pranked?

"Sure wish I'd thought of this before your hearing, then you could tell 'em you had insurance. Though I did tell Judge Middleton four days ago, when I did the paperwork, and yes, I can do my own paperwork on occasion. You're a good, hard worker, Ro. We're happy to have you around."

Tears fill my eyes. I blink rapidly hoping to disperse the bastards before they fall, desperate to be strong, unemotional, professional.

It's no use. I fail. One salty drop breaks free and trails down my cheek. "Thank you, Edmund." I sniff. "You have no idea how much this means to me."

His eyes are glassy too, and I swear he wipes his nose to hide the fact. "Don't thank me. Like I said, you earned it. Now, go tell your boyfriend next door, then get back here. We got work to do."

Jumping to my feet, I dash around his desk, catching him off guard, tackling him with a bear hug. "Yes sir!"

His warmth fills the room, and he pats me on the shoulder.

I pull back, sniffling, grinning, laughing as I run for the door. "I'll be right back."

Edmund blows his nose. "Watch yourself on those stairs across the street," he yells after me. "Your health's on my dime now."

Skipping, bolting, I breeze through the diner, past the grill where Eli fries eggs, past my office booth where a stack of bills awaits, past Sarah who pours coffee for several elderly women discussing crochet patterns, past Ernie and the Burts who argue the merits of duct tape, and past Rachel at the register ringing up Officer Brent's soda, destined for Sam. I shove open the door, flying like a bird, my worries forgotten...

I tumble onto the sidewalk straight into Judge Middleton.

Oh, crap the bed.

Shocked, winded, I clutch his winter coat, steadying us both by its lapels. His bowler hat is pitched forward on his face. It rests on his nose, mocking me.

I let go of his coat. "I'm so sorry, Judge. Please, accept my apology."

Thin gloved fingers push the hat where it belongs. "Ms. Andrews," he starts, "must you insist on mowing me down?"

This is not good. In a world teeming with fantastic hobby options, why is mine attacking old men with mama thighs?

Recovering, I beg forgiveness. "Again, sorry, Judge. I have great news to share with Sam, and I'm in a hurry to get back to work."

The judge raises an eyebrow. "News?" It arches upward, framing his disgust.

I deflate.

This man has the power to wreck my sanity, my children, my life, our lives, and I almost knocked him in the gutter. Again. I force a smile. "Edmund's offered to make me a permanent employee. With insurance."

Judge Middleton unbuttons his coat and nods. "Yes, he told me. Congratulations." Reaching into his coat, he removes the second envelope I've encountered this morning. He clasps it close to his chest and my heart stops.

Forgetting to inhale, my head spins. Stars dance before me. Soon, they may fall from the dark sky taking me with them. Should I grab the judge's coat lapels again, perhaps steady myself before I fall? No, landing face first on the frozen concrete would be more appropriate.

The judge interrupts my thoughts. "Ms. Andrews, I've decided to alter the original custody agreement."

For the second time this morning tears threaten my composure, but this time joy is nowhere to be found. My babies' faces—sweet, cautious Nicholas, rambunctious, playful Aaron, feisty, little Maddy— my world, my life, my babies swirl before me. The stars fall. A hand finds me, steadying me by my arm.

"I recognize a good person when I meet one and, better yet, a good mother too." Judge Middleton's voice breaks through the oxygen-deprived fog swamping my brain.

Blinking rapidly, I fight hard, trying not to cry.

Judge Middleton extends the envelope. "Congratulations, Ms. Andrews, and good day." He tips his hat and enters the diner leaving me alone on the sidewalk.

Paper cuts be damned, I rip open the envelope.

Judge Middleton, my neighbor nemesis, the man I've irritated to no end with cats and trees and borderline physical assault, has granted me full custody and raised Peter's support payment too.

I've won.

~ * ~

My feet fly, propelling me up the grain elevator steps two at a time, paying no heed to the ice, then burst through the office door. Bursting with joy, I make a beeline for Sam.

He's at his desk when the door bangs open, and concerned, half rises, all sexy and hunky and mine.

I sob, shake, and run. Zipping around the desk, I fall upon him, and we collapse together backward into his chair, nearly tumbling to the floor. I plant kisses on his cheeks, his neck, his lips. Emotions too strong to put into words pour from me, emotions I can only express by grabbing this man and holding this man and running my hands across every square inch of this damn, fine, sexy man.

All is right with the world. Evil has been banished, good prevailed, my babies are mine, and I'm in Sam's arms.

It's time to live again.

Sniffling indelicately, I manage to frame words, putting his confusion to rest. "Judge Middleton gave me full custody, Sam. I won! And guess what?" I lift my head from his chest. "Edmund's making me a permanent employee. He's giving me health insurance too."

Strong arms engulf me, and he cradles me tight "That's great, sweetie, I'm so happy for you. I never doubted it for a second. Judge Middleton is a good man, and you," he continues, "are a great mom. You deserve it, all of it."

I lay upon his chest, listening to his heartbeat. "Thank you, Sam, and thanks for being patient with me. This whole thing sucked, including the timing."

Calloused fingers find my locks. He strokes my hair, murmuring softly, "It's over now, time to celebrate. We can spend tonight with the kids, but tomorrow, you're mine. My place. I'll cook."

I grin. "I'll bring the wine and dessert."

"Sweetie, you are the dessert."

I peer at Sam. He leans into me. We breathe as one as he tilts my face toward his. Our lips meet, part, and mingle. Once again, he kisses me, and the world as I know it ceases to exist.

~ * ~

Fluorescent bathroom lights accentuate every fine line and enlarge every pore. I slather on moisturizer and squint. How long until this takes affect?

Clutching my miracle jar, I jostle for position with Mom, who's also going out, but won't provide details. It's dinner date night with Sam, I'm nervous, and Mom, being Mom, is being annoying.

"If you need it," she pouts and draws on lipstick, "I have a four-blade razor you can borrow."

Giving up, I ditch the jar and focus on the hot rollers instead, pulling one free. A fat, loose, reddish blonde curl frames my face. "I shaved, Mom."

She admires her reflection. "Only your legs?"

I remove another one. A perfect curl tumbles beside my ear. "No, other things."

"I'm not talking about your armpits, Ro. Did you shave your junk?"

More curlers gone, more perfection. "Women don't have junk," I muse.

"Oh, whatever you want to call it. You know what I mean. Did you?"

Should I tag her with an elbow, send her lipstick flying across her face? It's a thought.

Instead, I grill her. "Why do you keep asking me this? It's like you're obsessed with my crotch."

Finished, she caps her lipstick, thwarting my revenge. "No, I'm not. Besides, the only other time I asked is when you had a date with Charlie. I knew you wouldn't put out for him. Ugh." She shudders. "He wasn't your type."

"Yet, you pushed me to go out with him."

Self-satisfied, she smirks. "It got you on a date with Sam, didn't it?"

Removing the last roller, I ignore her dig and I run my fingers through my curls separating them gently. Perfection. Finding Mom's reflection in the mirror, I press, "You asked before my first date with Sam too."

"No, I didn't."

"Yes, you did."

"No, Ro, I didn't." Mom gives me a pointed look in the mirror.

I admire my wavy locks, happy to be goading her. Maybe I

have a hobby after all? I chuckle then say, "That's it, I'm buying you gingko. Your memory is shot."

"Don't you dare and quit changing the subject. Did you trim the shrubbery?"

Turning my head, I admire my reflection. "Mom, I not only trimmed the shrubs, I paid a gardener to rip them out by the roots, and that," I wince, "wasn't fun."

Joy spreads across her face. "Sweetie, I'm so proud of you! Way to go, kiddo."

Wow. This is the absurdity of my mother. To think, as a child I thought the key to her heart was good grades and macaroni necklaces.

Checking her cell phone, she drops it into her purse, then removes something else in the process and lays it on the counter before me.

A condom packet.

Oh, dear lord, why does she have this?

At the hint of round latex hidden behind suggestive marketing, I blush. "Seriously?"

Closing her purse, Mom chuckles. "I would give you two, but I'm running low and might need one myself."

Ick.

Grateful it's ribbed for my pleasure I slip it in my jeans' pocket and will my wandering mind to not go there even while I contemplate her lack of details. "Okay, Mom, where are you going and who with? Tell me, for safety's sake," I demand. "There are men out there with pits in their basements. Seriously, if some sicko shoves you in one, you could break a hip."

Unconcerned, thoroughly amused, she only laughs, dabbing perfume on her wrists, clucking like a happy hen. "Ha, nice try, little one. I'm off. Have fun on your date, and when I say have fun, I mean get laid. Ride the cowboy, kiddo. I would."

Before I can answer, Mom whips out the door, swirling in boho print and dragging a patchouli cloud behind her on the way to the kitchen.

Thank heaven for disappearing moms and good hair days. Both are too few and far between.

Embracing the peace and quiet, I study my reflection and enjoy the view in private. Much has changed since I came to this rundown farmhouse, this wacky town, and this brand-new life. Stronger, happier, more confident, I feel invincible. The glow in my cheeks is real, my face radiates joy, and the hole in my heart is healing.

Or better yet, I should say, healed.

One last re-apply of deodorant for confidence's sake, I follow my mom's path to the kitchen. There my precious, happy babies sit, chattering around the kitchen table, doing their homework while Olivia offers sippy cups to the twins and makes their favorite: mac and cheese. Justin bursts through the door, home from work, and I pass through, bound for my car.

Eyebrows raised, curiosity etched on his face, my brother peeks out the window. "Mom and Judge Middleton…who'd of thunk it?"

In mid-goodbye kiss, I hover above Maddie, fish lips protruding, halted in my tracks. "What?"

He sets his lunch box on the stove, snags a fork and stabs at the mac and cheese. "You heard me. Mom just drove away with Judge Middleton. She waved at me and said don't wait up."

Mom and the judge?

And a condom?

Double fricking ick.

Though it does explain the whole Katie-and-Milton business during court.

Banishing yet another disturbing mental image, I finish kissing my babies one by one, then slip on my coat. "She never ceases to amaze me."

Olivia fills plates at the stove and passes them to Justin. "She's something else. We've got to teach her how to blog. She'll set the world on fire. Anyway, you go enjoy yourself too."

Justin lifts a plate high above Aaron, teasing him, before setting it in front of Maddy. "Yeah, but don't do anything I wouldn't do. Or what Mom would…or, worse yet, will."

"Well, that's a horrifying thought, bro." I laugh. "See ya!"

Happy, horny, and practically skipping, I bee bop from the kitchen with a wave, a smile, and Sam on my mind.

Everyone needs joy in their lives.

Even moms.

~ * ~

A light burns bright on the front porch when I arrive. The door opens, and my cowboy greets me, all rugged and sexy and handsome as hell and ushers me inside. A red denim, button-down shirt clings to his muscular torso, dark-washed jeans hug his magnificent ass and strong thighs, and I ascend to an ethereal plane, bubbling with joy, awash in want, hungry, desperate, alive.

Every cell in my body ignites, catches fire, and I make silent plans to rip those shirt buttons off with my teeth. Thank God for fluoride toothpaste.

"Hi, Sam," I purr.

He leans in for a tender, succulent kiss.

I kiss back, griping denim with wandering, exploring hands.

In need of oxygen, we break apart, and he motions me in. "Hi, Ro," he replies. "You're early, and I couldn't be happier."

"I may have set a land speed record getting here."

A fire burns in the living room fireplace, a candle burns on an end table, and I burn down below. China, silver, and glass twinkle in the glowing light upon a table near the kitchen. Soft music floats from a speaker somewhere, and something delicious floats on the air.

Oh, hell, yes. My cowboy can cook too. "Something smells wonderful." I take off my coat. "You should write a blog, give Olivia a run for her money."

"Thank you, but, no, the crockpot did most of the work." He takes my coat and tosses it onto a nearby chair. "How's your writing coming? Did you finish the post you were working on? The one about plastic wrapped toilet seats?"

I shrug. "I did, my seventh post is online now. Some days it's easy, others not so much. I don't have many subscribers, but, again, seven posts, and I'm getting a few comments and likes. Plus, I'm still not sure if this is my thing. It's fun, though."

Shaking my head, I continue, "I may never find my thing, but I did find out Cam Whitmore's ready to sell Petunia, so now I'm obsessed with adopting her. Crazy, huh."

"Petunia?"

"His grandkids' pot-bellied pig? Oh, she's adorable. They've outgrown her which means, yay, opportunity for us. I want to see if I can train her to sit in the cart and have Oscar pull her around. Wouldn't that be hilarious!"

A huge grin lights Sam's face, and he chuckles. "Yes, it would, and hold that thought, sweetie." Taking my wrist, he steers me into the kitchen. A stack of books anchors a pile of papers on an antique hutch. "Take a look."

Titles catch my attention. "What's this?" I ask, lifting a book. Animal husbandry, grant writing for idiots, free money for nonprofits, how to run an animal rescue, and other assorted topics stare back. "Sam, are you starting an animal rescue? Oh, my gosh, how wonderful! Can I help? Please?"

He wraps strong arms around my shoulders, drawing me close. Sam murmurs into my ear, "They aren't for me, babe. They're for you."

"Me?" I pull back, confused. Vanilla, leather, and pine waft over me.

"Yes, you." His fingers trail along my arm to my shoulders, my hair, then sweeps it aside. "I think you've found your thing. You just don't realize it yet." His hungry lips find my neck. "When your husband abandoned you and your children, you saved them. You saved yourself."

Trembles erupt within me at his touch. "I didn't have a choice."

Sam's hot, supple lips nibble along my neck, setting my skin on fire. "You could have ignored Judge Middleton, Ro, but you didn't. At every turn, you showed him kindness, compassion, patience."

He traces hot, tiny circles below my ear lobe with his tongue. Instantly, I convulse. "About that," I croak, my voice husky, quivering, "Mom's got me beat."

Still Sam doesn't stop. "You rescued a dog."

My breathing is fast, ragged. "Okay, you've got me there."

Hot, damp kisses trail along my neck. "You rescued a goat."

Waves of want wash over me. "Umm…"

"Not to mention a pony," he mumbles, relentless, "and let's not forget the ass."

"Trust me, I won't forget the ass," I moan.

His lips find my earlobe. "Last, but not least, Ro," he murmurs, "you rescued me."

My body goes nuclear. I want him, need him. Nothing—small children, fainting goats, toy helicopters, toxic exes, annoying moms—nothing will stop me from getting at Sam.

I spin around and grip his shirt, steadying myself, panting, needing Sam. "Can the books and the crockpot wait?"

He takes my hand, raises it to his lips, kissing my palm, my wrist. For a split second, I swear I black out. Dinner forgotten Sam leads me to his bedroom.

The night is ours.

~ * ~

Whenever Mom mentioned sex, she always went for the cliché and possibly, in her experience, clichés did the trick. Maybe for her it is like riding a horse or riding a bike or whatever, and, excuse me while I pluck my eyes out from that visual.

Ick, ick, ick. Mom sex. The worse.

For me and Sam, we need a whole new cliché-free language for the ground we're covering. We're in brand new territory. At least, for me, it's never been like this.

Ever.

This, for me, defines the difference between having sex versus making love.

Even on our honeymoon, Peter and I never made love. We had sex. I didn't understand it then, but I sure do now. No, Peter and I, we were together for reasons neither of us could identify at the time, but it certainly wasn't love. For a time, when we were young, sex was enough, companionship was enough, joint sharing of a household, bills, and responsibilities was enough. Eventually, though, only emptiness remained, and nothing was left but obligation.

Guess what?

Obligation doesn't feed the soul.

Suddenly, I forgive Peter.

Crazy, huh.

As for Sam and me?

Oh, my God, as for Sam and me, we make love.

When he takes me into his bedroom, I expect to be awkward, self-conscious, out of practice.

But I'm not.

Fully in the moment, I'm confident, aware, sexual, ready. I find each button on his sexy red-cotton shirt and undo them with purpose. Seeing his chest, hearing his pounding heart, recognizing it only hints at the quality of this good, decent man excites me more than the prospect of mere sex. I drift toward his belt buckle. He caresses my back with trembling care. Lifting my sweater, he peels it upward, over my head, over my arms, releasing my curls, relieving my cares, releasing my fears, leaving me standing, panting, quivering, in my jeans and my one brand-new, lacy, push-up bra.

There's urgency, so much urgency. Years of loneliness, of the separation singleness imparts upon people, has built to a crescendo. We need that connection, that release.

It's time to tear down those walls.

There's an intimacy to making love that never existed for me until this moment. It's palpable and more real than I've ever experienced.

Easing his belt from his waist, I toss it aside, then pop the button on his jeans, knowing what I want, determined to get it. Delicately, he lowers my bra strap, kissing my shoulder. He finds the snap, unhooks it with ease, wrenching it from my body.

I press myself against his warm skin, reveling in his touch, my naked breasts against his chest. Our breathing grows ragged, rising and falling in disjointed waves. Gripping his zipper, I release the tension, releasing Sam. His fingers find my jeans' button. They claw at it, work it open, tug at the zipper. I'm desperate, I want him so. Our jeans fall to the floor, he takes me in his arms, and lifts me high. My legs lock around his waist, and we attack each other like animals, kissing, groping, touching, burning, feeling, loving.

Sam lowers me to his bed, and I cling to him, not wanting to release him from my arms. With gentle fingers, he removes my panties. His tighty-whities fall to the floor. I whimper, begging him to fall upon me, to take me, to love me, to complete me.

And Sam, my cowboy in shining chaps—the man I didn't think I needed until I really knew him—makes love to me on his bedsheets.

Every ounce of joyous energy coursing through us threatens to blow me to pieces, spilling out into our lovemaking. My heart stops, my breathing stops. I exist only in that one deep, lingering, life-altering moment, entangled with Sam, every cell attuned to this precise second.

Forget physics, my friends. *This* is how the Big Bang must have happened.

Somewhere, out there, in a parallel dimension beyond my grasp, my joy just gave birth to the energy that became another universe.

Bang

You're welcome, future aliens.

You're welcome.

Acknowledgements

To my amazing partner, Daren, for helping me find love again, to my besties, Michelle and Melissa, for always being there with a good laugh and a stiff drink, and to my writing mentor, Léonie Kelsall, who guided me through this crazy process called writing a novel. Without you, Lee, these words would still be stuck in my computer.

About the Author

Everyone has a purpose in life, and Robin Winzenread discovered years ago that her unintended role in the world is that of comic relief. From being stalked on a port-a-potty by a possum to getting a tiny crab stuck in her ear while scuba diving in the Florida Keys to actually losing her shoe on the road while driving to a job interview, Robin decided the best way to make sense of these crazy mishaps is to write about them.

Fortunately, the hilarity in her life continues so more stories will follow soon along with, possibly, therapy. And maybe even a good, stiff drink.

Robin loves to hear from her readers. You can find and connect with her at the links below.

Website: https://robinwinzenread.com
Twitter: https://twitter.com/RobinFritz
Facebook: https://www.facebook.com/robin.w.fritz
Pinterest: https://www.pinterest.com/RWplusF/
Instagram: https://www.instagram.com/robinfritz86/?hl=en

~~~

If you enjoyed *Some Assembly Required*, then you'll love *Heart of the Holidays*, a perfect group of holiday stories read to fall in love with.

HEARTWARMING TALES
OF THE SEASON

LOVE, LAUGHTER, LIFE

TURN THE PAGE
FOR A PEEK!

Heart of the Holiday

At Christmas, You Always Tell the Truth

For a long time, spotlight-avoiding attorney, Janelle Jackson, has loved her playboy law practice partner, Matt Masterson. She is the stalwart brains, and he is the flashy muscle—a perfect partnership. At least, until her one-sided romance sends her into a tail spin.

Hope for the Holidays

Christmas is the worst time of the year for Hope Hardcastle. Recovering from a disastrous divorce, every thought, every child's voice reminds her of the daughter she was forced to leave behind. Worse, her new neighbor is a handsome single guy with a daughter about the same age as her own. Speaking to them is an exercise in pain, so it's easiest to ignore them and hope they'll go away. But that's easier said then done.

Seven Days in December

A withdrawn, fiercely independent widow, Jody is determined to stay in her home, even in the dead of winter. But then an ice storm knocks out the electricity, and her generator fails. Faced with the prospect of a week without power, she reluctantly moves to a shelter at the local school. Surrounded by caring people and a possible romance, as the outside world thaws, so does her heart.

Noella's Gift

Holly Harper hates Christmas. The season full of commercialism has left her feeling cold and bitter. When she finds a little girl freezing and alone she feels warmth spark in her heart. She's determined to keep the child until Christmas is over. Will the little girl help Holly find joy in the season or will her heart be as cold as the winter winds?

Underneath the Mistletoe

Faith Jenkins has lost her faith in Christmas. Not only did she never celebrate Christmas as a child, but last year, a few days before the holiday, she was dumped by the man she thought was "The One". To save herself from further heartache, she's vowed never to let another man into her heart. The holidays have other plans.

Out Now!

What's next on your reading list?

Champagne Book Group promises to bring to readers fiction at its finest.

Discover your next
fine read!

We are delighted to invite you to receive exclusive rewards. Join our Facebook group for VIP savings, bonus content, early access to new ideas we've cooked up, learn about special events for our readers, and sneak peeks at our fabulous titles.

Join now.

CPSIA information can be obtained
at www.ICGtesting.com
Printed in the USA
LVHW091254120120
643351LV00001B/213/P